# A HEARTFELT CONFESSION

"When you asked me if any of the guard took lovers, I thought you might have sought a companion for your bed."

Ember nearly choked on her own breath. Fortunately Barrow continued speaking, sparing her the embarrassment of an attempt at spluttering a response.

"And it was that day"—Barrow paused, holding Ember in his gaze—"that I was forced to admit my jealousy. Though I thought I could fight my own desires, I learned quickly that my only choice was to keep myself away from you."

"I thought you despised me," Ember said.

"Despised you?" Barrow said. "How could you think—"

"You left me," she answered sharply. "You were my teacher, my friend, and then you were gone. What else was I to think?"

"I thought you would take me to be a brute no different from Alistair," Barrow continued.

"You are nothing like Alistair. I longed for you to come to me." Ember leaned toward him, her pulse thrumming with the boldness of her words.

"I still feared you," Barrow told her. "What would happen if I . . ."

He rested his hand on her knee. Very slowly, Barrow's touch moved up her thigh, following the curve of her hip and finally resting on her waist. He spread his fingers wide, pressing firmly from the bottom of her rib cage to her lower back. Ember didn't break from his intent gaze, but her every breath was short and trembling.

## OTHER BOOKS YOU MAY ENJOY

| | |
|---|---|
| *Belladonna* | Fiona Paul |
| *Bitterblue* | Kristin Cashore |
| *Bloodrose* | Andrea Cremer |
| *Eon* | Alison Goodman |
| *Fire* | Kristin Cashore |
| *The Inventor's Secret* | Andrea Cremer |
| *Nightshade* | Andrea Cremer |
| *Rift* | Andrea Cremer |
| *Snakeroot* | Andrea Cremer |
| *Spirit Walk* | Richie Tankersley Cusick |
| *Venom* | Fiona Paul |
| *Wolfsbane* | Andrea Cremer |

# RISE

## A NIGHTSHADE NOVEL

# ANDREA CREMER

# RISE

### A NIGHTSHADE NOVEL

**speak**

An Imprint of Penguin Group (USA)

SPEAK
Published by the Penguin Group
Penguin Group (USA) LLC
375 Hudson Street
New York, New York 10014

USA * Canada * UK * Ireland * Australia
New Zealand * India * South Africa * China

penguin.com
A Penguin Random House Company

First published in the United States of America by Philomel Books,
a division of Penguin Young Readers Group, 2013
Published by Speak, an imprint of Penguin Group (USA) LLC, 2013

THE LIBRARY OF CONGRESS HAS CATALOGED THE PHILOMEL BOOKS EDITION AS FOLLOWS:
Cremer, Andrea R.
Rise / Andrea Cremer. p. cm.—(Nightshade)
Summary: "Everything Conatus stands for is at risk, and Ember must involve herself in a deception
that ultimately brings about the Witches' War"—Provided by publisher.
ISBN: 978-0-399-15960-2 (hc)
[1. Knights and knighthood—Fiction. 2. Supernatural—Fiction.] I. Title.
PZ7.C86385Rj 2013 [Fic]—dc23
2012012263

Speak ISBN 978-0-14-242494-0

Printed in the United States of America

1 3 5 7 9 10 8 6 4 2

*For Charlie, Richard, and Lyndsey:*
*Those Musketeers have nothing on you guys*

The road to hell is paved with good intentions.

—Saint Bernard of Clairvaux

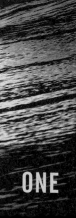

ONE

**ALISTAIR COULD REMEMBER** screaming only once before, at least since he'd become a man. The shrill cry had forced its way from his throat when he'd been pinned to the floor of the wine cellar. Three hobgoblins held him down, cackling, while a fourth stretched its long, clawed fingers toward his eyeball. That scream had been a brittle, strangling yowl of horror.

The sound escaping his lips now was brighter than shattering glass, jagged shards of pain and loss. Ember was gone.

Less than an hour earlier, restless after the events of the day—and of the night—Alistair had gazed at the stone ceiling in his cell. His pallet was unsympathetic to his pains, offering no ease or comfort to lull him into slumber. With eyes open, Alistair didn't see the rough-cut gray blocks above him. Neither did he see darkness when he closed his eyes.

An image had burned itself upon his vision. Skin revealed as linen slipped from Ember's slender but strong shoulders. Weeks with Conatus had chiseled her arms, making them hard as a man's, but Alistair remembered the softness he'd glimpsed. Her hair was fire, flames licking the snow of her naked body, its sudden curves appearing as her garment fell.

It was a scene stolen from his very dreams. Ember baring herself to him. Wanting him. Alistair would have given his soul to relive the moment. And change the way it had ended.

No matter how often he turned in bed or summoned other thoughts—for there was much to think on: Lady Eira's plans had been set in motion and everything was about to change in Tearmunn—he failed. Ember's bare skin, captured in the glow of candlelight, held him hostage.

Unable to bear the torment another minute, Alistair rose from bed. He hadn't bothered to change from his uniform into a sleep shirt. With Conatus reeling from Sorcha's death and Eira taking control of both the Circle and the Guard, the night portended chaos. Alistair had even kept his sword belted to his waist. Should a fight arise, he would be ready to assure Lady Eira's successful ascension to sole rule of their order.

As he left his cell, Alistair briefly considered seeking out Eira. Perhaps she had need of his help maintaining order. But he readily dismissed that thought. Should she desire, Lady Eira would have no qualms about summoning him. Having given this brief attention to duty, Alistair succumbed to the siren song that called him through the dim corridor.

Passing the few doors that separated his cell from Ember's, Alistair paused in front of her door. What took place within this chamber once he entered would determine the nature of his relationship with Ember. Alistair knew this truth. He leaned against the door, letting the image of her half-clothed figure slide into his mind's eye, coaxing him to action.

Ember must have known he was the one at the door earlier that night. Only a trusted friend would intrude upon her at such a late hour. She hadn't dropped her gown in surprise. The chemise had been falling, released with purpose by Ember's own hand. She'd been waiting.

Alistair refused to believe Ember had anticipated the arrival of another. How could she?

Despite the sick twist of his gut the thought provoked, Alistair couldn't stop the needling doubt following his question. Barrow had come upon them. The knight had disrupted what Ember's skin promised Alistair.

Could Ember have been waiting for Barrow?

Alistair's roiling stomach tangled itself into a hard knot. No. It wasn't possible. Barrow had abandoned Ember. He'd cast her off, forsaking his role as her mentor. And hadn't Alistair restored his own friendship with her in the wake of Barrow's rejection? Hadn't he and Ember grown ever closer, slowly returning to the intimacy and trust they'd shared as children?

That history, the knowledge that he knew Ember better than anyone else, assured Alistair of what he'd always believed. Ember was bound to him, and despite her characteristic stubbornness, she loved him. They would marry, and she would be his. Alistair could imagine no other role for Ember in his life, and his loyalty to Lady Eira had secured his future with Ember. Eira had promised to bring changes to Conatus, which Alistair would soon take advantage of. No longer heralding ties to those monk warriors, the Knights Templar, the Conatus Guards' vows would be of fealty to Lady Eira and Lord Bosque Mar and nothing more. The new order offered Alistair all he desired.

Fortified by this thought, he rapped lightly on the door. And waited. He knocked again, daring to use a bit more force. With Sorcha's sudden death, most of the Guard would be away from their cells, holding a vigil in the hall below. Waking someone was of small risk, and since Ember had kept away from the gathering of knights when he'd sought her out earlier that evening, Alistair wagered that she'd remained secluded in her bedchamber.

Even after more insistent knocks, Alistair couldn't hear Ember stirring within. Perhaps her sorrow over Sorcha had driven her into deep sleep. Or still grieving, Ember might be weeping in her cell, too ashamed to share raw emotion with another. Alistair thought Ember all too concerned about showing a brave face to the world. She was strong enough. Maybe a bit too strong. Ember could be a knight of Conatus if it suited her. But she was still a woman.

Convinced that Ember was most likely hiding her feelings, as she was wont to do, Alistair slowly opened the door. As her dearest friend, it was his place to comfort her. He thought of pulling her into his arms, of stroking her auburn tresses to soothe her. His body tightened when his mind pushed its musings further, making him imagine his hands pushing the loose neckline of Ember's chemise over her shoulders. Watching it fall as it had a few hours before. This time Alistair would catch her hands in his own if she feigned modesty. He would clasp her fingers tightly and look upon her body as he longed to.

In the darkness of Ember's cell, Alistair clenched his jaw so he wouldn't groan. The idea of offering solace to Ember as she mourned had been muscled out by desire that felt as old as his bones. He moved forward, slowly through the black.

"Ember," Alistair whispered.

She gave no answer.

He started toward her pallet, hands outstretched. As he reached to rouse her from sleep, clouds peeled back, uncovering the moon. Translucent beams stretched through the narrow window, giving light to the cell.

Alistair stared at the pallet. The wool blanket lay in a crumpled heap at its center. The bed was empty. He was reaching toward nothing.

The shock of embarrassment was trampled by sudden rage. Where could Ember be?

At the vigil? Her presence there would make sense. After all, Sorcha had taken up the role of Ember's mentor after Barrow had forsaken it. But if Ember intended to spend the night hours honoring her dead friend, why had she been readying for sleep when Alistair last saw her?

Ember wasn't one for complacency. If she hadn't been able to sleep, she might have left her cell. But Alistair doubted she'd joined the knights' vigil. Ember would be more inclined to contend with her sorrow directly. She could be out walking the grounds. Or riding that horse she loved.

Twin spikes of fear and agitation lodged in Alistair's chest. Foolish girl. Lady Eira hadn't yet been able to bring Ember into her fold. That made the young warrior vulnerable. It would take time for Eira to quell the panic in the village, to reassure them that Conatus had been cleansed of its wicked elements and a new reign of justice was about to begin.

A sudden, unwelcome vision crowded out Alistair's fantasies. An unwanted sound filled his ears. Ember's screams. Her pale skin blistering and blackening, splitting open like old, dry leather. Her hair engulfed in real flames. Villagers dancing as they reveled in bloodlust, having captured and punished another witch. For what woman but a witch would ride out alone in the blackest of night?

Alistair was running before he reached the courtyard. Once outside, he sprinted to the stable, praying he wouldn't find what he suspected. Rushing along the stalls, Alistair pulled up at Caber's holding pen. Seeing that the stall was empty, Alistair bent over, spewing curses and trying to determine his next move. How could she be so reckless?

But Alistair knew Ember's wild nature would compel her to gallop off without thoughts of safety. He craved nothing more than to tether and tame her.

Frustrated, Alistair resigned himself to saddle his own horse and go out in pursuit. He couldn't risk Ember falling afoul of witch-hunters.

Before he'd reached the tack room, Alistair abruptly halted, going silent and perfectly still. A flicker of movement had slipped into his peripheral vision. Alistair drew his sword, turning to face the shape that cowered in shadows.

"Show yourself," Alistair said.

"Begging your mercy, my lord," a quaking voice answered.

"Fitch?" Alistair peered at the hunched figure. "Is that you?"

"It is, Lord Hart!" Fitch gave a cry of relief.

Alistair kept his sword at the ready. "Why are you skulking in the stables?"

Fitch crept forward, grunting with the effort. In the dark, his body appeared wide and misshapen. When he walked, his feet scraped across the dirt—or so Alistair thought. A moment later, Fitch was close enough for Alistair to see why Fitch had been hiding.

He was dragging a body.

With a hiss of breath, Alistair jumped back. "What is the meaning of this?"

"Please, Lord Hart." Fitch let the body go and dropped to his knees.

Alistair grunted in disgust to see a knight of Conatus groveling. He jerked away when Fitch reached as though to grasp Alistair's tabard.

"What I've done was to serve Conatus. I swear!" Fitch shook his bloodied fists at Alistair. "They've gone mad. They'll destroy us!"

Making sure his blade was between the cowering knight and himself, Alistair took a closer look at the unmoving man beside Fitch.

"Mercer." Alistair breathed the knight's name. Mercer's face was bloodied, his flesh swelling as it took on violet and gray hues. It was well known that Mercer and Fitch had long been friends. What could have provoked Fitch to attack a fellow knight?

As if sensing Alistair's scrutiny, Mercer groaned. Fitch lifted a hand to strike.

"No!" Alistair's command stopped Fitch's blow. They both watched Mercer, but the knight remained unconscious.

"You did this?" Alistair forced the tremor out of his voice.

"I had to." Beads of sweat stood out on Fitch's brow. "He's a traitor, Alistair. They're all traitors."

Alistair didn't know whether to take Fitch's use of his familiar name as a good sign or not. But the word *traitor* made his knuckles whiten as he gripped his sword hilt tighter.

"Speak quickly, Fitch," Alistair said. "Or I shall deal with you only as a cur who dishonors his companions with unprovoked violence."

"Take me to Lady Eira," Fitch pleaded. "She favors you. She'll grant me an audience if you ask. When Mercer wakes, he can be questioned and my words will prove true."

Alistair grimaced. "I'll take your confession and pass it on to Lady Eira. I'd sooner see you wait in the barracks for her judgment."

"No." Fitch fell over in the dirt when Alistair took a menacing step toward him. Fitch lolled on the ground like a beaten dog showing its belly. "Begging your pardon, Lord Hart, but I fear that I might be implicated in this treachery. I only wish to tell Lady Eira myself so she can see my contrition and restore me to my station. I risked my life to overpower Mercer so I would have proof of this conspiracy against Conatus. Please consider that."

Alistair found it difficult to feel anything but contempt for this man. Yet his bloodied hands and Mercer's limp form promised an intriguing tale. And if this treachery he spoke of was true . . .

"Very well," Alistair told him. "Lady Eira will hear your words. Now get up and stop shaming yourself with this pitiful display. I need your help to carry Mercer."

Fitch scrambled to his feet, casting a fearful glance at Mercer as though the unconscious man might revive and grab him.

Alistair seized Fitch and gave him a rough shake. "Act like the Guard you're supposed to be, Fitch. Take his feet and lead the way. I'll carry him at the shoulders."

Fitch turned away from Alistair and kicked Mercer's legs apart.

Tucking a calf on either side of his waist, Fitch lifted the unconscious man's lower half while Alistair took care of his torso.

"That's good," Alistair told Fitch. "Head into the courtyard. And be quick about it."

A man twitching and quavering the way Fitch did wasn't someone Alistair wanted at his back. The two knights, one tall and wary, the other bent over as if on the verge of being sick, made their way across the courtyard.

"She's likely in the great hall," Alistair said, directing Fitch to the manor. "And if the Circle is with her, all the better. If traitors are in our midst, it's a matter to be addressed without delay."

Fitch muttered something unintelligible in response, but Alistair didn't bother asking him to repeat himself. He was already questioning his decision to bring Fitch to Eira. What if the man had taken ill and the madness of fever had turned him on his friends?

Still proving his worth to Eira, Alistair detested the thought of raising alarm without reason. It was the cool touch of fear, light on his skin, that kept Alistair moving at a swift pace toward the great hall. No matter how unstable Fitch might appear, something real lay beneath his words. Something real and very wrong.

The corridors of the manor were still. The Guard would be occupied with their vigil, and the staff must have sought their beds for the night. All for the best, Alistair thought. Too many questions were bound to chase after a pair of knights carrying the broken body of one of their fellows. With Sorcha's death raising alarm only a few hours earlier, further bad news could incite panic throughout the keep.

When they reached the thick double doors, Alistair pivoted to the side, bracing Mercer against him while he freed his other arm and pulled the door open. He took care to leave space only wide enough to carry the body inside.

"This is a private session!" Claudio's shout stopped Alistair in the doorway, leaving Fitch and the other half of Mercer still in the hall.

Despite his many years as one of two Circle members hailing from craft, Claudio still bore the strength of years working with his hands. He strode toward Alistair.

"Peace, Claudio," Lady Eira called to him. "Lord Hart is welcome here."

Claudio hesitated, but didn't counter Eira's words, and Alistair quickly pulled the rest of Mercer, and Fitch along with him, into the room.

"What's this?" Claudio gaped at Mercer.

Alistair glanced back at Fitch. "Let's put him down. And then shut that door."

They laid Mercer on the floor while the other occupants of the hall gathered around. Fionn, per his office as a cleric, carried a scroll in his hand. He gazed calmly at Mercer as though the unconscious man were a puzzle to be solved.

Lady Eira spoke first. "What happened to Mercer?"

Before Alistair could answer, Fitch blurted out, "Have mercy, my lady. I swear I'll confess all."

"What do you have to confess, Fitch?" Eira asked, her voice cool.

"I've done wrong. I thought to betray the cause. But I know I was misled now. I seek to make amends." Fitch gulped, but when he opened his mouth to speak again, he suddenly yelped.

A hand had wrapped around Fitch's ankle. Mercer's eyes were open. With a jerk of his arm, Mercer pulled Fitch off balance. Fitch tumbled to the ground, and Mercer was on him, snarling like a wildcat.

Claudio shouted in surprise and backed away from the struggling pair. Fionn ran across the hall to take cover behind the sacred tree. Eira didn't move, but neither did she try to interfere.

"Traitor," Mercer spat as he struck Fitch. "I'll see you in hell for this."

"I'm no traitor." Fitch grasped Mercer's tabard, trying to shove Mercer off. "You're mad for believing them. They'll be the death of us."

"Stop!" Cian's clear voice rang out.

Alistair, who'd been about to grasp Mercer from behind and wrestle him away from Fitch, wheeled around. He hadn't noticed Lady Eira's sister in the hall. Cian leapt from the far corner of the room and closed the distance between herself and the tangled knights in a few long strides.

With a movement of such grace and strength that it stunned Alistair, Cian took hold of Mercer and Fitch—one in each hand—and threw them in opposite directions. Mercer rolled over once before jumping to his feet. He had no weapon to draw, but his fists were raised. Fitch, either reeling from Cian's sudden intervention or still shocked that Mercer had regained consciousness, fell back onto his hands and heels.

Cian's sword hissed out of its scabbard. "What is this talk of treachery?"

Mercer stared at her, and without breaking her gaze, he pointed at Fitch. "There is your traitor."

When Cian glanced at Fitch, his eyes bulged. He began to crawl backward like a crab. "You . . . you—"

"Yes, traitor." Cian moved toward Fitch. "You should fear me."

When Alistair realized Cian's intention, he rushed at her. "No! Wait!"

He didn't reach her in time. Cian brought her blade down in a clean arc, and Fitch's head toppled from his body.

"Damn your impatience!" Alistair watched blood pour out of Fitch's severed neck. "He was the one who came to me seeking aid. Why would you kill him?"

Unruffled by Alistair's fury, Cian said, "Your companion claimed he had a confession to make. One must sin to require confession. Fitch's face spoke to me plainly of his guilt. I've no doubt that his sins were great."

Alistair was shaking with outrage when she walked away from him.

Mercer stood still, face pale and fists raised. His expression was resigned, as though he expected to meet the same end by Cian's sword.

"You've seen how we deal with traitors." Cian spoke slowly to Mercer, holding his gaze. "Perhaps you would like a chance to confess, and if your contrition proves genuine, you'll be shown mercy."

Drawing a sharp breath, Mercer said quietly, "You cut him down like a common thief. I desire none of your mercy, and I have nothing to confess."

"Very well." Cian raised her sword.

"Put down your sword, Cian," Eira commanded. "When did my sister become a barbarian?"

Cian paused, glancing at Eira. "Death is the penalty for traitors."

"Of course it is," Eira answered. "But we've yet to learn the cause of these accusations."

"Lord Hart brought the men." Cian turned to Alistair. "I assume he has the answers we need."

Alistair jumped forward, speaking as quickly as he could. "I found Fitch in the stables. He'd beaten Mercer senseless and claimed there was a conspiracy against Conatus."

"Is there any truth to his story?" Eira asked him.

Alistair looked with regret at Fitch's headless body before he answered. "I don't know, my lady. Fitch desired to make a full confession to you personally. That's why I brought him here."

"You shouldn't have killed him," Eira told Cian. "It was reckless."

Cian returned Eira's stare without flinching. "To my mind,

they're both traitors. The only difference between the two is that Fitch was clearly the coward. I took his head to make a point. A necessary one."

"You let your temper get the best of you, and you dishonor yourself by making excuses for it." Eira regarded her sister coolly. "Go with Alistair and take Mercer to the stockade. Secure him there until we know the truth of this."

Cian pursed her lips and then said to Alistair, "Wait here. I'll bring irons to bind him before we go to the stockade."

Alistair nodded. The chaos in the room gave way to an uneasy quiet. Alistair heard Fionn retching behind the tree.

Claudio approached them cautiously. He eyed Mercer, gauging whether any threat remained.

Mercer stared blankly ahead, giving no sign of worry that Alistair stood close by with his sword drawn in case of any trouble.

"You're going to question him, then?" Claudio asked Eira.

"I know one more suited to the task than I," Eira answered. "I'll ask Lord Mar to join us shortly."

Eira walked in a slow circle around Mercer, looking the knight up and down. Her smile made Alistair shiver.

TWO

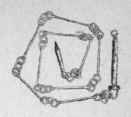

**STEAM ROSE FROM THE** horses' bodies, mirroring the mists that veiled the hillsides. The sun wouldn't show her face today, Ember thought. Though it was still night, Ember could almost feel the weight of low clouds pressing down upon them.

Leaning into Caber's strides, Ember tried to gather her wits. The stallion's hooves threw clods of damp soil into the air with each strike against the earth. Though the wind brought tears to her eyes, Ember had a hard time shaking the sense that she was caught in a dream. This breakneck flight from the Conatus keep of Tearmunn was too wild and frightening to be real.

But it was that fear, churning beneath her ribs, that made Ember all too aware that this midnight ride was not the stuff of dreams. Glancing over at her companion, Ember tried to muster courage. She could barely make out Barrow's features in the dark, but she could see well enough to take in his unusually rigid pose astride Toshach. He kept his eyes on the path ahead, urging Toshach to an even faster pace. As she watched Barrow, conflicting impulses wrestled within her. Barrow seemed incapable of fear. He led them into the night without hesitation. Ember trusted him. In brief moments when the terror of what she'd done released her from its grip, she reveled in the knowledge that she was riding abreast of the man whose company, whose touch, she'd come to believe was something she would never have. No matter how much she wanted it.

Joy surged in Ember's blood, like lightning strikes, but that ecstasy was chased away by the chill of doubt. They were running from friends. From sworn allies, beside whom she'd fought and bled. From a duty she'd come to believe was sacred. How could it be that they were fleeing Conatus? For years, Ember had longed for a life other than that which her father had planned for her. At Tearmunn, Ember had been granted that once-impossible dream, and she'd only begun to glimpse the wonders that serving Conatus offered. Now, only a few weeks since she'd arrived in Glen Shiel, she was running away from everything she'd ever wanted.

Everything except the knight who rode beside her. If it weren't for Barrow, Ember wondered if she would have been able to leave Tearmunn.

Despite her faith in Barrow, Ember wasn't at ease with the events of the last several hours. It had all happened so fast, and in a blur of such confusion. From the heat of Barrow's kiss in the woods to the attack on the village that had led to Sorcha's death, the night had brought Ember heaven and hell. And then there had been Alistair's unexpected appearance in Ember's cell. Her mouth went dry when she remembered the way he'd stared at her, his face tight with desire as he took in her half-naked form.

It hardly seemed possible, but Alistair's words had been even more disconcerting than his intrusion in her chamber. Not only had he spoken of them being together, as lovers, but he was in a frenzy over Conatus itself—the plans Eira had laid, the possibilities of a new order. None of it had made sense.

Ember wanted to face the night with courage, but as the hours of hard riding took their toll, she fought a losing battle against her uncertainty over the choice to leave. Though she tried to remember the reasons she'd been compelled to join the small band of rebels in their escape, Ember wished that the bearer of ill tidings had been someone in whom she had as much faith as she did in Lukasz and

Father Michael. But their informant had been a stranger, a wood-cutter whose mind seemed frayed at best.

Could any of what that disturbed man had told them be true? Ember would readily admit that Eira exuded strength and ambition, but how could she survive—a rare woman among the leaders of Conatus—without such traits? What could drive her to do anything to put those things most sacred to her at risk?

As Ember pondered these questions, she felt her confidence slipping away. A shout rose in her throat. She could stop this. All she needed to do was call out to Barrow and halt their mad dash from the keep. But when Ember looked at her companion, the panic swelling in her chest lessened. How could she behave with such cowardice?

*"That is all your strength and none of mine,"* Barrow had told her just before they'd fled Tearmunn.

He'd said more, as well: *"And that is why I love you."*

The memory of his words, the quiet strength behind them, kept the early morning chill at bay. Ember welcomed the fresh resolve that she could be the warrior Barrow believed she was.

A sudden shout jolted her out of her thoughts. Toshach had stumbled and squealed, either in pain or fright, knocking into Caber's shoulder. Barrow had called out as he worked to steady Toshach. Caber pinned his ears back, but Ember quickly checked the young stallion before he could bite the other horse.

Reining Toshach in, Barrow slowed their pace to a walk. The horses blew clouds of hot air, and their chests were lathered from the hard run. Barrow kept Toshach moving forward. He sat tense in the saddle, waiting. A moment later, he swore and swung down from the saddle.

Ember brought Caber to a halt, watching as Barrow knelt by Toshach's right foreleg.

"He's favoring this foot," Barrow told her without looking up. "If we keep riding, he'll pull up lame soon enough."

Barrow cursed again. "I'm sorry, Ember. I knew it was a risk to press the horses this hard at night. It's too easy for them to be injured by stones or branches on a path they can't see."

"What should we do?" Ember asked, trying to remain calm.

"I have the means to make an herb poultice that should give Toshach some relief," Barrow answered. "But we'll need to rest him for a few hours, and when we continue, we'll be traveling much more slowly."

Ember nodded, swallowing the hard lump in her throat.

"We've covered a lot of ground," Barrow said. "With luck, this delay shouldn't put us in any more danger than we already face."

He scanned the valley floor that buttressed the narrow path. "Let's head to that copse of pines. We shouldn't stay in the open."

Barrow led Toshach from the path and toward the cluster of trees. Ember stayed in the saddle but followed at a slight distance. Caber snorted and tossed his head, confused and frustrated by the sudden change of pace. Leaning forward to rest her head against the stallion's neck, Ember murmured soothing sounds until Caber's protests subsided.

When Barrow led Toshach into the copse, the pair suddenly vanished from sight. Arriving just behind them, Ember was grateful for the shelter the trees provided. Huddled together as if for comfort, the tall pines bent inward. At their upper reaches, the branches and needles tangled together. Ember might have wagered that if she jumped from the top of one tree toward the center of the ring, the branches were so tightly woven they'd break her fall, catching her in a net of fragrant greenery.

"Should I unsaddle him?" Ember asked as she swung out of Caber's saddle.

Barrow shook his head. "We're not likely to be surprised by an enemy, but it would be foolish to take anything for granted. We should be ready to leave at a moment's notice."

Ember settled for freeing Caber of his bridle and giving his ears a good scratching. Barrow gathered herbs and a strip of cloth from Toshach's saddlebags. He laid the cloth flat on the ground, measuring the herbs into a heap at the center. He hunted the soil until he found a stone that matched the size of his hand and, adding a bit of water from one of the skins, crushed the herbs into a paste.

"Ember." Barrow beckoned her to join him as he crouched beside Toshach's injured leg.

She knelt alongside him as Toshach watched them, flicking his ears in curiosity. Barrow held the poultice in one hand and gestured for Ember to crouch beside the stallion. He pressed her palm against the muscles just above Toshach's fetlock.

Toshach snorted, and Barrow spoke to him gently. "Easy, old boy. We're only trying to help."

Barrow looked at Ember. "Do you feel that heat?"

Ember nodded. Beneath Toshach's coat, his muscles radiated a strange warmth that pulsed against Ember's skin.

"That's the injury," Barrow told her. "The only way to cure it is a good rest, but the poultice will ease the swelling and some of the pain."

Ember watched as Barrow wrapped the poultice tightly around Toshach's leg. When he finished, Toshach whickered, lowering his head and blowing into Barrow's face.

"I know, friend." Barrow laughed. "It's not your fault." He patted the stallion's bowed neck.

Toshach swished his tail and wandered to the spot where Caber was foraging for spring shoots.

Though the copse of pines felt well protected, it was also very dark. Ember rubbed her arms, trying to chase away the sense of isolation that crept over her.

"We can't risk a fire," Barrow told her. "I'm sorry for the chill."

"Don't worry about me," Ember said. "Of course we must stay hidden."

Though she didn't want to, she shivered. The tremor hadn't been brought on by cold, but by a heightened awareness that many more nights of hiding awaited her.

Tentatively, Barrow reached out for Ember. She smiled, surprised that he'd worry she'd do anything other than step into his embrace.

Once Ember was close, Barrow folded her into his arms. She took a deep breath, noticing the way the astringent scent of pine mixed with the warm spice of his skin. He held on to her, his fingers running over her hair, down her neck.

Ember lifted her chin. Barrow looked down at her. She could barely see his face in the darkness. Raising her hand, she found the curve of his cheek and let her fingertips run over the rough stubble of his jaw. When she touched his mouth, his lips parted in a sigh.

"Kiss me," she breathed, taken aback at her willingness to voice her desire so boldly.

But Barrow was already bending close. She felt his breath on her lips for the barest moment before his mouth touched hers. Her hand moved from his face to wrap around his neck as he kissed her hungrily, discovering the contours of her lips and neck with his teeth and tongue.

Ember's limbs began to quake. She gripped Barrow's shoulders, no longer trusting her legs to hold her upright. As she swayed, Barrow slid his arm around her waist and lifted her off her feet. He was still kissing her when he took them to the ground. Ember looked up at the tangle of branches that stretched over their hiding place like a canopy of ebony lace. Barrow paused, looking down at her, hesitating.

Grasping the front of his tabard, Ember pulled Barrow to her. When his weight pushed her against the earth, Ember swallowed a moan.

"Ember." Barrow kissed her temple, her ear. His hand moved over her, tracing the shape of her body from her collarbone to her hip. His other arm slid between her back and the ground, lifting her up against him.

"Please," she murmured, shuddering as this strange longing took hold of her body.

Barrow unbuckled the leather belt that held Silence and Sorrow. It fell away and he slipped his hand beneath her tabard and then her shirt. His fingers rested briefly on her stomach, making her draw a sharp breath. His lips touched hers softly as his hand moved up. When he found the edge of the cloth that bound her breasts to her ribs, he traced the line of fabric.

Ember swore, and he laughed.

"I didn't know that was a word you used, Lady Morrow."

"Only when it's appropriate," she answered. "I'll have to take my tabard and shirt off. There's unwinding to be done."

She felt his smile when he kissed her again. "Perhaps . . . or . . ."

Barrow's hand moved away from the tight wrapping of cloth around her chest, his fingers traveling along her skin, over her stomach and down. Ember went very still, suddenly unable to breathe.

Her hips moved, and she drank in the cool night air, its contrast sweet against the heat of her blood.

Ember reached for Barrow's hips, drawing up his tabard. Her palms molded against the strength of his thighs. She slid her fingers up, wanting to learn what it was to touch him.

But before she could, Barrow pulled back and, instead of holding her, knelt beside her.

Startled, Ember scooted up to rest on her elbows. Not sure if she should worry or just shout at him, Ember did neither, because Barrow spewed out such an array of curses that she almost blushed.

"Barrow?" Ember rolled onto her side, watching him.

"By all that lives on earth and in heaven," he said roughly. "There is nothing I want so much as you."

She reached for him, and Barrow pulled her into his arms, but when Ember tried to kiss him, he turned his face from her.

"This isn't the time for us, Ember," he told her. "Not here."

Ember laughed. "Do you honestly believe I'm still attached to the thought of making love only in a feather bed? I'm not a spoiled noblewoman, Barrow. You know that."

"That's not it," Barrow said. "I would make love to you here, in a bed, in a river. No place would thwart my desire for you."

"Good." Ember moved to kiss him again. This time his lips lingered against hers, but not for long.

"The only thing that could stop me is putting you at risk." Barrow held her slightly apart, his hands strong on her shoulders.

"What risk?" Ember frowned, her body thrumming from his touch and her frustration growing from being kept at bay.

"That you could conceive," Barrow said quietly.

Silence filled the small space between them. For a time, Ember could hear only the rapid beating of her heart.

Finally Barrow said, "To father your child would be a great honor, Ember. But this is a dangerous time. If you were to become pregnant, you might fall ill as some women do. And you must be strong now, ready to fight."

"I know," Ember answered. She couldn't imagine carrying a child in her belly. Not now. Perhaps not ever.

When Barrow's fingers lightly touched her cheek, she covered his hand with hers.

"Does that mean . . . I can't be with you?" Ember asked, not sure she had the will to keep her distance from him.

"No," Barrow said quickly, with a forced laugh. "Merciful God, no."

"But—"

Barrow laughed again, pulling her against him. "You don't remember?"

"Remember what?"

"You asked me once if members of the Guard ever took lovers."

Heat rushed into Ember's cheeks as she recalled the conversation, the confusion she'd felt that day, and how much had changed since.

Barrow continued, "I told you to seek advice from Sorcha about getting herbs that would allow you to make your choices without risk of a child."

"I never—I didn't—" Ember spluttered. Barrow was the only man she'd wanted in this way. When he'd passed her training to Sorcha and kept himself distant, Ember had assumed that he held her in disdain. A child with a misguided infatuation. Only when he'd drawn her into his arms amid a downpour, beneath the shelter of a great oak, had she learned that he returned her feelings.

"Sorcha and I never talked of these things," Ember finished awkwardly.

"Mmmmm." Barrow made a sound that blended frustration and disbelief. "When you asked me if any of the guard took lovers, I thought you might have sought a companion for your bed."

Ember nearly choked on her own breath. Fortunately Barrow continued speaking, sparing her the embarrassment of an attempt at spluttering a response.

"And it was that day"—Barrow paused, holding Ember in his gaze—"that I was forced to admit my jealousy. Though I thought I could fight my own desires, I learned quickly that my only choice was to keep myself away from you."

"I thought you despised me," Ember said.

"Despised you?" Barrow said. "How could you think—"

"You left me," she answered sharply. "You were my teacher, my friend, and then you were gone. What else was I to think?"

"I thought you would take me to be a brute no different from Alistair," Barrow continued, "who tried to force his way into your bed."

"You are nothing like Alistair. I longed for you to come to me." Ember leaned toward him, her pulse thrumming with the boldness of her words.

"I still feared you," Barrow told her. "What would happen if I . . ."

He rested his hand on her knee. Very slowly, Barrow's touch moved up her thigh, following the curve of her hip and finally resting on her waist. He spread his fingers wide, pressing firmly from the bottom of her rib cage to her lower back. Ember didn't break from his intent gaze, but her every breath was short and trembling.

"I could ease your fears," Ember murmured.

"Yes." Barrow kissed the crown of her hair. "But only when the risk is mitigated."

Ember turned her face up. Barrow looked down at her, taking her chin in his hand. After a moment, he kissed her, letting his mouth linger on hers, tasting her. He didn't push her away when she moved closer, settling onto his lap and wrapping her legs around him.

When their lips parted, Ember was breathless. Barrow's fingers dug into her hips. She didn't want him to let go.

"When we reach Krak des Chevaliers, I'll find someone who knows of the herbs you need." He let all his breath out in a huff. "Believe me, I'll find someone."

"Good." Ember backed away, toying with the lacings of his chausses.

He caught her hand, pulling her fingers to his lips and kissing them softly. "I only have so much will, Ember. Be kind."

That made her laugh, and to demonstrate her kindness, she moved to sit beside him, her arms and legs no longer holding him hostage. Barrow smiled, and she nestled her head against his chest, afraid to look at him as she next spoke.

"I never knew I could want like this."

Barrow didn't answer, but he pulled her closer, letting his finger circle the hollow of her throat.

With a blush, Ember asked, "Is it . . . supposed to hurt? Wanting you? Because it does. A little."

Barrow's deep laugh rumbled in her ear. "Be assured that I share in your suffering. Now rest. I'll wake you in an hour or so to take over watch."

Ember thought to protest, but the warmth of his body drained the tension from her mind and muscles. Her eyelids fluttered only once before she nodded against Barrow's chest and slept.

THREE

**EIRA PACED THE GREAT** hall, her right hand grasping and releasing the hilt of her sword in agitation.

"Tell me again," Eira said to Cian, who was standing near the sacred tree.

Cian sighed. "You know the names."

Eira cut a sharp look at her sister. Frustrated that she couldn't silence the buzz of fear that chased her like a swarm of flies, Eira tried to recall the moments of this night when she'd felt triumphant.

Before tonight, only Alistair had witnessed her ability to summon Bosque. But less than an hour ago, the Circle had witnessed her power . . . and trembled. Claudio and Fionn had already been present, and Eira summoned Thomas and Ewan—who'd joined the Guards' vigil as a sign of the Circle's grief and respect—to the great hall. The gathered leaders of Tearmunn watched as she spoke the invocation, standing in the pool of Fitch's blood that stained the floor.

When Bosque appeared at her side, bowing to her, Fionn had collapsed to his knees. Claudio stood his ground, but Eira noticed the throbbing pulse at his temples. Ewan took several steps back, making the sign of the cross, and Thomas gave a startled cry. Cian's sword hissed out of its sheath; she held her ground, muscles quivering as she prepared to attack.

Bosque took Eira's hand, kissing the tips of her fingers. "My lady, I am here to serve you."

"Circle of Tearmunn, I would present to you Lord Bosque Mar," Eira announced without breaking Bosque's silver gaze.

It was the narrowing of those liquid metal eyes that drew her gaze to Cian.

Eira laughed at her sister. "You needn't have drawn your sword. Here stands our greatest ally."

Cian hesitantly returned her weapon to its sheath.

After her demonstration, Eira gave orders that they should write to their peers across Conatus, bringing more of the order into the fold, and had sent the other Circle members away—all save Cian, whom Eira wanted nearby. It was a relief to finally confide in her sister, though Cian's response had been much cooler than Eira had hoped.

Eira and Cian had taken Bosque to the stockade, where Alistair stood watch over Mercer. She asked Bosque to stay with Alistair, confident that Bosque would have no trouble loosening Mercer's tongue. And how much the better for young Alistair to bear witness. Eira had great confidence in the boy. Trust burgeoning into affection. If she'd ever had a nephew—or perhaps even a son—she imagined he would be much like Lord Hart.

That thought settled her mind a bit as she focused on the problem at hand. Eira stopped her pacing and glared at Cian. "I've asked you to tell me their names. Never mind that you've spoken them before."

Cian answered wearily. "Lukasz, Kael, Barrow, and Ember—all from the Guard. Fitch and Mercer would have made their party six."

"And you're certain no others supported them?" Eira asked. "None of the clerics or craftsmen?"

If the traitors had taken a cleric capable of weaving, Eira dreaded the possibilities. Lukasz and his band of fellows could already be in Asia.

Cian crossed to Eira, placing her hands on her sister's shoulders. "Calm yourself, Eira. The few who fled did so suddenly and in the dead of night. They had little time to plan, much less win allies."

Eira twisted out of Cian's grip. "We can't be too careful. This is a delicate time."

"Now that they're away, what do you have to fear?" Cian asked. "You have the greater force, not to mention the security of the keep."

"Are you such a fool?" Eira snapped. "Those who are away are the best of the Guard. For God's sake, the commander is among them."

"And what is it that you fear Lukasz will accomplish?" Cian frowned at Eira. "Is there anything he can do, given the power you've already demonstrated?"

"If I know Lukasz, he'll seek aid from other Conatus strongholds," Eira told her.

"But we will infiltrate those fortresses before your commander has even left this shore," Bosque Mar interrupted as he entered the hall with Alistair Hart at his heels. "Conatus is yours to rule."

Eira noticed the tightening of Cian's jaw when she answered Bosque. "And is that my sister's fate? To rule Conatus?"

The tall, dark-haired man's reply was serene. "Eira's fate is whatever she wishes it to be."

Cian turned to Eira. "Are you to rule us?"

"We will rule, just as we have before," Eira told her calmly. "But without suffering the petty whims and greed of those we once were beholden to—like Abbot Crichton."

"Do you doubt your sister's vision?" Bosque stepped to Eira's side, but leveled his gaze on Cian.

"My sister will always have my love and loyalty, Lord Mar." Cian spoke through gritted teeth. "But what's happened constitutes a revolt and will carry heavy consequences."

"The consequence for those loyal to Conatus will only be a great reward," Eira told Cian. "But for those who stand in our way—"

"Will you truly make war on your own?" Cian broke in. "Can you take the sword to Lukasz, who has so long been our friend?"

Eira pursed her lips, giving Cian a measured look. "I hope that our commander may yet see how shortsighted his actions are. If he repents, I will gladly welcome him home."

"My advice is that you bring him home before he is lost to us completely," Bosque interjected.

Cian's brow knit. "And how will you find them? Dawn is still hours away."

"The dawn is of no consequence," Bosque said. He turned to Alistair, who was standing quietly aside.

Eira noticed that while Alistair's back was straight and his shoulders set with strength, his face was pale and his eyes were empty.

"Has Mercer revealed the route they've taken?" Eira asked Bosque, though a new concern for Alistair's health unsettled her.

"I would give this task to Lord Hart," Bosque told them in a quiet, soothing voice. "For though the commander's flight threatens our cause, it is this young knight who suffers the most from his companions' departure."

Alistair gave the barest of flinches.

Bosque approached him, speaking calmly. "Is this not true, young knight?"

Clearing his throat, Alistair said, "It is, my lord."

"When that which is most precious has been stolen from you, there is even greater pleasure in taking it back." Bosque smiled at Alistair.

Alistair looked at Bosque, a desperate hope etched on his face.

With a frown, Cian interrupted. "I ask again, how will you find them?"

Bosque ignored her and instead considered Alistair's stricken expression. "I would ease your pain, Lord Hart. Do you crave a hunt?"

"A hunt?" Alistair repeated.

"You're the son of a nobleman," Bosque answered. "Surely you've enjoyed hunts with your father and brothers."

"I have, my lord," Alistair said, though his brow furrowed in confusion.

"I'll need something that belongs to the one you seek," Bosque told Alistair. "Can you provide such an item?"

"I—yes," Alistair said, the doubt in his voice giving way to excitement.

Bosque smiled at him. "Collect it and join us in the courtyard."

Alistair gave a short bow and dashed from the hall. Bosque pivoted to stand squarely facing Cian.

"If you wish, I can show you exactly how we will find your runaways," Bosque told Cian.

"The courtyard, you say?" Cian asked, and Bosque laughed.

"To bring my hunters here would be quite hazardous." Bosque glanced at the wooden beams of the ceiling. "And to lose such a lovely hall would be a shame."

Cian cast a questioning glance at Eira, but Eira had no answers for her sister. When Bosque offered his arm, Eira took it and let him lead them from the hall. She could see hesitation and fear written on Cian's face, but she knew her sister would soon understand and come to love the wonders Bosque Mar wrought.

For her own part, Eira was no longer anxious about Lord Mar's mysterious plans or his strange confidence in solving complex problems. She'd witnessed his finesse, his power, his control so many times over that she felt an almost childish joy in anticipating what he might manifest next.

Cian would come to know that same crackle of expectation, and then the two sisters would wield the great weapons Bosque provided. All would be as it should. Eira was certain of that.

When they entered the courtyard, Alistair was already there. He hurried to Bosque, and when the tall man held up his open palm, Alistair dropped a delicate object into Bosque's hand.

Eira recognized the necklace, and she knew Bosque would as well. He'd enchanted the pendant himself, promising Alistair that Ember would face no threat from the wraiths sent to attack the village. Assuring Alistair of Lady Morrow's safety had been tantamount to securing his allegiance.

A similar pendant had been given to Sorcha, but for a different purpose. When Eira had spoken to Sorcha, she'd presented the necklace as a peace offering. A token to remind Sorcha of the bond that women warriors shared, and an apology from Eira for the arguments they'd had about the future of Conatus. Sorcha had graciously accepted the necklace, not knowing that it meant her doom.

Sorcha's fate could have been Ember's. Had Ember reached the village and attempted to take on Bosque's wraiths only to have the shadow creatures submit to her, as they did to Sorcha, the villagers would have taken Ember for a witch too. Thus, Eira's task of the night had been to find the girl and keep her out of harm's way. That had been easy enough, though Eira hadn't found Ember alone—but she had determined to keep what she'd seen from Alistair. The boy was brokenhearted enough, thinking that Ember had gone with Lukasz, but Eira knew that the girl's reasons for leaving were likely more tied to the strength of Barrow's embrace than her loyalty to the commander.

"Lady Cian, if you'd bring me a torch." Bosque gestured to Eira's sister.

Cian fetched a torch from one of the sconces that framed the manor's door, and Bosque took it from her. His gaze lingered on the dancing flame. Cian gasped when Bosque thrust his hand into the fire. He didn't flinch as his skin crackled and sizzled. When he pulled his hand free, the flames crawled over his blackened fingers like a living glove.

Making a fist, Bosque swung his arm in several arcs. His fiery hand left a trail of flame and smoke. Rather than dissipate, the flames formed a circle, swirling crimson and gold, shimmering with heat.

With fingers still alight, Bosque pointed his hand at the center of the blazing ring. His words were strange, rasps and clicks syncopated over the low bass of his voice.

Eira squinted at the circle of flames, confused by what she saw, for she could swear that within the fiery ring lay the black depths of a tunnel. As she peered into the dark core, something winked at her, like the flicker of a candle in a draft. Then two small points of light caught her eye. Then three. The tiny dancing flames grew larger, taking form as they drew closer.

Cian gave a cry, and both sisters jumped back as fiery bodies leapt from Bosque's circle.

Alistair stood his ground, but his eyes were wide as he watched three shapes circle Bosque. Though flesh and blood had been traded for fire and smoke, there was no mistaking what these creatures Bosque had summoned were. Wolves.

Where fur should have been, flames licked the bodies of the beasts. When they opened their mouths, plumes of smoke spewed out. With each step, they left charred paw prints on the earth.

Bosque lowered his flame-covered hand, and the wolves approached. With tongues of fire, they licked his fingers, showing submission. Only when Bosque's hand no longer burned did the wolves step away and return to circling the tall man.

Eira glanced at Cian, who was staring at Bosque's hand. Eira knew why her sister was riveted. The blackened skin, burning for so long, had healed, leaving no trace of damage.

*If only you knew that Bosque's power to heal also saved your life,* Eira thought.

That secret Eira withheld for safekeeping. She hoped to win Cian over without relying on the fact that her sister owed Bosque her life. But if need be, Eira would reveal that truth in time.

"Your hounds, my lord." Bosque smiled at Alistair.

"What are they?" Alistair breathed. The wolves' fiery bodies were reflected in his gaze.

"Lyulf—loyal and ferocious, a precious resource drawn from my homeland. The fire and flesh with which I summoned them gives them purchase on this world," Bosque told Alistair. "But they can't survive here without a constant source of heat. You must act quickly, lest you lose them."

"How long will they last?" Eira broke in. "A few hours' head start is nothing to scoff at."

"Indeed," Bosque replied. "And none of your horses will bear the company of the Lyulf." He turned to Alistair again. "Thus, I have another gift for you, my lord."

There was no fiery circle called for this time. Bosque reached into the darkness itself, and where there had only been shadow, the shape of a horse materialized.

The stallion—if it could be called that—was familiar to Eira. Bosque's steed had always put her mare, Geal, on edge. The horse was eerily beautiful, but frightening. Eira didn't know if she'd be eager to claim the shadow steed as a mount.

Alistair, however, gazed at the horse with eyes that swam in dark dreams of possession.

"He will carry you, and the wolves will run at his side," Bosque told Alistair. "You will move through time in a way that the horses of this world cannot. It will be an exceptional hunt."

Despite Alistair's apparent confidence, Eira asked, "Your stallion will obey him?"

Bosque stroked the shadow stallion's nose. "The horse does my bidding. He will listen to the boy."

At a gesture from Bosque, Alistair strode to the stallion's side. Without further command, he climbed into the saddle and took the reins. The horse stood calmly, barely giving his new rider notice.

"Once I put the wolves on Lady Morrow's scent, they will be off,"

Bosque said to him. "And the horse will follow the wolves' trail. Do not lose your grip on the reins or attempt to stop him and dismount. The means by which you travel puts you at risk for being forever lost, should you stray from the intended path."

Alistair blanched, causing Eira to smile. Though she wanted the young knight to be courageous, his quick sense of mortal peril reassured her that he wasn't simply a brave fool.

"If I can't leave the horse," Alistair said with hesitation, "how will I fight?"

"Leave the fighting to the wolves," Bosque answered. When Alistair looked away, Bosque continued. "They will know to leave Lady Morrow unharmed. Your task is to collect her while the Lyulf engage her fellows. You must play Hades to her Persephone."

A brief smile crossed Alistair's mouth. "Very well."

Cian stepped forward, shaking her head. "Do you send your wolves to kill, then? What of mercy, of prisoners to question?"

"You already have a prisoner to question," Bosque answered. "Do you wish to show mercy to such a small band of traitors?"

Cian broke his gaze, casting a pleading glance at Eira. "Do you wish to send monsters after your fellow Guardsmen? You would give them this doom?"

"I would remind you that they are no longer our fellows." Eira gave her sister a steely gaze. "And did not your own blade offer Fitch the same justice that I send after his collaborators? Lukasz and his followers chose their own fate. Mercy cannot be granted when it is not deserved."

As the two sisters faced each other, both of them stonelike in anger, Bosque dangled Ember's pendant from its chain. One by one, the three wolves came to him, sniffing the gold and ruby necklace. Satisfied that the Lyulf had her scent, Bosque tossed the pendant to Alistair.

"Keep this with you," Bosque ordered. "If the wolves and your mount halt and look to you for instruction, it may mean they need to take the scent again."

Alistair nodded, though he regarded the fire wolves with wary eyes.

"If they come close, you'll suffer burns," Bosque told him. "But I can heal you upon your return. It's unlikely that you'll need to call them to you. Rarely do Lyulf lose a scent, and then only if the one they seek is warding their hunt by spellwork—but this night the prey does not know of the hunter's approach."

"Yes, my lord." Alistair slipped the pendant into the pocket of his cloak.

"The night wanes," Bosque said to him, ignoring the still-silent sisters.

When Eira finally sighed, turning away from Cian to answer Bosque, Alistair and the wolves were gone. Only the lingering shimmer of heat and acrid perfume of smoke remained.

FOUR

# "EMBER, YOU MUST WAKE."

Barrow took both of her hands and pulled Ember to her feet before her eyes were fully open.

"Of course," she said drowsily. "How long should I let you rest?"

"I wish I'd woken you for that reason," Barrow told her. "You've slept barely an hour, but something is amiss. Look to the west."

Ducking out from under the cloak of pine trees, Ember searched the valley floor. Where the glen curved sharply, putting the path they'd taken out of sight, a haze of rust infused the heavy mist. The strange light shifted, its hues bathing the dark hillsides in copper and bronze.

Ember would have named the colors a harbinger of dawn, but morning came from the east, and the east was presently at her back.

"What is it?" she asked in a whisper.

"I don't know," Barrow answered. "But I dare not hope for something good."

Without speaking further, Ember and Barrow sought the horses, who were dozing nearby.

Barrow patted Toshach's neck. "I'd wanted to give you more rest, but I'm afraid we can't wait."

Toshach whickered and stood patiently as Barrow put on the bridle.

Ember was already astride Caber when Barrow mounted.

"We'll stay off the path," Barrow said, "keeping the cover of the forest if we can."

Ember looked at Toshach, and Barrow answered her question before she asked it.

"I'd like to start at a walk," Barrow told her. "Whatever those lights are, they're still well behind us. If they gain too much ground, we'll have to run and hope for the best." He rested his hand on Toshach's shoulder. The stallion snorted and tossed his head.

Barrow laughed, reaching up to scratch Toshach's ear. "I know you'd be happy to run, old boy. But the harder we press you, the longer it will take to recover from your injury."

Caber was restless as well, keeping Ember busy as he pranced and tried to catch the bit in his teeth.

"You were sound asleep a few minutes ago," Ember chided the young horse. "Settle down."

Caber continued to snort and shake the reins as Ember gripped them, but the riders set out at a fast walk. The horses threaded their way through the forest's edge so the strange lights in the west remained in partial view. Every few minutes, Barrow turned in his saddle, frowning.

"It is getting closer," he said. "But I can't make any guesses at what it is."

Putting his heels to Toshach, Barrow brought them to a trot. Ember's pulse sped, jumping in her throat each time she glanced over and saw the grim set of Barrow's jaw.

He turned in the saddle again, and the sudden sharp intake of his breath made Ember turn as well.

The lights had cleared the glen's curving shape. Though her vision was partly blocked by tree trunks and branches, Ember's mouth still went dry at what she saw. Rolling down the valley floor was a thundercloud, its black shape like roiling smoke, the darkness broken by flashes of lightning that exploded in the colors of flame and blood.

The storm cloud moved with impossible speed, racing toward them.

"Run!" Barrow shouted.

Toshach leapt forward, his hooves tearing into the ground. Given free rein, Caber bucked once for good measure and then broke into a flat run. The two horses galloped side by side.

Ember kept her eyes ahead, too afraid to look back. She knew the cloud was getting closer because she could hear it. But the storm cloud didn't thunder after them—the noises within it could only be called snarls.

Barrow urged Toshach to a breakneck pace. Caber's ears flattened as he stretched his neck forward to match Toshach's stride.

The horses both squealed when, from very close behind, there came a howl, long and echoing through the glen. One wolf's cry was joined by two more. Toshach's eyes rolled, showing their whites. Caber jerked his head down sharply, ripping the reins from Ember's hands. She grabbed his mane, reaching for the flapping leather cord.

Before she could grasp it, Toshach gave a loud bellow. With horror, Ember turned to see Toshach falling. Barrow could do nothing as the stallion fell to his knees. The force of their pace sent Toshach somersaulting, rolling over onto his neck, back, flank. Ember screamed as Barrow was pinned between horse and earth. Dragging his rider along, Toshach skidded over the ground, at last coming to a stop.

The sound of the other horse's distress brought Caber's head up, and Ember threw herself forward, grabbing the reins and wheeling him around. When the stallion saw what was coming for them, he reared, striking the air with his hooves. Ember grabbed the pommel, managing to keep her seat as she stared in disbelief.

The storm cloud had slowed, but only because it was upon them.

Shapes were forming within the swirling smoke and fire. Wolves—and behind them, a dark horseman.

When Caber's feet returned to the earth, she forced him to the spot where Toshach struggled to his feet. Barrow lay on the ground close by, unmoving.

"Please don't run from me," Ember whispered to Caber as she jumped from her saddle. She wouldn't have blamed the young stallion for fleeing. Ember's every bone shrieked at her to run. And she did run, but it was toward Barrow.

Before she could get there, a flaming creature burst from the cloud. The wolf was made of fire. Ember didn't know how it could be possible, but her eyes told her the beast was real, her nose breathed in its scent of char, and even at this distance, her skin felt the touch of its heat. Entranced by the sight, Ember failed to watch her step and, catching her foot on a root, she stumbled. Expecting this sign of weakness to lure the wolf to her, Ember rolled to a crouch, drawing Silence and Sorrow from their leather sheaths.

The wolf, however, paid her no mind. Its pitlike eyes fixed on Barrow's still form. Hungry, the beast let its jaw drop open, and it drooled liquid fire that sizzled on the damp ground.

"No!" Ember tensed, ready to jump between Barrow and the wolf. Her chest constricted, knowing that Silence and Sorrow were forged to battle creatures of flesh. This molten wolf seemed unlikely to fear a blade . . . or any weapon Ember could imagine.

About to push off on her heels, Ember suddenly rolled to the side to avoid being trampled by Toshach's hooves. The stallion shrieked as it bore down on the fire wolf. The wolf snarled, gnashing its blazing fangs.

Toshach reared. His ears were pinned back. When he landed, he stamped the earth, squealing at the fire wolf.

The wolf sprang, and Toshach reared again. As the stallion's hooves struck the wolf, Toshach's clarion call became a bellow of pain. The wolf's jaws closed on the horse's throat, and he collapsed, his whinny cut off before his body hit the earth.

Ember took up the felled stallion's cry. Heedless of the wolf, Ember threw herself on top of Barrow. She laid her head on his chest. When she heard his heartbeat, she could breathe again. Ember moved into a crouch, Silence and Sorrow held low and away from her body to fend off attack, no matter how futile such a defense might be.

Toshach's corpse made a barrier between Ember and Barrow and the fire wolf. The wolf stood still, assessing its work. As it waited, two more wolves joined it, standing at its flank.

Ember's mind was a blur. What she faced was worse than any nightmare that had stolen her sleep as a child. Wolves made of fire.

Their black eyes were on her, yet they didn't attack. Ember stayed very still, her muscles burning with tension.

From behind the wolves, the dark rider approached.

Ember risked looking away from the wolves. When she saw who sat astride a horse that was smoke to the wolves' fire, she thought she would retch.

Alistair looked at the gaping hole in Toshach's throat. The stallion's flesh had burned away, revealing the bones of his jaw.

"I am sorry about Toshach," Alistair said, though he seemed to be speaking to the air rather than to Ember.

When Alistair did look at Ember, his face was calm. "They won't hurt you."

Ember stared at him, only realizing after a moment that he was referring to the fire wolves. The wolves continued to stand their ground, giving no sign that they wished to menace Ember. Though their black eyes seemed hungry when they looked at Toshach's body . . . and Barrow's.

Forcing her cracked voice from her throat, Ember managed two words. "Alistair, please."

He winced and then clenched his jaw. "I do what I must."

"What you must?" Ember kept her body covering Barrow's, growing convinced that should she leave him, the wolves would be on him in an instant. "You would destroy me?"

"I've already told you that the Lyulf won't attack," Alistair said. "Not without my command."

He straightened, taking an imperious stance. "You understand little of what's happening, Ember. I remain your friend. Let me help you."

"You hunt with monsters," Ember spat. "I understand that well enough."

"I acted only to protect you," Alistair said. "You know of my love for you. I would do anything for you."

"You attacked us," Ember argued. "Your wolves killed Toshach. And I know if I leave Barrow, they will kill him as well."

"Barrow is a traitor. And he deluded you into following him on a path that will mean your death."

Ember bit back her reply. Defending Barrow, making plain her love for him, would only incense Alistair.

"You must come with me, Ember," Alistair urged quietly. "It's the only way."

Feigning indecision, Ember dropped her gaze.

When she didn't speak, Alistair said, "You've been misled. If you return to Tearmunn, you'll see what's truly happening. I told you that Lady Eira wished to speak with you, but the traitors reached you before she could. And I've been forced to this."

"I know you love me, Alistair," Ember said, choosing her words carefully. "And you know me better than anyone. You've known me since we were children."

"I do know you," Alistair replied. "That's why you must listen to me and not to those who would use you for their selfish purposes."

Ember looked up at him. "Maybe I've made the wrong decision, but to leave Tearmunn was my choice."

The smile that had begun to touch Alistair's lips vanished.

"To know me is to know how bullheaded I am," Ember hurried on. "I won't lie to you, Alistair. You attacked us. Toshach stumbled, but it could just as easily have been Caber. I could have been killed, no matter your intentions."

"You are unharmed." Alistair spoke through gritted teeth, and Ember knew she had little time.

"I believe that you want to protect me, but I can't return with you tonight," Ember said. "Not like this. If I return, it must be my choice. Don't you see?"

Ember held her breath as Alistair stared at her.

"And why would you return by your own will when you fled the keep this very night?"

"I made the choice to leave in grief and confusion over Sorcha's death," Ember told him. "Lukasz is my commander, and his words were convincing . . . but I had little time to make my choice."

Alistair nodded, and Ember pushed on to the riskiest bit of her ploy. "Barrow isn't dead, but he's gravely injured. I must get him help."

"What happens to Barrow doesn't matter," Alistair said.

"I know you have a quarrel with him," Ember returned. "But he was my friend, and I will not abandon him."

She glanced at the fire wolves. "Nor will I leave him to your hellhounds."

Alistair was silent, and Ember knew he was uncertain of what to do. The wolves stirred, growling their discontent.

"If I give you my word that I go not to join Lukasz, but instead to my sister in France," Ember said, "will you leave me in peace?"

"And then what?" Alistair asked bitterly.

"Then I will have the time to know my own heart," Ember told him. "Both about the lady Eira and Conatus, and about you and me."

Alistair peered at her. "You and me?"

"I can't forget our history, Alistair." Ember spoke softly. "And all you've done to prove your love for me. You take great risks on my behalf."

"I would never do less," Alistair answered. "I swear to you."

"Then let me swear to you that I go to my sister." Ember's pulse was pounding. "To leave Barrow with a healer and seek the answers I must. I may yet return to Tearmunn and to you, but then it would be my choice. If you take me there by force, I will not forgive you."

Ember wondered if she'd pushed him too far, for Alistair was quiet a long while. The wolves' growls were louder now, and they snapped at the air with their flaming jaws.

Alistair reached into his cloak, then tossed something in the air. It sailed toward Ember, and she reached out to catch it. Opening her hand, she shivered when she recognized the pendant Alistair had given her. A gift from Lady Eira.

"That was given as a sign of Lady Eira's faith in you," Alistair said. "Let it be a sign not only of my faith as well, but also of my love. Think on us and on your future, Ember."

"Thank you." Ember's limbs wanted to collapse in relief, but she dared not move with the wolves so close.

"I pray that you'll make the right choice," Alistair told her, his face grim. "If you do not return to Tearmunn within the month, you will become the hunted again. And I will no longer protect you."

Wheeling the shadow horse around, Alistair didn't look back at Ember. The wolves howled in protest, their cries becoming whining snarls as they followed him, tethered by some invisible leash. Alistair put his heels to the dark horse, and in a blur, the wolves and rider became a cloud of smoke and blood lightning that soared eastward up the glen and finally faded from sight.

FIVE

**WHETHER IT WAS A FEW** minutes or hours, Ember couldn't be sure, but for a time she couldn't move. She dropped onto her knees beside Barrow and stared into nothing. She had a vague sense of being cold, but the chill was negligible compared to the hollowness beneath her ribs.

Caber finally roused her from the stupor. She didn't know what the stallion had done during the fight: whether he'd bolted and just now returned, not knowing where else to go, or if he'd been paralyzed by shock as he watched his friend Toshach die.

Wherever he'd been and whatever he'd witnessed, Caber now approached Toshach tentatively. Ember watched as the young stallion whickered to the fallen horse. Caber blew out on Toshach's neck, whinnying softly, then giving a low squeal of sorrow. Stomping the ground twice with his front hooves, Caber snorted and jumped away from the dead horse.

"I'm so sorry." Ember heard her own voice before she'd made the decision to speak. Caber looked at her, tossing his mane and whinnying in distress.

Shakily, Ember stood up. The stallion came to her outstretched hand. His nose was velvet soft on her palm.

"He did it to save Barrow." Her words came out thick. "And now Barrow needs our help."

Though it took a good deal of coaxing and pleading, Ember managed to convince Caber to lie on the ground alongside Barrow. Even with Caber's back in close proximity, Ember struggled to drag Barrow into the saddle. She held his body in place as she urged Caber to his feet.

After she'd collected the saddlebags from Toshach's body, Ember scrambled into the saddle behind Barrow. Easing Caber into a walk, Ember held on to Barrow with one arm. She tried to keep her mind blank. Fear that moving Barrow at all was harming him further threatened to unravel her determination. Though his heartbeat was steady and his breathing normal, Ember couldn't know the extent of his injuries. A broken rib or crushed organ would mean his body was bleeding on the inside, invisible wounds that nonetheless meant death. But what choice did she have?

Ember had briefly weighed the option of riding ahead in hopes of bringing help to Barrow, but it seemed much more dangerous to leave him unconscious and alone than to risk moving him. Moving at a plodding pace frustrated her so that her bones ached, but a faster gait than walking would jostle Barrow too much.

Steeling herself, Ember loosened the reins, letting Caber take up a swift walk without allowing him to trot. Dawn was breaking over the hills to the east, and Ember rode toward the light, praying that the coast was as close as the promise of morning. Despite her exhaustion, fear kept Ember alert. She surveyed the landscape, always watching for the landmarks that Barrow had mentioned would mark their path to the sea. Should she miss any of them, Ember knew she'd easily lose days wandering aimlessly in the hills.

When the sun had crested the top of the glen and spilled pale gold and rose light down the slopes, Ember caught her first glimpse of the eastern coast: a dark, roiling blue. The sight filled Ember with more foreboding than hope. As Caber kept up his steady gait, the vast blue expanse rose up to meet them, stretching farther and farther into the east. Ember's mind was full of brittle thoughts, too easily broken into sharp bits of emotion that cut her to the core. She had almost reached the sea, but then what? Their tiny band would sail to a strange land and hope for aid? The cause already seemed lost to her.

Caber snorted, his ears flicked, and a moment later, he gave a loud whinny. Ember straightened in the saddle, striving to calm the stallion, who'd begun to prance. Another whinny returned Caber's call, drawing Ember's gaze to the woods that lined the path.

Keeping a tight hold on the reins, Ember watched the forest edge. If bandits hoped for an ambush, she'd be hard-pressed to protect Barrow and fight them off.

When a gray mare carrying Lukasz emerged from the shadows followed by Kael and his mount, Ember gave a shout of relief. She jumped down from Caber's back and waved the commander over to them.

"We thought the worst when you were delayed," Kael told her. His eyes rested on Barrow's unmoving form, and he was already climbing from his saddle.

"He's alive," Ember said, answering Kael's unspoken question. "Toshach fell, and Barrow was crushed beneath him."

Lukasz dismounted, and the two men lifted Barrow from Caber's back, setting him carefully on the ground.

"Were you attacked?" Lukasz asked. "Was Toshach struck down?"

"Yes, but the fall happened when we tried to flee," Ember said. "Toshach had pulled up lame, slowing us. When we were forced to run, he managed a short while but then he broke down."

"Who pursued you?" Lukasz spoke to her as Kael unbelted Barrow's sword and lifted his tabard and shirt.

Ember's mouth went dry when she saw the mottled skin of Barrow's chest and abdomen.

"Ember," Lukasz said, drawing her gaze from Barrow.

"Alistair," she answered. "He had . . . creatures with him, hunting us. Wolves made of fire. They moved with impossible speed, as if riding a storm. We couldn't outrun them."

Kael swore, and Ember feared he'd assessed Barrow to be beyond help, but the blond knight was looking at Ember.

"Fire wolves?"

She nodded. "Barrow was unconscious, and the wolves would have been on him. Toshach attacked the wolves before they could reach Barrow. A horse had no chance against them. I don't know if anything could hurt them."

"Like the shadow creatures," Lukasz said quietly. "Beasts we do not have the means to fight are being raised against us by Eira."

"How did you escape?" Kael frowned at Ember.

She hesitated, not knowing if the truth would suffice as an answer. Her cheeks grew hot when she told Kael, "I took advantage of Alistair's favor and was able to convince him that, given time, I might return to Tearmunn."

Ember looked at Kael, expecting him to doubt her tale. But Kael offered her a wry smile.

"Enough said." He shot a knowing glance at Lukasz. "I suffered many, many hours listening to Alistair proclaim his love for you."

Ember's blush deepened.

"It served our purpose," Lukasz added. "You were wise to exploit that weakness."

The commander's words did little to ennoble Ember's strategy, but at least they understood why it had worked.

"Did Alistair reveal how our flight was discovered?" Kael asked her. "Were we betrayed?"

"He didn't say," Ember answered. "But with Barrow's injury, I was forced to continue at a slow pace. Fitch and Mercer never overtook me, as they should have."

Kael sighed. "We'll assume them lost, then?"

"We must," Lukasz said. "We waited longer than I like in the hopes that we weren't alone in making an escape. Though Alistair was persuaded to give you freedom, Eira will soon send others after us."

A thin voice trilled from the forest. "My lords? Is it safe?"

Kael groaned. "For a minute I'd forgotten about him."

"Kindness," Lukasz chided, but he smiled at Kael. "The man's been through much."

"And we haven't?" Kael replied. "I've had pudding made of stronger stuff than him."

Lukasz laughed quietly, then called out, "Come to us, Sawyer! There's no danger here."

Ember watched as the woodcutter who'd revealed the extent of Eira's treachery scuttled from the forest. Sawyer hurried to join them. He huddled on the ground next to Lukasz. The man's entire body was taut and quivering.

Bobbing his head in deference to Ember, Sawyer let his eyes roam over Barrow's bruised torso. For a moment, the trembling of his limbs ceased and the wild bulging of his eyes relented.

"If I may, my lord," Sawyer asked Lukasz, "have a closer look?"

Kael rocked back on his heels. "For what purpose?"

"My mother was a healer," Sawyer answered. "I've not her skill, but I might be able to help some."

"If you could tell us how severe the injuries are, we'd be in your debt," Lukasz said, making space for Sawyer to kneel beside Barrow.

With light, probing fingers, Sawyer worked his way over Barrow's shoulders, chest, and abdomen. Ember winced when he touched the purple and red contusions that webbed over Barrow's skin. Sawyer bent down, placing his ear against Barrow's chest, listening. He rose and carefully lifted Barrow's head, molding his hands to the shape of Barrow's skull.

Ember noticed that, while he was occupied, Sawyer's tremulous character vanished. He ministered to his patient with calm, steady movements. Purpose offered a salve for his fear, putting his mind at ease.

"He's had a good knock on the head," Sawyer told them. "Quite the lump back here. No blood, though."

"What about the rest?" Ember pointed to the bruise on Barrow's torso.

Sawyer shrugged. "I can't say for sure, but my mother told me that if a man's heartbeat is strong and his breath doesn't sound like he's half drowning, then he's got a chance. Best thing is to give him rest."

Lukasz and Kael nodded, apparently satisfied by Sawyer's assessment, but Ember wished Sawyer could offer more assurance.

"He'll get rest on the ship," Lukasz told Sawyer, but he glanced at Ember, sensing her concern. "And when we reach Krak des Chevaliers, their healers will attend him."

"Yes," Ember replied, because there was nothing else to say. All she could do was wait and hope that Barrow's wounds would mend.

"My mare will bear the double burden of myself and Barrow till we reach the port," Lukasz said. "She's a stouter horse than Caber."

Kael and Lukasz carried Barrow to the commander's horse. At Ember's side, Sawyer had reverted to his former state. He twitched as he stood, often muttering under his breath. Pity for the woodcutter filled Ember.

"Perhaps you could ride near me," she said to him, "and tell me more of your mother's work."

"As my lady wishes," Sawyer answered. "My horse is still tethered in the forest, where we were waiting."

Sawyer yelped when Kael slapped him on the shoulder. "And that's why you should go get the beast."

With a whimper, Sawyer scampered away.

"You should be gentler with him." Ember frowned at Kael.

"Ride with him for as many hours as I have, and we'll talk." Kael grinned at her.

As they continued to make slow but steady progress toward the sea, Ember kept her word. She rode alongside Sawyer, engaging him with questions. At first the woodcutter seemed reluctant to converse, but as Ember asked him to recount his memories of his mother, Sawyer began to relax. The frightened whine with which he often marked his words faded. He smiled as he recalled the days of his childhood. Ember was careful with her questions, making sure to keep his mind on the distant past and well away from the trauma of recent days.

Though Ember had believed the coastline promisingly close, they had farther to travel than she'd thought. Only as dawn broke on the second day of their sojourn did they reach the port of Inverness.

Kael rode at the head of their small band while Sawyer and Ember moved to ride abreast of Lukasz in the hopes of sheltering Barrow's dire state from inquisitive gazes. Kael guided them to the harbor, which reeked of brine and kelp.

"Do you want to secure our passage, or shall I?" Kael asked Lukasz.

"Go ahead," Lukasz told him. "We'll likely need to make a shorter voyage to one of the French ports before we can find a vessel that will travel as far to the east as we wish."

Kael swung out of the saddle, giving charge of his mount to Ember. His horse hardly needed tending. All their mounts were so exhausted that they were more than pleased to stand and doze while Kael found a ship.

From where he was slumped in the saddle against Lukasz, Barrow stirred, groaning, and then went still.

"Oh!" Ember was ready to dismount, but Lukasz stayed her with his hand.

"It's a good sign," Lukasz told her. "I think he'll wake soon, but there's nothing to be done right now. Stay where you are, lest you draw unneeded attention to us."

Grudgingly, Ember remained in the saddle, though she kept a close watch on Barrow, hoping for another sound or movement.

Kael returned in less than an hour, looking quite pleased with himself.

"Well?" Lukasz asked him. The commander appraised Kael's self-satisfied smirk uneasily.

"Found a ship," Kael told them. "She'll take us to Bordeaux."

"And is there a berth for us where Barrow can rest?" Ember tossed the reins for Kael's mount back to him.

"There is, my lady." Kael flashed a coy smile at her.

Lukasz's eyes narrowed further. "A merchant vessel?"

"They have some cargo," Kael said. "But the ship will mostly be filled with passengers."

"What sort of passengers?" Lukasz asked.

"Humble pilgrims," Kael answered. "Like ourselves."

"Kael—" Lukasz began, but Kael's laughter cut him off.

"Protest if you like, but it's a fine plan, and you know it," Kael told the commander. "Joining the Bordeaux to Constantinople pilgrimage will give us a perfect cover for travel. The sailors will be far less likely to remember a few additional pious passengers than they would a small group of knights paying good coin for transport."

"A merchant's vessel would be faster," Lukasz said.

"Faster isn't better in this case," Kael told him. "Arguing is just a waste of our time, and it keeps poor Barrow from his berth. Besides, the pilgrim vessel sails tomorrow morning. The first merchant ship to depart leaves in two days."

Lukasz held Kael in a stony glare for a few moments before he said, "Very well. Lead on."

SIX

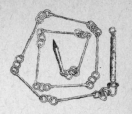

**ALISTAIR FOUGHT NOT TO** cower in the face of Eira's cold fury.

"You let her go." The quiet slither of her words was much worse than if she'd been screaming at him.

"Yes, my lady," Alistair answered, ready to accept punishment. He couldn't muster words to defend his actions. Bosque's shadow steed had carried him back to Tearmunn so swiftly that he'd had little time to contemplate the consequences of his choice. When the strange void the horse traveled through had vanished, revealing the familiar slopes of Glen Shiel, Alistair had gazed at the Conatus keep, feeling it tower over him like his doom.

Despite Eira's incredulous expression, Alistair held fast to his reasons for giving Ember her freedom. Ember had spoken true: Alistair knew her well. Though the temptation to seize her, restoring her to Tearmunn as a captive and his personal trophy, had been overwhelming, Alistair knew that victory would have been bittersweet and short-lived. Ember couldn't be conquered or coaxed. If she were to return to the keep and accept his affections, it must be by her own will.

Alistair didn't believe Eira would take to his pleas of true love kindly. He stood in awe and fear of the warrior woman. She was the greatest of leaders, and he would follow her to the ends of the earth, for to be at Eira's side was to know true power. But Eira's strength was rooted in ambition and fearlessness, and Alistair doubted she'd ever felt the flames of love that burned in his blood at any thought of Ember Morrow.

"I ask your forgiveness, my lady," Alistair said quietly. "I am sorry to have earned your anger."

Eira snorted, half turning from him to look at Cian as though for guidance.

Cian stood quietly. Her face showed lines of tension that Alistair read as disappointment.

"Your actions are difficult to understand, Lord Hart," Cian said. "Do you have doubts about my sister's plans for the order?"

Eira's eyebrows shot up and she wheeled on Alistair. "Do you?"

Dropping to one knee, Alistair said, "Never, my lady. I am yours to command."

"A reprieve is in order."

Alistair looked up in surprise to see Bosque coming toward him. He'd been silent as a statue upon Alistair's return to the great hall. Alistair could see that Bosque had been listening to all that was said, but Bosque hadn't spoken until now.

Eira frowned at Bosque. "A reprieve?"

"His deeds tonight may have been misguided, but his loyalty to you remains true," Bosque said with an air of finality.

Meeting Bosque's steady gaze, Eira slowly nodded. She stepped back when Bosque moved to stand before Alistair.

"Rise, Lord Hart."

Alistair stood up. Bosque was unsettlingly close, his silver eyes boring into the young knight.

"Do you know where the traitors' path leads?" Bosque asked.

"Ember goes to her sister's new home," Alistair told him. "The estate of Count de La Marche in France."

Eira broke in. "Does she go alone or with the others?"

"I can't say," Alistair answered. "I only know that Ember gave me her word that she would seek refuge with Agnes."

"And you trust the lady Morrow's word?" Eira made a low noise of disgust.

Alistair fell silent. He didn't know if he fully believed what Ember had said, but he'd believed her enough to let her go. His heart had assured him the risk was worthwhile.

"Whether she reaches that destination or another, she travels to the coast," Bosque offered. "And will take to the sea."

"Yes," Alistair said. "It would seem more likely that she sails with Lukasz and Kael rather than alone."

"And what of Barrow?" Cian interrupted. "You haven't spoken of him. Was he not with Lady Morrow?"

Alistair cast a grim smile at her. "He fell."

"He's dead?" Cian paled.

"He may well be," Alistair answered. "His horse went down and rolled over him. He lay ashen and unconscious when I left them."

"Whether Barrow or his corpse travels to the coast is of no moment," Bosque told them. "Another matter must be attended to first."

He fixed his silver eyes upon Eira. "The ritual that we discussed."

"What ritual?" Cian asked.

"Can we spare the time?" Eira ignored Cian's question, speaking to Bosque. "If you truly believe they can be intercepted, we should leave now."

"There is no need to hurry," Bosque told Eira. "Once they're upon the sea, they are mine. When you've performed this task for me, we can even seek our beds and ride to the coast on the morrow."

Bosque's smile reminded Alistair of an assassin's knife blade flashing under moonlight. He wanted to ask what Bosque meant, and he feared for Ember's life. Fists clenched, Alistair remained silent. After what he'd done, he could request no more favors without the risk of undoing Bosque's pardon.

As if sensing Alistair's distress, Bosque laid a hand on the knight's shoulder.

"It seems fitting, Lady Eira," Bosque said, "that these two—your most loyal knight and your own blood—are here to bear witness as you ascend."

Eira's quick glance at Alistair told him that she wasn't as assured of his fidelity as Bosque was, but she answered, "I suppose it is."

Cian moved warily toward her sister. "What is this, Eira? Of what does he speak?"

"It is the beginning," Eira answered.

"Wait," Bosque told Cian and Alistair. "And watch."

Cian lifted her chin in irritation at Bosque's order, but Alistair's pulse thrummed with anticipation as Eira took Bosque's hand and together they walked to the sacred tree.

Taking posts like sentinels on each side of the cedar's massive trunk, Eira faced Bosque. She kept her gaze fixed upon him as she drew a dagger from her belt. Alistair heard Cian's sharp intake of breath when Eira calmly drew the blade across her flesh. Blood welled instantly, filling Eira's palm like a cup.

Without breaking her gaze from Bosque's, Eira began to chant:

*In sanguine nostri mundi concurrunt.*
*Per sanguine porta patet.*
*In sanguine remane.*

Turning her hand, Eira let her blood pour over the width of the dagger. The crimson liquid flowed over the blade and dripped to the floor. Without speaking, Eira offered the dagger to Bosque.

Accepting the blade, Bosque likewise cut into his palm and echoed Eira's chant.

Alistair listened closely this time, silently translating the words from Latin to fully grasp their meaning.

> In blood our worlds meet.
> By blood the gate opens.
> In blood it remains.

When Bosque finished the chant, he bathed the dagger in his blood, drowning the sheen of the blade in rich red hues. Bosque stepped toward Eira, and she moved to meet him. They laced their wounded hands together upon the hilt of the dagger and turned to face the tree.

Moving in unison, Eira and Bosque suddenly thrust the dagger into the base of the tree, where the trunk split into roots. A sound filled the room that set Alistair's teeth on edge. It wasn't the crack of splintering wood, but a strange tearing of tightly woven fabric. Along with the ripping noise came a low wail, building into a screech that drove nails into Alistair's ears. Beside him, Cian doubled over, wrapping her arms around her head to block out the tree's scream—if that's what it was.

Then suddenly, silence.

Eira and Bosque stood beside the tree, but the sacred tree was no more. The golden bark had blanched—the surface of the cedar was white as the bone trees the Guard had come upon near Dorusduain. But more striking than the transformed skin of the tree was the wound at its base.

From the place where Bosque and Eira had stabbed the tree, stretching up to a height just above Bosque's head, was a gaping hole. It was wide at the base and tapered at its highest point. What had once been a living tree now appeared to be dead and hollow. Peering into the black gap in the trunk, Alistair perceived more than a simple hole. Strange lights moved within the darkness, illuminating the shadows with the dull green of an overgrown swamp.

Eira grasped the dagger in her left hand while she offered her wounded palm to Bosque. He covered her hand with both of his, healing the cut. His own injury had already disappeared.

"What have you done?" Cian spoke in a ragged voice that was much too quiet for anyone but Alistair to hear.

A bit shaken himself, Alistair looked at Cian. Her face was calm, and he wondered if he'd misheard her. They waited quietly as Bosque and Eira walked back to them.

"A task well done, my lady," Bosque said to Eira.

Unable to contain his curiosity, Alistair asked, "What is it? What happened?"

With a smile, Bosque nodded at Eira. "Show them."

Eira lifted her hand and traced a shape in the air. Flames trailed in her fingers' wake until a fiery symbol was suspended before her. The symbol shuddered, expanding, then contracting before a dark shape burst out of the flames, consuming the fire as it was born.

Alistair swore, jumping back from the shadow guard.

"How is it possible?" Cian's hand was on her sword hilt, but she stood her ground. The wraith hovered beside Eira, giving no sign of imminent attack.

Eira admired the creature of smoke and shadow. Her smile was full of pleasure while she gazed upon the thing she'd summoned.

Cian spoke again. "You command these creatures now?"

"As she should," Bosque answered Cian. "The power was hers to take and mine to give."

"But she gave you something in return," Cian said slowly. "Didn't she?"

"Your sister simply strengthened the bond we already share. In doing so, she opened a door between the earth and the nether," Bosque told her, gesturing to the split trunk of the sacred tree. "Now we may enjoy a true alliance."

"An alliance?" Cian was gripping her sword hilt now, her knuckles bloodless.

"An end to this war we've waged for so long, dear Cian." Eira spoke calmly, but a new fever burned in her eyes. "For that which we've toiled against now serves at our pleasure."

Cian released her sword, but her shoulders remained tense. "I don't understand."

"Then I shall explain," Eira replied. "But let us speak alone, as sisters."

"And will your creature accompany us?" Cian asked. Alistair assumed she referred to the wraith, but Cian's eyes flitted to Bosque.

"I said alone." Eira waved her hand and the shadow guard vanished.

Cian drew a slow breath. "You're powerful."

Eira's laugh was almost girlish, her cheeks flushed with exhilaration. "What's mine shall be yours, too. Come with me and learn."

Taking Cian's arm, Eira drew her sister to the door and into the corridor.

Still marveling at what he'd seen, Alistair moved as if in a trance. He thought to seek his bed and quiet his mind.

"A moment, Lord Hart." Bosque's call stopped Alistair from following the sisters from the hall.

Alistair waited for Bosque to approach. Just as Eira had seemed more wild and alive, Alistair saw that the tall man had been changed by the ritual. The silver of his eyes gleamed brighter; the air around him shimmered as though moved by a fire that burned within Bosque's form.

Seizing on an unexpected surge of courage, Alistair said, "There's more to it, isn't there?"

Bosque didn't answer, but watched Alistair calmly.

Encouraged that he'd met no resistance, Alistair continued. "Lady Eira can summon your creatures now, and can do so without your aid."

"Is her new talent something you envy, Lord Hart?"

It was Alistair's turn to remain silent.

With a stiff smile, Bosque told him, "Opening the rift imbued Lady Eira with power drawn from the nether. She can command some of those beings I rule."

"Only some?" Alistair asked.

"Eira is still human," Bosque answered. "Of this world. Though she's mingled her blood with mine, there are creatures who would overwhelm her. Those beasts can be summoned and commanded by my will alone."

Alistair considered Bosque's words, then said, "The Lyulf. Did I truly command them?"

Bosque's laugh was a low rumble. "You're clever, Lord Hart. That is why I see so much potential in you."

"The fire wolves obeyed me only because you ordered them to do so," Alistair said, a bit crestfallen. "And Eira would not be able to summon them to serve her."

"No," Bosque said. "The Lyulf are too purely linked to the nether to be ruled by a mere human."

Catching Alistair's flinch, Bosque quickly added, "Even one so great as Lady Eira or one so perceptive as you."

Alistair nodded and Bosque spoke again. "Opening the rift frees me to move through your world without being tethered to the one whose will first brought me."

"If you're free to leave Eira, why would you remain to aid us?" Alistair asked, taken aback.

"This is your world, Lord Hart," Bosque said. "Not mine. An alliance with an order as powerful as Conatus may serve Eira's purpose here, but it also serves my own purposes in the nether. That is my home, and while I will give all that I can to see Eira rule as she should and Conatus take its rightful place in this world, my aim is to secure my legacy in my world."

"I see," Alistair said quietly, though he was quite overwhelmed by the picture Bosque had painted of another world that existed—once separate, now connected to the earth.

"The rift offers another advantage," Bosque continued. "The Lyulf and my wraiths would have been the best weapons I could offer if Eira had rejected my offer of an alliance."

"You need yet greater tools of war?" Alistair balked. "No weapon can destroy Lyulf or wraith."

Bosque frowned. "None of your weapons, but that isn't the concern. Terrain is."

"Terrain?"

"Though in substance and power my world differs from yours, its landscape would have some familiar features," Bosque told him. "There are mountains of fire, deserts spotted with boulders clear as glass and sharp as razors, forests of choking vines. And the seas . . . with waters the color of the night sky."

Murky visions of this place swam in Alistair's head, as if Bosque were a painter filling the canvas of Alistair's mind with some imagined hell.

"Wars are fought on land and at sea," Bosque continued. "The wraiths and Lyulf serve no purpose when the battle takes to water."

Alistair's throat constricted as he remembered what Bosque had told Eira just before the ritual.

*Once they're upon the sea, they are mine. When you've performed this task for me, we can even seek our beds and ride to the coast on the morrow.*

"What will you send after them?" Alistair asked hoarsely. Fear for Ember's life needled him.

"In the morning you will see." Bosque gave him a measured look and said, "I would speak with you further about Lady Morrow. And the choices you made today."

Alistair's jaw clenched, but he nodded. It was like the man could read his mind.

"I've already shown my faith in you. You have a place of honor in this new order, and I would see you rise even higher." Bosque offered what almost looked like a gentle smile, though beneath his silver eyes, the expression was more frightening than reassuring. "But your passion for the girl sways you. It puts your future at risk."

Alistair turned his face, shame and outrage churning in his blood.

"I understand better than you surmise," Bosque told him. "You need her to come to you. It is not enough to simply take her."

Alistair looked up, his eyes suspicious, yet grateful. "Yes."

"That choice shows you to be more man than child, and merits respect. For your pains, I hope the lady finds her way back to you." Bosque paused before he added, "Should she not, you must let your love follow its natural course, allowing it to transform as it will. You'll be the stronger for it."

"Transform?" Alistair's brow furrowed.

"If your heart's wish is not fulfilled, the heat of your passion will instead burn as a cold fire." Bosque tilted his head, regarding Alistair with amusement as a father would a naive child. "That is what happens when love turns to hate."

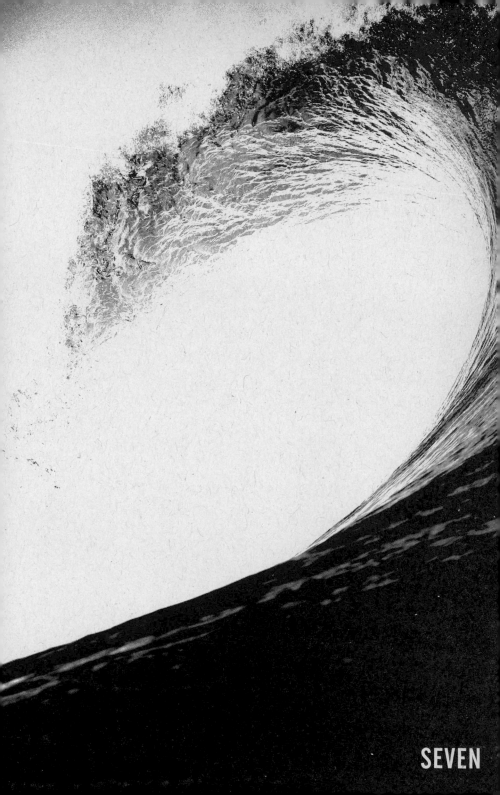

SEVEN

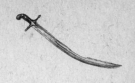

**ALL THE TALK EMBER** had heard of sailors described them as sour, drunken brutes. The crew of their ship, however, overturned those tales. Whether it was a reflection of their usual nature or an exception made out of respect for the holy mission of their current passengers, the burly men who occupied the ship were subdued and sober.

Ember learned quickly that she much preferred standing on the deck, where she could taste salt air and listen to the ship sluice through the dark sea. Belowdecks she suffered through the ongoing argument between Kael and Lukasz about whether or not they should actually join the pilgrimage upon reaching Bordeaux rather than seek another ship to carry their party east.

Their bickering tired her, but Barrow rested belowdecks as well. As much as Ember enjoyed the wind in her face, she didn't want to leave his side for long. Taking another deep breath of sea-tinged air, Ember sighed and descended to Barrow's berth.

Kael and Lukasz were there, still arguing. Sawyer was making do with the cramped space. He'd sorted through the herbs in Barrow's saddlebags, along with additional ingredients that Kael and Lukasz offered, rendering them into tonics that might bring Barrow some relief.

Occupied with crushing herbs and mixing them with water and

a touch of whisky, Sawyer worked happily, oblivious to the bitter voices that floated in the air nearby.

"I'm not asking that we go all the way to Constantinople with them," Kael said. "But if we join them on the route south through France, you know they'll stop at Sainte-Eulalie-de-Cernon, where we can remain."

"Or we can hire a ship and sail directly to Krak des Chevaliers," Lukasz answered brusquely. "Why delay?"

"It won't be a delay if the clerics at Cernon weave us a portal," Kael replied. "Walking through a door to the east will be much faster than sailing around Italy."

Lukasz stood up, shaking his head. "If we appear at Cernon requesting a portal, word will get back to Eira. She has many friends in France and fewer in the Holy Land."

"Barrow would benefit from the Hospitallers' skills," Kael said. "He doesn't need to spend another week aboard a ship."

"And carting him across the French countryside would be better?" Lukasz shot back.

Listening to the pair bicker, Ember wondered how their dispute could be so contrary to the tenderness she had seen them share the night of Sorcha's death. The secrecy Lukasz and Kael were forced to maintain must be a heavy burden, particularly now that death chased their every step. Perhaps arguing over their mode of travel offered the only release of the frustration they surely felt to be so close as they escaped from Tearmunn, yet to be unable to take comfort in each other because Sawyer had been placed in their care.

Ember doubted her resolve would be unshaken without the reassurance of Barrow's strong arms enfolding her and the warmth of his kiss to keep fear's cold embrace at bay.

Looking at Barrow where he lay in his berth, Ember gasped. His eyes were open and he was watching Lukasz and Kael as their fight droned on.

"I'll not be taking a cart anywhere," Barrow said, voice groggy.

"Thank God." Lukasz knelt beside Barrow. "How do you feel? Is there pain?"

Barrow pushed himself up onto his elbows, wincing. "There's pain. But not worse than I've had before."

"Good," Kael said from behind Lukasz. He glanced at Sawyer. "Is that tonic almost ready?"

"Yes, my lord," Sawyer answered without looking up from his work. "In a moment."

Coming fully awake, Barrow frowned as he took in his surroundings. "A ship? What happened? How long have I been away from you?" He gripped the sides of the wooden berth, eyes going wide. "Where is Ember?"

Ember rushed from where she'd been hovering in the doorway. "Here. I'm here."

She knelt opposite Lukasz, resting her hands lightly on Barrow's forearm.

Barrow tried to reach for her, relief etched on his face, but the movement made him draw a sharp breath of pain.

"You must be still, my lord." Sawyer stood over Ember. She looked up at the woodcutter in surprise, never having heard such strength in the man's voice. "And drink this until it's gone. I don't want to hear complaints about the taste. Just drink it."

Lukasz's eyebrows went up, but he told Barrow, "Our friend Sawyer has been ministering to you. He has some knowledge of the healing arts."

"Then I am in your debt, Goodman Sawyer." Barrow took the cup Sawyer offered, though his eyes stayed on Ember's face.

"Tell me what happened," Barrow asked her. "All I can remember is Toshach stumbling."

A lump formed in Ember's throat, painful as she swallowed it. "Toshach fell and rolled over you. You lost consciousness."

Barrow took a sip of the tonic and made a face, but as Sawyer had requested, he made no complaint and continued to drink it.

"They were on us before I could get to you," Ember told him.

"What was it?" Barrow asked. "Who pursued us?"

"Alistair." Ember took a deep breath and plunged into the tale. She struggled to keep her voice steady, watching Barrow's face pale as she described the fire wolves. When she told him what Toshach had done, Barrow looked away.

"The wolves would have killed you if Toshach hadn't stopped them," Ember said.

Barrow didn't answer. Neither did he ask how she and Caber had carried him to safety.

"We'll leave you to rest now," Lukasz said to Barrow. "I'll return later to further discuss our current predicament."

The commander stood, telling Sawyer, "Come with us. We'll find something to eat."

Sawyer nodded and followed Lukasz from the small room.

"Good to have you back, friend," Kael said, and then left with the others.

Still silent, Barrow lay on his back, giving no acknowledgment that he knew Ember was still there.

Ember took the cup from his hand.

"You need to finish this."

Barrow stared at the wood planks above him, his eyes full of unshed tears.

"He died because of my foolishness," he said quietly.

Ember placed her hand over Barrow's. "He died because we were forced to run in the dead of night."

When Barrow didn't reply, Ember dipped her fingers in the tonic and brought them to his lips. He started at her touch, but then clasped her wrist tightly in his fingers as he opened his mouth, half kissing, half drinking the tonic from her skin.

Shivering, Ember leaned down, pressing her mouth to his.

Barrow's tongue touched hers. His arm came around her back, drawing her against him. Through the kiss, Ember felt him tense with pain, and she quickly pulled away.

"Don't," Barrow whispered. "I can bear it."

"Your lie tempts me." Ember smiled at him. "But I won't risk hurting you. Please finish this."

She handed him the cup. Barrow sat up and drained it, shuddering as he swallowed.

"Vile," he told her. "Strange how I didn't mind when I sipped it from your fingers."

Taking the cup and setting it aside, Ember said softly, "Don't try to hold me . . . but I need to touch you."

Meeting her gaze, Barrow nodded and became very still. He sat quietly, watching as she reached for him. Their quiet breathing was the only sound as Ember moved her hands through his hair. She touched his neck, sliding her hands up and tracing the shape of his jaw with her fingertips. Then cupped his face in her palms.

As Ember spoke, her cheeks became wet with tears. "I am so sorry that you lost Toshach. But I cannot regret what he did, for I could not bear to lose you."

Barrow drew a ragged breath, lowering his eyes, and a few teardrops escaped onto his cheeks.

"I love you," Ember whispered. No words she'd spoken had ever felt so important or so frightening. "I have loved no one but you."

Barrow looked at Ember, and she saw that his deep gray eyes were the color of the sea upon which they now sailed.

"Kiss me, Ember."

She was careful to hold herself above him when she moved close. His mouth was gentle and warm, tasting her, breathing her breath. Ember's eyes were closed, her body caught between the sweetness of his kiss and the ache of needing more. She broke the kiss, murmuring, "Heal swiftly, for my patience is short."

"As my lady wishes," Barrow answered. His voice was drowsy,

and Ember realized that the tonic Sawyer had made most likely contained a sleep draught.

"Will you tell me now how you came to my rescue?" he asked.

Ember backed away slightly, wondering what Barrow would make of her tactic with Alistair. Lukasz and Kael had seen the expedience of her decision, but Barrow already bore a grudge toward Alistair when it came to Ember's affections.

"Because it was Alistair," Ember told him, "I was able to persuade him to let me go, but—"

She hesitated, waiting for his response. When he laughed lazily, Ember sat up, banging her head on the low wooden beam that curved over the berth.

"Ow!"

Barrow didn't react, and she saw how quickly he was drifting off.

Before his eyelids fully closed, he rolled out a few words, though exhaustion put strange lapses in his speech. "Poor lad. Of course he came after you . . . I would have . . . He can't have you . . . kill him . . . sorry bastard . . ."

Smiling, Ember stretched out on the bed beside Barrow, close enough so her body touched his but keeping her weight from leaning too heavily against his bruised chest. Their fingers laced together. Ember rested her chin on Barrow's shoulder, listening to his breath slow as the rocking ship lulled him back to sleep.

Her own eyelids heavy, Ember was about to let slumber take her when she heard a stirring at the door. Lifting her head, Ember met Lukasz's gaze. The commander paused in the doorway. He looked at Ember and Barrow lying together on the narrow berth. Ember started to rise, but Lukasz lifted his hand and gave a brief shake of his head. The commander stepped out of the doorway, pulling the door shut. As he did, Ember thought she saw him smile.

EIGHT

**ALISTAIR WALKED THE** perimeter of the great hall, taking note of the changes Eira had made in the chamber. No longer a gathering space for Conatus, Eira had commandeered the hall for her own purposes. The room now served as a meeting place for the Circle but felt more like a throne room in which Eira held court. A massive, ornately carved ebony chair had been placed in front of the dead tree that harbored Bosque's rift. The glossy black polish of the thronelike seat offered a stark contrast to the bone-white, lifeless trunk. Alistair didn't know where the chair had come from, though he suspected it had once belonged to Abbot Crichton.

Eira had other chairs and a table carved in the shape of a crescent moon added to the hall as well. The inner curve of the table faced Eira's seat and the rift, while the outer edge featured much more diminutive chairs for the rest of the Circle. There was no chair for Bosque. Whenever Eira received visitors, the tall man stood at her side, just behind her left shoulder. Alistair did have a seat, one of the plain chairs designated for Circle members. At Eira's decree, Alistair had been named to the Circle, a new voice for the Guard in the absence of the commander. No one had complained.

These changes suited Alistair. He much preferred that the order be ruled by a single, strong voice. Eira had explained how often accommodating the diverse opinions of the Circle had weakened Conatus. Better to be finished with such a burdensome form of leadership. While building her vision for their future, Eira, enforced by Bosque's power, would not make any concessions.

But that didn't mean the transition to a new order would occur without incident, unexpected turns of events that were sometimes helpful and sometimes irksome. Such was the case with the two things that delayed their travel to Inverness into the afternoon. The first delay was of the irksome sort.

Mercer was dead. When the guard had opened his cell to give the prisoner his morning meal, Mercer lay unmoving on the floor, his glassy eyes open wide.

Though by no measure a devastating loss, Mercer's demise was nonetheless frustrating. He'd given up no useful information, despite Bosque's extraordinary means for extracting desired answers. More troublesome were the questions that remained about how Mercer's life had come to an end.

"You cannot trust your peers," Bosque told Eira. "Someone took the traitor's life."

Eira cast a doubtful glance on Mercer's corpse, which she'd ordered to be brought to her in the great hall for further examination. "Perhaps his body couldn't withstand the torment. Many men die under the torturer's care."

Bosque smiled briefly. "No."

"How can you be sure?" Eira asked.

"My wraiths can feed off a man for years," he told her. "They would not be so careless with a fine meal. And they do not kill prisoners without my command."

Alistair peered at Mercer's stiff body. "There are no marks on his body."

"Poison is the assassin's favorite weapon," Bosque answered him. "Who had access to the prisoner's food?"

With a shrug, Alistair told him, "Any number of people. The kitchens aren't guarded. It would have been easy for someone to add a fatal seasoning to the meal without garnering attention."

"That is what I suspect happened," Bosque said. "It would be wise to question the kitchen staff."

"When you say question—" Alistair looked to Eira, wondering if Bosque meant to set his wraiths on the cooks.

Catching Alistair's meaning, Bosque smiled. "Fear not, young Lord Hart. I only use extreme measure on those whose actions have earned that reward. Until we have the suspected assassin identified, a simple review of the persons who were in the kitchen when Mercer's last meal was prepared will do."

"I'll have Cian do it," Eira said. "She seemed reluctant to travel with us to Inverness."

"And why is that?" Bosque asked her.

"Hunting her fellow Guardsmen turns my sister's stomach, I'm afraid," Eira said. When Bosque raised an eyebrow, Eira added, "She'll come around."

"I'm sure," Bosque replied, though Alistair thought his tone skeptical at best. "Perhaps Claudio should assist her in the task."

"If you think so," Eira said. "It *would* add more weight to the investigation if two Circle members conducted the search."

Bosque nodded. "Give the orders and meet us at the stables. We'll depart when—"

A sharp rapping at the door stopped their conversation.

"Come!" Eira called.

One of the guards posted outside the great hall stepped into the room. His eyes briefly passed over Mercer's corpse, and he swallowed visibly.

"Pardon me, Lady Eira," he said. "But a visitor has arrived and pleads that she must be seen."

"Very well," Eira said.

The guard cleared his throat. "My lady, the visitor asks not for you, but for Lord Hart."

Eira turned to Alistair. "Are you expecting a guest, Lord Hart?"

Alistair shook his head, but his heart gave a wild flail of hope.

Perhaps in reaching the coast, Ember had looked over the sea and realized how pointless the voyage would be.

"Lord Hart?" the guard asked, shifting his weight as he hovered near the door.

Opening and closing his mouth, Alistair couldn't find breath to answer.

"Send the visitor in," Eira answered with a laugh. "Lord Hart is taken by surprise and can't find his voice."

The guard bowed and slipped out the door, returning a moment later with a slight figure who was covered head to toe in a traveling cloak. The visitor lifted pale, trembling hands and pushed back the cloak's hood.

The face revealed wasn't the one Alistair had hoped for, but was nonetheless familiar.

Agnes Morrow hurried forward and then awkwardly dropped to her knees.

"My lord Hart, I am your humble servant who begs for your mercy and the refuge of this place," Ember's sister said.

Taken aback, Alistair reached down to help her rise. "Lady Morrow, you need not kneel before a longtime friend."

As Agnes turned grateful eyes on him, Alistair saw how colorless her skin was and the way her face was pinched with weariness. He wondered if the illness she'd experienced upon her last visit to Tearmunn had worsened.

"Why are you here, Lady Morrow?" Alistair asked. "I thought you would be settling in at your new French estate."

"And why pleading for refuge?" Eira cut in. "Are you not the daughter of a lord?"

Agnes wobbled a bit when she curtsied to Eira. "My lady, I have brought dishonor upon my family and have been cast out."

"What?" Alistair couldn't believe her words. If any daughter merited Lord Morrow's ire, it was Ember. Agnes had always been the obedient child.

Eira's eyes narrowed. "Dishonor?"

Hanging her head, Agnes murmured, "Yes, my lady; thus, I come to you asking for mercy and shelter. I may no longer claim my former station. Whatever work you might find for me I would do with a thankful heart."

"Don't be ridiculous, Agnes," Alistair said, flustered. "You will not shame yourself through common labor. Your father is known to have a quick temper and often speaks rashly. Whatever the quarrel between you is, we will resolve it soon enough."

Eira stepped closer to Agnes. "Push back your cloak."

"My lady?" Agnes looked at her with wide eyes.

"You heard me." Under Eira's hawkish gaze, Agnes seemed a trembling rabbit.

With shaking hands, Agnes unfastened her heavy cloak. She let it drop into a heap at her feet, lowering her head once more.

Eira looked Agnes up and down, her eyes stopping on the unmistakable swell of Agnes's belly. "You're with child."

Alistair began to swear, drawing startled looks from Eira and Bosque. Struggling to compose himself, Alistair said, "Lord Mar and Lady Eira, if you'd please give me a moment alone with Lady Morrow."

Eira seemed ready to object, but Bosque laid his hand on her shoulder.

"Of course, Lord Hart," Bosque told him, leading Eira from the hall.

When they were gone and the door closed, Alistair came to Agnes, taking her hands.

"Is it as I suspect?" he asked, his throat tight.

Agnes began to cry. "I thought he loved me."

"My brother is brash," Alistair said, peppering his words with another round of curses. "Too quick to make declarations he has no intentions of following through . . . but how were you to know that?"

"When I arrived at Château de Lusignan, I had convinced myself

I could still become the count's wife." Agnes struggled to speak through her tears. "I insisted on keeping my own ladies-in-waiting, and with their help, I was able to hide my condition through the wedding. But in the marriage bed, there was nothing—" Agnes broke down.

"The count returned you to your father?" Alistair asked when her weeping subsided.

She nodded. "The marriage was annulled, of course, and my father was furious. My mother pleaded with him to have mercy, but his condition of letting me stay was to confess the name of the father."

"And why didn't you?" Alistair had little sympathy for his older brother's actions.

Henry had indulged his desire for Agnes fully aware that he would marry another. The arrangement for their father's second son to become the husband of Lady Howard of Yorkshire had been made when they were small children. Lady Howard's estate was much greater than Lord Morrow's, though the lady herself was half as pretty as Agnes. Henry had taken full advantage of his proximity to Agnes, and distance from Lady Howard, as long as he could. Once the time for the wedding had arrived, however, Henry discarded Agnes without explanation or apology.

That Agnes would continue to protect Henry's name bespoke her love for him . . . and her naiveté. Though he wouldn't tell Agnes for fear of breaking her heart even more, Alistair wagered that if Henry were to face accusations of fathering an illegitimate child, he would deny the bastard was his without care that it meant bringing further shame to Agnes.

Though Alistair couldn't undo his brother's churlish deeds, he could honor his family and Agnes by protecting her now.

"You will have your refuge, Agnes," Alistair told her. "I give you my word—which is much truer than Henry's."

He guided her to a chair. "Wait here. I'll return shortly."

Alistair left Agnes sniffling at the crescent table to join Bosque and Eira where they waited in the hall.

Before speaking to them, Alistair addressed the guard at the door. "Go find a maid to show Lady Morrow to a room in the manor and attend to her. Make sure she understands this is her new position. Someone else will take over her former responsibilities."

"Yes, my lord." The guard bowed and went to find a maidservant.

Eira locked eyes with Alistair. "You're giving orders now?"

"I'm helping a friend," Alistair said, unwavering. "It's the chivalrous thing to do."

"Send her to a nunnery," Eira said with a snort. "We're in the midst of our own troubles and can't worry over the health of a girl and her bastard. Chivalry be damned."

"Lady Eira," Alistair said through clenched teeth, "I would not argue with you, but I ask that you not insult Lady Morrow. She is a naive girl, misled by another. The dishonor is not hers to bear."

"But the child is," Eira answered coolly.

"If I may." Bosque's smooth voice slipped between them. "Lady Morrow's arrival presents an advantage, not a burden."

"How?" Eira turned on him, seething.

"I can think of two things," Bosque told her. "If you'll forgive me for saying so, your sister, Cian, seems reluctant to embrace the changes you've made in Conatus."

Eira didn't answer him, but she nodded.

"Perhaps an act of charity would reassure her?" Bosque said.

"It might," Eira said. "And the second thing?"

"Of course the utmost care will be given to a lady of Agnes Morrow's station and to someone in her condition," Bosque replied. "But that same care might also be provided for a valuable hostage."

"What?" Alistair said sharply.

Bosque silenced him with a glance.

"A hostage?" Eira frowned at Bosque.

"Lady Morrow may have been disowned by her father, but I'm certain he expected nothing less than for Conatus to protect her," Bosque explained. "And in protecting her from public shame, we're doing him a service."

With an assessing gaze, Bosque said to Alistair, "Your interest in the lady's condition suggests an intimate knowledge of the situation."

"The child isn't mine," Alistair replied. "I swear it."

Bosque didn't look away, and Alistair relented under the force of the man's silver stare.

"My brother Henry." Alistair's shoulders slumped. "He took advantage of her long infatuation."

"And your brother is now married?" Bosque asked.

Alistair nodded. "He is a lord in Yorkshire."

Turning to Eira, Bosque said, "As you plot your new course and break from the rule of the church, you'll want the support of nobles—both in coin and men. Use every advantage you have."

"I can see the wisdom of what you say," Eira told him. "Lady Morrow will be given a home in Tearmunn."

"Alistair will send a letter to Lord Morrow, informing him of our generosity," Bosque said. "And he will also request that Agnes send a letter."

"What would you have Agnes say to her father?" Alistair asked, thinking that such a letter would find its way into Lord Morrow's fire without being read.

Bosque smiled at him. "The letter is not for her father. She will write to her sister."

Alistair gaped at Bosque, who said, "If your absent Ember keeps her word, she will go to Château de Lusignan. Should she arrive there to find her sister missing and a letter explaining what's happened, the younger lady Morrow might be persuaded to return to Tearmunn more quickly than otherwise."

"Yes," Alistair breathed, a sudden fever washing over him.

"If she survives," Eira muttered, earning a warning glare from Bosque and a fearful look from Alistair.

"That lies in the hands of fate," Bosque said. "As do Alistair's hopes."

"My lords and my lady." The guard had returned with a maidservant.

"See to it," Eira told Alistair. "And I'll deal with the other task we discussed. We'll meet in the stables thereafter and make our way to Inverness."

Alistair had thought that Bosque would employ his mystical means of transport to speed their trip to Inverness, but it was not so.

"The rift frees me to do many things," Bosque explained to Alistair and Eira. "But that form of travel presents great risk to you. One companion I can watch over, but with more there is too much chance someone would be lost in the nether."

Shuddering at the thought of becoming trapped in Bosque's world, Alistair happily endured the journey to Inverness. Relying on the speed of their horses, they reached the coast well after dark of the following day. The night sky was clear; stars looked down on them like a million witnesses.

Upon Bosque's advice, they'd left the road before they reached Craig Dunain, traveling north to an isolated shoreline west of the port of Inverness. They left the horses a short distance from the rocky coast, tethering Alistair's and Eira's mounts so the beasts would not attempt to flee from Bosque's shadow steed.

With little wind, the firth lay calm, mirroring the midnight blue sky.

The delays of the day and Bosque's refusal to leave Alistair—

freeing herself and Bosque to travel in the nether—had put Eira in a foul mood.

"Have we lost too much time?" Eira asked as they walked to the stone-covered beach.

"No," Bosque answered. "I welcomed the delay. This work is better done at night."

Eira made a noncommittal sound, but Alistair gazed worriedly at the firth's dark waters. He'd put Agnes to writing her letter to Ember before they'd left Tearmunn. Now his mind was fixed on her words and how they might bring Ember back to him.

*But not if she is lost at sea.*

Alistair pulled his eyes from the water and found Bosque watching him.

"Ember will soon face trials wrought by her choices," Bosque said. "For your sake, I hope she is able to overcome them."

Alistair nodded, not trusting himself to speak. He sent the stars a silent wish to watch over Ember and carry her safely to France. As to her companions, Alistair could just have easily wished for their demise. He laid the blame for her imminent endangerment at the feet of Lukasz and Kael . . . and especially Barrow. If Barrow escaped the sea with his life, the only sweetness Alistair would find in his being spared was the thought that he could slay Barrow himself one day.

"Wait on the beach," Bosque ordered Eira and Alistair. "Do not touch the water until I return."

Without another word, he stripped off his clothes, revealing a warrior's body. The long lines of his muscles and grace of his movements made Alistair think that Bosque's magic wasn't his only weapon. The strange man might prove a worthy adversary on a martial practice field.

Forgetting herself, Eira gave a startled cry as Bosque brazenly tossed her his shirt, chausses, and breeches. Bosque stood tall, facing her, though he was fully naked. "You blush like a maid, Lady Eira. I'm surprised." He grinned, and Alistair wondered how Bosque could see a rosy hue paint Eira's cheeks in this darkness. "Still, I trust you can keep my clothes dry?"

She stood paralyzed, staring as he turned and waded into the sea. Alistair watched in disbelief. The firth's waters were cold enough to kill a man, yet Bosque appeared as comfortable as if he'd entered a hot bath.

Having reached waist-deep water, Bosque suddenly dove, vanishing beneath the blue-black surface. Only the slight ripples at the place he'd submerged gave evidence that the water had been disturbed. The night was silent. Alistair and Eira stood transfixed, waiting.

Bosque didn't surface. When he'd been underwater twice as long as any man could manage without drowning, Alistair forced himself to speak.

"Can he survive this? Should I swim out to search for him?" Alistair didn't relish the thought of following Bosque into the sea. The water would cut like knives of ice.

"He said not to touch the water," Eira said. "We must obey."

Alistair threw a startled look at Eira, surprised to hear her speak of obedience to anyone. Even Lord Mar.

"There."

Alistair's gaze followed Eira's pointing finger.

Far from shore, the dark waters of the firth stirred. It began as ripples like those Bosque had created when he dove. Concentric circles formed in the water and began to move, turning in on themselves. Soon the sea was churning, and where the firth had been still and dark, it frothed into a violent maelstrom. The vortex of water roared, a gaping and hungry mouth.

Alistair gave a startled cry when, from the center of the whirlpool, a huge tentacle lashed out. Then another. A massive dark shape broke free of the maelstrom, swimming east toward the open sea. Alistair stared after it. If not for the tentacles, he would have thought the creature a whale.

"How do you like my kraken?" Bosque, dripping seawater, was wading back to shore. "She has no rival in the sea."

Alistair could only nod. Bosque smiled his approval. The night was cold, and Bosque's skin was slick as a seal's, but he neither shivered nor were his lips frigid blue as they should have been.

Shaking water from his thick, dark hair, Bosque turned to Eira. "Is my lady Eira also pleased with the night's task?"

Eira didn't answer his question, instead shoving the contents of her arms at him. "Your clothing, Lord Mar."

Bosque took the clothes but didn't move to put them on, instead standing before Eira, watching her closely. She managed to hold his gaze for a moment, but then looked away.

"Is my body so objectionable?" Bosque asked her, stepping into his breeches.

Still turned from him, Eira said, "Of course not."

"Then why won't you look upon me?"

"Why do you care?" Eira asked, lifting her chin in defiance as she faced him. Her face showed visible relief when he tied his chausses and slid his shirt over his head.

Alistair coughed. He was not eager to know where this conversation would lead.

"Yes, Lord Hart?" Bosque turned his attention to putting on his boots.

"Your kraken hunts the traitors' vessel?" Alistair asked with a slight frown.

Bosque shrugged. "In its own way, yes."

Feeling a twist in his gut, Alistair asked, "How will it know what ship to wreck?"

"It will not know," Bosque answered. "The kraken will sink them all."

"All of them?" The shock in Eira's question echoed Alistair's.

"At least all she finds before she desires to return to her slumber in caverns at the bottom of the sea." Bosque stood up, fastening his cloak. "That will be in a week's time, possibly a day or two longer."

"But there are countless ships that sail the western sea to the French ports," Eira said softly, bowing her head and falling silently into her own thoughts.

"I'm certain there are," Bosque answered.

Alistair waited for Eira to object, to ask Lord Mar to find a way to send the kraken after singular prey instead of destroying an entire herd.

When Eira lifted her face to the night sky, she began to laugh.

NINE

**BY THEIR SECOND DAY** at sea, Barrow insisted on going above deck to breathe fresh air. Ember had assumed she'd be the one who was most concerned about Barrow's recovery, but Sawyer kept a close eye on the knight, like a watchful mother hen. Barrow indulged the woodcutter's attention, though Ember could tell the knight wearied of Sawyer's insistence that he spend more time in his berth than walking about the ship.

The four of them stood in the small room. Barrow was sitting up, shirtless, as Sawyer inspected his chest. The dark contusions had lightened but taken on sickly yellow hues. Sawyer assured Ember that the change was a good sign, despite its unpleasant appearance. Though he continued to offer Barrow tonics to help his healing, the concoctions no longer put the knight to sleep.

While Barrow adjusted to his restricted movements, the rest of them were making other accommodations. Packing away their Conatus tabards, Kael bartered his way to more inconspicuous clothing. Much to Ember's chagrin, that meant she had to trade in her fighting gear for a peasant dress.

While she scowled at Kael, he said, "It's either the dress or you wear a helmet all the time so no one wonders why a girl is going about in men's clothes."

"The disguises are only necessary so long as we're among the pilgrims," Lukasz reassured her. "You can dress in the manner of the Guard when we're away from these strangers."

Ember grudgingly took the dress.

"There's a good lass." Kael grinned at her.

"Even if I'm wearing a dress, I can still hit you," Ember told him.

Lukasz laughed and asked Kael, "Did you learn anything useful while you procured our new clothing?"

"Nothing more than what we already know," Kael answered. "The French and English keep their focus on the Welsh uprising. Some say the French have taken to raiding the English countryside, and French vessels bear Welsh soldiers to war."

"Owain Glyndwr proves himself a capable king and diplomat," Lukasz mused. "And a festering thorn in England's side."

"Good news for us," Kael replied. "With the attention on Wales, the pilgrimage route shouldn't be hindered by armies tramping about France."

"We should make landfall tomorrow," Lukasz said.

"We'd be there tonight if the captain didn't keep so close to the coast," Kael added.

Lukasz shook his head. "A balinger doesn't love the open sea."

"Why don't you all go measure our progress so I can don this lovely dress," Ember said, pushing Kael toward the door.

Laughing, Lukasz followed Kael.

"My lord, remember, you must rest," Sawyer tittered at Barrow. "Be patient as you heal, lest you aggravate the wounds."

"Thank you, Sawyer." Barrow nodded.

Handing him a brimming cup, Sawyer said, "And drink this down."

Barrow grimaced but accepted the tonic. Sawyer made a quick bow to Ember and left the room.

Holding the dress, Ember glanced at Barrow and then at the still-open door.

"You don't think Sawyer would give me something that impedes my recovery," Barrow said. "Because he's awfully fond of practicing his medicines on me."

"Don't be wicked." Ember laughed. "Drink the tonic and be grateful Sawyer possesses healing skill."

Barrow made a sullen face, but he took the tonic in a few swallows and set the cup aside. "He could at least sweeten it with honey."

"And where would he get honey?"

Barrow shrugged, and Ember frowned at him. "Aren't you going to leave?"

"Didn't you hear Sawyer?" He leaned back on his elbows. "I'm to rest."

"You want to stay," Ember said slowly.

Barrow didn't answer, but the barest of smiles graced his lips. Ember closed the door.

Without speaking, Ember laid the dress on the bedside table. She removed the belt upon which Silence and Sorrow were secured and hung the leather strap and weapons from a wall hook. After pulling her tabard over her head, she folded it and set it beside the dress. Standing in her kirtle and chausses, Ember looked at Barrow. He continued to watch her, silent.

Ember slowly lifted her kirtle and the soft chemise beneath, sliding them over her head and shoulders. Placing the kirtle with her tabard, Ember reached for the tight cloth binding her chest from under her arms to her low ribs. Loosening the fabric, Ember unwound the long strip of linen and let it drop to the floor.

When the bands of cloth fell away and Ember was bare from shoulder to waist, Barrow let out an audible breath.

"Do you want me to cover myself?" Ember's fingers were at the lacing of her chausses, but she could easily don her chemise again before undressing her lower body.

"That is the last thing I want," Barrow answered quietly.

Nodding, Ember worked free the knots at her waist, then pushed down both her chausses and breeches and stepped out of them.

She reached for the dress, but Barrow murmured, "Wait. Let me look on you for a moment longer, my love."

His eyes slowly moved over her, and Ember's skin tingled. She was quiet, but her thoughts were of how much she wanted his hands to linger upon her body as his gaze did.

When she couldn't bear the ache any longer, Ember retrieved her chemise and slipped it on. The dress was stiff, gray wool with a scooping neckline that revealed the embroidery at the top of her pale chemise. Ember reached around to tighten the dress's lacing.

"Let me help you," Barrow said. "Turn around."

Giving him her back, Ember let Barrow take the laces from her hands.

"I am a novice." Ember heard the smile in Barrow's voice. "How tight should this be tied?"

"The dress is meant to fit close to my figure," Ember told him, "but it shouldn't pinch or bind."

Barrow pulled the laces until the bodice was snug at her waist and molded to the curve of her breasts, rounding them against the thin fabric of her chemise. It wasn't an uncomfortable dress, but it was strange to have her feminine attributes so emphasized when the Guards' wardrobe strove to minimize them.

When she felt Barrow tie a knot at her lower back, she turned to face him. Her smile was impish. "You'd be a fine lady-in-waiting."

"I like to think I have many hidden talents." He laughed, but his eyes were taking her in again.

"Do you prefer the dress to my other garb?" She smoothed the gray fabric of the skirt.

"You are comely, no matter what clothes you wear," Barrow said. "As well as when you wear none at all."

He leaned in and lightly brushed his lips over hers. Ember put her hands on his chest, wanting to feel his bare skin. She touched him lightly, wary of his bruised flesh.

"Does it pain you?" she asked, fingers carefully following the pattern of colors that marbled his skin.

"Much less than it did." Barrow watched her hand move over his chest and stomach. "When you touch me, I could forget altogether that my body still mends."

"That would be unwise," Ember said, regretfully pulling her hand away.

"So would this."

Ember gave a startled cry when Barrow tucked his arm around her back, his other below her knees, and lifted her. Careful to hold her away from his bruised body, he brought her to the berth and set her down on her back. Barrow knelt over her.

"You're meant to be resting, Lord Hess," Ember chided, smiling up at him.

He leaned down. "And, alas, I cannot exert myself the way I wish."

Ember parted her lips when he bent to kiss her.

"Let me show you," he said, "that I am not entirely infirm."

Sliding his hand under her back, Barrow lifted her hips. His other hand pulled the heavy wool skirt up to Ember's waist. He reached for the hem of her chemise.

"But we must wait," Ember breathed, catching his hand as it moved up her thigh.

"Some things must wait." Barrow kissed her cheek, then her throat. "But not all things."

His mouth lingered at the swell of her breasts before he continued down. Ember closed her eyes when Barrow pushed her chemise over her hips. His lips touched her inner thigh. Higher.

Ember's hands tangled in the bedclothes as Barrow coaxed her body into revealing its secrets. And though Ember knew that the art of love offered even more than this, she hardly believed that it could be so.

Much later, after Barrow actually had rested, he and Ember joined Kael and Lukasz at the ship's rail, gazing westward to watch the sea swallow the sun. Though the wool dress offered enough warmth against the stiff breeze, Ember had donned a cloak so she could wear her belt while still keeping Silence and Sorrow hidden.

Barrow's arm wrapped around Ember's waist, and she leaned into him. Kael glanced at them, chuckling and nudging Lukasz with his elbow.

"Let them be," Lukasz said with a smile. Ember watched the commander's fingers meet Kael's beneath the ship rail, and her heart warmed at the sight, though she worried at the burden of secrecy they were forced to bear. While Barrow seemed unafraid to show his affection for her, Kael and Lukasz could never risk the same.

Kael leaned toward the commander, whispering. Lukasz laughed quietly to himself, and Kael left the rail to go belowdecks.

"You look much better, my friend," Lukasz told Barrow, still smiling at whatever Kael had said.

Barrow nodded. "I feel it too."

"Good." The mirth faded slightly from Lukasz's face. "I doubt it will be long before you're needed in a fight."

"That seems likely," Barrow answered. "I'll be ready."

"Enjoy the twilight," Lukasz told them. Then he too went below.

Ember watched the commander disappear into the dark inner compartments of the ship.

"Do you know?" she asked Barrow.

"I've been injured before," Barrow answered. "I'll recover soon enough. Don't worry."

"That's not what—" Ember paused. "I was speaking of Lukasz and Kael."

Barrow tensed, casting a sidelong glance at her. "What of them?"

She turned to face him. "You do know."

He didn't answer her, so she pressed him further. "How long have they been lovers?"

"Hush, Ember," Barrow said. "How did you learn of this?"

In a low voice, Ember told him, "I saw them together. After Sorcha's death."

"And have you spoken of this to anyone else?" Barrow asked.

"No." Ember frowned at him. "Of course not."

Barrow leaned out over the railing, visibly relieved. "Good."

"What did I do to trouble you?" Ember had thought her question simple.

"What you saw is not something to be spoken of where others might overhear," Barrow told her.

Ember's brow furrowed. "I meant no harm, only wondered—"

"Your wondering could cost their lives, Ember. You're forgetting your history, Conatus's history, why the Templars burned."

When he saw the pained look on her face, Barrow pulled her closer to him. "I know you meant no harm, but what you saw and now know about Kael and Lukasz must be kept secret."

She laid her head on his shoulder, thinking about the loss she would feel if she were forbidden to enjoy the comfort of his embrace lest others see it.

"It feels wrong," Ember said.

"Love is love," Barrow answered sharply, dropping his hand from her waist and pulling away from her.

"Not that!" Ember's cheeks reddened at his suggestion she would pass judgment on their companions. "What I intended to say was that it feels wrong to be filled with happiness when so much strife and sorrow surrounds me."

"Ah," Barrow said. "That is a much more fitting sentiment, but if guilt over your joys is a burden, I'm certain we can find a priest in France so you can give confession."

"Are you so impious as to make fun of my lamentation?" Ember teased.

"Piety has nothing to do with it," Barrow answered with a brief smile. "I simply think that wringing your hands over the evils of the world will drain your heart of its courage. We must embrace what happiness is granted us when we can, or else we spend our lives awaiting the next sorrow."

Ember grasped the ship's rail, pondering Barrow's words as she looked out over the sea. The sun was an orange sliver on the horizon. Its rusty light threw a distant island into stark relief.

"What if we sailed there?" Ember looked at Barrow. "And made our refuge on an island, hidden from the world."

"I doubt you'd be willing to forsake the world for long," Barrow said. "Of what island do you speak?"

Ember pointed to the dark ridge of land that rose from the painted sea, but her arm was outstretched toward nothing. The waters lay flat all the way to the horizon.

Frowning, Ember said, "I saw an island. Just a moment ago."

"A trick of light and shadow," Barrow told her.

But as Ember watched the sun disappear, the last of its light spilling up into the western sky, the dark island reappeared. Larger this time. Ember squinted into the distance. Though the ship sailed away from the island, she could swear it was closer.

"There it is!" Ember pointed, and Barrow looked out to sea. As he did, the island sank below the waves. "But what—"

"I think your island is a whale, my love," Barrow said.

"I've never seen a whale," Ember told him, delighted. She leaned out over the railing, hoping to catch another glimpse of the beast.

"Be careful, Ember," Barrow said. "If a swell pitches the ship, you could lose your footing."

"I'm holding the rail," she answered. The whale hadn't resurfaced, and she sighed, but as she was about to turn away from the sea, the remaining light of the sunset captured a shadow below the ocean's surface.

Ember drew a startled breath and stepped back. The whale was massive, twice the size of their ship.

"Do you see something?" Barrow was still searching the distant waves.

"It's gone below the ship," she answered. "I just saw it beneath us."

"What?" Barrow's alarm brought her eyes to him.

Before she could ask what put such panic in his voice, the ship lurched. Ember fell against the railing and Barrow stumbled backward toward the center of the deck.

The ship pitched violently again, and Ember flew over the rail. She plummeted into the frothing waters, which were stirred by some unseen force.

If she hadn't been submerged, hitting the water would have made Ember scream. The sea was filled with frigid talons that slashed her skin. Kicking hard, she forced her way to the surface, gasping for breath and grateful that she'd forced Alistair to teach her to swim.

Waves manifested without wind roiled around her, making it difficult to keep her head above water. She heard screaming as she turned to swim back to the ship, but then she screamed too.

Huge tentacles were wrapped around the balinger from prow to stern. Some of the crew slashed at the thick appendages with their swords to no avail. The ship groaned as the shrill sound of splintering wood pierced the air. Pilgrims surged from belowdecks, flinging themselves to the sea's mercy.

"Barrow!" Ember couldn't see him on the deck or in the water.

A terrible screech and boom filled Ember's ears just before the ship buckled. The great tentacles had torn the ship in two. It released the severed prow in favor of ripping what remained of the hull to pieces. With horror, Ember watched as the monster's sucker-covered limbs grasped not only timber but bodies, some living and shrieking, some limp. Some people were dragged beneath the waves; others, tossed far out to sea.

Then she saw Barrow. He was floating on the water, faceup but unconscious.

With a cry, Ember swam toward him. Her limbs no longer felt cold; they were on fire, and Ember knew how dangerous that was. She forced herself to move through the waves while wreckage swirled around her. Reaching Barrow, Ember hooked her arm through one of his and prayed she had the strength to tow him to shore.

Struggling through the waves and forcing herself to shut out the cries of other victims, Ember dragged Barrow toward the coast. The fire devouring her skin had diminished to a dull needling. Her limbs felt so heavy.

"Ember!"

The call came from behind her. Ember turned to see Lukasz swimming toward her.

When the commander reached them, he looked grimly at Barrow. "Did he take water into his lungs?"

"I don't know," Ember said. "When I found him, he was floating on his back."

"We'll hope for the best, then," Lukasz said. "Let me help you."

Threading his arm beneath Barrow's opposite shoulder, he began to swim.

"Kael?" Ember asked.

"He's getting help," Lukasz answered. "Don't stop moving. The ocean will kill us as quickly as that beast."

Ember obeyed, though she was alarmed when Lukasz steered them back toward the shipwreck. The creature was still hunting for intact sections of the ship to obliterate, and it had taken to plucking men and women from the water as well.

"What about Sawyer?" Ember's teeth had begun to chatter.

"I don't know," Lukasz said. "Kael and I were in the berth when one of those tentacles tore the beams from above our heads. Sawyer wasn't with us, and I've seen no sign of him."

A sharp whistle sounded in the waters ahead.

"Here!" Lukasz shouted, then he said to Ember, "Kick hard. We have to catch them."

Following the commander's intent gaze, Ember saw their goal. Kael cut through the water with hard strokes, but he wasn't alone. Four long necks bobbed alongside him. The horses' eyes were rolling, wild with fright.

Lukasz and Ember swam at a diagonal, working hard to intercept Kael and the horses, who were swimming directly for the coast. Though she wanted to be strong, Ember groaned with pain, fighting to keep her arm and legs moving.

"Courage, Ember," Lukasz said, his jaw clenched against the cold slap of waves. "When we reach the horses, we'll have relief."

They were closing the distance, but Ember could feel her body shutting down as the cold sea cocooned her limbs.

Feeling her slow, Lukasz said, "Call out to Caber. He may hear and wait for you."

In desperation, Ember shrieked, "Caber!"

She whistled and called his name again. The stallion's chestnut head turned in her direction. Caber gave a shrill whinny. His nostrils flared.

"Again," Lukasz ordered.

"Caber!" Ember saw that the stallion hesitated, watching her as Kael and the other horses continued toward the shore.

"Good," Lukasz said, and Ember could hear how strained he was. "Now swim."

With all she had left, Ember plowed through the water, matching the commander's furious pace. When they reached the horse, Ember wept.

"Hold on to Barrow and to Caber's tail," Lukasz told her. "He'll follow the other horses and tow both of you to the shore."

Freed of Ember and Barrow, Lukasz swam quickly ahead.

"Go, Caber!" Ember cried out. The stallion whinnied, his legs churning beneath the waves. Not trusting her grip to hold, Ember wrapped the length of Caber's tail around her forearm. The horse dragged them through the water.

Ahead, Ember saw Lukasz reach Kael and the other horses. The two men grasped the tails of their mounts and let the swimming horses pull them toward the coast. With the single purpose of swimming taken from her, Ember dared to look back.

The ship was gone. Floating timber and scattered debris were the only evidence that a vessel had once sailed. The turbulent waters had stilled, and Ember searched the wreckage for signs that the beast remained. But its flailing and grasping tentacles had vanished beneath the waves. As dread filled Ember at the thought of what lurked in the darkness below, Caber's feet hit ground. He snorted and dragged Ember and Barrow into the shallows.

Despite reaching the shore, Ember couldn't find the strength to move. She held Barrow against her, relieved when Lukasz and Kael splashed through the water to reach them. Giving up Barrow to Kael's care, Ember succumbed to her own exhaustion as Lukasz pulled her from the grasp of the frigid sea.

TEN

**EIRA'S IMPATIENCE WITH** her sister was unbearable. When Cian had asked to meet alone in their former quarters, Eira had known this fight was inevitable. It seemed that anytime Bosque or Alistair was absent, Cian was determined to question everything that Eira had worked for. At least today Eira had questions of her own.

"You've learned nothing?" Eira asked her sister.

Cian let her head drop back against the top of the chair. Eira noticed the new lines of strain and exhaustion on her sister's face.

"Not for lack of trying," Cian said.

Unwilling to show softness, Eira answered, "Try harder."

Cian sat up. "Is it your wish for me to hand over our entire kitchen staff to your pet monsters? Perhaps they'll at last confess the secret blend of herbs for the savory stew you crave."

A wave of fury rose in Eira's chest, but she forced it back. "Sister, the creatures are the means to an end. That is all."

"And Lord Mar?" Cian asked. "What is he?"

"An ally." Eira turned away, angry and unsettled by Cian's question.

Rising from her chair, Cian came to Eira's side and took her hand. "I fear this course you've plotted, Eira."

Eira clasped Cian's fingers. "Why must you question everything I do? Can't you see how much good has come of this?"

"Tell me what's good," Cian said. "You have power, yes. More come to you each day from all corners of the world to swear their allegiance. But it isn't for love of you."

"I have never needed love," Eira snapped, shaking her hand free of Cian's.

Cian sighed. "You still have mine."

"I know." Eira relented. "And you have mine. But I swear your reluctance to embrace this new path is pointless. This constant bickering wearies both of us."

"I only wish to fully understand the nature of an alliance with Lord Mar," Cian said. "You quickly forget that he is lord of all that we have sworn to destroy. That is the mission of Conatus."

"You don't understand because you keep me and Lord Mar at a distance," Eira told her. "If you'd join us—as Alistair, Thomas, and Claudio have—you'd know the wonder that it is to command the nether beasts."

Cian shook her head, but Eira pressed on. "You refuse to see all that's changed. Lord Mar's aid transforms our purpose. He is no longer forced to scavenge our world for what he needs. We are no longer beholden to the Church or to kings. We rule all, including Bosque's minions. His servants bow to us, serve us."

"But he still has need of this world," Cian said. "His creatures still find nourishment here, do they not?"

"Yes." Eira's shoulders ached from tension. They'd had this argument so many times. "But we decide—"

"You decide." Cian cut her off. "You and this Bosque. How can you trust him so?"

"Because I know him as you do not." Eira's mind flashed to the forest outside Dorusduain. She remembered cradling Cian in her arms, her sister's body broken beyond repair. If not for Bosque.

A polite knock was followed by the sound of Alistair's voice. "Lady Eira?"

"Come in, Lord Hart," Eira answered. She ignored Cian's low sound of disgust.

Alistair entered the room, offering a short bow to the sisters.

"The clerics who wish to make the oath have assembled in the great hall," Alistair told them. "Lord Mar awaits you there as well."

Eira cut her eyes at Cian. "I'm so pleased that our scholarly peers have come forward, embracing the path of visionaries."

"How many?" Cian asked quietly.

"Seven," Alistair answered. "Though in speaking to Hamish, who brought their request, I believe more will partake in the ritual soon. They're waiting to see how the first fare."

"So many sheep." Eira laughed coldly.

"That's hardly fair," Cian said. "Caution does not bespeak cowardice."

Eira turned hard eyes on her sister. "So speaks the queen of caution." With a smile, she continued, "I think I have a fitting task for you."

Cian didn't respond, but her lips thinned as she watched Eira.

"We've been waiting for the sheep to come to us," Eira said. "But are we not the shepherds?"

"My lady?" Alistair asked.

"Lord Mar offers an incredible gift to those who swear fealty," Eira told him. "Why share it with only a few when all could benefit?"

She turned to face Cian. "I have a new task for you, sister. Since your attempts to find Mercer's assassin have been fruitless."

Cian wore a stony expression. "What would you have me do?"

"Take Lord Hart and Claudio," Eira said. "The three of you shall be emissaries of the Circle to all of Tearmunn. Let the clerics, craftsmen, and Guard know that at sunset on the morrow, they are invited to join our new order. To become part of the future."

Cian nodded slowly.

With a smile, Eira said to Alistair, "Lord Hart, you will take note of all who refuse this gift."

"You're forcing loyalty." Cian's face had gone pale. "There is no honor in that, sister."

Eira approached her sister and, without warning, slapped her hard across the cheek. "You will not speak to me that way again."

Alistair's eyes were wide, but he stayed silent.

"We're awaited in the great hall," Eira said, passing him as she went to the door.

He nodded and followed while Cian stood silent in the room, her hand pressed to the red welt on her face.

As Eira and Alistair descended the staircase, Alistair said, "Forgive me, Lady Eira, but was it necessary to shame your sister so?"

Eira glanced at him. "My sister behaves as a child, and until that changes, I will treat her so. Her doubts are like a sickness that will spread dissent through Tearmunn. It forces me to deal harshly with her."

"Yes, my lady," Alistair said.

"What do you think of your new task?" Eira asked him. Her fury at Cian had inspired the idea of forcing the whole of Tearmunn to swear fealty, but as her anger waned, she recalled the plan with a measure of uncertainty.

"It's wise." Alistair's unwavering tone reassured her. "Lord Mar spoke to me of forming a new command within the Guard. And that will require more of our number who can summon nether creatures."

"Lord Mar has already spoken to you of this?" Eira asked in surprise. She knew Bosque favored Alistair, but she was taken aback that he would have approached Alistair about new plans for the order without speaking to her first.

"Only in passing," Alistair responded quickly. "He wondered if I would aspire to lead the Guard."

"And would you?" Eira smiled at him, wondering how far the young knight's ambitions stretched.

Alistair ducked his head, suddenly shy. "If it would serve your greater purpose, my lady."

"It may," Eira replied thoughtfully. "See who among the Guard are eager to join us. Report to me what you make of them and how you would proceed as their commander."

"It would be an honor." Alistair's boyish grin made Eira laugh. He was young, but so hungry for acknowledgment. It was no wonder, given that he was the third son of a nobleman, left with only a name and not even the scraps of an estate to inherit.

When they reached the great hall, Eira paused. "Alistair, have you written to your family since Lady Morrow came to us?"

A blush colored Alistair's cheeks. "I have not, my lady."

"Send them a letter," Eira told him.

Alistair's eyes widened. "What would you have me say?"

Eira touched his cheek. It was an odd gesture for her, almost motherly. "Our task is to secure loyalty within Conatus, but also to ensure subservience without. Starting with Abbot Crichton, we've demonstrated that we shall not be ruled by the Church. Who else might contend with us?"

"The nobles," Alistair answered. "You would begin with my family?"

"They should know how far their son will rise in our ranks," she told him.

Alistair nodded, his face alight with sudden pride.

Eira continued. "You should write to your brother Henry as well."

When Alistair's delight became a scowl, Eira said, "Listen to me, Alistair, and you will have joy in your brother's folly."

"How?" Alistair asked her.

"Lord Mar already showed us the way," Eira told him. "We care for Agnes as a hostage. It seems to me that Ember isn't the only one who would be concerned for her sister."

Alistair shook his head. "You place too much faith in my brother's character. He will call Agnes a whore before he acknowledges the child."

"Do you not think we have the means to persuade him otherwise?" Eira said. "If Henry behaves with dishonor, I believe a visit from Lord Mar would be in order."

"That would be interesting." Alistair laughed.

"Your family will bring us noble houses in Scotland and England," Eira told him. "They will be the first to align with us, but not the last."

When Alistair dropped to one knee, Eira was surprised and delighted. He took her hand, kissing it.

"Wherever you lead, my lady," Alistair murmured, "I shall follow, for the world is yours to take."

"Yes." Eira helped him rise. "It is."

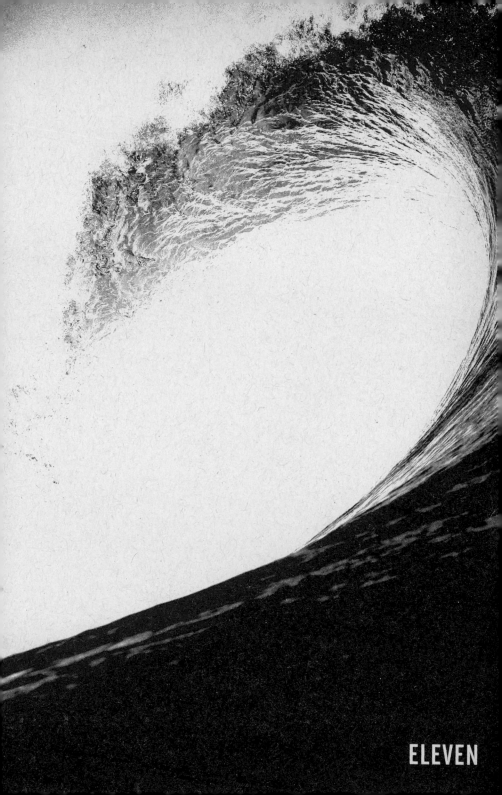

ELEVEN

**EMBER WOKE TO** comforting warmth. The bonfire, a ramshackle pile of driftwood, spit and crackled as it burned. She sat up, turning when she felt a hand on her shoulder.

"How are you feeling?" Barrow asked.

With a cry of relief, Ember threw herself on him. Barrow grunted and flinched.

Ember pulled away. "I'm sorry."

"Don't be," he answered. "The day when these bruises are healed can't come soon enough."

"Good to see you awake and less blue in the face, Lady Morrow." Kael sat on the other side of the bonfire.

"Thank you," Ember said with a rueful smile.

"That's twice Ember's saved your life, Barrow," Kael told him. "I thought you were the one teaching her to be a warrior."

Barrow grimaced. "The last few days haven't been my best as an instructor."

"You do have a tendency to get knocked out at inopportune times," Ember teased.

"A terrible habit"—Barrow returned her smile—"that I promise to break."

"Glad to hear it." She laughed, searching the beach near the campfire for her other companions. "Where is the commander?"

"Guarding the horses," Kael told her. "They're the most precious cargo to survive the shipwreck. We can't risk them being stolen."

"How did you save the horses?" If she closed her eyes, Ember could still see the heaving deck, spikes of timber jutting toward the sky as the ship was halved.

"A stroke of luck," Kael said. "We were belowdecks when the roof of the berth was ripped away, leaving only sky above our heads. Lukasz went to find the two of you. I went to the horses. I reached them just as the ship broke up, and fortune smiled on us. The beast opened a hole to the sea that let me swim out with the horses. If that hadn't happened, we'd have drowned."

"And Sawyer?" Ember asked, looking for any signs of him elsewhere on the beach.

"He wasn't with us at the time of the attack." Kael bowed his head. "We found his body washed ashore. At least we were able to bury him."

Ember nodded, but her chest was tight with grief.

"He was a good man, but troubled by the evil he'd seen," Barrow said quietly. "I would hope that he's at peace now."

"What was that thing?" Ember asked, forcing her sorrow aside.

"Some would call it Leviathan," Kael told her. "Others a kraken, Lothan, Scylla, or Tethys. It has many names, though I wouldn't claim to know the true one."

A part of Ember wanted to ask plaintively if the myths of sea monsters were true, but she'd seen enough of myth come to life since her arrival at Conatus to quell that impulse.

Instead she asked, "Have you fought this creature before?"

Barrow said, "You cannot fight Leviathan."

"Especially not when you're unconscious." Kael grinned at him.

"True enough." Barrow laughed darkly. "Even bearing the greatest of weapons, however, the kraken has the advantage."

Kael shifted forward. The bonfire cast a strange mask of light and shadow on his face. "We haven't encountered a sea monster ourselves before now. The records we have of their attacks are rare. From what we know, the kraken keep to the open sea, taking ships infrequently and more infrequently leaving survivors to tell the tale."

"It doesn't bode well," Barrow said.

"What doesn't?" Ember asked.

"This attack happened close to shore," Kael answered. "On this sea route, ships are lost to storms, war, or pirates, but not to Leviathan."

Ember took in the strain on their faces. Battle-worn knights made fearful.

"You think it was sent after us?" she asked.

Kael nodded. "If wolves of fire hunted you on land, it isn't hard to believe that the greatest of sea monsters was awakened from the deeps to continue the chase."

Pulling her knees to her chest, Ember shivered. "How is it that these things—beasts of fire, shadow, and legend—come to life now as never before? What has changed?"

"That we must learn," Barrow said quietly, "before we are destroyed."

Kael stood, brushing sand from his clothes. "And now that you're awake, we should be on our way. Something is hunting, and I'd prefer to let it believe us dead than have it come after us again."

There were few other survivors. Of the forty souls who embarked from Inverness, only two sailors and five pilgrims besides the four Conatus refugees had escaped to the shore. Ember watched them huddle around their own fires as she, Barrow, and Kael went to join Lukasz and the horses.

"Any trouble?" Kael asked as they crested the beach slope and found the commander.

"The two crewmen who made it to shore came skulking," Lukasz told him. "But they didn't stay long."

"Reaver's good that way." Kael laughed.

"Who?" Ember frowned at Kael.

Lukasz answered her. "The name of my sword." He patted the hilt of the massive claymore strapped to his back.

When Caber caught sight of Ember, he snorted, coming to her and bumping her shoulder with his nose.

"Thanks for getting me to shore, friend." She stroked his neck.

Barrow stood beside her. "He's very loyal to you."

Ember smiled at him, clasping his hand in hers, but couldn't bring herself to speak. The sorrow she saw in his eyes was too much. If Caber had died, Ember knew the loss would cut her deeply. Yet she'd known the stallion only a short while. Barrow and Toshach had been bonded for years. Barrow returned her smile sadly before going to his new mount, a roan gelding Lukasz had hurriedly purchased in Inverness before they'd set sail.

"Do you know where we are?" Barrow asked the commander as they mounted.

"A fairly good idea," Lukasz told him. "Shortly before the wreck, one of the crewmen told me they'd sighted the Île de Ré on the southern horizon. That means our best hope is La Rochelle."

Kael shifted in his saddle, agitated. "Will the cache still be intact?"

"If the knights at Cernon have honor, it will," Lukasz answered. "I've not had need of the sanctuary before now. We'll have to chance it."

The commander led them forward at a trot. Ember reined Caber close to Barrow's mount.

"What is this place we're seeking?"

Barrow's mouth set in a grim line. "A slender hope, but as the commander said, the best we have. In the twelfth century, until their demise, La Rochelle was a Templar stronghold and the home of their fleet."

"And now that the Templars are gone?" Ember asked

"When the order was condemned for heresy, a group of Templars collected what they could of their wealth and arcane knowledge and loaded ships," Barrow continued. "They made their escape so as not to burn with the rest of their brethren."

"Where did they go?" Ember checked Caber as he tried to nip Barrow's gelding.

Barrow glanced at Caber's pinned ears. "Not friends yet, are they?"

"He misses Toshach," Ember said, then bit her lip, regretting her words.

"So do I," Barrow said quietly. Then, after a breath, he continued, "The story of their escape remains a mystery. It may even be a legend. If the Templars on those ships did land on another shore, they've kept the location a secret."

He leaned forward to pat his mount's neck as the roan became irritated with Caber's threatening posture, nostrils flaring and head tossing. "Easy, now."

Ember reined Caber slightly farther from Barrow's horse. "If we don't know, how does that help us?"

"The story of the Templars' voyage was passed down to Conatus," Barrow answered. "But we received another tale as well: that because La Rochelle offered salvation for a few of the persecuted, it would forever remain a sanctuary for those of our order in need. This place is reputedly protected by Templar spellwork so that only warriors loyal to their cause may enter."

"Why did Lukasz mention Cernon?" Ember asked.

"La Rochelle's sanctuary was created over a century ago," Barrow said. "The Guard of Cernon are supposedly its caretakers, but given the mythic nature of the story, we can't be sure they've maintained it—if it ever existed. Though the Templars were destroyed, Conatus was never in danger. We haven't had need of such a place."

"Until now," Ember said quietly.

They traveled in silence, at a steady but restrained pace to avoid straining the horses after their ordeal at sea. When the sun reached its midday pinnacle, Lukasz brought them to a halt. The horses had their fill of ripening spring grasses while their riders took turns resting. Their provisions lost to the sea, Ember tried to ignore her rumbling belly. If her companions could bear hunger without complaint, she was determined to do the same. Though as she watched Caber relish his mouthfuls of greens, she wished that the grasses could feed her too.

Lukasz took them overland, in sight of but not on the main road. Though they traveled without speaking, Ember could feel the tension that bound them together. The sight of other riders sent ripples of alarm through their party, palpable enough for the horses to sense it, making them snort and prance nervously.

As they neared La Rochelle, the road became more congested, and Lukasz deemed it safe enough for them to blend in with the other travelers. Bedraggled as they were, Ember supposed they didn't appear too strange for road-weary pilgrims.

Stout walls formed a barrier between La Rochelle and the countryside. The stone fortifications were enhanced by tall towers that cast watchful shadows over the city. Lukasz led them southwest through the narrow streets. The pungent scent of seawater permeated the city. Though the town corridors still bustled with people, dusk had long since fallen, and the merchants had closed their stalls for the day. Ember's stomach had grown vengeful claws, but her hopes for encountering a baker selling bread were rapidly waning.

When they reached the harbor, Lukasz dismounted and waited for the rest of them to do the same. Leading the horses along the waterside until it became a canal that eased between the stone buildings, Lukasz pointed at a tall church.

"Saint-Sauveur," he told them quietly. "The sanctuary we seek is there."

They passed by the bell tower, turning down a side street barely wide enough to accommodate the horses. The corridor ended abruptly, leaving Lukasz to stop in front of a carved stone façade. Two torches blazed in sconces, throwing their firelight onto an image taller than the commander. A pair of knights rode together on a single horse, the words *Sigillum Militum Xpisti* ringing the life-size soldiers and their steed.

"The Templar seal." Peering at the image of these brethren in arms, Ember contended with admiration and sorrow. The legacy she aspired to fulfill was one that had ended with blood and fire. So many lives lost.

"I hope this works," Lukasz said.

Standing before one of the torches, he swiftly passed his hand through its flame. As they watched, the firelight blazed anew—its flames silver-white. Stone grated on stone, and the two riders slowly pulled away from them into a hidden recess.

Lukasz ducked into the shadows, reemerging a few moments later. "There's a short staircase, but it opens into stables below. We can bring the horses."

"Stables underground?" Ember looked at Barrow.

He shrugged. "It's a refuge for knights, and knights have horses. See?" He pointed at the Templar seal.

"Hilarious," Ember replied drily.

"I only speak the truth," Barrow said seriously, but his eyes were laughing.

Barrow and Kael blindfolded the horses so no time was wasted coaxing the animals into the dark stairwell. Lukasz entered last, taking the white-flamed torch with him. When they reached the bottom of the staircase, the great stone seal groaned, returning to its original place.

Kael glanced at Lukasz. "I hope you know how to open that up again."

"You'll just have to trust me," Lukasz told him. "Get the horses settled."

The light from Lukasz's silver-bright torch revealed an open space. Ember couldn't discern whether it was a natural cave or a man-made hollow. Iron rings were bolted into the rock walls, offering tie offs for the horses.

Barrow found a pitchfork in a nook as well as fresh hay and a sack of grain.

"Someone's been keeping this place in order," he told them. "And a good thing that is. Our horses hardly need a meal of moldy hay and rotten grain."

As Barrow apportioned food for the horses, Kael and Ember took turns leading their mounts to a carved stone trough into which bubbled a steady stream of fresh water. When the horses were unsaddled and fed, Lukasz beckoned the other knights to follow him.

Opposite the stairs, the cave narrowed into a short tunnel that ran up against a solid wooden door. Finding it unlocked, Lukasz opened the door and led the way into another open space.

As torchlight illuminated the room, Kael clapped his approval.

"I'm glad the horses aren't the only ones provided for."

The room was small, but furnished with all they could desire. A table and six chairs were laden with bread and fruit. Six pallets were tucked against the walls. Ember went to a tall wooden cupboard, where she discovered dried meat, herbs, and a cloth-bound hard cheese. Her mouth watered while her stomach cramped with hunger.

"There's wine." Kael hooted with delight as he opened a barrel.

Ember brought the meat and cheese to the table while Lukasz prepared a fire in the hearth.

"Where do you think the smoke is released?" Barrow asked the commander.

"Somewhere inconspicuous," Lukasz answered with a wry smile. "Or the purpose of this place is ill served."

Though ravenous, Ember forced herself to eat slowly, chewing her bread and cheese thoroughly instead of wolfing down large chunks as she wanted to. The lack of talk at the table confirmed that Ember's companions were as hungry as she.

The silent meal was interrupted by the sound of a key turning in a lock. Ember jumped up in surprise. She'd been so fixated on her rumbling stomach that she only now noticed the second door in their hiding place—the door that was slowly opening.

Lukasz brandished the knife he'd been using to eat. Leaving his chair, Barrow pounced onto the table's edge, using its surface to propel his jump to the pallet where he'd left his saber. Ember and Kael rushed to the wall where the door was opening, placing themselves behind the door so they'd be hidden from whoever had turned the key.

"*Qui est ici?*" The question floated from behind the half-opened door.

Tilting his head at the sound of the speaker's voice, Lukasz spoke. "Jérôme? Is that you?"

"Lukasz?" the hidden man replied, and the door opened a bit further.

Tension melted from the commander's shoulders. "Yes. You don't how glad I am that you've come to meet us."

When Lukasz let his knife fall to the table, Kael and Ember retreated from their hiding place, and Barrow rose from where he'd been crouched by the pallet.

The door swung open, and a lanky knight with long chestnut hair gathered at the nape of his neck came into the room. Lukasz rounded the table to receive the French knight's embrace.

"It's good to see you, friend." Jérôme's voice lilted with his accented English.

"The same," Lukasz answered. He gestured to his three companions. "My fellow knights, Barrow Hess, Kael MacRath, and Ember

Morrow. It's my honor to present Jérôme Fauré, Cernon's finest Guard."

"Your praise is undeserved." Jérôme shook his head. His gaze lingered on Ember, and his eyes narrowed slightly. She wondered if he found the presence of a woman among Conatus's knights unsettling. She knew women of the Guard were a rarity, but she didn't know how exceptional her role might be.

"You've always been too humble, Jérôme," Lukasz answered. "We're indebted to you for the food and shelter. Our need is great, and we feared that the sanctuary of La Rochelle might have been long neglected."

Jérôme nodded, his smile short-lived. "You were right to be anxious. Until very recently, La Rochelle was viewed as a worthless vestige of days long past."

"What changed?" Kael asked.

"So much, it seems, and so quickly," Jérôme said. "I feared this place might be needed, so I took it upon myself to restore its provisions."

"Alone?" Barrow returned to the table.

With a sigh, Jérôme told him, "Yes. I regret to confess I cannot trust my brethren as I would like. I took over the watch at La Rochelle, which had been an unfilled post for some years, but I did so in secret."

"How did you explain your presence here?" Lukasz frowned. "You don't have duties at Cernon?"

"The Guards' tasks at Cernon are rapidly shifting," Jérôme said. "Our commander requested an emissary be sent to the city to lay groundwork for reasserting Conatus's control of the harbor. My sister's husband lives here and is a wealthy merchant with ties to the region's nobility. I volunteered for the post—to learn more of what my superiors have planned, as well as to ensure that this sanctuary was made available to any who found themselves exiled."

The implications of Jérôme's words choked the room.

"You were expecting us, then?" Lukasz asked when the silence had become too much to bear.

Jérôme took a cup from the table and filled it at the wine barrel. "I considered the task preparing for the worst."

"We're the worst, then," Kael muttered. "Wonderful."

"What do you know?" Lukasz returned to his chair, and Jérôme sat opposite the commander.

"Only that the darkness creeping across my homeland now began in yours," Jérôme said. "I hope you can tell me how that came to be."

"One of our Circle," Lukasz told him, "the lady Eira, pursued a dangerous course that has overtaken Tearmunn."

"It's gone much further than that, but I knew not that a woman was behind all of this." Jérôme took a long pull from his cup. "Though I confess it doesn't surprise me."

"I beg your pardon?" Ember moved to stand beside Lukasz.

Arching an eyebrow at her, Jérôme said, "It's well known that women fall to the devil's temptations more readily than do men."

"Is it?" Ember glared at the French knight.

Barrow approached Jérôme, hand on his saber's hilt. "You will apologize to Lady Morrow. Or my blade will defend her honor."

Jérôme stood up, reaching for his scabbard.

"Stop!" Lukasz raised his hand. "I will not have quarrels between allies that are so few. Jérôme, Lady Eira is an exception, not a rule by which to judge all women. Even now, Eira's sister, Cian, works at great risk to support us from Tearmunn." He stood and placed his hand on Ember's shoulder. "Lady Morrow is among the bravest knights I've had the privilege to fight beside."

"Very well, I shall hold my tongue when it comes to women's weaknesses." Jérôme offered Barrow a haughty smile. "You should be grateful I call your commander my friend."

"Jérôme." Lukasz pointed to a chair, and Jérôme returned to his seat.

Barrow stood by, his hand still gripping his sword hilt.

"Be at peace, Lord Hess." Lukasz watched Barrow until he let go of the hilt. "Fill wine cups for each of us, Kael. We will drink together as befits brethren—and sisters—in arms."

Lukasz pulled out the chair beside him, gesturing for Ember to sit at his right hand. Barrow took the chair on the commander's left. After distributing brimming cups around the table, Kael sat beside Jérôme.

Lifting his cup, Lukasz intoned, "To driving back the dark."

They raised their glasses to his toast, but after drinking, Jérôme murmured, "I fear it is too late for that."

"What's happened here?" Kael asked Jérôme.

Jérôme leaned back in his chair, his former arrogance overwhelmed by weariness. "We've had many visitors from across the sea."

"From Tearmunn?" Lukasz frowned at him.

"Yes," Jérôme answered. "One of the eldest members of your Circle—the cleric called Thomas—has been here several times."

Barrow scowled into his wine cup. "I thought Thomas better than this."

"He wasn't alone," Jérôme said. "He came with an official missive from the Church, carried by your abbot."

"Crichton?" Kael gaped at Jérôme, then shook his head. "I thought he was a prisoner in his own manor."

"Apparently Eira has seen fit to send him out in her stead," Barrow replied. "Albeit on a leash."

"Thomas does most of the talking," Jérôme added. "My sense is that the abbot's presence conveys the Church's interest in the changes at work in our order."

"What message did Thomas bring?" Ember asked, weathering the snide look she earned from Jérôme.

"He spoke of a great discovery at Tearmunn," Jérôme told them, making a show of addressing Lukasz rather than Ember. "A mystery solved that would forever change our place in the world and end our struggle against the dark creatures with which we have so long contended."

Barrow didn't look at Jérôme, but asked, "Did anyone have ears to hear this message?"

"Many," Jérôme answered in irritation. "To Thomas, my companions at Cernon showed great respect, and the abbot they were all too happy to fawn over."

"I'm sure Abbot Crichton welcomed their attention." Kael drained his cup and went in search of another.

"What did they ask of you?" Lukasz stood up, following Kael to the wine barrel.

Jérôme handed his empty cup to the commander when he passed by. "To prepare the way for the future."

Lukasz placed a full cup of wine in front of Jérôme.

"Thank you," Jérôme said. "I hope you noticed that I provided a barrel of very good wine."

"We noticed," Kael said, pointing at his newly brimming cup as he settled into the chair beside Jérôme.

Jérôme took a sip of his wine, then continued. "Thomas said he and the abbot were the forerunners of much more important visitors. When these guests he spoke of come to Cernon, we're to partake in a ritual that will imbue us with new power."

"It must be Eira who's coming," Barrow said quietly.

Lukasz nodded. "And this Bosque Mar she's summoned."

"Who?" Jérôme's brow furrowed.

"Lady Eira has become obsessed with harnessing the power of the nether," Lukasz told Jérôme. "And she seems to have fulfilled her desire by allying with a stranger. A man who calls himself Bosque Mar."

Swirling the red liquid in his cup, Jérôme said, "Thomas made no mention of Lady Eira or this Bosque Mar. He only warned us that with great change comes resistance and that we must be watchful for any who would stand in the way of our ascension."

"That would be us." Kael laughed darkly.

Jérôme half smiled. "You don't say."

"Were no objections raised when Thomas spoke of these things?" Ember asked Jérôme.

"Think of where you sit." Jérôme spoke harshly. "Where you find refuge. The Templars were destroyed by the ones they served, by priests and monarchs who had been their most ardent supporters. Many in Conatus live in fear that one day we shall meet the same fate. Your Eira has become their champion. Like a weed, she sends tendrils out in every direction. Finding fertile ground, they take root."

"This new allegiance grows out of fear, not honor." Barrow spat the words.

"Fear holds more sway than honor," Jérôme told him. "Does that truly surprise you?"

"I had hoped my brethren of Conatus would prove better," Barrow answered.

Jérôme tilted his cup at Barrow. "They are but men, prone to sin and selfishness."

"And yet you're here," Ember said quietly.

Jérôme met her steady gaze and smiled slowly.

Unflinching, Ember went on, "Does that mean you still have honor?"

"I'd like to think so." Jérôme's laugh was brittle. "I trust my instincts, and my heart whispers that the future Thomas heralds is forged of blood and shadow. I will not align myself with that which I took a sacred oath to fight."

"Nor shall we." Lukasz raised his cup. This time they drank their toast in solemnity.

"I came here tonight to warn you." Jérôme wiped his mouth. "The houses of Conatus offer no refuge. Lady Eira's emissaries have traveled far and wide, spreading their message. I doubt there is any keep where word of your arrival wouldn't be swiftly dispatched to Tearmunn."

Barrow leaned forward. "Are you telling us to hide?"

"For now," Jérôme answered.

"We're not cowards," Barrow snapped.

"I'm sure you're not," Jérôme replied. "But I hope you're not fools either. If your whereabouts are known, you'll be hunted. You can't hope to make a stand if you're forever running from Eira."

"He's right," Lukasz said to Barrow, who sat back in his chair, though his jaw remained set in anger.

Jérôme spoke to the commander. "There are others like me who see the evil in this. And more still who have little care for our sacred mission, but see the rise of a powerful order of knights—the Templars restored—as working against their interests. These merchants and nobles will aid us when called upon."

"It's a start," Kael said. "But it sounds like you're preparing for a war."

"Is that not what this is?" Jérôme finished his wine.

Lukasz passed a hand over his tired eyes. "Not yet. It may come to that."

"And I would have an army ready," Jérôme replied.

Barrow leaned forward. "An army will do no good against the creatures at Eira's command. These things are not known to us, and our weapons cannot harm them."

Jérôme straightened in alarm. "Is this true?"

"It is," Lukasz answered. "We don't know how to battle this new enemy."

Taking a long breath, Jérôme said, "Then that is your task. I will continue to gather allies, but you must find a way to fight the creatures Eira has brought into our world. Search for a place where you can get word to the East. The old Templar fortresses have libraries that house the mysteries of our order. You might find the answer within those ancient texts."

"I'd hoped to reach Krak des Chevaliers by ship," Lukasz told him. "But our vessel sank after it was attacked by Leviathan."

Jérôme's eyes went wide. Recovering, he said, "Let us pray that Eira believes you lie at the bottom of the sea."

"That's indeed what I've been praying for." Kael's speech was a bit slurred, and Ember noticed he'd refilled his wine cup yet again.

Lukasz rested his head in his hands. "But where to go?"

"I know where we might find refuge," Ember offered quietly, her idea forming as she spoke.

Barrow looked at her in surprise. "Where?"

Ember met Barrow's gaze, steeling herself, for she knew he wouldn't like what she was about to say. "I have a promise to keep."

Kael and Lukasz exchanged a worried glance.

"You don't mean—" Kael began.

"Yes," Ember cut him off. "I told Alistair I would go to my sister at the Château de Lusignan."

Barrow was shaking his head. "If he believes you go there, how could it possibly be a safe place for us?"

"Because Alistair expects I'll go there only if I've left you," Ember told him. "I can ask Agnes to write to him, and she'll tell him I've arrived alone if I ask her to. She wouldn't betray your presence."

Lukasz turned his wine cup in his hands. "That may work."

"Is the Count de La Marche friendly to Conatus?" Ember asked Jérôme.

"He has little interest in our work," Jérôme told her. "Our dealings with him have been limited."

"Good," Ember said. "Then he's unlikely to report our arrival."

Jérôme shrugged. "True enough."

"I don't like it." Barrow sulked.

Kael traded his half-full wine cup for Barrow's empty one. "Of course you don't, my friend. But that's not because it's a poor idea."

Barrow took the cup, but gave Kael a puzzled look.

"Drink up, Lord Hess." Kael winked at him. "Jealousy doesn't look good on you."

TWELVE

**WHEN EMBER WOKE,** Lukasz was already sitting at the table with Jérôme. The French knight had left them to rest while he went to gather additional provisions they'd need for the trip to Lusignan.

Ember rose from her pallet and went to join them. When she sat, Lukasz tore a hunk of bread from a loaf and handed it to her.

"Break your fast with us, Lady Morrow."

Still drowsy, Ember chewed on the bread while the commander and Jérôme continued their conversation.

"It will take you the day to reach the château," Jérôme said. "But if you follow my advice, you shouldn't have trouble."

"That's Ember's decision," Lukasz answered. "I won't make it for her."

Ember looked up from her breakfast. "What must I decide?"

Jérôme stood up and went to collect a bundle that had been left near the tunnel to the stables. Barrow and Kael were stirring on their pallets.

"Wake up, you two!" Lukasz called to them. "We should be on the road at dawn."

With yawns and some grumbling, Kael and Barrow made their way to the table.

Kael groaned as he sat down. "I hate riding on a sour stomach."

"Then you should drink less," Lukasz said, offering Kael a skin of water and a hard smile.

"You can be a cruel man." Kael took the water.

Lukasz's smile softened. "I know."

Barrow sat beside Ember. He quietly accepted the bread and cheese she offered. Beneath the table he rested his hand on her knee, his thumb grazing her lower thigh, and Ember was suddenly very much awake.

At the end of the table, Jérôme unwrapped the bundle to reveal tightly packed clothing. He separated the pieces. He pulled out chausses and breeches, shirts and cloaks. What made Ember choke on a bit of bread was the appearance of a gown.

Jérôme shook the rich emerald-green brocade until it unrolled to its full length and held the dress up for Ember to see. She bit back a groan.

"Does it please you?" he asked. "I thought it would match your eyes."

Ember didn't answer him, instead holding him with a cold gaze.

With a sigh, Jérôme said, "I am not jesting, Lady Morrow. I brought the gown for a purpose. You cannot go to your sister's husband in that ragged dress you're wearing."

"I thought not to go in a dress at all," Ember answered.

Jérôme's eyebrows went up. "Well, that would be interesting."

Ember made a sound of disgust, and Barrow rose, his hands becoming fists. Before he could speak, Jérôme said, "Peace, friend. I meant no harm—I only thought to lighten the spirit of this dark morning."

"Sit down, Barrow." Kael threw a hard bread crust at Barrow. "It's too early for chivalry. You're making my headache worse with such noble posturing."

Barrow stared in surprise at Kael, but after a moment he laughed. "I shall spare your aching head, then."

"Ember." Lukasz took up the conversation. "Jérôme discussed a tactic with me, and I think you should hear it."

Ember looked at the French knight.

"Do you want to arrive at Count de La Marche's estate as a noble-woman or a warrior?" Jérôme said, gesturing to the dress and then the pile of men's clothes. "I leave the choice to you, but consider to whom the count will respond more warmly—a contingent of knights or his wife's noble sister and her retinue."

She looked at the two sets of clothing. Resigned, Ember reached for the dress.

Jérôme nodded his approval, but his expression wasn't gloating—a good thing, for if he had watched her acquiescence with a snide smile, Ember would have wanted to don a pair of breeches just to spite the Frenchman.

"It's the wiser course, Ember," Lukasz told her. "You can dress here. We'll take the clothes Jérôme brought for us and change in the stables. Then we'll ready the horses and wait for you."

He stood up, gesturing to Barrow and Kael. "Come on, then."

"I haven't finished my breakfast," Kael said, pointing to a half-eaten wedge of cheese.

"Bring it with you." The commander disappeared into the tunnel with Jérôme behind him, his arms full of clothing.

Muttering under his breath, Kael bound up the bread loaf and cheese in a cloth and went after them.

"What you wear doesn't change who you are," Barrow whispered in Ember's ear. "Never forget that."

"Thank you," she said.

He kissed her lightly and left the table.

"Barrow," Ember called after him. When he turned, she said, "I also haven't forgotten what happened the last time I exchanged my warrior's clothes for a dress."

"Nor have I," he said, smiling. "Would that our companions weren't awaiting me, or I would give you more to remember."

He disappeared into the tunnel, and Ember hugged the silk brocade to her body, letting the warmth of the memory she did have wash over her. After finishing her bread, Ember spread the gown on one of the pallets. She couldn't deny that the dress was beautiful. Its deep green hue reminded her of the dark pines that covered Scottish hills.

Ember pulled off her rough wool dress and put it aside. The silk brocade was as pleasing to her hands as to her eye. The gown slid on easily. Its low, broad scooping neck revealed her chemise at the bodice and shoulders. Ember grimaced, knowing that the dingy pale cloth contrasted poorly with the fineness of the green silk, but there was nothing to be done about it.

The lacing for this gown was at Ember's side rather than the back. She tightened the cords, tying them off when the silk wrapped her torso in a snug embrace.

Just as she couldn't improve the state of her chemise, Ember had little luck tidying her hair. She pulled her fingers through its length until her auburn tresses were free of tangles and decided that was good enough.

The sound of a man's cough drew her eyes to the tunnel opening. Jérôme stood watching her, a playful smile on his lips.

"I see there was a noblewoman hiding beneath the peasant dress," he said. "And a beautiful one at that."

Rather than reply, Ember belted on Silence and Sorrow, fastening a cloak over her dress so the weapons would be hidden.

Jérôme stepped aside to give her entry to the tunnel. "Your companions await. I must leave by the other door, but I'll see you at the canal shortly."

He bowed deeply when Ember brushed pass him, but she didn't bother to acknowledge the gesture. Her patience with the arrogant knight had worn too thin, and she didn't trust her tongue to be anything other than venomous.

When Ember reached the subterranean stables, the horses were saddled, bridled, and once again blindfolded.

Lukasz led their ascent, carrying the white-flamed torch that had burned ceaselessly since the commander had taken it up. When he reached the top of the staircase, the stone slab groaned its way open. They led the horses out into a city filled with the lavender-gray light that warned of dawn's approach.

Returning the torch to its sconce, Lukasz spoke quiet words and swept his hand through the white fire. Ember blinked and the flames had returned to their normal colors. The Templar seal that hid their sanctuary closed, restoring the appearance of a solid wall.

"Jérôme awaits us at the canal on the other side of Saint-Sauveur," Lukasz told them.

They retraced their steps along the narrow side passage, entering the streets of La Rochelle. A thin veil of mist hung over the canal. The other knights mounted, but Ember struggled to find a way to get her foot into the stirrup without pulling her skirts up to her waist.

"Let me help." Barrow had swung out of his saddle and now was behind her. He grabbed her around the waist and lifted her up, allowing her to slip her leg over the saddle with ease.

"Thank you," she said, rearranging the bothersome skirts so they fell properly over her legs as she sat astride Caber.

Barrow smiled at her. "Of course, my lady." His hand slid beneath her skirt. For a moment, he seemed to be making sure her foot was secure in the stirrup, but then his fingers were on her bare calf.

"I find it troubling," he said in a low voice only for her, "to be so close and yet so rarely be able to touch you."

"Yes." Ember gripped the reins as Barrow's hand moved slowly up her leg. "It is troubling . . ."

"Lady Morrow, are you ready?" Lukasz called to them.

Barrow laughed quietly, leaving Ember's leg tingling when he returned to his horse.

Jérôme waited for them between the church and the waterway, holding the reins for not one but two mounts.

The first, a dark brown steed, stood quietly but cast annoyed glances at its equine companion, a filly who couldn't seem to keep still. The filly whinnied when she saw other horses approaching and tossed her head so that Jérôme had to take a firmer hold of her reins.

"You're not alone?" Kael asked Jérôme.

The Frenchman shook his head. "I've simply brought the last of the provisions you need for your journey. Lord Hess, could I trouble you to leave your saddle?"

Barrow dismounted and came forward, leading his roan.

Jérôme nodded at the filly. "Her name is Tempête."

"The storm." Barrow looked the filly over. "Appropriate for a silver dapple."

"Her coat is less cause for the name than her spirit," Jérôme told him. "How do you like her?"

"She's a beautiful filly," Barrow answered. "Lithe. I imagine she's a runner."

"Her speed rivals the wind." Jérôme glanced at Lukasz. "I was told you lost a fine stallion."

Barrow's shoulders tensed, but he nodded.

"Please accept this filly as a gift," Jérôme said to Barrow. "A symbol of our alliance."

Taking the reins of Barrow's roan, Jérôme offered those of the high-spirited filly. Ember found it hard to take her eyes off the young horse. Though the sun had yet to rise, each time Tempête moved, her coat rippled like lightning flashing within the depths of a thunderhead.

"Your mount is serviceable," Jérôme said to Barrow. "But a knight of Conatus needs a warrior's steed. A companion. Though I must warn you, Tempête is as much a challenge as an offering. Perhaps you're not up to the task?"

Barrow watched the skittish filly dance on the path. He accepted

Tempête's reins from Jérôme, and the silver steed eyed him as he approached. Her nostrils flared, and she gave a shrill whinny, warning the knight off.

"Lukasz regards your horsemanship to be the best he's ever seen." Jérôme observed Barrow's slow movements as he drew nearer to the filly. "None of my Guard can master Tempête. She favors her own will over her rider's wishes. Your commander suggested that you might succeed where others have failed."

"That they tried to master her was likely the problem," Barrow answered, though his eyes never left the horse.

Ember leaned over to Lukasz, whispering, "Is now the best time to give Barrow such an unpredictable mount?"

"He needs this," Lukasz answered. "Our friend suffers greatly from the loss of Toshach. And despite Jérôme's narrow mind toward those of your sex, I would prefer that he be in Barrow's favor. Jérôme may be careless with his speech, but he is matchless with his sword."

Tempête snorted and stamped the ground. Though Ember couldn't make out his words, she could tell Barrow was quietly speaking to the filly. When he was standing close enough to touch her, he paused, standing completely still but murmuring all the while. Tempête reared, giving a shrill whinny. Her hooves trampled the ground a hair breadth from Barrow's feet, but he didn't move. She reared again, her neck snaking through the air.

Tempête pawed at the earth, but her squeal died in a low whinny of confusion as all her antics failed to provoke the tall knight standing before her. Bowing her head, she stretched her nose toward him. He remained still as Tempête blew into his face, shoulders, and chest. Her ears flicked in curiosity.

As she took in his scent, Barrow slowly reached up and laid his hand on Tempête's neck.

"I think he's the first man she hasn't taken a bite out of," Jérôme said to Lukasz.

The commander smiled. "When I told you of his skill, I wasn't exaggerating."

"I can see that," Jérôme replied.

Tempête was bobbing her head with delight as Barrow scratched between her ears.

"A fine gift," Barrow said without turning away from the horse. "I'm honored to accept."

Lukasz clapped Jérôme on the shoulder. "Thank you for offering shelter and supplies. We were in dire need."

"I wish you well on your journey," Jérôme said, handing Lukasz a sealed letter. "Send word through my sister of your whereabouts. I will keep you informed as I continue to draw allies to our cause."

The knights mounted their horses, with the exception of Barrow, who was still speaking quietly to Tempête.

"I would leave you with one last thought," Jérôme said to Barrow. "You won't like my words, Lord Hess. But I mean no offense."

"Say on," Barrow told him as he moved from standing in front of Tempête to her side, rubbing her neck and shoulders all the while.

"You should leave the lady with her sister." Jérôme glanced at Ember. "In what's to come, there's no place for a maid who plays at swords because her father offered Conatus enough coin to take her. I know well how such arrangements work."

"Thank you for the horse," Barrow said, swinging into Tempête's saddle. The filly reared, but Barrow kept his seat with ease. "As for the lady, she does not wield swords, and she's saved my life twice. When you see her take the field—as one day you shall—you will beg her forgiveness for your hastily spoken words."

Turning to Ember, Jérôme said, "I hope his faith in you is not misplaced."

Biting back some choice words, Ember instead put her heels to Caber, and the stallion trotted away.

THIRTEEN

**ALISTAIR KNEW HE** wasn't as happy as he should be. He'd done everything that had been asked of him. Young as he was, Lord Mar and Lady Eira looked to Alistair for advice over that of any other member of the Circle. Not even Cian was treated with the esteem Alistair enjoyed.

His swift ascension had been noticed by his fellows in the Guard. Battle-seasoned knights bowed when he passed. They came to him in private, asking for his help in gaining favor from Lady Eira.

All around him, servants, scholars, craftsmen, and warriors acknowledged Alistair's place of honor in the new order at Tearmunn.

But he took little joy in any of it.

He'd woken this morning covered in sweat. The result of another night where dreams held him captive, tormenting him. No matter what had taken place in his waking hours, when Alistair gave himself over to sleep, he became a player, acting out an impossible scene.

It was the night that he'd visited Ember's room and found her gone. But in this dream, Ember hadn't fled with Barrow. When Alistair entered her cell, she sat on her pallet, waiting for him. Her plain sleep shirt had been traded for a sheer chemise.

As he watched, she rose, and the delicate garment slipped from her body. Ember stepped out of the chemise and lay on the bed. Her arms reached out to him, her face full of yearning.

Alistair approached slowly, savoring the moment for which he'd waited so long and suffered so much. Her skin was so pale in the shadows, but held an inner gleam, a promise subtle and alluring as moonlight.

His skin was hot with anticipation as he knelt over her. Though he had fleeting thoughts that he should treat her gently, be patient, he couldn't wait any longer.

But as he reached for her skin, his fingers found no flesh to caress. His hand passed through Ember's body, meeting with the rough fibers of the blanket beneath. He could still see her. She lay before Alistair, waiting, wanting him. Her lips parted, breaths short and shallow.

Grasping for her shoulders, Alistair collapsed against the bed. Ember was there, but she was not. He couldn't hold her. Couldn't touch her. Longing wrenched his limbs as though he were being stretched on a torturer's rack.

He flung the length of his body on top of hers, but he pressed into an empty pallet. Alistair writhed and sobbed, unable to quell the desperation of his heart or the terrible hunger of his body.

It wasn't the sort of nightmare from which he woke suddenly, sitting up on his pallet in a moment that cleanly severed the dream world from the real. This dream lingered, clinging to his skin like a foul odor. Ember's face, the cream of her skin, the fullness of her lips—every detail followed him long after he'd left his bed. Each time reigniting the slow burn of unquenched desire in his body.

He moved through his days with methodic precision. All his tasks were accomplished without flaw. But each night the dream returned, and the next day he felt more like the husk of a soul than a man of muscle and bone.

On this morning, Alistair made his way to the great hall. Eira had summoned him to gauge the fealty of craftsmen, who would be next to take their oaths. It had gone well with the clerics. Of the forty men and women who devoted their lives to studying esoteric tomes, devising spells, or improving their practice of healing arts, most had been allured by Eira's promises for the future. A few had declined, but Thomas had carefully noted their names, and appropriate steps had been taken.

If anyone had noticed the disappearance of three or four of their companions, none found courage enough to speak of it. As power shifted, Alistair observed, the residents of Tearmunn proved more likely to let the new current carry them rather than fight against it.

When the guard posted at the doors to the hall let Alistair pass, he wasn't surprised to find Lord Mar waiting within. Lady Eira's absence, however, was a surprise.

"Good day, Lord Hart." Bosque stood beside the sacred tree. Though Alistair had assumed the dead tree would begin to rot, the huge trunk, along with its sprawling branches and roots, hadn't deteriorated at all. Instead the sacred tree had ossified in its new form, as though a life-size ivory sculpture of a cedar of Lebanon had been commissioned to occupy this room.

Alistair nodded a greeting to Bosque, but looked over his shoulder, expecting Eira to appear in the doorway at any time.

"Lady Eira contends with an unforeseen dilemma," Bosque said. "She'll be delayed."

Alistair abandoned his watch of the door, walking toward the tall man. "What's wrong?"

"The way you travel"—Bosque stroked the bone-white trunk of the tree like it was a favorite pet—"has been disrupted."

Frowning as he tried to discern Bosque's meaning, Alistair said, "I haven't heard of any trouble at the stables."

With a quiet laugh, Bosque told him, "The problem is not your horses. It's your clerics."

"Do you mean the portal weavers?" Alistair's eyes widened. "What's happened to them?"

"They can no longer, as you put it, weave." Bosque showed little concern over what Alistair considered grave news.

"Your scholars and magicians are distraught," Bosque continued. "But as I assured Eira, they will soon know much greater power than the simple act of opening a door."

"Those doors take us all over the world—" Alistair began to argue, but taking in Bosque's placid smile, he instead asked, "Did you know this would happen?"

Bosque left the tree to stand face-to-face with the knight. "I knew there would be consequences. The power I give is drawn from the nether, not the earth, whence Conatus called forth magic. Where there is one, the other cannot be, as oil remains separate from water."

"None of the old magics will work?" Alistair asked. His eyes found the black abyss that maimed the sacred tree. "Because the rift is open?"

"You have new power." Bosque shrugged. "Greater power that doesn't require concessions to this world."

Alistair didn't fully understand. As a knight, he had limited experience with the arcane practices of the clerics and would never claim to understand the intricacies of their spellcraft. Yet the loss of portals and, with them, the ability to travel great distances in an instant troubled Alistair.

Sensing Alistair's agitation, Bosque folded his arms across his broad chest. Alistair was uncomfortably aware of how tall and imposing Bosque was. He took a step back.

"What do you want, Lord Hart?" Bosque asked, his silver eyes intent.

Alistair tried to answer, but stumbled over his words. What did he want? Ember's body flashed across his mind, leaving bitterness in its wake. *Only what's been denied me.*

"I believe your talents haven't been put to as much use as they could be," Bosque said. "I'd like that to change, but I would prefer that you choose the task that fully demonstrates your worth."

"My lord?" Alistair shook off the frustration that built from thoughts of Ember.

Bosque walked in a slow circle around Alistair. "You are often distracted, Alistair. And something clearly pains you."

Alistair nodded and heat crept into his neck. Lord Mar displayed no weakness, no vulnerability. Shame at how easily he could be provoked by unrequited love churned beneath Alistair's ribs.

"Passion is a great force," Bosque told him. "Harness yours, set it to good purpose, and I believe the results would be astonishing."

Grinding his teeth out of impatience with himself, Alistair asked sullenly, "How can I do that when my passion is wasted on—" He stopped himself, choking on the rage he felt toward Ember.

"It is only a waste if you let it be," Bosque said. "As for the woman—I can't help you until she reappears."

"If she's alive," Alistair muttered, his anger spiraling into a hollow sadness. It was always like this when he thought of Ember: he loved, hated, and mourned her within the space of a heartbeat. It was agony.

Bosque ignored Alistair's comment. "There have been moments of triumph. Your triumph. That is what you must build your legacy upon."

Alistair stared at him. "A legacy?"

"You will have a great legacy, Alistair," Bosque said quietly. "But it must begin with a demonstration of your cunning."

As Alistair mulled over Bosque's words, Bosque continued. "Can you tell me when you felt strongest since you joined Eira? The most powerful?"

"When I rode the shadow horse and ran with the Lyulf," Alistair answered without pause. The memory of rushing through time on a river of darkness, of seeing the fire wolves put Ember and Barrow at his mercy, made Alistair's pulse spike.

Bosque nodded. "Consider this: I've told you that the Lyulf are beyond human mastery."

The feverish light in Alistair's blue eyes diminished. "I remember."

"But there are many beasts in my dominion that are not," Bosque said.

Meeting Bosque's searching gaze with a furrowed brow, Alistair said, "You would have me command other creatures of the nether?"

"I have given you pieces to a puzzle, Lord Hart," Bosque answered. "That is all. Even I don't know what picture will emerge when you put them together."

Bosque returned to the tree. He dipped his hand into the rift and drew forth shadow that ran from his cupped palm like water.

"What I have is yours for the taking," Bosque said without turning away from the tree. "Tell me what you will do with this gift."

A rush of images filled Alistair's mind. Shadow and fire. The howl of wolves. A village in chaos. A forest of bone.

And Bosque. Summoned by blood. Yet with his own blood, drawing Cian's broken body back from the edge of death.

*What I have is yours for the taking.*

*I've been acting the child,* Alistair thought. *When one as powerful as Bosque sees the man I should be.*

Then he smiled, knowing his dreams would be different that night.

*The man I shall be.*

FOURTEEN

**ONCE THE CITY WAS** behind them, Lukasz set their pace at a swift gallop. Ember was surprised at how glad she was to be free of La Rochelle. The walled city and its fortified harbor were impressive and beautiful, but what she'd learned there had left a chill in her bones.

The horses appeared delighted to be out of the cavelike stable in which they'd spent the night. Whether it was the appearance of the sun or the warm winds full of lush green scents, their hooves pounded the road east tirelessly. Despite the fast pace at which the commander led them, Caber remained restless. Grabbing for the bit, so that Ember had to take extra care in handling him, he made it obvious that he wanted to run faster yet.

"Would you settle down!" Ember chided the stallion, who insisted on tossing his head, pulling hard on the reins. Intermittent low whinnies rumbled from his chest.

Barrow eyed Caber's arched neck. "He's showing off. When this filly comes into season, we'll have a problem."

The silver horse Jérôme had given to Barrow moved as though she were floating above the ground. Her strides were effortless, though they'd set out at a fierce gallop.

"Perhaps we should let him burn off some of that aggression," Barrow said to Ember.

"What do you have in mind?" Ember asked. Tempête sensed a change in her rider and snorted in anticipation.

Barrow grinned. "If I signal you, just try to catch me."

Easing the reins, Barrow let Tempête's stride lengthen until she was abreast of Lukasz's mare. Ember could see the two knights speaking, but their words were drowned by the horses' hoofbeats.

The commander laughed, and Barrow turned in his saddle. Catching Ember's eye, Barrow pointed to the road ahead. Tempête bolted before Barrow had fully turned to face the road. Caber went wild beneath Ember, and she swore under her breath.

"All right, lad," she said through clenched teeth as Caber bucked, his back legs kicking at the sky. "Let's chase them."

She loosened the reins, and Caber stopped thrashing between strides, startled to find he no longer fought Ember for control.

"Go on!" she called to him, leaning forward. "Look how far ahead she is!"

Caber bellowed and his hooves shredded the ground as he took off in pursuit of Barrow and Tempête.

Kael and Lukasz gave shouts of encouragement as Caber tore past their mounts. On the road ahead, Tempête flashed like lightning. Her speed was as impressive as the grace with which she ran. Though deadly quick, her limbs moved fluidly, her body flowing like a river. Ember didn't know if Caber would catch the filly.

But where Tempête was built for speed, Caber was driven by pride and determination. Ember could scarcely believe it, but stride by stride, he gained ground. Like Ember, Barrow seemed to have assumed it would be some time before the pursuers caught them. When Caber gave a trumpeting call as he closed on Tempête's flank, Barrow's head whipped around in surprise.

Laughing at his startled expression, Ember put her heels to Caber, challenging the stallion to overtake Tempête. The silver filly, equally alarmed by the sudden race she'd become part of, snorted and put on a fresh burst of speed. She pulled ahead of Caber, but he refused to concede. Caber matched Tempête's stride until the filly and stallion were running side by side, a storm of hooves, manes, and tails whipping in the wind.

The riders crested a hill, horses still neck and neck, and Barrow finally reined in Tempête. Caber, who was more interested in keeping close to the silver filly than continuing at his furious gallop, didn't give Ember any trouble as she slowed him. They continued at a milder lope, then a trot, and finally an easy walk. Caber was a bit lathered from the run, but Tempête, looking as if she'd only taken a quick turn around the pasture, showed no signs of weariness.

Barrow pulled on the reins again, bringing Tempête to a stop in the middle of the road. He looked back toward the hill they'd just topped. Kael and Lukasz were hidden on the other side.

"Good run," Ember said, a bit breathless with the exhilaration of the ride.

With a smile, Barrow maneuvered Tempête close to Caber and then reached for Ember. He didn't quite pull her from the saddle, but almost. Ember couldn't worry about falling from her horse when Barrow's arms were around her and he was bending to kiss her. He braced her against him with one arm while his other hand tangled in her hair.

Ember dropped Caber's reins so she could run her hands over Barrow's neck and shoulders. His kiss was full of the desperate ache that overtook her limbs. She needed to be closer to him.

A shrill whinny sounded, and Barrow was pulled suddenly from Ember's arms. Fortunately Ember grabbed Caber's reins and righted herself in the saddle before the stallion began to prance in a circle, snorting at Tempête. From the way her ears were pinned back and her nostrils flared, Ember could only guess that Tempête had grown tired of standing so close to Caber.

"Who won?" Kael shouted to them.

Their companions had just crested the hill and loped up to join them.

"I think it was a draw," Barrow answered, offering Ember a knowing smile.

Ember laughed. "That sounds about right."

Setting out at a steady lope, their party continued through the French countryside. They made idle chatter as they rode, jokes and laughter accompanying the rhythmic hoofbeats of their mounts. As the sun made its arc across the spring sky, watching over their journey, Ember could almost forget that they were exiles.

The first shadows of dusk had fallen when the Château de Lusignan rose before them. Ember's breath caught. She'd heard her father's extensive boasts about how grand her sister's match had been, but Ember had taken most of his claims as bluster.

She'd been wrong.

The château claimed a broad swath of the countryside. Fortified by an outer wall and a second inner wall that featured barbican towers, the castle warned away intruders and at the same time proclaimed the wealth and standing of its occupants.

"Your sister married into great fortune," Barrow observed.

All Ember could do was nod. Timid Agnes was the lady of this massive estate. Had marriage and the accompanying responsibilities changed her sister? Had Agnes found joy in becoming a countess?

The chaos of recent events had kept Ember from considering anything other than her own circumstance. Now that Agnes's home lay before her, Ember was eager to be reunited with her sister. The happiness of their reunion was paired with a new springing hope that the advancement of her sister's position would mean Agnes could give them real aid.

"This bodes well for us." Ember voiced her thoughts to Barrow. "My sister remains in good standing with my father. Perhaps, learning of what's happened, he will rally to our cause."

"Your father casts his lot with the physical world, the world of men." Barrow frowned. "Not with the mystical war we wage. I doubt he can help us."

"He has powerful friends," Ember pressed. "Even if he alone can't provide assistance, at least he could rally the Scottish nobles against Eira."

Barrow still seemed doubtful, but Lukasz spoke up. "Whatever help is offered, we will accept gratefully."

They reached the outer walls of the castle just as twilight overtook the sunset. Passing by the households that were clumped between the outer and inner walls, they made their way to the gate that led to the count's manor. The estate bustled with activity. Servants hurried about their tasks. The ringing of a blacksmith's hammer caught Ember's ear. Fires roared in the open kitchens. Hens and roosters avoided crossing paths with the massive hunting dogs that roamed the courtyard.

When Lukasz dismounted, the rest of the party followed suit. The commander called to a nearby servant. The man approached the tall knight apprehensively. After they exchanged a few words, the servant hurried to the manor.

"Should we follow?" Ember asked.

"If we're playing at nobility, we must wait to be invited," Lukasz said. "The count should offer you an official welcome and make a show of his hospitality."

Kael grinned, rubbing his stomach. "I hope that show involves a roast pheasant."

Ember laughed, the rumble of her own stomach reminding her that dinner would be appreciated.

The manor door opened, and Ember handed her reins to Barrow, expecting to run into Agnes's open arms. But her sister didn't appear, only a man. He was dressed more finely than the servant whom Lukasz had sent into the great house, but not richly enough to be the count.

He walked straight to Ember. A thin man with a close-clipped beard and a pinched face.

Though Ember had a fair command of French, she was still relieved when the count's man spoke to her in English.

"His excellency will not see you," he told her. So much disdain filled his gaze that Ember had to look away. She sensed Barrow moving closer, looming over her shoulder so as to remind the manservant that he contended not only with a young lady.

Lukasz crossed to stand at her elbow. "Lady Morrow merits a more gracious welcome than this. Is your master so lacking in manners?"

The servant snorted, his lips curling.

"If the count is indisposed, I understand," Ember said quickly. "I only wish to speak with my sister."

The servant thrust his chin out, his face sour. "Your sister is not here."

"Not here?" Ember stared at him. "But she must be. She's the count's wife. Has he sent her to court?"

That Agnes could have gone to Paris hadn't crossed Ember's mind. She ground her teeth, knowing that a side excursion to the French court wasn't possible.

"The lady Agnes is returned to her home in Scotland," the man continued. He began to smile at Ember, his mouth twisting in wicked delight. "On my lord's wedding night, he discovered to his horror that his bride was not . . . pure."

Barrow stepped around Ember, menacing the servant. "Take care with your words, sir, lest you find yourself lacking a tongue to speak them."

The Frenchman grimaced, but didn't back down. "My tongue speaks only the truth." He squinted at Ember. "Your family was too disgraced to tell you?"

"Tell me what?" Ember asked, more anxious for her sister's well-being by the minute.

"Your sister, the lady Agnes Morrow, was with child."

Ember rocked back, as if the servant had delivered a blow.

Lukasz spoke in a low, dangerous tone. "I will ask this but once: do you besmirch the elder lady Morrow's name, or are you speaking the truth?"

The servant eyed Lukasz's height and the hilt that peeked over his shoulders. "I do no dishonor to the lady's name," he said. "That was her own doing."

"Ember." Barrow put an arm around her shoulders, seeing that she'd gone weak in the knees.

A bit of the Frenchman's haughty demeanor left when he saw how distressed Ember was. Clearing his throat, he offered her a letter.

"My master received this letter and now gives it to you, for whom it was intended." With a curt bow, he half turned toward the manor. "And that will be the extent of his hospitality. You will find an inn on the road leading north from the château. It should provide accommodations suitable for your party."

Whether their purpose now lacked its former urgency or out of respect for Ember's shock, Lukasz led them on at a plodding pace. Ember didn't remember Barrow helping her into the saddle, nor the way he folded Caber's reins into her left hand. Her right hand clasped the unopened letter to her chest.

Ember had little sense of how much time passed before they reached the inn, only that the evening had grown dark. Numbly, she slid from Caber's back. Barrow guided her to the entrance while Kael and Lukasz made arrangements for the horses. Settling Ember at a table, Barrow went to speak to the innkeeper.

Breaking the letter's seal, Ember opened the pages and recognized her sister's handwriting. The ink blurred as Ember stared at the words, too afraid to read them and know what had befallen Agnes.

A cup plunked in front of her on the table.

"Drink this," Barrow said.

Ember started to shake her head, her thirst and appetite smothered by worry.

"Drink it, Ember." He took the letter from her, putting the cup in its place.

Too wearied to argue, Ember took a large swallow and immediately began to cough. The liquid burned all the way down her throat and lit a fire in her belly.

Wheezing, she pushed the cup away and glared at Barrow.

"You weren't supposed to drink that much, lass." He couldn't quite hide his smile. "But it did the job."

Tempted to throw the rest of the drink in his face, Ember had to admit that the concoction had pulled her out of her stupor. "What is it?"

"Aqua vitae," Barrow answered. "Much stronger stuff than wine. You needed a bit of a jolt."

Kael and Lukasz joined them at the table. Ember glanced around the small inn. The main floor held a cluster of tables and chairs, only one other of which was occupied. The clothes of the pair of men sitting there suggested they were merchants. A large fireplace warmed and cheered the room, and the air held a pleasant mix of scents: spice, smoke, and hops.

The innkeeper appeared at their table with a platter of cold roast duck and a pitcher of ale. They ate quietly. When the meat was gone and they were sipping at their cups of ale, Barrow placed the letter in front of Ember.

"You'll have to read it," he said. "We can't tarry in Lusignan when the count offers no sanctuary."

Ember nodded, though her heart was hard and cold in her chest. She began to read. Soon her hands were shaking. The pages dropped from her hands and tears escaped from the corners of her eyes.

"You must tell us what has taken place," Lukasz said to her quietly. "Whether it concerns our fate or simply to unburden your spirit."

Covering her face with her hands, Ember squeezed her eyes tight, willing herself to speak through her horror.

"She carries an illegitimate child," Ember told them, "and my father has cast her out of his house."

"He cast out his own child? Where is she now?" Kael asked, his usual mirth replaced by outrage. "Is she destitute? Without shelter or sustenance?"

When Ember answered, she looked directly at Barrow. "Agnes has gone to Tearmunn."

Lukasz bowed his head. "She writes to you as a hostage, then."

"No." Ember tried to keep her voice steady. "She speaks only of the care she's been given . . . by Alistair in particular."

She glanced at the pages again. "The child was fathered by Alistair's elder brother Henry."

A growl of disgust erupted from Barrow's throat. "Does Alistair hope to protect his brother from dishonor?"

Frowning at Barrow, Ember said, "Agnes says little of Henry, only that she went to Tearmunn with nothing and has been treated as if she retains her noble station."

Ember hesitated, then quietly she said, "My sister asks when I return to Tearmunn. She is afraid and heartbroken and begs for my presence."

"No." Barrow stared at her in alarm.

"She is my sister," Ember replied. "And she has wandered unknowing into a lion's den. I must go to her."

Lukasz covered her hand with his. "Consider this, Ember. Your sister might have been coerced into putting these words to the page. What if the letter is only a snare set for you?"

"Yes," Barrow said urgently. "Lukasz speaks reason, Ember. Take heed."

"I know Agnes well." Ember pulled her hand from Lukasz's. "These are the secrets and sorrows of her heart. The letter is not a trap."

"That doesn't mean that her welcome at Tearmunn is not a ploy to lure you back," Kael argued.

Ember sighed. "I can't argue with that, but it doesn't change that she has gone to the keep and I must follow."

"Why?" Barrow demanded. "How can you aid your sister by putting yourself in danger?"

Lowering her gaze, Ember spoke softly. "I won't be in danger. Not if I return on a premise besides that of sisterhood."

"For what other reason would you put yourself in the hands of our enemy?" Kael asked her.

Fixing her eyes on Lukasz, but not daring to look at Barrow, Ember said, "For the reasons that Alistair wishes. The reasons he didn't take me back to Tearmunn by force the night he hunted us with wolves of fire."

"You can't be serious," Barrow hissed through his teeth.

"There could be more to gain here than my sister's well-being." Ember continued to speak to the commander, though she could feel the weight of Barrow's gaze.

Lukasz nodded, and she went on. "We've been cut off from Tearmunn, and Jérôme tells us that Eira's influence is spreading well beyond our home. Without support from the other sites of Conatus, you have no means to communicate with those within Tearmunn who would resist Eira."

"Cian will find a way in time," Lukasz told her, but Ember heard the edge of doubt in his voice. "She'll send word . . . somehow."

"But soon enough?" Ember pressed. "Eira works quickly. While we hide, she rallies more to her side. If I go to Tearmunn, I can serve as an envoy to our allies within the keep."

"And how will you send word to us," Kael asked, "when the others cannot?"

"They know not where you are, or what you do," Ember answered. "I already have the means to reach you—through Jérôme's sister in La Rochelle. I think you should return to the city and seek refuge in her home. If she's already assisting Jérôme, it seems unlikely that she'd turn you away."

Quiet overtook the table. Glancing at each man's face, Ember could tell she'd convinced Lukasz, Kael remained uneasy, and Barrow was a lost cause.

When she could bear the silence no longer, Ember said, "In the morning I ride to Cernon. Once there, I'll inform Jérôme of what's happened and inquire about his sister providing you shelter."

"You want us to hide in a merchant's house while you throw yourself into the fire?" Barrow said angrily.

Ember steeled herself before she replied. "You won't just be hiding. You will be working with Jérôme to consolidate a resistance. When you're ready, we can move against Eira. You from without, I from within."

"You are not the Trojan horse, Ember," Barrow told her.

"This is my will," Ember answered, holding his gaze.

Lukasz took a deep breath. "Barrow, I know it pains you, but Ember is right. We need a way into Tearmunn, to understand what Eira is planning."

"Isn't that why Father Michael and Cian remained?" Barrow said, fists clenching. "And what of Fionn and Lora?"

"They know not whether we survived the journey," Kael interrupted.

"And we don't know what has befallen them," Lukasz continued, nodding at Kael. "Have you so soon forgotten that we were pursued on the very night we fled the keep? Our rebellion was discovered before it began. Our friends may be imprisoned, or worse."

Barrow pushed his chair back from the table, slamming his way out the inn's door without another word.

Lukasz and Kael exchanged a long look.

"I'll go after him," Kael said, standing up. "You wouldn't think it, but Barrow has something of a penchant for drama."

He patted Ember's shoulder. "You're a brave lass, Lady Morrow."

Ember offered him a weak smile. She'd spoken with certitude, but now that Barrow had stormed out and the implications of her words were sinking in, Ember began to feel much less than capable of following the path she'd set for herself.

"He doesn't, you know." The commander's voice brought Ember back to the table.

"What?" She rubbed her tired eyes, hoping to clear her thoughts.

Lukasz smiled. "Have a penchant for drama. Neither is he quick to anger. Barrow fears for you, that is all."

"I don't mean to hurt him," Ember said.

"He knows that." Lukasz stood up, leaving her at the table, and went to speak with the innkeeper. Ember toyed with her empty cup, wondering if she should follow Kael and try to reason with Barrow.

Lukasz returned to his chair, pressing an iron key into her hand. "Your room is upstairs—the key opens the westernmost door. And the innkeeper's daughter will bring a copper tub and heated water so you can bathe."

Ember shook her head. "I don't need such fine treatment."

"We still travel as your ladyship's retinue," Lukasz told her. "It's wiser that we keep up that appearance."

"If I'm to reach Cernon tomorrow, I must rise early." Ember rose and took Lukasz's hand. "I'll say good night now."

"Good night, Lady Morrow." Lukasz clasped her fingers. "And remember Kael's words."

"What were those?" Ember asked, thinking of Kael's jests.

"You're very brave," he answered. "I think we may soon all owe your courage a great debt."

Taking leave of the commander, Ember climbed the stairs and went to her room. Like the simple comfort of the inn's main floor, her chamber was sparely appointed with a bed and a table with a single chair. She'd no sooner settled onto the edge of the bed than a tentative knock brought her to the door.

Opening it, she was greeted by a girl no more than ten years of age. A little bit of her brown hair peeked out from beneath the kerchief that covered her head. She looked up at Ember with large eyes and a shy smile.

Ember stepped back and the girl carried in a copper tub half as big as she was. After setting the tub down, she took a bundle from inside the basin and set it on the floor. The girl gave Ember a folded cloth that she'd held tucked under her arm and then hurried from the room, returning a few minutes later with a pail of steaming water. The girl poured the scalding water into the tub. After several trips back and forth, the tub held sufficient water for bathing.

The girl looked at the full tub, the cloth bundle, and then at Ember. When Ember smiled and nodded, the girl beamed, gave a little curtsy, and left the room, swinging her pail.

Alone and exhausted, Ember fought her way out of the heavy brocade gown and slipped off her chemise. She stepped into the copper tub and then knelt. The steaming water covered Ember to her waist. Gooseflesh rose on her arms from the chill of the room on her bare skin, while her lower body basked in the bath's heat. Reaching over the side of the tub, Ember collected the bound cloth, unwrapping it to reveal a rough lump of soap. Despite its misshapen appearance, when Ember sniffed the soap, she found it bursting with the scent of lavender.

Ember set to scrubbing herself from head to toe, washing away days of travel by land and sea. With her skin free of dirt and her hair heavy, sopping wet, for a moment Ember let her body melt, forgetting the fears and strains that she still carried. The tub wasn't large enough for her to lie down, but she leaned over, resting her forearms along the curved edge of the bath and laying her forehead against them. Steam caressed her face, and she took deep breaths of the cleansing hot air.

Another reluctant-sounding knock at the door roused Ember

from her dreamy repose. Assuming that the girl had returned to see if Ember was through with the tub, or possibly if she wanted more water heated, Ember stood up, gathered the plain sheet of linen the girl had provided, and gave herself a cursory drying. Wrapping her body in the cloth, Ember went to the door.

"Who is it?"

"Barrow."

Ember glanced over her shoulder at her discarded dress, but swiftly abandoned the idea of putting it on. She opened the door only slightly, keeping herself hidden behind it.

"Ember?" Barrow asked, still in the hall.

"Come in quickly," she said, pulling the door open a bit farther.

Barrow stepped inside, and Ember closed the door after him. His brow was furrowed until he looked at her. Barrow's surprise was quickly replaced by a mischievous half smile.

"I had a bath," Ember said, straightening so she'd look more dignified. As dignified as she could when wearing only a sheet of undyed linen.

Barrow answered gravely, though his eyes danced with mirth. "I can see that."

He took a step toward her, but Ember backed away. She hadn't forgotten his angry departure from their table. His words had left a sting that still festered.

Watching Ember's defensive movement, Barrow also took a step back. His gaze avoided her warning glare. "I'm sorry."

"For what?" Ember asked. She didn't want his apology if he thought she'd somehow reverted to playing the part of a noble maid who was offended by his advances.

"For letting my love for you become possession," he told her. His voice was quiet, regretful. "What I desire can't stand in the way of the greater purpose we serve."

Lifting his eyes to meet hers, Barrow said, "I won't lie to you. I don't want to see you do this."

"I know," Ember answered. "But you understand why I must?"

He nodded, and she went to him. Barrow folded Ember in his arms, resting his cheek against her wet hair. He held her quietly for some time, but when she felt him tense, Ember asked, "What is it?"

"I'm afraid my jealousy is a beast I find difficult to tame," he said with a sigh.

Ember stepped back, lifting her hand to touch his face. "You have nothing to be jealous of."

His eyes were tight with strain, and Ember's fingers slid along the tense set of his jaw. "Tell me what's troubling you. Is it something more than my return to Tearmunn?"

"It's what that return means for you," Barrow told her. His arms tightened around her back.

She smiled at him. "I don't think I'll be in as much danger as you believe. People would always rather see me as a spoiled noble-man's daughter than a soldier. All I have to do is be what Jérôme thinks I am."

"That doesn't worry me." Barrow continued to hold her close, but he looked away from her.

"Then what does?"

"Alistair." Barrow's teeth were clenched when he spoke the other knight's name, making the word sound like a growl.

Ember started to laugh, but when she saw fear in Barrow's averted eyes, she stopped. Rising to her tiptoes, she kissed his cheek and whispered in his ear, "You have nothing to fear from Alistair."

"Not I. You." One of Barrow's hands came up to cradle her head. "I fear for you."

Though a part of Ember wanted to push him away and laugh again, the way he held her sent a cool prickling of fear through her veins.

"Why?" She wrapped her arms around Barrow's neck, letting the full length of her body press into him.

Barrow was silent, his arms strong around her so that, while her toes brushed the ground, she was no longer standing on her own.

"Tell me." She curled her fingers in his dark hair.

"Ember, you go to him with words of love on your tongue. Of loyalty to his cause." Barrow set her down and walked away. For a moment, Ember worried he would leave, but he turned back to face her, and she saw how ashen his face was.

"What will you do when he seeks to claim the love you offer?"

Rather than walking to Barrow, Ember went to the bed. She settled on it, keeping the linen sheet wrapped around her body and tucking her legs beneath her.

"I understand your fears, but I would try to assuage them."

Barrow stayed near the door, frowning at her.

"Please, come sit with me." Ember held out her hand, and Barrow came to the bed. He took her hand, sitting on the edge of the feather-stuffed tick but not moving to embrace her.

Holding his fingers in a tight clasp, Ember said, "I will give him only what I must to persuade him of my love, but nothing more."

Staring at the floor, Barrow asked in a hoarse whisper, "And what do you think that will be?"

"Sweet words," Ember said quietly. "Brief embraces and light kisses."

Barrow shook his head. "I worry that you underestimate Alistair's obsession with you. He sought your bed before you were willing."

"I haven't forgotten," Ember answered. "I will never forget, nor will I give Alistair any chance to attempt such folly."

"Then how will you—" Barrow looked at her, frowning.

"Two things work in my favor," Ember told him. "The first is Agnes. Her illegitimate child, fathered by Alistair's own brother, offers sound reason for me not to share my bed with him before marriage. The second is my own virtue. As I will have reembraced my role as a proper noblewoman, that serves the same purpose as my sister's misfortune."

A little color returned to Barrow's face. "And you think he'll be persuaded?"

"I do."

Barrow dropped his head, covering his eyes with his hands. "I don't want this. I wish I could be stronger for you, Ember. But I'm not."

Ember crawled to him and rested her chin on his shoulder. "I would be more troubled if you sent me to Alistair with a cheerful heart and good tidings."

A low sound rumbled from Barrow's throat that Ember slowly realized was laughter. When he turned to look at her, he was smiling.

"You have a marvelous spirit," he said. "Like none I've ever known."

Ember leaned in, kissing him. His arms came around her waist, and she tangled her fingers in his hair while her tongue tasted the sweat and spice of his jaw and neck.

Barrow's voice was tight when he said, "I can tarry here. Or find a room of my own."

"If you think I will spend this night without you, you are a fool." Ember's lips returned to his.

"Hopefully not a fool," he answered, with a slight smile. "But I know too well that my penchant for jealousy makes me weak when I must be strong."

"Meaning?" Ember frowned.

"I would stay with you," Barrow told her. "But we should seek sleep. If you kiss me again, I will be too tempted to take things further than we dare."

Ember nodded, a tightness gripping her limbs. Though she didn't voice her thoughts, Ember knew she couldn't overcome that same temptation. She also knew Barrow thought her resolve greater than it was. A part of Ember had hoped he would share this last night making love to her, possessing her as he wanted to before she went to Tearmunn professing a false love.

But those were impulses she couldn't give in to. As much as she wanted him, Ember reluctantly conceded her own desires' defeat. What lay ahead bore far more import than indulging in one night's passion.

So Ember let Barrow pull the heavy furs over their bodies. She stayed wrapped in her linen sheet. He slipped off his boots, but otherwise remained clothed. Their one concession to love was the intimacy of their slumber. As Ember's eyes closed, she could feel Barrow's breath on the back of her neck. His body curled around the length of hers, and his arm held her close. She twined her fingers with his.

"I love you," Ember whispered, frowning at the strange echo she thought she'd heard. Until she realized that Barrow had whispered the same words in her ear within the same breath she'd spoken them.

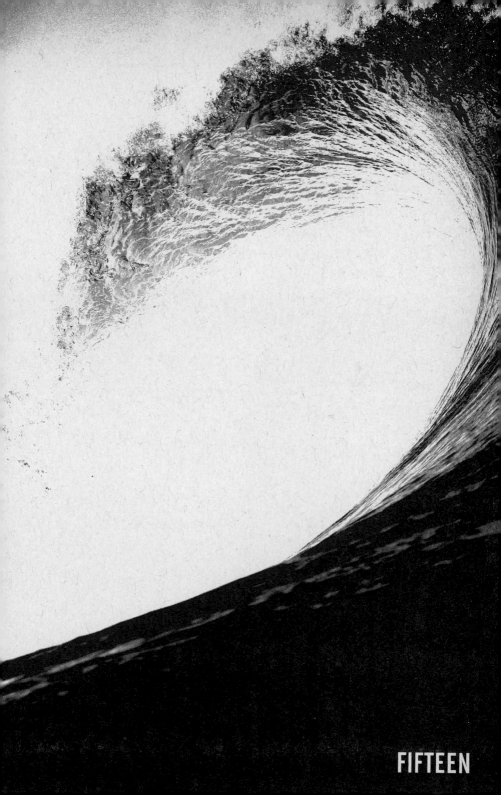

FIFTEEN

# BOSQUE'S TASK OFFERED Alistair a welcome distrac-

tion, but it wasn't always enough. Though he'd set himself to spending long hours in the scribes' quarters, jotting notes and sketching visions of his ultimate goal, his mind still found occasion to wander until it came upon Ember.

He'd made an effort to avoid confronting his worst fears about her. As Eira sent her emissaries to entreat their counterparts across Europe and Asia to join her, they'd had a few reports about what might have befallen the small band of rebels who fled Tearmunn. A rash of shipwrecks had plagued the western European coast, with the few survivors relating strange tales of their doomed voyages. Some spoke of a terrible sea monster that attacked their ship, while others recalled only a maelstrom suddenly appearing beneath their vessel, the vortex pulling the crew and passengers into a watery death spiral.

The stories of chaos and death abounded, but no reports of stranded knights appeared in the flurry of news, leaving Alistair to wonder about Ember's fate. Setting his quill on the desk, Alistair stretched his arms back. His muscles had grown sore from maintaining a hunched position so long.

"Interesting work."

Alistair gave a yelp. He hadn't heard Bosque enter the library, but now the tall man was leaning over his shoulder, peering at the drawings Alistair had scratched out on a length of vellum.

Recovering himself, Alistair turned to face Bosque. "Will you sit? I have some ideas I'd like to share with you."

"I'd be honored." Bosque settled into the scribe's desk next to Alistair's.

Alistair handed Bosque a sheet of notes he'd already cut from the vellum scroll. He waited while Bosque's eyes flitted over the page.

"An ambitious plan."

"But possible." Alistair considered putting his words to Bosque as a question, but had decided to do so would make him sound doubtful about his work.

"Yes." Bosque set the page on the desk. "What do you need from me?"

Picking up the quill, Alistair stroked the length of the swan feather to calm his nerves. "If you've found any of the clerics who have sworn fealty to Eira particularly skilled, I'd like to have their names."

Bosque nodded, but watched Alistair expectantly.

*Of course he knows that's not all,* Alistair thought. Bosque had an uncanny ability to sense things that remained unsaid.

"And . . ." Alistair's mouth had gone dry. "Your blood."

Though Alistair hadn't known what reaction to expect, he didn't know what to say when Bosque simply tilted his head, as though amused.

"It's the key to their healing," Alistair continued, tapping his quill on the page.

"I understand," Bosque replied. "That's very clever."

Alistair ducked his head in respect. "Thank you, Lord Mar."

Rising, Bosque said, "Hamish has considerable power, but has been disconsolate since losing his ability to weave. He needs a new focus for his magics. I will send him to you."

Bosque placed his hands behind his back, taking a turn around the desk. "You should find somewhere to put your enchantments through trials. It should be hidden. I'd suggest the catacombs beneath the chapel. Father Michael can show you the entrance; it is known only to a few within the keep."

"I'd like to begin the trials," Alistair said, gazing at the sketch he'd just finished. He glanced at Bosque and his heart convulsed with fear. "But who—"

Bosque answered before Alistair had finished his question. "The stockades have begun to fill with those whose reluctance to join us has made them suspect. Start there."

"We don't need them for questioning?" Alistair asked.

"I'll send you those who have nothing to offer us but cannot be trusted to go free," Bosque told him. "They are prisoners now and will remain prisoners under your . . . care. Be prepared to receive them on the morrow."

Alistair stood and gave a quick bow. "I will, my lord."

As he passed Alistair to depart the library, Bosque said, "I'm pleased you didn't limit your vision. Ambition is the fertile soil in which true power can be cultivated."

When Bosque was gone, Alistair settled back into the desk. He found he couldn't return immediately to his drawing, due to the shaking of his hands. It wasn't fear that caused the tremor through his limbs, but excitement crackling beneath his skin. Not only had Bosque been pleased with his work, but he believed it would come to fruition.

*My vision. My creation.*

Lifting his still-trembling hand, Alistair delicately touched the image on the vellum. At a glance, the sketch might have appeared to be someone's dream of strange knights who rode to war upon wolves.

But wolf mounts were not what Alistair aimed to create. Not at all.

Alistair opened and closed his fingers several times, hoping to still them.

"Lord Hart!" A servant burst into the library. "Lord Hart! You must come!"

Jumping to his feet, Alistair rushed to meet the breathless servant. "What is it?"

"In the armory," the boy panted. "A portal has opened."

"From where?" Alistair asked. He grabbed the boy's shirt, tugging him along as he made quick strides through the manor.

"They didn't tell me," the servant answered.

Alistair grunted in frustration, his mind a rush of possibilities. Eira had been waiting for a portal to open. They would send a group of emissaries through, to continue the work that the first envoys had begun. No longer able to open portals at Tearmunn, they'd been forced to rely on conventional means of travel, slowing their ability to reach the furthest outposts of Conatus.

"Has Lady Eira been alerted?" Alistair asked as they crossed the courtyard.

The boy wheezed, trying to catch his breath. "I think they sent another servant."

"If you don't know for certain, then make sure." Alistair let go of the boy and shoved him in the direction of the manor. "Go to the great hall."

The servant darted away, and Alistair broke into a run. He slammed his way through the barracks, ignoring the startled cries of the servants he plowed over as he bolted to the armory.

A cluster of guards and clerics had gathered there, and Alistair had to push his way through them to reach the portal. He stopped when he reached the edge of the crowd, pausing to take in the shimmering doorway. Two guards with weapons drawn had taken up sentinel posts on each side of the portal. They stood up a bit straighter when Alistair approached.

"When did it open?" Alistair asked them.

"About ten minutes ago," one of the knights answered. "Lady Eira's orders were followed—two of the Guard went through so the portal would not be closed."

"Very good." Alistair gazed at the gleaming door. "Has anyone come through?"

The other knight shook his head. "Not from their side yet. I suspect the appearance of two of ours on the other side the moment the door was open shocked them, and they wanted to know why. Our men will explain quickly enough."

"Where is it?" Peering at the door, Alistair could see the hazy image of a room not unlike the many halls of Tearmunn, but no identifying details were in view.

"I'm not sure, my lord," the knight answered.

A knight wearing the Conatus tabard came into sight on the other side of the door, followed by a hooded, cloaked figure. Alistair stepped back, making way for the travelers to pass through the portal.

When the knight emerged in the armory, he eyed the gathered crowd and his two armed counterparts with surprise.

"Have things gone so badly here that you expect enemies to come through our portals?" the knight asked, his words inflected with a heavy French accent.

Alistair stepped forward. "Not so, my friend. We are well. I am Lord Hart, commander of the Guard at Tearmunn."

The Frenchman's mouth twitched when Alistair named himself commander, but he didn't offer a reply.

"May I have your name?" Alistair pushed his cloak back, putting his sword hilt in plain view.

"Jérôme Fauré, of the Cernon Guard," the knight answered. "I took it upon myself to conduct a lost soul back to your keep."

Jérôme moved aside, beckoning to the hooded figure waiting on the other side of the portal. From the sway of the stranger's hips, Alistair took Jérôme's companion to be a woman.

"Who seeks us?" Alistair asked Jérôme, frowning as the woman passed through the shimmering door. Her cloak and hood flared with light as she left the door.

From beneath the shadow of the hood, she answered Alistair, "A friend."

Though the voice was familiar enough to make Alistair's throat constrict, his heart didn't dare to hope until slender hands pushed back the heavy wool hood.

Ember sank to her knees before Alistair and began to weep.

SIXTEEN

**AGNES HAD ALWAYS BEEN** more likely to cry than Ember, but now Ember found it all too easy to summon tears. She'd been saving them.

At each moment before she stepped through the portal to Tearmunn, Ember had held back her ever-welling sorrow. When she'd disentangled herself from Barrow's arms before sunlight touched their room at the inn, Ember had bitten back tears. Riding away from her companions, she'd swallowed the hard stone in her throat. Meeting Jérôme at Cernon, she'd conveyed the events at Château de Lusignan and her plan to return to Tearmunn without giving any sign of her distress.

But now she was here, facing Alistair, who needed to believe that she came back to him full of remorse and perhaps even shame. So Ember closed her eyes and called up each moment of fear and sorrow that haunted her. And the tears came.

Through her blurred vision, Ember looked up at Alistair, but he stood frozen, staring at her.

Ember bowed her head, suddenly terrified that she'd presumed too much feeling on Alistair's part. What if in the space of days since he'd let her go, he'd regretted his decision? What if his brief moment of empathy had turned into wrath, and all he would offer Ember now was retribution?

As she choked on a sob provoked by her newborn fear, Ember felt hands grasp her shoulders.

Alistair helped her stand. "It doesn't befit a lady of your station to grovel like a servant."

His words were flat, making Ember clutch at her cloak, her anxious fingers digging into the wool.

Bending close to her, Alistair asked in a low voice, "Why have you come here, Lady Morrow?"

Ember drew Agnes's letter from her pocket, giving it to Alistair. "I went to Château de Lusignan and was given this."

Alistair took the parchment from her hand. "You went to La Rochelle."

"My lord." Jérôme drew Alistair's attention. "I would return to my duties if you will take the lady into your care."

"You may return," Alistair told him. "But the portal must remain open until you receive other orders."

Jérôme frowned, glancing at the open doorway behind him. "Lord Hart, the clerics cannot sustain a portal for long. Its very presence draws from their spirit."

"I'm aware of that." Alistair gave Jérôme a hard look. "The order stands."

Squaring his shoulders, Jérôme asked, "Does Tearmunn give orders to all of Conatus now?"

Ember tensed, knowing she couldn't risk trying to warn Jérôme off his line of questions. She silently willed that he would abandon his rebellious tone before doing himself harm.

"Not Tearmunn." A woman's clear, strong voice filled the armory. The crowd massed around the portal parted, opening a path for Eira. "The orders are mine."

To Ember, Lady Eira had always been fierce and intimidating, but in the time Ember had been away from Tearmunn, those characteristics had been amplified tenfold.

The warrior woman of the Circle drew all eyes as she strode to the portal. Her bearing was imperious, her eyes sharper than a hawk's. At her shoulder stood a tall man whose appearance struck Ember as naggingly familiar, but she couldn't recall where she would have seen him before. His hair was dark as freshly turned earth, which emphasized the green-gold tones of his olive skin. His face was hard, sharp lines and a full, sensuous mouth. And his eyes were on Ember. Silver eyes that stopped her breath.

Beside them, Jérôme bowed low. "My lady Eira. All Conatus marvels at your deeds."

"Do they?" Eira's smile was knife thin. She placed her hand on Alistair's elbow. "I see you've met my commander, Lord Alistair Hart."

"Yes, my lady." Jérôme offered a cursory bow to Alistair. "I apologize, my lord. As you were unknown to me, I treated your words with reservation. If I'd known your orders came from Lady Eira, I would not have questioned them."

Alistair met Jérôme's words with silence, but Eira answered, "These small confusions will doubtless happen in such a tumultuous time for our order."

"Indeed," Jérôme replied.

"Tell your Circle that I will only keep the portal open long enough to send an envoy through to Cernon," Eira told Jérôme. "They will be ready within the hour."

Jérôme bowed again. "I will give them your message."

"My orders," Eira said.

"Of course." Without looking at Ember, Jérôme returned to the doorway.

With the French knight gone, Eira looked from Alistair to Ember.

"Lady Morrow," Eira said quietly, "I hadn't expected to see you again."

Ember ducked her head and tried to gather her thoughts. Her

pulse was frenzied. She'd hoped to have some time to persuade Alistair of the reasons for her return before she faced Eira. Knowing that Eira responded favorably to strength over fragility, Ember forced herself to look directly into Eira's eyes.

"I have returned to reap whatever my actions have sown," Ember said, hoping the steadiness of her voice contrasted with her tear-streaked face to present an image of remorse and courage. "For good or ill."

"We were quite grieved when you left us," Eira replied. "What could have led you to such a reckless act?"

Ember kept her chin lifted. "I was misled by those I placed my trust in. I was wrong."

Smiling, Eira raised her hand, commanding those gathered in the armory to listen. "Speak again, Ember, for all to hear."

The room fell silent. Ember's fists clenched, but she spoke loudly. "I fled this keep in the company of men who spoke ill of Lady Eira. In the time I've been away from Tearmunn, my home, I've paid dearly for this sin against Lady Eira and Conatus, and I've returned in the hopes of absolution."

"Absolution requires penance," the tall man behind Eira said, and Ember shivered under the silver light in his eyes.

She forced herself to answer him. "Then I shall do penance." She looked at Eira. "As my lady commands."

After giving Ember a measured gaze, Eira said, "I'll consider your words, but for now you are Lord Hart's charge."

Ember curtsied, and Eira took Alistair's arm, pulling him aside into a quiet conversation. Keeping her head bowed, Ember stared at the armory floor, but all the while she could feel the tall stranger's eyes upon her.

Then suddenly she knew he was closer, standing not a hand-breadth away.

"Lord Hart speaks highly of you." His voice was low and rich.

Without looking at him, Ember said, "Then he does me honor."

A quiet laugh, with a ring as silver as his eyes, floated around Ember's head. "I wonder, Lady Morrow, will you show him honor?"

Startled by his question, Ember looked up, only to be met by his eyes, which flared like lightning. The stranger didn't speak again, but neither did he release her from his gaze until Alistair returned to them.

"Lord Mar." He addressed the tall man. "May I introduce you to Lady Ember Morrow?"

Quelling the shudder that wanted to ripple through her limbs, Ember gazed at the man whom Lukasz had named as the source of this rising dark. Lord Mar. Ember dug her nails into her palms, forcing herself to be still. Bosque Mar.

"You may," Bosque answered. His eyes moved slowly up and down Ember, as if searching for something, and made her want to squirm. Even as his examination progressed, Ember couldn't tell if he viewed her as a simple curiosity or a threat.

"Ember, this is Lord Bosque Mar," Alistair told her. She could hear the touch of awe in his voice. "He provides Lady Eira counsel."

Ember curtsied to Bosque, trying her best to make it seem she had no knowledge of him. "Whence did you come to Tearmunn, Lord Mar?"

Bosque didn't answer, and Alistair took her arm. "You haven't earned such questions yet, Ember. Come with me."

The crowd parted again when Alistair pulled Ember out of the armory. As their whispers followed her, Ember searched their faces, looking for any sign of her allies. She could find neither Cian, nor Lora, nor Father Michael.

Alistair's grip on her arm was tight, but not bruising, as he took her across the courtyard. Though she hadn't expected to remain in the barracks, restored to her position in the Guard, Ember was relieved that Alistair steered her to the manor and not the stockade.

What unsettled Ember the most was his silence. Since he was a boy, Alistair had chatted as constantly as a babbling brook. He hadn't said a word to her since they'd left the barracks. Accustomed to Alistair initiating most of their conversations, Ember didn't know how to react to his taciturnity. She worried that speaking would provoke his anger, but she also was afraid that if she waited too long to tell the tale she'd concocted, it would lose its sense of urgency and verity.

As they entered the manor and began ascending the stairs, Alistair still hadn't spoken.

Maybe he wanted to hear her tale only when they were alone, Ember thought. But why then did he take her to the manor and not to his cell in the barracks?

Alistair stopped in front of the first door at the top of the stairs. Opening the door, he stepped back.

"I'll come for you later."

Ember stared at Alistair, not understanding why he would leave her in this room. Alone.

"Ember?"

At the sound of her name, Ember stepped forward to look into the room. Sitting in a chair facing the door was Agnes.

Forgetting Alistair, Ember gave a small cry and ran to her sister. She didn't hear the door close and lock behind her.

Holding Agnes close, Ember was reminded of how many of her sister's traits she found comforting. The silk of her pale blond hair, the rose of her perfume. But Ember noticed the change in her sister as well. Her cheeks and breasts were plump and less girlish, and while they were pressed close, Ember could feel the swell of Agnes's stomach.

"Where have you been, Ember?" Agnes asked when they'd finally let each other go.

Ember knelt beside the chair where Agnes rested. "Alistair didn't tell you?"

Agnes shook her head. "Only that you were away and that he couldn't be sure of when you'd return."

Taking in this news, Ember hesitated. Should she reveal the truth? Could she trust her sister with these secrets?

Her mind still divided, Ember changed the course of their conversation. "Are you well?"

Agnes's lower lip trembled, but she didn't begin to weep again. "As well as I can be. The sickness that troubled me when we were last together has passed."

She placed her hand on her belly. "Sometimes I feel him kick."

"Him?" Ember watched Agnes smile sadly.

"Of course I don't know," Agnes answered. "But I wish for a boy, only for the child's sake. This is a world for men, I think. Not women."

Ember's throat tightened. "Henry treated you with dishonor."

"He did." The hardness in Agnes's reply surprised Ember. It wasn't a tone she'd ever heard in her sister's voice. "But I was as much the fool for believing his words of love to be anything other than flattery."

"Don't judge yourself so harshly," Ember countered, taking Agnes's hand. "Henry knew you were infatuated with him and took advantage."

"Infatuated." Agnes sighed. "That's a good word for it."

"I didn't mean to insult you," Ember said quickly.

Agnes smiled at her. "I know you didn't. I wish I could be like you, Ember. You're so much stronger than I am. So unafraid to take what you want from the world."

"I have more fears than you know," Ember answered. "But my greatest fear is for your welfare. Tell me what's happened since you arrived."

"Very little." Agnes shrugged. "Alistair asked that I stay in my room so as not to be in the way of the keep's business. He's been so kind to me."

"Alistair?" Ember wanted to fire a barrage of questions at Agnes, but she forced herself to be patient.

"Of course, Alistair." Agnes gave a little laugh. "I came here hoping to be shown pity. I would have worked for my food and shelter, but Alistair would hear none of it."

"He's making up for Henry," Ember muttered, unable to keep the bitterness out of her voice.

Agnes blanched, and Ember regretted her words.

"I'm sorry, Agnes," Ember said. "It's just that . . . since I've been at Conatus, Alistair and I have had some quarrels. He's made my role here difficult at times."

"I find that hard to believe," Agnes told her. "He adores you."

Ember looked away, trapped by her own words. If she was to convince Alistair that she'd reconsidered her feelings for him, she would need Agnes to believe it too. Or she could tell Agnes the truth.

For the moment, Ember simply said, "I know."

"So it's simple lovers' quarrels then?" Agnes's cheeks were rosy with mirth, and Ember was glad to see that, despite her misfortunes, Agnes hadn't fallen into despair.

Angling for ambivalence, Ember didn't deny Agnes's question. "So you stay in your room. What else?"

"There can't be much else if I'm always here," Agnes quipped. "But I have a maidservant who cares for me and serves meals. When I need fresh air, she walks with me through the courtyard, and Alistair seems not to mind. He looks in on me every day. Sometimes even Lord Mar comes to ask after my welfare."

Ember gripped Agnes's hand too tightly, and Agnes cried out. Dropping her sister's fingers, Ember said, "I'm sorry, Agnes. You startled me."

"With what?" Agnes shook her fingers to loosen them.

Ember chose her words carefully. "Lord Mar is a stranger to me. I find it odd that he would take an interest in my sister."

"I think it simply a kindness," Agnes answered. "He is close to Alistair and Lady Eira. Perhaps he takes an interest in what matters to them."

"Perhaps."

Agnes leaned toward Ember, her smile conspiratorial. "He's rather fascinating, isn't he?"

"Lord Mar?" Ember wrapped her arms around herself, suddenly cold.

Nodding, Agnes whispered though there was no one to hear them. "I've never seen a man like him. So tall and strong. He's not as lovely as some men, but still handsome. His face is just . . . compelling. Those eyes."

Ember couldn't stop herself. "They don't frighten you?"

Rather than laugh at her, Agnes paused to consider the question. "They might if he hadn't been so gallant each time I've spoken with him."

"What do you talk about?" Ember frowned, fearing what the answer would be.

"He asks about our family and my health. He wanted to know about the father of my child, so I told him about Henry." Agnes blushed. "I know it isn't fitting for me to speak of these things to a near stranger, but I have so few friends now."

Ember asked, "What did Lord Mar say about Henry?"

"It was strange," Agnes answered wistfully. "He said that Henry's dishonor would haunt him all the days of his life."

"You don't think Henry feels any shame?" Ember couldn't put such heartlessness past Henry, but she wanted to believe otherwise.

Agnes folded her hands in her lap. "It wasn't what Lord Mar said. It was how he said it."

When Agnes paused, her gaze going to the window where rain battered the glass, Ember asked, "How did Lord Mar say it?"

Agnes looked at her sister. "Like a promise."

SEVENTEEN

**ALISTAIR SLIPPED THE IRON** key into his pocket, but he didn't return to the stairs. He stood in front of the door to Agnes's chamber for a long while, unmoving.

*Why did she return?*

Alistair had imagined Ember coming back to him too many times to count. Now that she was here, real, he was stricken with doubt. Tugging his hands through his dark curls, Alistair resisted the urge to unlock the door and take Ember from her sister so he could demand the answers he wanted.

But Agnes was the reason Ember was here. It had to be. As much as Alistair coveted the thought that Ember came to him, it was the letter that had brought her to Tearmunn.

And yet. And yet.

Ember had gone to Château de Lusignan, as Alistair had asked. She'd returned to Tearmunn and had given testament to those gathered in the armory that her decision to leave had been misguided.

And she'd come alone.

*Where are the others?*

To hope for even a moment that Ember had come back to him and not simply for Agnes's sake seemed too great a risk. Forcing himself away from the door, though unconvinced he'd accomplish anything else of worth that day due to the distraction of his mind, Alistair returned to the manor's ground floor.

When he reached the bottom of the stairs, he was surprised to find Bosque waiting for him.

"Would you be inclined toward a hunt, Lord Hart?" Bosque asked.

"When?" Alistair found it strange that Bosque would suggest a hunt amid so much activity in the keep.

"Now." Bosque took a few steps toward the manor door, then turned, waiting for Alistair to follow. "If you'll join me, we'll find special prey. Our bounty will aid your work immensely."

Bosque exited the manor, and Alistair hurried to catch him.

"My work?" Alistair asked when he reached Bosque.

"You will have your prisoners for trials tomorrow morning." Bosque kept up his swift, long strides toward the stables. "But they alone will not be enough."

"No." Alistair had to jog to keep up with the taller man. "You're taking me to hunt wolves, then?"

Bosque cast an amused glance at him. "How else did you think to procure the animals?"

"I was going to send woodsmen out to set snares," Alistair answered.

"This task is too important for servants," Bosque said when they were just outside the stables. "Ready your horse."

"Will you bring the hounds?" Alistair tossed the question over his shoulder as he went to gather Alkippe's tack.

Bosque called to him, "We'll have no need of hounds whose only hope is the destruction of our quarry."

Alistair grimaced at the foolishness of his question. To begin his trials, he needed wolves whole and alive, not torn to pieces by a pack of hunting dogs. When Alkippe was saddled and bridled, Alistair led his mare from the stable. Bosque had already mounted the shadow steed. Alkippe balked, snorting, but Alistair hadn't expected the mare to behave otherwise. No matter how many times Alistair rode out with Bosque, Alkippe wouldn't settle with the shadow mount near.

Once when Alkippe was particularly troublesome and Alistair had grown weary of battling the reins, he'd suggested that Bosque might be better off using one of Guards' mounts when in the company of other horses. Bosque had thrown back his head, laughing deep and long.

When he finally answered Alistair, it was to say, "Would you give up your mount upon the offer of a much lesser beast?"

Bosque's question had made Alistair hunch up with shame. Alkippe had always filled Alistair with pride. She was as fine a mount as any in Conatus's stables. Even so, Alistair couldn't fault Bosque's assertion. To ride the shadow steed was to harness a storm.

Swinging into the saddle while Alkippe sidled away from Bosque's mount, Alistair asked, "How shall we hunt when we aim not to kill?"

"I hadn't wanted to speak of it to you until I found what I'd been seeking," Bosque told him.

"And what was that?" Alistair checked Alkippe when she began tossing her head.

"You'll see soon enough." Bosque glanced at the restless mare. "Keep her close."

Alistair nodded, gritting his teeth as he forced Alkippe to ride abreast of Bosque's horse. He found himself wishing there were a way to explain to the mare that by fleeing the company of Bosque's steed, she would doom herself and her rider to wander lost in a space between worlds. Since reason wasn't an option, Alistair had to resign himself to the ongoing struggle between him and his mount as the air around them swirled, veiling the two horsemen in mist.

"Are you pleased by Lady Morrow's return?" Bosque's question took Alistair by surprise.

Still struggling to answer that question for himself, Alistair said, "I'm glad she lives." That was true enough.

Bosque laughed quietly. "Those weren't the words I expected."

Wearied by his own doubts, as well as his mount's agitation,

Alistair cast his fears upon Bosque. "I don't know if I trust her. That she would come for Agnes I understand, and though I want more from her, I dare not assume."

"The lady must have done your bidding, though," Bosque offered. "Had she not gone to La Marche, she would never have received her sister's letter."

Alistair nodded at Bosque's recitation of the possibilities he'd been mulling over since Ember appeared.

"You've been steadfast and cunning," Bosque continued. "I've promised you rewards. Do you not think Lady Morrow should be among them?"

Alistair barked a laugh, imagining Ember's reaction to being called a reward. Bosque watched him, waiting for a reply.

"On that front, what I think has never mattered," Alistair said, his laughter growing tinny. "Ember's mind has ruled our friendship, always keeping it from growing into something more."

"But she has changed. Thinking herself an Amazon, she discovered she is only a frightened maid," Bosque told him. "The world has treated her brutally, and now she seeks a protector. The walls of a fortress won't serve well enough for a trembling girl. I believe she'll look to you in her need . . . if she speaks the truth about her motives for returning to Tearmunn."

"And if she lies?" Alistair blew out a frustrated sigh. "So much is at stake. I fear I can't indulge my hopes when they might undermine Eira's plan."

"Nobly put," Bosque replied. "But why should the burden of trust fall to you?"

"Could it be any other way?" Alistair glanced at Bosque.

With a shrug, Bosque said, "I don't see why not. Take what you want from Lady Morrow. Be the hero she longs for. Leave the matter of truth versus lies to me."

"Do you think she returned for love of me?" Alistair knew he sounded like a lovesick boy, but Bosque's words enlivened a mad hope within him.

"I don't know." Bosque didn't look at Alistair, but he smiled into the mist. "I shall enjoy finding out."

Alistair shifted in his saddle, uneasy at the thought that Bosque could harm Ember as he investigated her trustworthiness.

"There is one more piece of advice I would give you," Bosque said, turning to gaze at Alistair. The silver flare of his eyes illuminated the mist.

"Please."

"Be hard on her," Bosque told him. "Ember knows of your love for her and yet takes it for granted. Make her believe you are lost to her. Force her to win you back. What she has fought for she will more likely treasure."

Before Alistair could question him further, Bosque leaned forward, peering at the gray veil that enveloped the riders. "Ah. This is it."

The mists parted, revealing thick clusters of pine trees and a mossy bank that hugged a shallow stream.

"We'll leave the horses here," Bosque said, sliding from the shadow stallion's back. He waited as Alistair dismounted and tethered Alkippe to a tree.

Bosque led them across the rippling brook and up a slope. The forest grew quiet as they walked. When they reached the top of the rise, Bosque halted. Alistair's eyes followed the other man's pointing finger, which directed his sight to a hollow beneath the trunk of a great fallen tree.

"There," Bosque said, his voice rich with satisfaction.

"A den?" Alistair frowned.

"Wolves are much like men—they are ruled by kings and queens." Bosque gazed at the gap below the tree trunk. "Without the pack leader, chaos ensues."

Bosque turned to Alistair. "To complete your vision, you need an alpha wolf's blood."

"And that's why we're here?" Alistair squinted at the den, but could see only darkness.

"Partly." Bosque held a bloodied rabbit in his hands. Alistair had no idea where the dead rabbit had come from. "She lies within. And she is hungry. Her pack went to hunt for her."

"And if they come back?" Alistair asked him.

"They aren't coming back." Bosque motioned for Alistair to be still. "Wait here."

While Alistair watched, Bosque laid his kill just beyond the den's opening and crept to the other side of the massive dead tree. They waited.

Alistair couldn't remember the last time he'd been still for so long. His limbs twitched, eager to move again. Bosque held his position as if he'd been carved of stone.

A flicker of movement within the den's shadow drew Alistair's gaze. A stirring of shadows became a shape. The shape became a head. The female wolf emerged from the den, hovering at its edge. Her body was heavy, teats peeking out from the fur of her belly.

Cubs. And from the looks of the mother, she'd very recently given birth.

Alistair wanted to shout in triumph. It was exactly what he needed.

Bosque never failed to keep his promises. This was special prey.

The she-wolf sniffed the air. Her ears and eyes were alert, seeking danger. Hunger won out over caution, and the wolf proceeded from the safety of her den. She'd taken the rabbit carcass into her jaws when she suddenly yelped. Dropping her meal, she scrambled back to the den. Her head and shoulders were engulfed by the dark opening when her back legs went out from under her. The wolf collapsed on her side and lay still.

Bursting from his hiding place, Alistair rushed toward the den. He didn't know what had made the wolf fall, but he lamented the thought that he'd lost her at the same moment she'd been found. Perhaps she'd already been sick.

Alistair knelt beside the tunnel and wrapped his arms around the wolf. Her fur was thick, a mottling of gray hues. Running his hands over her fur, Alistair's fingers met with something cool and hard. Something metal.

Wrapping his hand around the slender object, Alistair pulled it from the wolf's shoulder. He peered at the dart's needlepoint tip.

"Take care not to prick yourself, Lord Hart." Bosque was standing beside him.

Alistair swore under his breath, then said, "You move without a sound." He offered the dart to Bosque. "This is yours?"

"A favored weapon," Bosque answered. He showed Alistair a slim length of wood that had been hollowed in the center. "Poison on the dart took the wolf down."

"You killed her?" Alistair couldn't imagine why Bosque would have wanted the wolf dead.

"Of course not," Bosque replied. "More of the poison would have taken her life. What I used knocked her senseless. You didn't want her chewing through the nets on the ride home, did you?"

Without waiting for Alistair to answer, Bosque crouched down and gathered the wolf into his arms. He lifted her effortlessly.

"Go into the den and gather the cubs into your cloak," Bosque told Alistair. "They'll be small enough to bundle within the fabric until we return to Tearmunn."

Alistair poked his head into the dark tunnel. The tiny mewling sounds of the cubs calling for their mother filled his ears. His shoulders barely fit into the den's entrance, but the hollowed space widened as he squirmed deeper into the earth. Blinded by shadows, Alistair used his ears to locate the cubs. Covered in fur soft as down and barely larger than his hand, the wolves were easy enough to gather into his cloak before he pulled up the corners into a sack.

He found Bosque watching the den's entrance expectantly as Alistair crawled back into the daylight with this squirming, whimpering bundle.

"We should return." Bosque started down the slope. "On the ride home, we'll discuss the mother's feeding and the process for weaning the cubs off her milk."

Alistair followed, numbed by the onslaught of events. Ember's arrival. Prisoners and wolves stashed beneath the manor, awaiting his purpose. Forcing his mind away from unwieldy questions about what the future held, Alistair focused on the mundane: hopping over the creek, preparing for the ride home.

As they neared the horses, Alistair laughed quietly.

"What is it?" Bosque glanced over his shoulder.

"Between your horse and the wolves." Alistair grinned. "I wonder if Alkippe will survive the return trip to Tearmunn."

Bosque's smile matched Alistair's. "Would you like to wager on it?"

EIGHTEEN

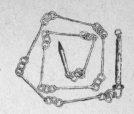

# EMBER WOKE AS A HAND covered her mouth.

"Don't scream."

The cry welling in Ember's throat died, but only because she recognized the speaker's voice.

When Cian saw that Ember wouldn't panic, she rose from her crouch. Taking Ember's arm, Cian pulled her from the bed where she'd been sleeping alongside Agnes. Cian handed Ember a heavy cloak, which the younger woman fastened over her sleeping gown. They quietly stole from the room.

The seasoned warrior took Ember only so far as a few doors along the manor corridor to another chamber. Hurrying inside the door that Cian had opened, Ember clasped her fingers in front of her lips so she wouldn't give a joyful cry.

Father Michael sat at a desk on the far side of the room, watching her in the soft glow of light cast by the lantern at his side. Though she stayed quiet, Ember flung herself at the elderly priest when he stood up, wrapping him in an embrace. Father Michael staggered back from her unexpected greeting, but soon he was clasping her tight.

"My heart is glad to see you well, Lady Morrow."

Embarrassed by her unrestrained display, Ember let go of Father Michael and scuttled back, bowing her head in respect.

"I take it that your response to Father Michael means your little speech this afternoon was an act?" Cian asked from behind Ember.

Turning to answer, Ember noticed for the first time that Cian was fully armed, despite the late hour. And her hand was on the hilt of her sword. Ember stiffened, realizing that Cian might have believed that Ember would betray their secret.

"It was," Ember told Cian.

Cian relaxed slightly, but kept a close watch on Ember. "Have you returned only to see to your sister?"

"I did come to ensure Agnes's safety." Ember pulled the cloak tighter around her. "But that is not all."

"Sit, child." Father Michael gestured to another chair, and Ember gratefully accepted his offer. Cian remained close to the door.

The priest's kind eyes put Ember more at ease.

"What can you tell us of the others?" Father Michael asked her.

"Barrow, Lukasz, and Kael are in France," Ember said. "Sawyer was lost at sea. I don't know what became of Fitch and Mercer. They never joined our party on the road from Tearmunn."

Cian grunted in disgust. "Fitch proved spineless. He betrayed Mercer and would have revealed our presence."

"How did you stop him?" Ember's eyes were wide.

"I killed him before he could tell his tale," Cian answered, and Ember flinched, knowing that if she'd been suspected of the same, Fitch's fate would have been her own.

Father Michael folded his hands on the desk. "We must know, Ember. Does it go as badly abroad as Lady Eira's boasts would make it seem?"

Reluctantly, Ember nodded. Any comfort she'd taken in seeing Cian and Father Michael faded as quickly as the glimmers of hope on their faces.

"They all go to her." Cian shook her head. "And there is naught we can do."

"We must not despair," Father Michael said calmly, though Ember saw a great sadness in his eyes.

Cian met his gaze, but didn't answer.

"What of Tearmunn?" Ember asked. "Have we no allies here?"

"Those who would join us have either been cowed by fear into submitting to Eira's will," Cian told her, "or they are locked in the stockade."

Ember spoke, though she was afraid to learn more. "Lora? Ewan?"

"Ewan remains part of the Circle, but he cannot delay taking the oath for much longer without risk of being put in irons," Father Michael said. "Lora has disappeared. I pray that she simply fled the keep, knowing she would be imprisoned for refusing to give Eira fealty. But I fear something worse has befallen her, for I find it hard to believe she would have left without sharing her plan with us."

Made restless by this news, Ember stood up. "I know it wouldn't be ideal to forswear oneself." She glanced with guilt at Father Michael. "But couldn't the oath be taken falsely?"

Father Michael answered, "If it were so easy, I would gladly absolve those who pledged themselves to Eira's new order, but the oath is much more than words. It changes those who take it."

"Changes them how?" Ember frowned at the priest.

Cian hissed through her teeth. "It binds them to him."

Her brow still furrowed, Ember looked at Cian.

"To Bosque," Cian said, anticipating Ember's question.

"Lord Mar?" Remembering the reach of his silver gaze, Ember fidgeted, suddenly anxious.

"He calls himself lord," Cian told her. "And he walks and speaks as a man, but his body and his words are an illusion that he used as a net to snare my sister and those guileless enough to be drawn in by his promises."

"What does he offer?" Ember asked.

"What men desire the most," Father Michael said. "An easy path paved in gold."

Ember shifted her weight, unable to fight the cold seeping beneath her skin. "But there must be a cost."

"The cost is everything we are," Cian said. "The sacred tree is profaned. We are cut off from the magics that sustain us."

Father Michael nodded, looking at Ember. "Any who take Eira's oath lose the gifts offered by this earth. All we've studied. The crafts we've honed."

"Then why would anyone take this oath?" Ember asked.

"The price wasn't clear at first," Father Michael said. "It wasn't until the clerics found themselves unable to weave portals that we learned how strong this Bosque's poison is."

Ember looked back and forth from knight to priest, trapped by her own disbelief. "And there was no outcry against this?"

"By then Eira had too many followers for those who balked to sway," Father Michael said.

"And my sister's pet had other enticements to assuage those who were disturbed by the loss of their magics," Cian added.

Ember's mind beckoned images that she'd buried, knowing that to revisit them would be like opening scabbed-over wounds. The shadow creatures in the forest.

Watching as Ember went still, Father Michael said, "I wish I could allay your fears, Ember, but your mind has settled on the truth. Those who take Eira's oath are instructed in arts darker than those practiced by any conjurer the Guard ever hunted."

Appalled as she was, Ember could understand how Bosque had lured so many followers. Whoever commanded an army of invincible warriors had no earthly enemy to fear.

"But to do this, Eira has allied herself with the very thing Conatus is sworn to destroy," Ember protested weakly. The appeal of power aside, Ember couldn't forget Eira's strength and courage. Her thirst for justice.

Cian slumped against the door. Like Eira, Cian had been changed in Ember's absence. But while Eira seemed taller, more alive, Cian had diminished. Her eyes were tight with lines and deeply shadowed, her skin sallow.

"The fault lies with me," Cian said.

Father Michael shushed her.

"No." Cian looked away from the priest. "I knew how thin Eira's patience wore with Crichton's abuses and the fight to give women more power in Conatus. I didn't watch her closely enough. I didn't see."

Cian closed her eyes, and a tear slipped along her cheek.

"Eira made her own choices," Father Michael said, "as we all must do—and one day she will answer for them. But that burden does not rest upon your shoulders."

"Is there anything we can do?" Ember thought of Barrow, Lukasz, and Kael, exiled in France and awaiting news. Thus far, Ember had nothing but grief to offer them.

Father Michael rose and went to Cian, taking her hands in his. "Please sit, my lady. I know how rarely you rest."

Cian let him guide her to the chair, and she sat, silent but shedding no more tears.

Turning to Ember, the priest said, "We search day and night for a means to defeat Bosque, for he is the vessel that carries us into shadow."

"That's what the others do as well." Ember nodded. "They're at a safe house in La Rochelle."

"Not the hidden sanctuary?" Father Michael asked in alarm.

"No," Ember told him. "We sought refuge there after our ship was wrecked, and a longtime friend of the commander's, a knight by the name of Jérôme Fauré, came to us. He gave us aid but also told us that any site associated with Conatus or the Templars would be unsafe."

"Your ship sank?" Cian broke in. "When you said Sawyer was lost at sea, I didn't think . . . how?"

"A sea monster," Ember answered. "Barrow called it a kraken, Leviathan. It tore the ship to pieces."

"By God's mercy alone, you survived." Father Michael made the sign of the cross.

Ember couldn't disagree. That she'd made it to the beach with Barrow in tow was nothing less than a miracle. "We made it to shore, but we lost everything except the horses."

"Another mercy," Father Michael said. "Without horses, you might not have reached La Rochelle."

Returning to her hidden companions, Ember said, "Jérôme advised Lukasz to try to contact the clerics of the Holy Land. He believes that only the oldest, most secret tomes will reveal the means to defeat our enemy."

"I hope he's right," Cian said. "We've found nothing here. At least nothing good. So far we've learned more about Bosque's power by his own hand than our studies."

"Have you received word from Lukasz?" Ember asked. "Will he be able to safely contact you if they find something?"

"We're still working on that," Father Michael admitted. "The success with which Eira has recruited followers took us by surprise. Your friend Jérôme was right. Any of the usual places we'd send word have been compromised. Perhaps this safe house in La Rochelle will suffice."

"That's what Lukasz hoped for," Ember replied.

"How do you plan to fit in here, Ember?" Cian said bitterly. "Do you think to return to the Guard?"

"No," Ember answered. "I serve Lukasz, not Alistair."

"You speak like a true knight of Conatus." Cian's tone remained sharp.

Ember stood up straighter. "Do you think I am not?"

"Eira favored you," Cian answered her. "And those Eira favored have become her greatest supporters."

Nodding, Ember said to Cian, "Alistair spoke of Eira's hopes for me, but I never aspired to win her admiration. All I wanted to do was serve Conatus with my blades."

"And how will you serve Conatus now?" Cian asked.

"I must convince Alistair that I returned not only for Agnes, but for him," Ember said calmly, though her heart gave a heavy thud as she spoke. Before she'd come to Tearmunn, her plan had been nothing more than words spoken with conviction. Now that she was here, she would have to act.

"That's a dangerous game." Cian returned Ember's steady gaze. "Are you prepared to see it through?"

"I have to be." It was the most truthful answer Ember could give.

Father Michael clasped his hands as if in prayer, holding them to his chest. "It's a great risk you take, but if you gain Alistair's trust, it may help us immensely."

"That thought occurred to me as well," Cian added.

Ember forced herself to smile, affirming their words. Inside she was a jumble of doubts and second guesses. Since her return, Alistair hadn't so much as looked at her with warmth. Her offers to aid them by becoming Alistair's confidante might prove empty.

Cian rose, gesturing to the door. "I'll take you back to Agnes's room. You've had a long journey already, and I'm afraid the road ahead grows only rougher."

Before she followed Cian's direction, Ember asked, "This oath. Does Eira not press each of you to take it?"

"My faith is my shield," Father Michael told her. "I cannot take an oath that would compromise the vows I've already taken in the service of the Church."

Ember suddenly was very afraid for him. "And Eira doesn't object?"

"Fortunately, Eira and Bosque see me as a doddering old priest and not a threat," Father Michael said. "Since they think I have nothing to offer them, they care not whether they take something from me."

A bit relieved, Ember looked at Cian.

"I currently enjoy a reprieve," Cian said. "Due to my general stubbornness and the fact that I am Eira's sister. But my time will come."

For several heartbeats, Ember found her eyes locked with Cian's. She realized that they shared a common goal beyond that of saving Conatus: each woman remained within Tearmunn at her peril, all in the hopes of saving her sister. Cian broke their gaze first, reaching for the door handle.

"If I need to speak with you . . ." Ember trailed off, thinking herself ill advised to go knocking on Cian's door or sneaking into Father Michael's humble quarters near the chapel.

Cian and Father Michael exchanged a knowing look.

"Where else, my child?" The priest smiled at Ember. "Confession."

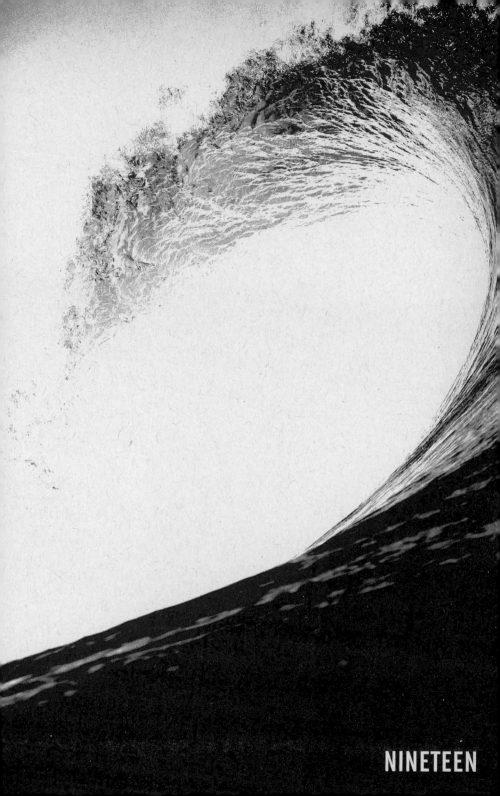

NINETEEN

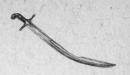

# A WEEK PASSED BEFORE Alistair sought Ember's

company. In those seven days, Ember became increasingly convinced
that she'd traveled backward through time. Had it not been for the
sight of the steep highland slopes that she could spy from Agnes's,
and now her own, window or the fact that Ember and her sister had
grown into women and were no longer young girls, Ember could
have been convinced that she was again at her father's estate, living
out the life that she'd known most days of her childhood. Even her
dresses were familiar. On Ember's first morning after her return to
Tearmunn, all the chests her father had insisted accompany Ember
to the keep had appeared.

Ember wasn't happy at how quickly she remembered why she'd
hated the days spent cooped up in her father's manor. Since their
movements were restricted, Agnes had suggested that they embroi-
der clothing for her unborn child. Wanting to please her sister,
Ember assented before she recalled how much she despised working
with a needle and thread.

When enough of her fingers were bleeding from tiny, invisible
needle pricks, Ember gave up. Her embroidery sat in her lap,
unfinished, while Agnes chatted or sang sweet songs. Ember gazed out
the window, knowing she must be in this room, in this keep, but wishing she were not. After the first clandestine night visit, Ember had no

further contact with Cian or Father Michael. Though she offered Agnes placid smiles, Ember's thoughts more often than not were of Barrow. Sometimes she closed her eyes, trying to remember what it was like to pass the night in his arms, waking to the scent of his skin on hers. She captured brief glimpses of his face in her dreams—the softness of his lips and the rough stroke of stubble on his jaw, the color of his eyes as dark as the winter sea, the strength of his hands.

Knowing she couldn't lose herself in the fantasies of elsewhere, Ember tried to keep her attention on Agnes. Surprisingly, given the circumstances, Agnes blossomed with her pregnancy. The sickness that had plagued her early on had passed, and while her belly grew, so did the glow in her cheeks. Though Ember was happy to see her sister well, Agnes's condition raised troubling questions. Alistair had offered to care for her now, but when did his hospitality come to an end? Would he provide for her child as well? Would Agnes live forever at Tearmunn?

Even if such an arrangement had been made, Ember knew it wasn't viable. Tearmunn could never be a safe place for either Agnes or Ember. Not so long as Eira ruled and Bosque stood at her side. Because of this, Ember set herself another task. Not only must she find a way into Alistair's good graces, but she also needed a way out of Tearmunn for Agnes.

Ember pondered these two problems while Agnes embroidered the hem of a minuscule shirt. Both sisters looked up when the door opened. Agnes's maid curtsied and stepped aside. When Alistair walked in, Ember jumped to her feet, smoothing her pale blue gown. Bosque followed Alistair through the door, but Ember managed to keep a pleasant smile on her face.

Agnes set her embroidery aside and rose with much more dignity and grace than Ember had shown. Since it was her room and she was the elder sister, Ember deferred to Agnes, leaving her to greet their visitors.

"Good morning, Lord Hart and Lord Mar." She curtsied, and Ember mimicked her sister's action.

Alistair gave a brief nod. "Good morning, Agnes. I hope you are well?"

"I am, Alistair." Agnes blushed when she beamed at him, picking up her nearly finished shirt. "Look at what we've made."

Ember offered Alistair a wry smile. "My sister is being too generous with her use of *we*."

"I'm sure she is," Alistair answered, barely looking at Ember.

The smile vanished from Ember's face as quickly as if Alistair had slapped her. She didn't understand. Joking had always been their way, and his brusque manner was strange. Ember was surprised at how deeply it stung her.

Bosque came forward, leaning down to examine the hem. "How lovely. You must have delicate hands to create such fine needlework."

Agnes curtsied again. "You're very kind, Lord Mar."

"I hate to trouble you, Agnes, but I'd like to ask for a bit of time alone with your sister." Alistair didn't look at Ember, though he was speaking about her.

Under any other circumstances, Ember would have shouted at Alistair until his ears were red for treating her thus. But now she felt helpless; she could do nothing but stand quietly while plans were made about her. Her nightmares offered more kindness than this.

"Of course." Agnes put the shirt down, but clearly didn't know what to do with herself.

Bosque offered her his arm. "I thought I could take you for a walk around the grounds. The day is fine, and some air would do you good."

Agnes smiled up at the tall man as though he were the sun itself. Ember wanted to stomp her feet and scream. Wooden and miserable, she watched Bosque lead her sister from the room. Before he passed through the door, Bosque cast a glance back at Ember, one corner of his mouth curving up in a way that made Ember's legs quake. She dropped back into her chair, feeling cold and breathless.

"Are you ill, Lady Morrow?" Alistair hadn't moved from where he stood.

"No." Ember sat up, pretending she wasn't as unsettled as she felt. "I slept poorly, that's all."

"I'm sorry to hear that." Alistair made a show of looking the chamber over. "Perhaps you require a separate room."

Ember chewed her lip. A room of her own would give her privacy, both for attempting to win Alistair and for sneaking out in the night if need be. But she was also instinctively protective of Agnes and reluctant to create distance between them.

"I've shared a room with Agnes all my life," Ember told him. "You needn't make special arrangements for me now."

"No arrangements would be needed," Alistair replied. "We have an empty room that you may use if you like."

"I—" Again caught off guard by Alistair's cold demeanor, Ember struggled for a new approach to their conversation.

"And you might consider that when you shared a room with Agnes, you were both girls," Alistair continued. "If you haven't noticed, your sister is a woman with child, and you . . . well, I can't say what you are."

Ember blanched, completely unsure of herself. The man speaking to her now was nothing like the Alistair she'd known. Gone was the teasing boy who'd taught her to fight with a sword.

Alistair gave her a tired look. "You'll still have ample time to spend in Agnes's company, but you'll conduct yourself as a woman of your station should—at least on the surface of things."

"If you think it best—" Ember began, but then she could no longer help herself. A sob welled from the very pit of her stomach, bringing with it tears that required no playacting to summon. "Why are you acting like this?"

She felt exactly like the petulant little girl Alistair accused her of being.

Stiffly, Alistair said, "Ember, collect yourself. You're better than this."

That only made Ember sob again. Not only was she confused, she was mortified by her own unexpected outburst.

With a noise of disgust, Alistair finally broke from his watchful pose and came to her. Grabbing her arms, he forcefully lifted her to her feet.

"Stop, Ember." Alistair gave her a light shake. "You shame yourself with this display."

Ember couldn't halt her tears, but she choked back another sob. Through her blurred vision, she met Alistair's sky-blue eyes and found them judging her.

He held on to her arm with one hand while the other took her chin. His thumb raked tear tracks from her right cheek. Shaking his head in disappointment, Alistair frowned. "Why did you come back?"

Ember stared at him, her eyes brimming. "I thought you wanted—"

"When have you ever cared about what I want?" Alistair snapped.

"I was wrong." Ember had begun to tremble all over. "I didn't know."

Alistair's arm slid around her back, gripping her tight at the waist and hip. "Where did you go?"

"To La Marche." Ember tried to focus, to recall the story she needed to tell. Her mind was drowning in tears and cruel words. She could barely sense the room around them. All she could see was the piercing blue of Alistair's gaze.

Alistair's lip curled, haughty. "Why?"

"You told me . . . you said . . ." Ember was shaking so badly that she couldn't stand up. She didn't need to, as Alistair was now holding her against him.

"Did it ever occur to you that I might have regretted what mercies I offered you that night?" Alistair hissed into her ear. "Did a single thought cross your mind other than what would make your life the easiest? What you wanted?"

"Stop." Ember grasped Alistair's shirt, clinging to him. "Please."

"Tell me why you left the others." Alistair spoke in a low, harsh voice. "Are they dead?"

Ember's throat closed. Her head was spinning. What was she supposed to say? What should have befallen her companions? What story would keep them safe?

"Or did they leave you behind?" The sweetness of Alistair's question was like venom. "Did you prove too great a burden, the maid who held back such great knights of Conatus?"

Shutting her eyes, still burning from her tears, Ember said, "I left them."

Was that wrong? Should she have told Alistair they'd perished, drowned? Barrow's face glared at her, accusing. Ember buried her head against Alistair's shoulder.

"You're lying." Alistair's lips were at her ear, hot and unrelenting. "Tell me the truth."

Ember twisted her hands in his shirt, pulling her body closer to his. "I left them."

"Why?"

His face was warm against hers, and Ember didn't know how they'd come to be so close. She couldn't be sure of anything, except that if she let him go, she would fall.

"Because I was wrong to leave," she whispered, her voice cracking.

Alistair laughed, his breath beating against her neck. "You expect me to believe that?"

"I'm here now." Each word Ember spoke felt more pathetic than the last.

"You're here for Agnes," Alistair told her. "Which is the one noble act you've accomplished since you first set foot in Conatus. I can honor that." His fingers lifted her chin. "But you are not here for me."

Ember opened her mouth, but her protest died in her throat. She'd failed. Failed before she ever made the decision to return. Alistair despised her.

More tears stung as they gathered at the corners of her eyes, and Ember hated herself for it. She let her eyelids close in defeat. A moment later, she felt Alistair's lips on hers. The sudden warmth and silken touch of his mouth provoked an instinctive reaction from Ember; her hands released his shirt, sliding around his neck to pull him closer still. When his tongue slipped into her mouth, she didn't fight him, desperately needing a reprieve from his hostility. Seeking any sign that he still wanted her, she was not ready to face what it would mean if he didn't.

Alistair broke off the kiss suddenly. Ember's eyes were still closed when he pushed her back into her seat. He left the room without speaking or looking back at her.

Ember sat, gripping the arms of the chair. Her body still trembled as waves of heat and cold coursed through her. She stared at the door, terrified by the fact that she had no idea what had just happened.

TWENTY

**ALISTAIR HAD KNOWN THE** encounter would be a struggle, but it had been more trying than he'd imagined. He hadn't planned to kiss Ember, or more accurately, he had planned to avoid kissing her. In his first real interaction with Ember since her return, Alistair had hoped to show her only disdain.

Temptation had proved too great. The kiss had been provoked not because Ember had been molded against him, nor because he watched the way her breasts rose and fell with each short breath she took. It was her desperation that had pushed him over the edge. The way she'd held on to him as if her life depended on it.

In some ways, Alistair supposed, Ember's life did depend on him. But the way she had needed him to give her something. The smallest token that she remained of some worth to him. Ember had always been defiant. To see her quaking with fear made him feel stronger, more alive. And more determined.

Though he hungered for more of Ember, Alistair knew that giving in to his desire meant he would have to keep himself away from her again. At least for a length of days that would leave her ill at ease. He needed her to be unsure of him.

As usual, Bosque's advice had proven wise and effective. Alistair meant to spend the majority of his hours becoming the protégé that would give Lord Mar the most pride.

Making his way to the catacombs, Alistair nodded as he passed Father Michael working at a scribe's table in the chapel. The priest bowed slightly in response and then returned to his studies.

Alistair entered the cellar door, rapidly descending the staircase. He hurried past the wine casks. He hated being in this dark, musty room, so filled with memories of fear and humiliation. His trial against those wretched hobgoblins had been an exercise in cruelty, Alistair had decided. An unfair game set up for the entertainment of Lukasz and Barrow, who were predisposed to dislike Alistair because of his noble blood.

Though Kael had left with them, Alistair found it hard to fault his mentor, instead preferring to believe that, like Ember, Kael had been deluded by their lies. Behind the rows of wooden casks, Alistair ran his hands over the floor until his fingers found the iron ring. Alistair tugged hard on the ring, and the trapdoor groaned open, revealing another, much older staircase.

Happy to leave the cellar behind, Alistair disappeared beneath the floor, pulling the trapdoor shut. He was plunged into darkness but didn't mind, knowing it would soon abate. Alistair had made this journey often enough that he no longer had to follow the curve of the wall. He knew the precise angle and distance it took to reach the next door. Even in the pitch-black, Alistair had no trouble finding the door handle. He pushed the door open and entered the realm of the dead.

Before Bosque's instruction to use them, Alistair hadn't known of the catacombs' existence. He gathered that few in Tearmunn did. The ever-curving passage sloped steeply down as if the corridor led to Hades itself. Alistair had wondered upon his first entry into the catacombs how many years had passed since any man had fired the torches that now lit his path.

Alistair kept up his quick pace until he reached the lowest and last section. Here the narrow, tomb-lined corridor widened into an open chamber. More hollows had been carved in the rock of the chamber's four walls to offer holding places for sarcophagi. The most ornate resting places for the dead were featured on carved platforms at regular intervals.

Stepping into the broad chamber, Alistair took a deep breath, letting tension melt from his body. This was his workplace. The only solace he could find from Ember's pull.

Hamish was already at work. A mortar and pestle, bundles giving off pungent scents, and copper bowls of varying sizes were spread before the cleric.

Without looking up from his notes, Hamish said to Alistair, "The first one is dead."

"But you expected that," Alistair answered, leafing through his own pile of scribbled-upon parchment.

Hamish nodded. "The problem was in the merge. Too many organs or too few. I won't know until I open him up."

"You'll do that today?"

"Before the rot sets in," Hamish replied. "Do you want me to wait to begin the third trial? To see what I can learn from taking a peek inside the first?"

Alistair grunted, not liking the delay, but conceding that it was prudent. "Yes."

"Very well." Hamish picked up a serrated blade. "I'll get to it."

A high-pitched yip pierced the chamber, bouncing off the catacomb walls. Soon a chorus of whining barks were ringing in the air.

"They're hungry," Hamish said, looking at Alistair.

"That only means they're awake," Alistair answered drily. "They have two ways of being right now. Asleep and hungry."

Hamish turned to leave, but Alistair caught his arm. "How's the mother?"

"She's a bitch," Hamish answered.

Grimacing, Alistair told him, "Even the first time, that joke wasn't very funny."

Hamish grinned in return. "I still like it."

Alistair kept stony eyes on the cleric. "How is she?"

"Not fond of me, as usual." Hamish lifted his chin toward one of the walls. "Probably because I keep stealing her blood."

"She's not weakening, though?" Alistair's gaze moved to the sealed earthenware carafes that lined a shelf. In another place they might have been used to serve wine, but not here.

Hamish shook his head. "She's a fighter."

"Good," Alistair said.

Sticking a finger in his ear, Hamish shook the knife at Alistair. "Now will you shut them up?" he asked. He walked off, muttering under his breath.

The cleric's perpetual sour mood might have dissuaded Alistair from taking him on as a collaborator. Some days it still grated on Alistair's nerves, but Alistair couldn't deny that Bosque had been right in identifying Hamish's potential.

The cleric had studied Alistair's notes and sketches exhaustively. Within a week of his joining Alistair, Hamish had already brought the knight's vision to life.

Or a rough rendering thereof.

Alistair refused to be frustrated. Trials of this sort required patience, the willingness to fail and begin again.

Taking an opposite course from Hamish, Alistair moved through the chamber. The piping calls for food grew ever louder as Alistair walked. Pausing at the larder, Alistair collected strips of venison to fill the hungry bellies. There were other sounds in the room too, coming from the cages that were hidden in a corner chamber that was a smaller version of the main tomb. Alistair ignored those sounds, unpleasant as they were.

When the yips became more fervent and faster, Alistair knew they'd spotted him coming. He deposited the venison in the hollow closest to the holding pen, then continued on his way.

Alistair paused at the edge of the pen. Small paws tried to scramble up the sides of the pen as tails wagged furiously. Six furry faces and shiny black noses lifted, seeking his attention. Looking down at the wolf cubs, Alistair marveled at how much they changed with each day. The cubs, four males and two females, still tottered a bit as they jostled against each other, trying to reach him, but they moved with much greater control of their feet. Their eyes were bright and alert, ever observing their world.

Alistair opened the gate and joined the cubs, who swarmed around his feet. They were an array of shades ranging from mottled gray like their mother to the silver-white of the moon. Alistair scooped up the male who had steel-gray fur on his back but a white chest and stomach. He could easily hold the cub in one hand. The little beast wriggled, its yips mixing with tiny grunts and mewling. Alistair let the cub rest against his chest, and it gave itself over to licking his neck incessantly. The tickling sensation made Alistair laugh, and the cub barked in reply.

He carried the cub into the chamber from which plaintive cries emerged, picking up his stash of venison strips on the way.

*Concentrate,* Alistair reminded himself as he forced one foot in front of the other. *Focus.*

The feeding wasn't troubling, but the place the meal had to occur was. The cries fell silent when Alistair entered the room. Six cages had been placed in the chamber, three along each wall. The village children's wide, frightened eyes fixed on Alistair. Though he refused to look at his captives, Alistair could feel their stares, sense the quivering of the prisoners' limbs as he reached the center of the chamber.

Settling onto the floor with the cub in his lap, Alistair took his time feeding the cub small morsels of the raw meat. The gray-and-white wolf gulped the venison down greedily, his attention fully consumed by the bloody flesh. Not once was the cub distracted by the caged children who shrank against the bars at the back of their cages, away from the man and young predator in his arms. Alistair was pleased.

After the cub had his portion of meat, Alistair sat with the wolf. He let the cub play at chasing him or wrestling with his arm until it tired. Only when the little wolf climbed into his lap and curled into a ball to sleep did Alistair return him to the pen. Setting the sleepy cub down, Alistair picked up his sister. He went through the same cycle with each of the six cubs. He'd been with them each day since their birth. He would continue to be there each day as they grew. And with each meal, they'd become accustomed to the scents of the six caged children, as they needed to be.

It was Hamish's task to bring Alistair's vision to life. But Alistair's work would ensure its success.

TWENTY-ONE

**EIRA HAD HEARD AS MANY** complaints as she could bear for that day. The scraggly shepherd bowed as she promised for the twelfth time that day to address some villager's concern. Most of their fears were petty, born of superstitions that had run wild since Bosque's wraiths had attacked the village. Since Bosque kept her informed of what creatures had crossed over from the nether to the earth, Eira could quickly discern those of the villagers' tales that were true and those that were only their nightmares spoken in the light of day.

Other pleas brought before Eira were of a more serious nature. Those petitions were what provoked Eira to ask Bosque to accompany her to her chamber after she'd held court.

"I suffer through this on your advice," Eira told him after he'd closed the door.

Bosque nodded. "And though I'm sorry for your pain, I would give the same counsel if asked again."

"Why do you think the villagers matter?" Walking back and forth through the room, Eira stretched her arms and neck. She'd been sitting far too long that day. Casting her gaze toward the window, Eira wondered where Cian was and if her sister might be game for an hour or two on the practice field.

"The villagers do matter," Bosque told her. "If they fear you, they will submit to you, but if they love and fear you, they will fight for you."

"With pitchforks and brooms?" Eira arched her brow at Bosque.

"Don't underestimate them," Bosque replied.

"Very well," Eira said wearily. "What about the children?"

"What about them?"

Eira frowned. "Don't be coy."

"Children go missing all the time," Bosque said. "They drown in the lake. They fall from cliffs. They are lost in the woods."

Pursing her lips, Eira said, "What are Alistair and Hamish doing with them?"

"Making progress," Bosque answered.

"Are you trying to annoy me?" Eira's hands went to her hips.

Bosque smiled at her. "Perhaps. But more likely I seek to delay you."

"Why would you do that?" She went to her desk. The stack of parchments grew taller each day. Each new letter confirming the spread of her message across the known world.

"You know Lord Hart as a soldier," Bosque said. "But I've asked him to become an artist. This is his great work. I wouldn't have it spoiled for you because you saw an unfinished masterpiece."

"Hmmm." Eira looked up. "We still have little news from the Holy Land."

Bosque made a noncommittal sound. "I expect they'll resist the longest. The places where things begin often prove the most reluctant to let those things go."

When Eira didn't reply, Bosque laughed. "Why do I suspect you long for an uprising?"

Eira's furrowed brow gave way to a smile. "Is that what you think?"

"I think your hand would rather grip a sword than a quill," Bosque replied. "And I don't fault you for it. The business of politics is often dull."

Looking at him with curiosity, Eira said, "Are there politics in your world?"

"There is no war without politics," he said.

Turning away from her letters, Eira asked, "Will you speculate as to when I can see this masterpiece that Alistair creates?"

"Another week," Bosque answered. "Perhaps a few more days than that, but not long."

"I'm intrigued," Eira told him. "You've guarded this secret like a hoard of treasure."

"I assure you," Bosque said, "it's much better than treasure."

Eira laughed. "If you want to keep me from spoiling your great day of revelation, you shouldn't entice me with such promises."

"Alistair's work points to the future," Bosque said, brushing aside her playful tone with his newly serious manner. "It brings to mind something you should also be considering. Something to do with politics. And war."

"How so?" Eira began to unbraid her hair, which she'd bound too tightly in the morning; it had caused her head to ache.

Bosque watched as waves, copper bright, fell section by section upon Eira's shoulders. "Your legacy. I would see you secure it."

"My legacy," Eira murmured. She rubbed her temples.

"Who will rule when you are gone?" Bosque continued. "Though I assure you, that will be many years from now."

Though her eyes were closed, Eira smiled. "You are always so certain, Lord Mar."

"I am." His voice was much closer. Eira opened her eyes to find him standing before her.

Bosque's gaze lingered on her face. "I would like you to think about your heir."

Eira laughed. "An heir?"

When Bosque showed no sign of joining her bout of mirth, Eira said, "You spoke of Alistair. Is it your wish that I should name him my successor?" She didn't dislike the idea. Though he often frustrated her with his youthful whims and irritating obsession with Ember Morrow, Eira held Alistair in high regard. Her affection for him grew daily.

A hint of a smile touched Bosque's mouth. "You need Alistair to be your general, and in that role, he will serve you well, but someone else should take your throne."

Eira frowned at him. "Who?"

"Why not your own child?" Bosque asked.

She took a step back, half turning from him. Twisting her fingers in her loose hair, she said quietly, "My years to bear children are past. I chose another life than that of wife and mother."

Unsettled, Eira smoothed her hair back, intending to braid it once more. But Bosque was suddenly at her side, pushing her hand away.

"Leave it down," he said in a voice that reached beneath her skin, making her tremble.

She drew a startled breath when he placed his palm low on her belly. Leaning close, he murmured, "Life would still quicken within you."

"Why do you speak to me of this?" Eira couldn't move. No man had touched her, desired to draw close to her, before now.

*But he isn't truly a man.*

Her mind tried to grasp that small, fearful voice, but her body responded to the warmth of Bosque's hand and the caress of his breath on her neck. When she closed her eyes, attempting to focus, the image of Bosque appeared, emerging naked from the waters, rivulets of seawater chasing each other down the carved lines of his chest and abdomen.

Eira's eyelids fluttered open and she shook her head, trying to dispel the memory.

"Does my touch offend you?" Bosque asked. His fingers pressed into her as he slid his hand from her stomach to grasp the curve of her hip. Bosque drew Eira close. Her back fitted against his chest, and she could feel the strength of the body her mind's eye had memorized so well.

"I asked a question," Eira said, not wanting him to know how far off balance he'd put her. She laid her hand over his, thinking to push it away from her, but the moment her fingers touched his warm skin, they curled around his hand as if by instinct.

"Your future is also mine, Eira." He wound loose strands of her hair around his wrist like a serpent. "And our bond is already formed, joining our two worlds. I suggest only that there is a further path we might walk together."

"Do you want me as a lover?" Eira pulled away from him. "Or do you simply wish for me to bear your child?"

"Is there a reason I can't desire both?" Bosque asked. She kept her distance, and he didn't attempt to draw near again. "And the child will not be mine, but ours."

"I—" Eira stared at Bosque. Her skin was still flushed and strangely hot from their brief closeness.

"Consider what I've said." Bosque retreated to the door. "When I speak of this again, I'll require your answer."

When he'd gone, Eira went to her bed. She lay down and closed her eyes, pondering a question she never had expected to be asked.

**TWENTY-TWO**

**DAY AFTER DAY PASSED,** but Ember couldn't shake Alistair's visit from her mind; nor could she think of any prior incident in her life that she'd given such scrutiny. Once Alistair was out of the room, Ember had been able to catch her breath and collect her wits, only to find herself utterly bewildered by what had transpired.

In a matter of minutes, Ember had broken down, been reduced to a pathetic, weeping lump of a girl. All because Alistair had treated her more coldly than she'd ever believed he would, or could. His words had bruised her spirit as well as her heart. Though she didn't love him in the way he wished, Alistair had been her only friend besides Agnes throughout her childhood. He'd been the only one who hadn't chastised her for longing to wield a sword and become as accomplished a horseman as any boy.

Shocked and humiliated by her own naiveté, Ember had to admit that, while she had believed she would have to persuade Alistair that she had returned to Tearmunn for his sake as well as her sister's, she had never imagined that she would arrive to find him turned against her.

But what bothered her most of all was the kiss. It was too easy to remember the feeling of Alistair's mouth on hers and the way she'd responded. Ember recalled the first time Alistair had kissed her, how invasive his ardor had felt. This latest kiss Ember had wanted, but not because she wanted Alistair. In beating her down with his words, dashing her hopes to insinuate herself into his confidence, Alistair had rendered Ember a hollow shell, desperate to be filled with some affirmation. The kiss had served that purpose, and Ember was deeply shamed by her behavior.

Even so, she couldn't understand why the kiss had happened. As much as Ember longed for some sign that Alistair still cared for her, she hadn't brought her lips to his. Alistair had kissed her. If he despised her, as his words and manner implied, why would he want to kiss her like that? Perhaps, believing that Ember had at last returned his affections when his own had cooled, he'd offered the kiss as a final insult. A reminder of what she would now be denied.

The thought had been like a fist in her belly.

All Ember could do was wait for Alistair to return, and while she waited, she swore to herself that a scene like the first would never be acted out again.

But Alistair didn't return, leaving Ember to wonder if she was truly held captive in Tearmunn by her enemies or if she'd simply imprisoned herself.

Servants came and relocated Ember to chambers of her own. Bosque Mar did visit them again, informing Agnes and Ember that they were free to move through the manor as they pleased, but if they desired to go elsewhere in the keep, they must be accompanied.

Over the course of the next week, Ember and Agnes shared days that Agnes greeted with cheer and Ember found monotonous. While Alistair didn't appear, Lord Mar did visit them several times. On some occasions, he would converse with them for hours while Agnes embroidered and Ember sat with a needle and thread in her hands. Agnes chattered contentedly, showing no sign of being unnerved by the man's strange eyes or mysterious origin. Though Ember supposed Agnes knew nothing of Bosque's true nature, she nonetheless abhorred how easily Agnes accepted his invitations to walk the grounds of the keep or visit the scribes' library. For her own part, Ember found it difficult to speak at all in Bosque's presence. She made every effort to avoid making contact with his silver eyes. What Lord Mar's assessment of her was, Ember couldn't know.

When eight days had passed with no sign of Alistair, Ember began to wonder if he would ever visit again. Resting her forehead against the window, Ember stared down at the practice field. She watched pairs of the Guard battle each other. Her fingers twitched, wishing for the leather grips of Silence and Sorrow. She'd left her blades in Barrow's care, fearing that if they arrived with her at Tearmunn, the weapons would be lost forever.

Ember didn't turn at the light knock upon her door. "Come in, Agnes."

"My lady?" Ember whirled at the man's voice, the burgundy silk of her gown rustling with quick movement. A Guard stood in the open door. Ember worried at how many of the Guard were now strangers to her. Eira had been recruiting knights, expanding the Guard well beyond its traditional number.

"Your presence is required in the great hall." The Guard bid her follow him.

Ember left her room and descended the stairs at his heels. A flurry of possibilities swirled through her mind. Ember suspected any leniency she had been afforded upon her arrival had run its course and now she would face an interrogation.

The Guard opened one of the doors to the great hall, letting Ember pass, and closed it behind her. Only a few steps into the room, Ember froze, stunned by the changes that had taken place since her departure. Structurally, the room was the same, but had she not known that this had once been the Tearmunn hall in which she'd begun her initiation to Conatus, Ember might not have recognized it.

The hall had been transformed into a throne room, Lady Eira's throne room. The warrior woman sat in a high-backed chair elaborately carved from ebony. When Ember entered, Eira beckoned to her. Ember came forward but stopped again, gasping when she saw what stood directly behind the throne.

The cedar of Lebanon's lush green canopy was gone. The sacred tree's richly textured bark had been stripped away, as if the trunk and branches had been flayed. What stood in the tree's place was a monstrosity, pale as dry bones and devoid of life. At the base of the tree was a gaping wound. The tree's heart had been destroyed, leaving an empty carcass behind.

Gazing at the desecrated tree, Ember saw that what she'd assumed to be the gutted trunk teemed with movement. Shadows revealed edges of sickly green and dull bronze as they pooled and eddied within the dead tree.

"Welcome, Lady Morrow."

Ember gave a small cry, jumping away from Bosque Mar, who had appeared without warning beside her.

"I'm sorry to have startled you," Bosque said. His smile gave no sign of real concern for her. Pushing her forward, Bosque said, "You linger near the door when you've been invited to join us."

Ember walked quickly toward Eira so Bosque's hands would no longer be able to guide her. His touch made beads of cold sweat form on the back of her neck.

Ember's eyes kept returning to the nest of shadows that marred the sacred tree. Even without knowing what the darkness was, she feared it.

Alistair was standing at Eira's right hand. Bosque walked past Ember to take up a post on her left. Ember dared to look at Alistair; he met her gaze, but his face gave no indication as to whether he was pleased or displeased to see her. Ember couldn't stop herself from searching for any sign of emotion in Alistair's eyes, or any curve of his lips, and where there had been cold, heat immediately raced up her neck and into her cheeks. Staring at the floor, Ember clenched her fists. She didn't want to think about the kiss. She hadn't enjoyed it. Had she?

Keeping her head bowed, Ember didn't bother to turn when the door to the great hall opened and closed again.

"Ah, Father Michael. Thank you for coming." When Eira spoke the priest's name, Ember was so relieved, her knees threatened to cave. Gratitude filled her when Father Michael stopped at her side, holding her with his kind eyes.

"Good morning, my child."

Alistair had one arm propped on the top of Eira's throne. He leaned against the ornate chair, almost lounging. "Well, Father Michael, you said you had an urgent matter involving Lady Ember Morrow to discuss?"

Father Michael nodded. "I received a missive from Lord Mackenzie. He currently plays host to Ember's father and offers to act as a mediator between Lord Morrow and his elder daughter."

"To what purpose?" Eira asked the priest.

"The tongues of men love to wag over the misfortunes of their fellows," Father Michael answered. "Mackenzie knows of Agnes's sorrows and wishes to see her restored to her father's good will, provided for once again by her own family. Mackenzie has always been a clan leader who values loyalty over grudges. He believes it more honorable for Agnes and her unborn child to be acknowledged by her father than for Lord Morrow to continue to shame his own flesh and blood."

Bosque folded his arms across his chest. "And what does Lady Morrow think of this?"

"Of course I—"

"Lord Mar speaks of Agnes, not you," Alistair cut her off.

For a moment, Ember felt the rush of shame and confusion that had overwhelmed her when she'd last met Alistair, but before she pulled her eyes from him, she caught the way one corner of Alistair's mouth hooked up in pleasure at the way she reeled from his reproach.

Ember's self-doubt dwindled as outrage spread through her veins. Alistair was enjoying making her suffer. Wrapping her arms around her waist and bowing her head, Ember feigned the submission Alistair doubtless wanted to see. In truth, she was holding herself back, longing to pummel his smug face.

Still addressing Father Michael, Bosque said, "I've had the pleasure of spending many hours with Agnes and have found her to be quite happy here. Do you think it worthwhile to even attempt reuniting her with a father who has already shown his disregard for her?"

Ember listened to Bosque speak of Agnes with rising alarm. He showed far too much interest in Agnes's welfare, and Ember couldn't puzzle out why her sister would be of any consequence to him.

"There is wisdom in your counsel, Lord Mar," Father Michael answered. "But I am tasked to restore all lost sheep to the flock. Lord Morrow is quick-tempered and stubborn. He may well already regret his mistreatment of Agnes, but men too full of pride need help in righting the wrongs they've done. I would lend my aid to this cause and see the girl and her family reconciled."

"I won't send poor Agnes to a man who has abused her so," Alistair told the priest. "She is in good health and spirits here. If he harangues her again for her condition, it could endanger the lady and her child."

Father Michael bowed his head in assent. "Of course you're right, Lord Hart. That is why I ask to go as envoy to make peace with Lord Morrow. And I would bring Ember with me to speak on behalf of her sister."

"You want to take Ember to Mackenzie's castle?" Eira leaned forward on the throne, like a hawk looking down at prey from its perch.

"I am little more than a stranger to Lord Morrow," Father Michael said. "My words alone, I fear, cannot hope to soften his heart."

"But—" Ember hesitated; she looked to Father Michael with a frown. The thought of leaving the keep was more than appealing, though Ember feared she would put heels to her mount and run to the coast without looking back.

"Say your piece, Ember," Lady Eira ordered.

Keeping her eyes downcast to appear as timid as she could, Ember said, "I too would see my sister's honor restored and my family's wounds healed, but my own relations with my father are hardly ideal."

Father Michael touched her arm. When she lifted her eyes to meet his, she found his smile mischievous. "You forget your own transformation, Lady Morrow. Your father raged his way out of Tearmunn because you pledged yourself to the Guard. Now you've forsaken that role."

Ember nodded, and Father Michael said, "I remember that Lord Mackenzie once hoped you might become the wife of his son, Gavin. Perhaps that match could still be made, pleasing your father and Mackenzie."

"No!" Alistair straightened, all the haughtiness draining from his face. With that single word, Ember knew that Alistair had concealed his true feelings for her. Her pulse jumped both with renewed fury and a thrill of resolve. By letting his mask slip in that moment, he affirmed Ember's belief that she could make her way into his heart and thus be positioned to play a vital role when the moment of Eira's downfall was at hand.

Bosque checked Alistair with a stern look. Recovering his composure, Alistair said, "Ember remains under suspicion for colluding with traitors. Do you think marrying her off and releasing her from Tearmunn is wise?"

"Forgive me, Lord Hart," Father Michael replied, "but I'd been led to understand that Lady Morrow's story had been verified by the Circle at Cernon. Are you questioning their assessment?"

Though she wanted to smirk, Ember kept her face blank. Alistair glared at the priest, but didn't answer.

Father Michael took Ember's hands in his. "Would you consider making peace with your father by offering to marry Mackenzie's son and fulfilling his former wishes for you?" He squeezed her fingers tight, his gaze intent.

Ember's eyes widened at Father Michael's question. He'd planned for this moment, giving her an opening. Making them wait for her answer, Ember looked at her shoes and bit her lower lip while her fingers tangled together as if from anxiety.

"I would do this for my sister, if there is no other way." With those words, she stole a glance at Alistair.

As she anticipated, his gaze was fixed on her, fearful and hungry. When their eyes met, Alistair's lips parted, and he leaned forward as if he was about to come for her in that very moment.

Ember broke their gaze, returning to her timid pose.

"Lady Eira." Father Michael released Ember's hands and faced the throne. "Will you allow me to travel with Ember to Eilean Donan?"

When Eira hesitated, the priest added, "I've been told that a number of both the highland and lowland clan chiefs are assembled at the castle to settle disputes and discuss the succession. They offer a captive audience to which I could present the worthiness of your cause."

"I can handle the clans myself," Eira answered, her eyes narrowed.

"My lady, I have no doubt you can and will," Father Michael replied. He gestured to the empty chairs at the Circle's crescent table. "But you've sent the rest of the Circle as envoys into Europe and

Asia. I would speak for you closer to home if you would name me as another of your messengers."

Eira relaxed into her throne. "Very well, but I doubt you'll meet with success. Lord Morrow is a boor of a man. You can't travel without escort. Though I trust our brethren of Cernon, Lady Morrow's recent trespasses still cast doubt upon her. I wouldn't have you attacked on the road west and left for dead, Father."

Ember had to hold her breath so she wouldn't laugh at the suggestion that she could ever attack a man as good as Father Michael.

"I'll accompany them." Alistair had reassumed his disdainful attitude, but now that Ember knew his guise, she could look right through it. Still, she quickly averted her eyes and began to fidget as she had when he'd successfully undermined her sensibilities a week before. The more Alistair believed he was manipulating Ember, the better she could mold his actions to her own devices.

Father Michael took a step forward, lifting his hands imploringly as if begging for reprieve. "Lord Hart, I would not insult you, but consider this: we go to Lord Morrow in hopes of restoring his child. A daughter who has been shamed because of your brother's actions."

"I am not my brother," Alistair answered through gritted teeth.

"No one has suggested you are," Eira interjected. "But Father Michael is right. If you appear at Eilean Donan, all that will come of this is a brawl."

Silenced by Eira's judgment, Alistair went still, but his fists were clenched at his sides.

"I will serve as escort." Cian stepped from the shadows beneath the gallery, and Ember swallowed a gasp. Her attention had been held so fully by the transformation of the hall and those who stood at its center that she had never noticed Eira's sister lurking to the side of their conversation.

Cian approached Eira's throne, giving a short bow. "Like Father

Michael, I have not yet traveled as your envoy. I am happy to serve you thus now."

Ember was surprised when it was Lord Mar who answered Cian. "There is a reason you have not been sent abroad." His words carried more than the hint of an accusation.

Offering another stiff bow to Lord Mar, Cian said, "I have not adequately expressed my thanks for your patience regarding the oath."

"My patience is not endless," Bosque answered.

Eira raised her hand. "Stop this." She turned to Bosque, and an unspoken agreement seemed to pass between them.

Addressing her sister, Cian continued, "The clan chiefs know me. And as your sister they will acknowledge my right to speak for you."

Holding Cian in a speculative gaze, Eira finally said, "Yes." She looked to Father Michael. "When do you travel?"

"If it pleases you, I would travel on the morrow at dawn," Father Michael answered.

"Make your arrangements," Eira told him, then said to Ember, "Speak with your sister of these things. If she wishes to return to her family and Lord Morrow assents to reclaim her, I will send her to him, but I will not force her to return to a family that cast her off unless she chooses to go."

Ember nodded, taken aback by Eira's willingness to protect Agnes. The words weighed heavy on Ember's shoulders as she recalled why she had first admired Lady Eira. Though she could not understand the new course Eira plotted, Ember still saw the ferocity and determination that made Eira such a formidable warrior and exceptional leader.

"My lady." Ember made a low and graceful curtsy. Before she turned away, she let her gaze flicker to Alistair one last time. He watched her, eyes intent.

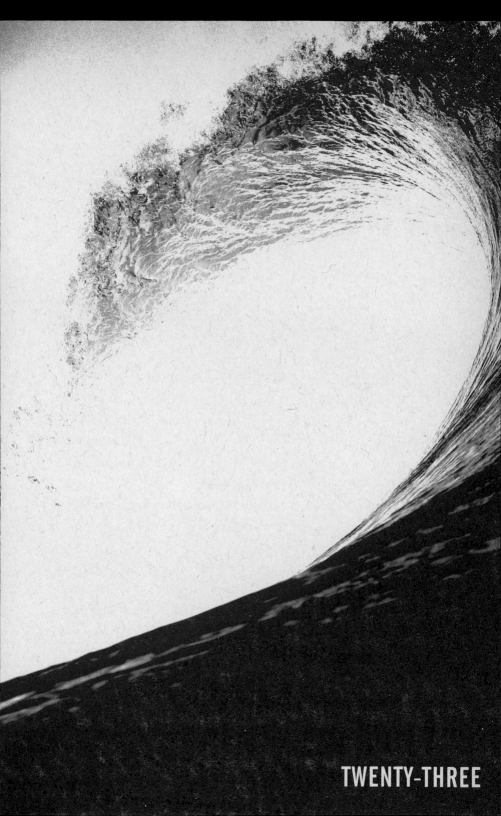

TWENTY-THREE

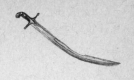

**LEAVING THE GREAT HALL** alone, Ember climbed the stairs slowly. With each step, her body felt more and more like it had been wrung out as clothes after washing. The stress of standing before Eira, Bosque, and Alistair, not knowing what they wanted of her, would have been enough, but new fissures in Ember's resolve were opening.

The small glimpse of Eira's former self had stirred Ember more than she wanted to admit. And witnessing the remnants of those characteristics Ember had envied in Eira provoked other memories she'd stored away. Memories of Alistair.

It was too easy to recall the joy she'd felt when he'd arrived at her father's manor, surprising her in the very place he'd secretly instructed her in swordsmanship. Her hopes for rising in Conatus had been hopes for both of them. Ember had always imagined they would fight together and care for each other, not as lovers but as friends. She knew Alistair had felt betrayed when she'd rejected his professions of love, but to Ember it was Alistair who had played the traitor. Alistair's desire for her forever altered their relationship. She could never return his feelings, and he would always resent her for that.

Though he had allied himself with Eira and Bosque, Ember couldn't forget the boy she'd grown up with. A boy she still cared for and was loath to hurt. The sweet triumph she'd known when she realized Alistair still loved her now tasted rotten. Yes, Ember would be able to go forward with her plan—a strategy that Lukasz, Kael, Father Michael, Cian, and even Barrow deemed cunning—but she couldn't stop the rising disgust she felt toward herself. Alistair's love had been twisted by his jealousy. It wasn't the love Barrow showed her; that rare passion that could only grow out of respect and admiration as well as the fire of attraction. But beneath the sullied layers of possessiveness and lust, Ember believed Alistair did love her. That love had spurred him to protect Agnes when most would have condemned her. Still, any warmth Ember felt toward Alistair was tempered by the likelihood that desire to protect his family name had also motivated him.

Nevertheless, that she must use Alistair's love as an implement of war unsettled her deeply. And yet Ember could see no other path.

"There you are!" Agnes peeked out of her room and rushed to meet Ember. "I've been waiting for you all morning."

"I was summoned to the great hall," Ember told her. "Will you sit with me? I must speak with you."

"Of course." Agnes beamed at her younger sister. "Let me get my sewing."

With a groan, Ember pushed through her chamber door, leaving it ajar for Agnes. She slumped into a chair, afloat in her growing self-pity.

Agnes closed the door behind her, settling into the chair beside Ember's.

"You shouldn't sit like that, Ember. It's uncomely. And you'll wrinkle your dress."

"I know" was all Ember said.

Shaking her head in disapproval, Agnes returned to her sewing.

"I'm riding with Lady Cian and Father Michael to the coast tomorrow," Ember told Agnes. "We're going to Mackenzie."

"At Eilean Donan?" Agnes's fingers flew as she embroidered, carrying on the conversation without erring on a single stitch. "Why do you go there?"

"Father is there," Ember said quietly.

Only a slight hitch in the rhythm of Agnes's needle and thread indicated her distress. "Is he?"

"Father Michael wishes to plead your case to him," Ember continued, watching Agnes closely. But Agnes didn't look up. Her face remained a picture of calm. "So you can be restored to our family and return to Father's estate."

"If Lady Eira and Lord Mar believe that wise, I am happy to go," Agnes said. "I miss Mother."

Ember frowned. "You don't question the counsel of Lord Mar?" Lady Eira didn't trouble Ember half as much.

"Why should I?" Agnes's needle slid up and down, up and down. "He has shown me nothing but kindness. I am grateful for him."

Ember sputtered. "You are a simpering child, Agnes. Have you nothing more to say about your own future than to leave such decisions to a stranger? How can you spend each day happy? Is all you need from life a spool of thread and a silver needle?"

The needle stopped. When Agnes looked up, Ember barely recognized her sister's face. Gone was her pacific smile; the rosy glow of her skin had dimmed.

"You have always been impetuous, Ember," Agnes snapped, "but I never thought you a fool."

Staring at Agnes in disbelief, Ember was rendered speechless. Agnes, it seemed, still had plenty of words to offer.

"Do you think I take pleasure in this?"

Ember shrank back as Agnes threw her embroidery the full length of the room.

"I—"

"Do you know what it is like to carry the child of a man who cast you off and yet still feel love for him?" Agnes hissed. "Do you think I can help but hate myself for that?

"I have nothing," Agnes continued, her voice quiet with rage. "No title. No family. I have no means to provide for myself or my child. I came to Tearmunn a beggar, carried here by a nag purchased with the little money Mother secreted to me before Father drove me from his home."

Agnes cupped her face in her hand, recomposing her expression into that open, innocent beauty that had drawn praise as long as Ember could remember. "I wear this mask because it is all I have to barter with. Would Alistair have taken me in if I came to him bearing bitterness and a withered spirit?"

Ember reached for Agnes's hands, but Agnes drew them back. "I feign happiness, for it is the only kind of joy that I have."

Though she tried to fight it, Ember's eyes flitted over her sister's belly.

With a broken smile, Agnes said, "No. I do not hate the child." She laid her palm against the swell of her abdomen. "Though I am ashamed that I cannot forget my love for Henry, because he doesn't deserve it, this child is innocent of his father's sin. I shall not forget that."

Agnes looked away, and her voice hardened. "And because of that, I will go wherever Eira wishes to send me, so long as I can find protection for me and my child. Whether that is to remain here, to return to Father's house, or to be packed off by him to become another man's wife—if any man would suffer to raise a bastard."

"Agnes!" Ember had never heard anything resembling a curse pass from Agnes's lips.

"Is it too much to bear when I speak the truth, dear sister?" Agnes said, chastising Ember with her gaze. "Shall I return to wearing my mask for you?"

Ember threw herself at Agnes. Tears welled in Ember's eyes.

"Why have you kept this from me? I love you. Have I been so poor a sister?"

With a sigh, Agnes touched Ember's cheek. "My love for you kept me from burdening you with my heartaches."

"Your pains are mine." Ember laid her head in Agnes's lap. "I would help you bear them."

"Oh, Ember." Agnes's voice was thick, but when Ember looked up, her sister's eyes were dry. Tracing the line of Ember's tears with her fingertips, she said, "I have no tears left, I think."

Her voice dropping to a hush, Agnes said to Ember, "Please don't pity me. I couldn't bear the shame of it."

"Never," Ember promised. Taking Agnes's hands, Ember said, "I must tell you something—"

She fell silent, hearing footsteps approaching the door. Ember quickly rose, rubbing her tear-stained cheeks. Agnes also stood up and hurried to collect the embroidery she'd thrown across the room.

The sound stopped, and both women looked to the door, but the knock they waited for didn't come. Instead Ember heard a faint rustling on stone.

"Oh!" Agnes picked up the scrap of parchment slipped under Ember's door before Ember had identified the source of the quiet sound.

"Do you often receive notes in this manner?" Agnes raised her brow.

Ember hadn't received any anonymous notes. That was part of the reason she was so eager to get her hands on the one Agnes had claimed.

Holding out her hand, Ember said crossly, "Give it to me."

"That's very rude," Agnes chastised Ember in a mocking tone. "I think I should read it, don't you?"

Ember frowned at Agnes, surprised by her sudden change in demeanor. "Are we simply moving on, then?"

"There's nothing more to say, Ember." A bit of sadness crept back into Agnes's voice.

But there was more to say. Before the note's writer had approached her door, Ember had been on the verge of confessing everything: Eira, Bosque, Barrow, Alistair—the coming violence Ember saw no way to avoid. By remaining at Tearmunn, Agnes would be in terrible danger. Agnes had to know the truth. But now Ember could only think of what might be written on the parchment in her sister's hand.

Agnes continued, "I will not act the helpless, fallen woman in your company any longer. Not when it's only the two of us."

"Good."

Without warning, Ember leapt forward and snatched the parchment from Agnes's fingers, twisting away from her sister and skipping across the room in victory. Agnes didn't bother to attempt to retrieve it.

"I'd ask what it says, but I know you won't tell me." Agnes went to the door. "I'm in need of a nap as it is."

"Agnes, wait," Ember said, then she glanced down at the note in her hand.

Standing with the door partly opened, Agnes looked back at Ember, her eyes questioning.

"Never mind," Ember mumbled, her eyes fixed on the parchment. "It's nothing."

Agnes closed the door, leaving Ember alone. Numbness crept over her skin, and she went to sit on the edge of her bed. She gazed at the single line of words scratched in ink on the parchment.

*Come to me in the great hall when the others have sought their beds.*

The note wasn't signed. Nor did it need to be.

TWENTY-FOUR

**WELL AFTER NIGHTFALL,** Alistair still wondered if leaving Ember a note had been a mistake. He didn't know what he would say to her. What he would do. But Alistair had been consumed by the notion that he couldn't let Ember leave Tearmunn without speaking to her first. Going to Ember's room would have been easier, but he needed her to come to him.

The manor corridors were quiet but for Alistair's footfall. He opened one of the doors to the great hall, but left it slightly ajar as he entered—a signal to Ember that he was within. Lacking torches or daylight, the empty hall proved as eerie as the catacombs in which Alistair spent most of his time.

Thin beams of moonlight cast their glow on the stained-glass windows, rendering colors dusky as wilted flowers. The moon's pale face offered light enough to see, but Alistair's gaze was drawn to another light source.

Walking toward the skeletal tree, Alistair peered into the rift. He'd been reluctant to examine it closely, knowing it was a gateway between worlds. Alistair had no desire to risk being dragged from the earth into the nether from which Bosque hailed. Alistair associated the rift with darkness, but by cover of night he witnessed the subtle play of light within the undulating shadows. Metallic threads appeared and disappeared within the gaping hole, chasing one another like glowing minnows in a black pond.

"Alistair?"

Ember hesitated in the doorway, the torchlight from the corridor outlining her body.

Alistair cleared his throat and took a deep breath before he answered, "Here."

Closing the door, Ember took cautious steps into the hall.

"Your eyes will adjust to the dimness," Alistair told her. His voice was steady, unlike the thrumming of his heart. She'd come. But now what?

Ember stopped just short of Alistair, but she looked past him at the rift. "What is it?"

"A door between worlds," Alistair answered. "Eira opened it to seal our fate with Lord Mar's."

Nodding slowly, Ember said, "He is not of this world."

"Has it taken you so long to realize that?" Alistair meant to tease Ember, but she flinched. He'd been too harsh with her, and now like a pup that had been beaten, she expected more abuse.

Alistair tried to make up for his gaffe by giving her an answer. "By joining forces with Lord Mar, Eira has increased our power beyond imagining. The beasts we once fought now serve us. It is truly a marvelous thing."

Ember didn't answer, but she stared at the ripples of light that moved through Bosque's gateway.

Finally she looked at Alistair. "You asked me to come here."

"I know." His throat tightening, Alistair hunted for his next move.

Ember's fingers laced together, twisting nervously against her gown. "I am sorry to have earned your hate, Alistair. I never meant it to be so."

Her words surprised Alistair enough to keep him silent, and she spoke again.

"I've watched for you on the practice field each day from my window, but have yet to find you there."

"I rarely take to the field," Alistair told her. "Bosque has given me a more important task that consumes my days."

Ember spoke with hesitation, her voice just quiet enough to show submission. "I wanted to see you and had given up hope that you would visit me."

"You wanted me to return to you?" Alistair asked.

Ember stared at her tangled fingers. "Only to tell you that I understand why your heart turned from me. I was naive to convince myself it could be otherwise."

Letting her words sink in, Alistair turned the conversation in another direction. "Do you look forward to visiting Eilean Donan?"

"I shall enjoy the ride and the highland air," Ember said. "I do not relish my father's company."

"And Gavin Mackenzie?" Alistair watched Ember's face closely, seeking any reaction.

"I've never met Lord Mackenzie's son," Ember answered, dropping her gaze. "I know not what to expect."

Alistair lowered his voice. "I remember a time when you agreed to run away with me rather than be married off by your father."

Ember began to smile, but the small sign of mirth quickly vanished. "I had reason to choose my words with less care. I no longer have the luxury of flouting my father's plans."

"You'll assent to him, then." Alistair had trouble controlling the anger that boiled under his skin. "And marry as he commands."

"What am I to do other than marry?" Ember cried, walking away from him. "I no longer fight with the Guard. I forsook my place in Conatus. The only advantage I have over Agnes is that no man's child grows in my belly."

"If you must marry, then marry me," Alistair said hoarsely, reeling from his own outburst.

Ember went very still.

Blood roared in Alistair's ears. What had he done other than give her another opportunity to crush his hopes? While she stood silently, her face hidden from him, Alistair ground his teeth.

"You are cruel to taunt me," Ember finally whispered.

A wave of emotions crashed through Alistair. He grasped Ember's shoulders, turning her to face him. "I say this truly." Alistair cupped her chin in his hand. "Marry me."

"After all that's happened"—Ember's voice shook—"everything I've done, you would still take me as your wife?"

"I have loved you since I was a boy." He stroked her hair; its fiery shade had become raven in the low light. "I can hardly remember a day before I loved you."

Ember looked down. Tears caught in her lashes before trailing over her pale skin.

Bending to her, Alistair tasted the salt water on her cheeks. He brought his lips to hers, a gentle touch. Ember's mouth opened, and he drank in her breath. Alistair kissed her slowly, waiting with each movement for Ember to respond. When she returned his embrace, Alistair struggled for control. He wanted to take her. All of her.

But he'd erred in that way before. Pushed her too soon. The wisest choice Alistair had made about Ember was letting her go. She couldn't be ruled, at least not knowingly. When Alistair had acted as the aggressor, Ember had pushed him away, thinking him a tyrant. Now he was her champion, and she welcomed his kiss.

Knowing these things, Alistair pulled Ember's arms from around his neck and forced her to take a step back.

"Will you let your father make you the wife of Gavin Mackenzie?"

Ember shook her head. "I will only become the wife of Alistair Hart."

"Ember," Alistair breathed.

"I will marry you, Alistair." When Ember reached for him, Alistair didn't try to stop her. When she lifted her face, he kissed her. Overwhelmed by the taste of her, the softness of her skin, Alistair gave in to his craving for Ember. His lips moved down her neck, lingering at her throat. But when his hands molded to the swell of her breasts, Ember stiffened.

"Are you afraid?" Alistair didn't move his hands, but kept them still. He could feel her heart racing. "Because it is not in my mind to hurt you, my love."

Ember swallowed hard, her pulse jumping at her throat. Not wanting to push her too far, and reminding himself that Ember was still a maid, Alistair conquered his impulse and slid his hands to her waist. Her breath eased, and Alistair kissed her tenderly.

"You have nothing to fear from me," he murmured against her lips. "I only want to please you."

She nodded, and he returned to the path his lips had taken over her skin. Then he knelt before her.

"Ember." Alistair wrapped his arms around her thighs, his cheek pressed to her stomach. He closed his eyes, reveling in the gentle tousling of her fingers in his hair. "My Ember."

For the first time Alistair could remember, he basked in the sense that all was as it should be.

"I don't want to leave you." Ember's voice was thick, whether with desire or regret Alistair couldn't tell. "But I must return to my chamber and ready for travel. We leave at dawn."

Alistair rose and kissed Ember once more. "Of course. We will speak more of this when you return."

Ember nodded and lifted his hand to her lips. "I am unworthy of your steadfast love."

After she'd kissed his palm, Ember stole from the room. Alistair stood quietly. He could still taste her, smell her. Alistair wanted to hold on to this night forever.

"Well done, Lord Hart."

Where Alistair would have sworn only shadows had been, Bosque stood.

"How long have you been here?" Alistair stared at the tall man.

"I am often here when I am not needed elsewhere." Bosque smiled at him. "You must be very pleased, having won your prize."

Alistair risked speaking in anger, realizing that Bosque had witnessed the entirety of his meeting with Ember. "You should have made yourself known. These were private moments."

Still smiling, Bosque shook his head. "It is unwise to keep secrets from me, Alistair. Our aims are so intertwined."

When Alistair didn't reply, Bosque said, "Will you truly begrudge my interest in your happiness?"

The initial shock of Bosque's appearance fading, Alistair quelled his objections. "I would be grateful if you didn't make a habit of spying on me."

"I wasn't hiding from you," Bosque answered. "You were the one too occupied with his own thoughts to notice I was in the room."

"That's one way of looking at it," Alistair said drily.

"It is," Bosque replied. "I am glad for your new arrangement with Lady Morrow. Upon her return, you must discover what you can about this journey she makes to the Mackenzie stronghold."

"Does it concern you?" Alistair asked. "A single word from you would have prevented their trip."

"To stop them is not my desire," Bosque told him. "I've often reaped greater rewards by assisting my adversaries instead of hindering them. The closer they are to their goal, the more likely they'll reveal their intentions."

Alistair glanced at the door, his happiness compromised by the implications of Bosque's words. "You think Ember is your adversary?"

"No," Bosque answered. "I'm not certain what your Lady Morrow is to me yet. My concern is with another woman."

"Cian?" Alistair went rigid. "My lord, I know Cian has been reluctant to embrace you, but she is Lady Eira's own blood."

"That is why she may be a threat," Bosque said. "Cian holds Eira back, encourages her to question me. She seeks to impede our work."

"Are you certain Cian wishes to undermine you?" Alistair asked. "She has a cautious spirit. I doubt her hesitation regarding the changes in Conatus are anything more than a reflection of that trait."

"I hope you're right," Bosque answered. "Learn what you can from Ember."

"Your will, Lord Mar." Alistair inclined his head, starting toward the door.

"Before you seek your bed—"

Alistair turned, wondering if Bosque ever slept. "Yes?"

Bosque walked toward the rift, gazing at it with what appeared to be longing. "It's good that you have what you want, but I spoke in truth when I said I haven't yet discerned what Ember's place will be among us. Don't let your heart run ahead of your instincts."

TWENTY-FIVE

**THAT THE CHILD HAD TO** die made Alistair uneasy, but he understood the necessity of it. He'd been relieved that Hamish had taken it upon himself to select the boy out of the six children, two girls and four boys all between one and three years of age, that had been stolen from the village. Alistair didn't know that he would have had the stomach for it. At least the toddler's death had been as kind as it could be. After the boy had been lulled to sleep by one of the cleric's tonics, Hamish had smothered the slumbering child.

Though the day's work was hardly pleasant, Alistair was grateful for it. The import of this task kept his mind from wandering to the previous night and his rancor over having finally won Ember's love only to have her ride away from him for several days.

While Alistair watched, Hamish set about draining all the blood from the boy's corpse. The young wolf beside Alistair sniffed the air, licking its muzzle at the scent of fresh blood.

"That's not for you." Alistair crouched beside the wolf, and it turned to lick his cheeks, making Alistair laugh.

Lord Mar stood near the sarcophagus, opposite Hamish.

"Will it hurt the wolf?" Alistair asked Bosque.

"The change will be confusing and no doubt unpleasant," Bosque answered. "But if Hamish is successful, no harm will come to the beast."

Alistair frowned, looking into the juvenile wolf's golden eyes. He held out his arm so the wolf could chew at the thick leather gauntlet Alistair wore. This wolf had five brothers and sisters. If Hamish failed, the work would continue. But Alistair had grown deeply attached to the cubs—all of which had grown from yipping balls of fur into gangly pups. He would mourn the loss of any of them.

Watching Alistair with the wolf, Bosque said, "Don't fear for your children, Alistair. Hamish will not fail. Will you, Hamish?"

Hamish grunted in reply, swapping a bowl brimming with blood for an empty one.

Knight and cleric had gone together seeking Bosque's advice. Alistair's work with the wolf cubs couldn't have been more edifying. That Bosque had described them as Alistair's children uncannily echoed the feelings that Alistair harbored for the wolves. He spent each day with them. He fed them, played with them, let them huddle around him when they tired of their wrestling and drifted to sleep.

Hamish's endeavors offered an opposite result. Despite his tireless studies and innovations with the trials, Hamish could not manifest a viable form of Alistair's vision. With each new attempt came new failures. Alistair and Hamish consulted, found fresh inspirations, and strove to complete their work again. And again they failed.

When Alistair decided Hamish teetered on the edge of madness because of his frustrations, the knight brought Hamish to Lord Mar. Bosque accompanied them to the catacombs to observe their work.

"I see the problem," Bosque told them within minutes of examining Hamish's notes and the outcomes of his trials.

"You do?" Hamish tugged at his ruddy, gray-streaked hair. From the look of it, Hamish hadn't picked up a comb in weeks.

Nodding, Bosque said, "Two bodies cannot exist in same space. Each will struggle against the other for dominance until they are both destroyed. That's what's happened here."

A strangling whine poured out of Hamish's throat. "Then we

attempt all in vain. Why did you not tell us that Alistair's creation has always been an impossibility?"

"Because it is not," Bosque told him. "You're simply viewing the world in too limited a way."

Since Hamish's eyes were bulging dangerously at the suggestion that his thinking was limited, Alistair quickly said, "What do you mean, Lord Mar?"

"You've been trying to force wolf and man into a single being in this world," Bosque answered. "When your very ability to manifest this creature requires the aid of two worlds."

"But we have your blood," Hamish spluttered.

"You're not using it correctly."

Alistair put his hand on Hamish's shoulder, restraining a further outburst.

"You only think of my blood for its value in letting the beasts restore their health," Bosque continued. "But you forget the other purpose it serves."

"The gate," Alistair said quietly.

Bosque smiled at him. "Of course. Consider the blood oath that all who follow Eira must take. Blood binds us together, strengthens the channel that flows between my world and yours."

Hamish's white-faced disbelief began to wane as fascination overtook him. "Bodies between worlds?"

"Yes." Bosque picked up a piece of parchment, gazing at the monstrous images Hamish had drawn. "The wolf in one, the man in the other."

"How can a creature be thus divided?" Hamish asked, a fever burning in his eyes. He grasped a blank parchment and quill. "Would it not be driven mad to exist in two planes?"

"Only the body is divided," Bosque answered. "Mind and spirit are always present in the body that lives in the active plane."

"The active plane?" Alistair frowned.

"The worlds where men and beasts are born, live, and die," Bosque explained. "Where we carve our wills into the fabric of existence."

Setting Hamish's bizarre sketches aside, Bosque said, "Your wolves will be created to serve you here, in this world. But the body that waits, a hollow vessel until filled with mind and spirit once again, must bide its time in an empty plane."

"Such places exist?" Hamish scribbled notes as Bosque spoke.

"Lord Hart has visited one such place several times."

"I have?" Alistair looked at Bosque in surprise.

Bosque laughed. "When you rode the shadow steed or traveled in the mist alongside me. The space between, which speeds the journey, is an empty plane. And that is the place you must invoke to bring your vision to life."

Hamish dropped his quill as his fingers trembled. "Can I accomplish this task?"

"I would not have sent you to Lord Hart had I any doubt that you could. The premise isn't difficult," Bosque told Hamish. "In the magics you've practiced, you could take from the earth but only if you gave in return. Now you will take what you need but keep it."

His bushy eyebrows hunching together, Hamish said, "Forgive me, my lord. I do not understand."

"How did you weave your portals?" Bosque asked. "Recite the principles to me."

"The old magic of Conatus was based in the elements of earth," Hamish answered, regret creeping into his words. "The doors could be woven by pulling various threads of those elements together, honoring the connections that bind the whole world together, like the roots of a single great tree."

Alistair ground his teeth as an unwanted memory of the sacred cedar flashed into his mind. The tree had been a living symbol of that magic before it had been altered to serve Bosque.

"To complete your work, you will again be pulling threads," Bosque told Hamish. "But instead of using threads from the earth, you will unravel the threads of life. You will take the essence of a creature's being and bind it to the body of another."

"Bind the wolf to the man?" Hamish spoke in awe. "But the bodies remain separate."

Bosque nodded, smiling in approval at the cleric. "The receiving vessel must be empty—the spirit gone and the blood drained. The wolf lives, its essence possessing the body."

"Why the blood?" Alistair asked.

"Blood binds, as I've already said," Bosque answered. "The emptied body will have to be infused with my blood to gain entry to the empty plane."

Turning his gaze on Hamish, Bosque asked, "Do you understand?"

Hamish nodded eagerly.

"Then let us see to it." Bosque led them from the room that reeked of death to the main chamber of the catacombs.

Now they stood around the sarcophagus, waiting for the child's body to give up the last of its blood.

"There," Hamish said, setting a third brimming bowl to the side. Taking a long, hollowed needle that was thin as a hair at its point and wide as a man's hand at its base, Hamish pierced the center of the boy's chest with its tip. With careful taps he hammered the slender spike into the child's heart. Keeping the needle in place with one hand, Hamish set a funnel over the base and looked at Bosque.

Holding his hand over the funnel, Bosque used a dagger to open a deep gash in his palm. His blood welled, dripping into the funnel. Bosque allowed his blood to run freely for about a minute before he closed his hand.

"That will be enough," he told them, looking at Alistair. "Now the wolf."

Alistair nodded, though his jaw was clenched. He moved around the sarcophagus to stand beside Hamish; the wolf followed.

Going to one knee beside the young wolf, Alistair said in a firm voice, "Be still."

The wolf watched him, ears perked up in curiosity. Alistair reached around the wolf, looping his arms around its back and chest. The wolf's tail began to wag in anticipation of a wrestling match.

Alistair looked at Hamish and nodded. The cleric's motions were somewhat familiar, like the dance that wove a door, but altered. Hamish moved more slowly than a weaving cleric would. His arms swept through the air in deliberate motions, as if he were gathering objects invisible to the rest of them.

Clasped in Alistair's arms, the wolf growled and then began to whine. Steeling himself, Alistair tightened his hold on the beast as it began to struggle. Its whining became more urgent. Alistair made soothing sounds, hoping to calm the wolf. He knew it didn't help that his pulse was flying, which the wolf could surely feel.

The wolf stopped squirming but continued to whine, the sound of its distress growing softer, but more plaintive. Alistair bent his head, thinking that if he laid his cheek against the wolf's shoulders, it might soothe the beast. But as he did so, the animal in his arms began to glow. The wolf's gray fur glimmered, becoming molten silver.

"Let the beast go," Hamish said, sweat pouring down his face. "The wolf must take possession of the empty body that awaits it."

Alistair released the cub, and it rose into the air. Where fur, flesh, and bone had been now was a creature of pure light, as if the moon had given birth to a wolf. While Hamish filled the air with a steady stream of chanting, the wolf cub floated away from Alistair to hover over the sarcophagus. It began to descend, and when its gleaming paws met with the dead child's cold skin, the wolf vanished.

Hamish dropped his hands and bent over, coughing and gasping for breath. Alistair leapt up and went to the sarcophagus. The child's eyes widened before it opened its mouth and began to wail in fear. Alistair gave a low cry when he noticed the boy's golden irises. The boy turned at the sound, his frightened gaze finding Alistair standing beside him.

Holding his breath, Alistair stretched his arms out to the crying child. Without hesitation, the boy crawled into his embrace.

TWENTY-SIX

**PERCHED AT THE JUNCTION** of Loch Duich and Loch Aish, the Mackenzie castle called Eilean Donan kept watch over land and sea. Cian, Father Michael, and Ember rode in silence, their mounts' hooves clopping on the stone bridge that joined the mainland to the castle's small isle.

The journey from Tearmunn amounted to less than a half day's ride, but for Ember the trip wore on and on. While the horse she rode upon was a sensible palfrey with a smooth gait, Ember missed Caber's lively spirit. Her companions traveled in silence, not deigning to speak of their errand to the western lord's castle nor of any other matters that burdened Ember's thoughts.

At several points on the road, Ember had looked at Father Michael with the intention of telling him about Alistair's proposal, seeking his advice as to how she should proceed. But Ember found that she struggled to bring any words from her throat. She didn't question the result of her meeting with Alistair in the great hall the night before, but speaking the words aloud made them real in a way Ember wasn't prepared to face. She had played upon Alistair's affections and earned the result she desired, but now Ember wasn't sure she knew what that would mean.

Mackenzie's stable hands awaited the riders inside the castle gate. When they had dismounted, one of Mackenzie's warriors escorted them to Eilean Donan's main hall. The somber gray stone of the keep enclosed corridors lined with dark wood, giving the castle an air of solemnity.

The hall into which they were led would have been dwarfed by Tearmunn's great hall, yet the room was filled to bursting with people. Ember saw quickly that not only were a handful of clan chiefs in attendance, but they had also brought large contingents of their warriors. Searching the crowd for her father, Ember couldn't find him or Lord Mackenzie. But among the clansmen, three figures stood out to her, all wearing dress that identified them as hailing from the kingdoms of the east.

Two of them were men, each wearing a steel helm with a spike at the crown of the head and a train of chain mail that covered his neck and shoulders. Their long, colorful robes offered only glimpses of the plate mail gauntlets and greaves beneath. Their female companion wore a flowing gray gown that fit more loosely than the European fashion. Her hair, neck, and shoulders were covered by a pale blue headscarf.

Beside Ember, Cian murmured, "They have come. I dared not hope it was true."

"Who are they?" Ember asked.

"The men are Mamluks," Cian answered. "The woman is a cleric; they secreted her to us at great risk to themselves."

"We aren't here to meet my father, are we?" Ember asked.

"Your father is here, and we will discuss Agnes with him," Cian told her. "But that meeting provided the excuse for our real reasons to journey here."

Father Michael had already pushed his way through the crowd to greet the strangers. The priest and the woman embraced, and Father Michael beckoned to Cian and Ember.

"Lady Ember Morrow and Lady Cian." Father Michael presented the two women. "Please meet Lord Kurjii and Lord Tamur, of the

Krak des Chevaliers Guard, and their most revered cleric, Lady Rebekah."

Kurjii and Tamur offered crisp bows. The knights reminded Ember of falcons, with their clear, sharp eyes and the talonlike sabers belted at their waists. The sight of the wicked, curving blades, so like Barrow's sword, made Ember's chest pinch. Rebekah's hair was dark brown shot through with threads of silver, her face deeply lined, and Ember guessed she was only a few years younger than Father Michael.

Ember curtsied, and Cian returned their bow.

"It's an honor," Cian said to Kurjii and Tamur. "Your reputations in the field proceed you."

"As does yours," Tamur answered. "And your sister's."

Kurjii nodded grimly. "We're deeply grieved that she has been seduced by this nether creature, Bosque Mar."

"He grows bolder by the day," Cian replied. "The way he looks at my sister terrifies me. She believes he answers her commands, but he thinks only to rule her."

"From what we've been able to discover of Bosque Mar, your suspicions are true," Rebekah told her.

Father Michael clasped his hands together prayerfully. "God be praised. You have found something, then?"

Rebekah smiled at the priest, but it wasn't a mirthful expression. "We have, but I fear we don't bring good tidings."

"But you have found a way to defeat him?" Cian asked the cleric.

"Possibly," Rebekah answered. "But only by cobbling together lore from some of the most ancient texts in our archives. There is no way to be certain it will conquer him."

"How is it that you've come here?" Ember asked.

Kurjii and Tamur exchanged a glance, and Cian said, "Ember is one of the Guard, forced to hide her true allegiance for our purpose. You may speak freely."

With a curt nod, Tamur said, "Hiding is what many are forced to do now. Those who openly hold to the true mission of Conatus have been labeled traitors. They rot in our dungeons. Or worse."

"Worse?" Ember asked.

"Lady Eira's clerics-turned-conjurers demand allegiance while shadow beasts hover at their side," Kurjii said, mouth turned down in disgust. "Any who resist or refuse to swear their fealty to her rule of our order are handed to the wraiths. Most who witness the torment abandon their convictions in order to avoid a similar fate."

Tamur sighed. "Upon their first arrival, Eira's emissaries implied the oath taking would be voluntary, but now they have no qualms about forcing an immediate choice. The orders came from Eira that any who question or delay joining with her are enemies. She dismantles a resistance before it can be gathered."

"Then what are you?" Ember asked Tamur. "If not resistance?"

"The last chance." Rebekah answered Ember, though her gaze met Father Michael's. "Before Conatus is lost."

A stirring of the crowd near the hall entrance turned Ember's attention to the door. The gathered warriors quieted, stepping back as Lord Mackenzie entered the room with Ember's father at his side.

But Ember's eyes fixed upon the trio that followed the two Scottish lords.

Tamur leaned forward, murmuring into her ear, "You asked how it was that we came here, Lady Morrow. It was due to the efforts of your former companions."

Lukasz, Kael, and Barrow halted just inside the door. Lord Mackenzie lifted his hands, commanding the attention of all assembled.

Paying the clan chief no mind, Ember was already pushing her way past burly warriors, elbowing them roughly to get through. As men grunted when she jostled and shoved them, Ember's advance gained notice.

Barrow saw her trying to reach him. His face paled, and he ran forward. Ember broke through the crowd and then she was in Barrow's arms. With the castle's lord, her father, and a hundredsome of Scotland's battle-hardened men watching, Ember drew Barrow's face to hers. Barrow held her gaze for a moment before he kissed her. Her fingers dug into his shoulders as she breathed the scent of his skin.

They only parted when Kael said loudly, "And I thought we'd come here to fight."

His words didn't make Ember blush, and while she forced herself to step out of the embrace, she took Barrow's hand, holding it tight, needing to feel that he was here, alive, safe.

"Well, then." Lord Mackenzie nodded at Barrow. "At least not all of the day's talk will be of sorrow."

Ember risked looking at her father. To her surprise, he hadn't transformed into a red-faced troll, but instead appeared to be on the verge of laughter. When he winked at Ember, she gasped.

Following her gaze, Barrow whispered, "I've been speaking with your father and am happy to report I'm out of his ill favor, as are you."

Ember glanced up at him, wondering exactly what Barrow had told her father.

"Would you like to kiss the lass again, Lord Hess?" Lord Mackenzie called to Barrow with a guffaw. "Or can we get to the business of war?"

Hearty laughter filled the room, and Barrow said, "I will always want to kiss the lady Morrow, but out of respect to your lordship, I will wait . . . for a while."

At that, Ember did blush, and the warriors roared, snickering and slapping one another on the back. Ember ducked her head, but Barrow slid his arm around her waist, holding her close.

"Rebekah!" Lord Mackenzie stretched his hand out, and the cleric came to join him. Addressing the crowd, Mackenzie said,

"Though I am proud to call myself chief of my clan, I am not such a fool as to believe myself master of spirits and devils. Whenever those foul things that are not men, yet prey upon them, have troubled those under my protection, I have called upon Conatus for aid. Now the very order that has kept the darkest of things from infesting our lands falls under the sway of nefarious forces."

Lord Mackenzie's arm swept the room. He paused to point at Father Michael, Cian, the Mamluk knights, Ember and Barrow, and lastly, Kael and Lukasz.

"A few brave souls would resist this rising dark that threatens not only their order but the future of all men. I have called you to this keep asking that your brawn and steel join in their fight."

His face darkening, the clan chief continued, "You may notice that not all of your clan brethren are here. Some have already pledged their hearts to Lady Eira and her devilish hordes. But I know each of you, know that your clans have been steadfast in the old ways. This new, rising tide will drown us all. Those who welcome it are fools."

A somber, but affirming titter passed through the crowd and Mackenzie nodded, pleased.

The Scottish lord pushed warriors aside until he stood next to Rebekah. Resting his hand on her shoulder, the clan chief said, "This woman brings us hope. Words drawn from the oldest of faiths and the chance to beat back wickedness that would rule us."

Bowing to Rebekah, Mackenzie stepped back, and the cleric lifted her voice.

"They surround man on all sides as the earth does the roots of the vine; a thousand are on his left, and ten thousand on his right side."

Pausing, Rebekah let her audience absorb the words, then said, "So our sacred texts speak of demons."

Warriors shifted nervously, glancing around the room as if the hordes Rebekah spoke of might materialize at any moment.

"We make the mistake of presuming that the worlds invisible to us can be nothing like this earth," Rebekah told them. "But through our study, we know that those strange worlds touching ours should be seen as a darker reflection of our own. We know well how kings and princes strive for power. When has there been a time without war in the land?"

Murmurs and nods answered her.

"So it is for those creatures that inhabit the nether realm," Rebekah said. "Like ours, their lives are ordered. Some beasts live like peasants, others make war in the way of knights. And like us, they serve at the pleasure of kings."

Rebekah bowed her head, as if overcome by great sadness. "One of our sisters has fallen under the sway of such a creature: a king of the nether who seeks to win the wars of his world by infiltrating ours. Lady Eira serves a creature who names himself Lord Bosque Mar. It is he whom we must defeat."

A grizzled warrior with two axes strapped across his back called out, "I do not like what Lady Eira has done, but we have all heard the tales of the shadow army she can summon. This creature she serves imbues her with power. All say that she is become invincible."

"No weapon can harm her wraiths!" another warrior shouted. "If we go to war against Eira, we offer ourselves up for slaughter."

Uneasy whispers and sullen expressions followed the objections.

Mackenzie motioned for silence. "Our swords may not kill these creatures, but Rebekah offers a way by which we may drive them back whence they came."

"How?" The question was shouted from somewhere in the crowd.

"The oldest of magics, drawn from the earth herself," Rebekah replied. "Any who ally themselves with Eira are tainted. The power upon which they draw is a disease to this world, and the earth would see the infection purged. Bosque Mar gained purchase of this world by opening a gate to the nether—a rift torn in the fabric of creation. We must heal the wound and thereby rid ourselves of this plague."

"We are not magicians," the ax-bearing warrior objected.

Mackenzie replied to him, "Nor need we be. But the gate of which Rebekah speaks lies within Tearmunn."

"Do you suggest we lay siege to Tearmunn?" the warrior shot back. "Eira will summon her wraiths to destroy us before we reach the keep's walls."

Nodding gravely, Mackenzie answered, "Your words are true. The attack must be a surprise, or we are defeated before the battle begins."

The room grew quiet. Ember looked at the stern but fearful faces of the assembled warriors and set her jaw, knowing what she had to do.

Slipping away from Barrow, Ember took a few steps toward the clan chief. "If I may, Lord Mackenzie."

"Lady Morrow?" Mackenzie's bushy eyebrows went up in surprise.

Ember's heart was slamming against her ribs. She clenched her fists, wishing she could have spoken privately with Barrow before this moment.

"I believe I can offer a way for the clansmen to enter Tearmunn without raising suspicion."

Mackenzie nodded, waiting for her to continue.

"Lord Edmund Morrow will summon them to the keep"— Ember looked at her father—"to attend his daughter's wedding."

"Good God, lass," her father said, thunderstruck. "How did you find a husband for Agnes?"

Ember shook her head. "Not Agnes. I speak of my own wedding."

Mackenzie and her father exchanged a doubtful glance. Behind her, Barrow coughed. When she turned, he was smiling at her.

"I'm pleased you're eager to marry me, Lady Morrow, but I don't think I'd be welcome at Tearmunn. Even as your bridegroom."

"No." Ember couldn't meet his gaze. "I do not speak of a marriage to you, Lord Hess."

Facing Mackenzie and her father again, Ember said, "Last night I agreed to become the wife of Lord Alistair Hart."

TWENTY-SEVEN

**EMBER WAS GLAD HER** back was turned to Barrow. She couldn't bear seeing his face.

"Alistair?" Her father's face gained a mottled purple hue. "You think I would give my younger daughter to the worthless brother of the cur who shamed my elder daughter by putting a bastard in her belly?"

"Of course not." Ember was glad to shout, wanting Barrow to hear what she was about to say. "I do not wish to marry Alistair, only to insinuate myself to his trust. He has long admired me. By assenting to become his wife, I gain freedom from suspicion about my reasons for returning to Tearmunn."

Edmund Morrow's face returned to a normal color, but he looked to Mackenzie for guidance.

The clan chief scratched at his beard while he thought. "A wedding. You are a nobleman, Edmund. You do have the right to call the clans to honor your daughter at a marriage feast."

"I would give my support to this strategy." It was Lukasz who spoke. The commander came to Ember's side. "The festive air of a wedding will provide ample distraction so that we can infiltrate the keep."

"Are we only to be wedding guests, then?" The ever-doubtful warrior laughed. "Shall I leave my axes at home?"

Rebekah answered him coolly. "I fear not, my lord. The spellwork required to close the rift takes time. Your weapons will be needed to draw Eira's forces away from a second, stealth party that will protect me while I perform the necessary rites."

"Make no mistake," Mackenzie added, "even with the advantage of surprise, the fight will be hard, our losses many."

Lukasz said to the man so full of objections, "Consider the choices. Risk your life now or wait for the wraiths to prey upon your families." The commander raised his voice. "I bear witness to the slaughter of Dorusduain! An entire village emptied of men, women, and children. Not a single soul was spared—all to satisfy the cravings of those beasts ruled by Bosque Mar and welcomed into this world by Lady Eira."

"Dorusduain!" A returning shout filled the room.

"Dorusduain! Dorusduain!" A chorus of booming voices echoed through the hall.

Mackenzie nodded his approval, letting the battle cries go on for some minutes before he once again lifted his arms to quiet the warriors.

"Your courage speaks of your honor!" Mackenzie let his gaze sweep the room. "Return to your clans and await news of Lady Morrow's wedding. When the date is set, I will send word of how the attack will proceed. Now, rest here and enjoy my hospitality. Food and drink will fill these tables within the hour."

A cheer went up from the crowd. As the mood of the hall transformed from tense to jovial, Ember returned to Barrow. His face was unreadable as she approached.

"I had no time to explain," Ember said. "Or to tell you what's transpired. I'm so sorry."

Barrow's smile was thin. "You shouldn't apologize, though I cannot feign happiness at this news."

"Nor does it bring me joy," Ember replied. "I do not love Alistair, though it pains me to deceive him in this way. Once he was my dearest friend, but he has been twisted by Eira and Bosque."

"It is a petty thing, but I would be more at ease if you despised Lord Hart." Barrow drew a long breath.

"I cannot hate Alistair," Ember said. "But my heart is yours alone."

Though sadness still touched his eyes, Barrow bent to kiss her.

"Betrothed to one man, yet kissing another?" Edmund Morrow broke into the tender moment. "Conatus has truly corrupted my younger daughter."

Ember turned a cold gaze on her father. Once she would have feared his judgment, but no longer.

Raising his brow at her withering glare, Edmund laughed.

"I tease you, Ember, and yet you throw daggers at me with your eyes."

"My memories of your humor must be faulty," Ember answered. "For I can only recall your reprimands."

"Ah, lass, you are hard on your father." Edmund sighed. "But I suppose I have earned your wrath."

Ember frowned at him. "Your good spirits are strange to me, Father. At our last meeting you condemned my decision to join the Conatus Guard."

"I still would see you married rather than charging into battle," her father replied. "But the grief of your mother at losing both her daughters in such quick succession has softened the gristle of my heart."

"You would restore Agnes to your home, then?" Ember asked. She had no interest in making peace with her father unless he planned to make amends with her sister.

"Aye," Edmund said, though he looked as if he'd swallowed something terribly sour. "I can't have joy in your sister's condition, but I know her to be a sweet, loving girl. That damnable Henry is to blame for her misfortune."

"You've treated her horribly," Ember said, unwilling to forgive him too easily. "And she suffered long for it."

"Will you torture me by harping on my poor judgments, Ember?" her father asked.

"I may," Ember answered, meaning it.

"You're a hard lass."

Ember nodded in answer. With a groan, Edmund looked to Barrow. "My daughter is swayed by you, Lord Hess. Will you speak on my behalf?"

Barrow smiled at him. "I've learned to trust in Ember's choices. I cannot spare you her wrath for fear of earning it myself."

"Very well." Edmund shrugged. "I will do my penance."

Lord Mackenzie joined them, saying, "I bid you come with me to my quarters. There are matters to be discussed away from this throng."

Following the clan chief from the hall, they were met by Lukasz, Kael, Father Michael, Cian, and the visitors from Krak des Chevaliers. Mackenzie led their small party through the castle, the din of the clansmen's feast fading to a murmur. When they were ensconced in Mackenzie's private quarters, the clan chief collapsed into a chair. His weary gaze rolled over to Cian.

"You have the clans, my lady."

"And you have our gratitude," Cian answered with a short bow.

"The wedding should take place as quickly as possible," Mackenzie said, looking at Ember. "Will your betrothed assent to that?"

Ember nodded, dread snaking through her belly. "I believe he will."

"We should consider that I have no love lost for those who rule Tearmunn," Edmund interjected. "If I seem too amenable to this arrangement, it could draw suspicion."

"Demand the amount that would have been your daughters' dowries instead be paid to you," Father Michael suggested. "Alistair has no fortune, but Eira and Bosque will see to it that his happiness is ensured. They will agree to your terms, and you will still appear to object to the marriage, but for your own greed."

"That sounds like me." Edmund smirked. "Doesn't it, Ember?"

"Yes," Ember answered truthfully. She'd remained skeptical of her father's change of heart toward herself and Agnes, and as she watched him, she realized there had been little change at all. What Edmund Morrow took joy in was vengeance. Thwarting Eira's plans constituted retribution for taking his younger daughter from his home and offering his elder daughter a place of comfort and honor when he'd denied her the same.

Wishing she could spit bile into her father's face, Ember instead kept silent. No matter his motivations, her father's cooperation was vital to their success. Until she could be rid of him again, she would have to pretend she believed her family fully reconciled.

"It's settled, then." Edmund beamed at her. "I'll send for your mother to join me at Eilean Donan. We will accompany Mackenzie on the day of the wedding."

"You're bringing Mother?" Ember gaped at him. "There's no place for her in this. What of the attack?"

Her father shrugged. "I do not wish to endanger my wife, but do you not think it would raise questions if your mother wasn't in attendance at your own wedding?"

She frowned. "Make an excuse. Say she is ill and cannot travel."

"And what of Agnes?" he replied. "Will you keep your sister from the wedding as well?"

Ember glared at him, caught by the truth of his words but hating them.

"Lady Morrow," Mackenzie offered gently, "none of us want harm to befall your mother or sister. I will assign one of my most trusted men to protect them when the battle begins."

Resigned to the strength of their argument, Ember asked, "And who will go to the rift?"

Kael smiled at her. "Those of us who wouldn't dare show our faces to congratulate you on your wedding."

"And how will you gain access to the keep?" Mackenzie frowned at the Conatus knights. "I know of only two entrances, neither of which would let you pass unnoticed."

"We have unusual means of travel that will allow us to bypass the guarded entryways," Lukasz answered.

"Hmpf." Edmund eyed Lukasz warily. "More of this magic, I suppose. I do not wish to know of it, for I blame such things for our current sorrows. Witches and sorcerers be damned."

"Not all magics bring evil to the world," Rebekah chided, earning a bitter glare from Ember's father.

"We'll rely on yours to close the gate," Mackenzie added.

Tamur spoke up, frowning at the group. "You are all familiar with this keep. Are you certain the room in which the rift is found will be unguarded?"

"My sister only posts guards at the door when she is holding court," Cian answered.

"Eira holds court now?" Kael's eyes widened.

Cian's jaw clenched, and she nodded.

"Her lust for power has overwhelmed all else," Father Michael said sadly.

"And this creature, Bosque Mar." Kurjii frowned. "Though he is not human, you expect he will be present to witness the marriage."

"Bosque has taken a special interest in Alistair," Ember answered. "I cannot imagine he would be absent for such an important event."

"I'm afraid that raises another matter," Father Michael said, his voice troubled. "Though I know not if it affects our plans, I would not be blind to a threat that may exist."

"What is it?" Lukasz asked the priest.

"As Lady Morrow says, Bosque Mar favors Lord Hart," Father Michael replied. "And he has put Alistair to work within the catacombs and given him the assistance of Hamish, who was once a formidable cleric."

Ember tilted her head, looking thoughtfully at Father Michael.

"Alistair spoke to me of this work. He said it was a special task given to him by Bosque."

"I fear what occurs in the tombs beneath Tearmunn's manor," Father Michael said. He met Ember's gaze. "Lady Morrow, though I do not wish to further endanger you, you are the most likely person to discover what occupies Alistair's days."

"I will do what I can," Ember said quickly. It wasn't that she was eager to take risks, but that the strategy they'd adopted at her suggestion would mean every day was a day closer to a wedding she didn't want. Uncovering the mystery of Alistair's work for Lord Mar would offer a welcome, if dangerous, distraction.

"Very well." Mackenzie grunted, pushing himself out of his seat. "I believe we have settled all that we can for now. A hard road lies ahead, and I suggest we feast while we can."

Mackenzie left the chamber and the others filed out after him. Ember began to follow, but a hand caught her wrist, holding her back. Barrow looked down at her. He'd been unusually silent, but Ember didn't have to ask why.

When they were alone in the room, he turned her to face him. His hands rested on her hips and he pulled her close. In silence, his fingers moved up the sides of her body, over her shoulders, down her arms to briefly clasp her hands. Then he slid his hands through her hair as he bent to kiss her. Ember knew their embrace would be brief, that neither their circumstance nor this castle afforded them time and space enough for the intimacy she craved. Nothing could be done to change that. When their lips parted, Ember felt a hollow ache beneath her ribs.

Barrow kissed her cheek before resting his forehead against hers. They didn't speak, and Ember didn't want to. Words wouldn't bring what she longed for.

TWENTY-EIGHT

**EIRA GAZED AT ALISTAIR.** The young knight had been holding his breath while she considered his petition. She briefly toyed with the idea of seeing whether he'd turn blue in the face before she gave answer. Love made such fools of otherwise worthwhile men.

"This is what you truly desire?" Eira asked, frowning at him.

"I know it's a large sum, my lady." Alistair gasped the words. "I'm sorry that Lord Morrow seeks to punish you because I would marry Ember instead of seeing her the wife of Gavin Mackenzie."

Eira tapped Edmund Morrow's letter on the arm of her throne. Ember's father was a pathetic, selfish man, but money was of little consequence to Eira. "That isn't what I asked."

"I love her," Alistair said quietly, lowering his gaze.

"Very well." Eira looked to Ember, who stood alongside Alistair. The young couple had requested an audience the moment Ember had returned from Eilean Donan, despite the late hour. Eira had deigned to see them in her own bedchamber and had summoned Bosque to attend the meeting as well.

The pair kept stealing glances at each other, like children who'd been caught breaking rules. Eira observed them with a mixture of amusement and befuddlement.

"Lady Morrow, your father asks for the wedding to take place while he remains at Mackenzie's castle."

"Yes, my lady." Ember smiled shyly at Alistair. "But I do not mind. I would sooner be married to Lord Hart than wait another day."

When Ember looked upon him with love, Alistair thought his heart would burst. "I also do not wish to wait."

Eira crumpled the letter in her hand so she wouldn't groan at their sickeningly sweet words.

"A week from today will provide enough time for arrangements to be made," Father Michael offered.

"Next Friday?" Eira glanced at Bosque, who as usual stood to her left. "What say you, Lord Mar?"

Bosque smiled at her, mischief dancing in his silver eyes. "I believe Lord Hart should not be denied his heart's desire. Let the wedding take place Friday."

Eira held his intent gaze, wondering what he was up to.

"I shall make arrangements." Father Michael bowed.

"Take Lady Morrow with you," Bosque told the priest abruptly. "We require a private audience with Lord Hart."

A flicker of discontent passed like a shadow over Ember's face, but she curtsied and followed the priest out of the great hall.

Alistair watched until they were gone, then turned to Bosque. "Is something amiss?"

"I don't know," Bosque answered. "What has she told you of the gathering at Mackenzie's castle?"

"That her father has changed little." Alistair's voice was gruff, indignant on his beloved's behalf. "He would have married her to Mackenzie's son but for her pleas to be wed to me. And as you know, he assented to that only by promise of payment."

"And nothing else?" Bosque frowned at Alistair.

"There's the matter of Agnes," Alistair offered.

Bosque laid his arm over the back of Eira's throne. "The bribe requested for Agnes should be denied."

"What?" Alistair replied in alarm.

"Don't fear for your wedding, Lord Hart." Bosque smiled at him.

"We won't revoke the offer to pay to restore Agnes to her father until after you and Ember are wed."

Eira turned in her seat to look up at Bosque. "You want to keep the girl here?"

Bosque nodded, his eyes thoughtful. "She remains valuable. Particularly as a means of preventing any missteps on the part of Alistair's new bride."

"You want to continue to hold Agnes as a hostage?" Alistair asked.

"That's one way of looking at it," Bosque replied. "But Agnes offers a rare opportunity for you, Alistair. I'm surprised you haven't thought of it yourself. Your mind is too full of love, I suppose."

Alistair grimaced, and Eira laughed.

Straightening in an effort to restore his dignity, Alistair asked, "What have I missed with regard to Agnes?"

"You've done a marvelous thing," Bosque told him. "And the reward you shall reap is a terrible army like the world has never seen. An army fearsome for its strength and its absolute loyalty to you."

"Thank you, my lord," Alistair said, but his brow was furrowed in confusion.

"But now you have only six warriors to raise for this purpose," Bosque said. "How do you propose to increase their ranks?"

Alistair opened and closed his mouth, but could give no answer.

Bosque smiled at Eira. "As I said, his mind is too full of love."

Eira nodded, but asked, "I confess I do not see how Agnes fits into his vision."

"Submission, duty, and loyalty are qualities not only of warriors that serve their king," Bosque said, answering Alistair rather than Eira. "Such traits are even stronger within families."

"Families," Alistair repeated.

"Witness Lady Morrow herself," Bosque told him. "She risked her life to return to her sister, to protect her . . . and to be with you, of course."

One corner of Bosque's mouth turned up, and Eira wondered if Bosque was mocking Alistair.

When Alistair still didn't speak, Bosque began to show frustration. "Agnes is with child. A child that will be devoted to its mother and to those to whom its mother submits."

Alistair's eyes suddenly went wide.

"Yes." A slow smile spread across Bosque's mouth. "I want you to continue your trials, Lord Hart . . . with Agnes."

"But Ember—" Alistair shifted on his feet.

"If you worry that my counsel would anger your beloved," Bosque said smoothly, "consider this: if Ember is to be your wife, she must serve you, obey you. How do you think she would respond to the miraculous work you've accomplished thus far?"

Alistair blanched, making it obvious to Eira that he'd kept his love for Ember strictly separate from his collaboration with Bosque.

"I agree," Bosque told Alistair. "She may not understand the greatness of it, only because it will be strange to her. But if you make her sister a part of it, she will be forced to accept what you've done."

"I will think on this, Lord Mar." Alistair's face had gone gray, but he bowed. "May I take my leave now?"

"Yes."

When Alistair was gone, Eira asked, "Are you worried that Lord Hart will falter in his loyalty?"

Bosque shook his head. "If he harbors doubts, they will fade with the novelty of his love."

"I hope you're right," Eira said. She stood up and stretched, weary from the long day.

"I am."

"Soon you and Lord Hart must show me this marvel he's created." Eira began to unbraid her hair, thinking to seek her bed.

"Alistair will take you to the catacombs soon." Bosque came close to Eira, and when he reached up to touch her loose copper waves, she became still. "He is wise to let the beasts know him alone, to trust him completely, before he introduces them to others."

Eira didn't answer. Bosque continued to stroke her hair.

"I should sleep." Her voice hitched when she spoke, and she stepped away from him.

"Why do you shrink from me?" His voice was like silk.

"I—" Her heart was beating much too quickly, making her breathless. She looked away, gazing at the window but not focusing on anything.

Following her retreat, Bosque stood very near, but didn't touch her. "Eira."

Laying his fingers against her cheek, he turned her face to look at him. "I have not known desire for a woman before you called me forth from the nether. Now I find it consumes me. I can think of little else."

Eira felt dizzy. She moved away from Bosque again, but her path led her to the side of her bed. She turned around and found herself facing him.

"Will you deny me?"

The doubts churning beneath Eira's ribs finally surfaced. "I confess, Lord Mar, I find your words of passion difficult to believe. No man has ever spoken to me thus."

"What man would have courage enough to believe he could win you?" Bosque laughed. "You exude power. Men are small creatures, easily cowed by those who challenge their sense of self-importance."

He leaned closer, his breath touching her cheek. "Men fear you, but I promise they have also wanted you."

She turned her face, and his lips met hers. Bosque pulled back, and Eira gasped when he took off his shirt.

"I haven't assented to share my bed with you." She put steel into her voice, but her gaze traveled over his broad shoulders, the strength of his chest and abdomen.

"And I haven't forgotten that." Bosque smiled at her. "But if you would consent to touch me, I would like to know the feeling of your hands on my skin."

Eira's fingers twitched, aching to trace the lines of muscle that covered his bare torso. She dared to rest her palm just below his collarbone. His skin was so warm under her fingers. Heat seemed to flow from the point of contact up her arm, spreading over her limbs.

"Lie with me, Eira," Bosque murmured, holding her in his gaze. "Perfect our union. Make it complete."

Slowly, waiting for her to object, Bosque reached for the front of her tabard. When she didn't try to stop him, he pulled the long garment over her head. He leaned down, kissing the spot where her pulse beat rapidly at her throat.

Eira's hand stole around Bosque's neck, her fingertips brushing his soft hair.

"I spoke to Alistair of the loyalty inherent within families, sealed by shared blood," Bosque whispered against her skin. "As long as a child born from the line of our union walks the earth, a gateway between this world and mine can be opened."

"How can you be sure I'll conceive?" Eira placed her palm on her stomach. She'd abandoned any thoughts of bearing a child years ago; the idea still struck her as absurd.

"There will be more at work here than passion," Bosque said, lifting his head to look at her. "There is also the power that I bring. Consent to this union of body and blood, and you *will* bear my child."

"No one has limitless power," Eira told him. When his eyes narrowed, she worried she'd gone too far. "I meant no insult."

"You are the only creature in this world or mine I would let speak to me thus," Bosque told her with a thin smile. "Your words are true enough. My powers do have limits, but in the matter at hand, those limits are naught." Regret, or perhaps sadness, crept into his eyes. "What I cannot do is grant you eternal life."

Taken aback, Eira said, "I never wanted immortality."

"Then you are unlike most men and women," Bosque told her. "When wizards and conjurers call upon the least of my creatures, immortality is often the first thing they demand."

He folded her hand in his strong grasp. "I can give you threefold years beyond other men, and in these years, you will not age. You will remain as you are now. Strong."

Moving his grip to her wrists, he pulled her closer. "Beautiful." His lips nearly touched hers.

Eira asked with hesitation, "If I will not age, why must I bear this child now?"

"I would give you leave to wait as long as you like," Bosque told her. "Were it not for the risk of losing you."

"You think I will try to sever our bond?" Eira couldn't imagine wanting to rid herself of Bosque. She craved his presence, felt lost when he was absent. She wouldn't name their bond one of love, but it was nonetheless powerful, irresistible even.

Bosque released one of her wrists and traced the line of her collarbone. "You are loyal, Eira. And we desire the same things. I do not fear your leaving. I know you would not abandon me, just as I would never forsake you."

"Then what do you fear?" Eira asked, trying not to be distracted by the light touch of his fingers on her skin.

"You are and always will be a warrior," Bosque answered. "And there are many battles to come. Though I can offer you powerful allies, helping to secure your victories, when my queen goes to war, she may lose her life."

Eira nodded. Bosque's words won him yet more of her admiration. Despite his hopes for her, he didn't suggest she stay hidden away in a keep, safely distant from any bloodshed. He wouldn't deny her true nature, her hunger for the fight.

As she fell silent, Bosque bent closer. His lips followed the path of his fingertips. The touch of his mouth on her skin stirred a new hunger in Eira, one she'd never expected to feel. Bosque trailed his lips over her throat and up her neck. His tongue flicked her cheek, and his teeth closed lightly on her earlobe.

"Tell me, Eira." Bosque repositioned himself, placing an arm on either side of her, trapping her against him. "What is it you want from me?"

Adrift in a sea of sensation—the sound of her quick breaths, the rising heat of her skin—Eira knew too well what her body craved, but her mind balked. She turned her face from him, trying to steady herself.

"Your touch is that of a man." Eira forced the words out. "But—"

Bosque finished for her. "You fear what I truly am."

Eira met his gaze. "I do . . . Should I?"

"I don't know," Bosque said, his expression thoughtful. "I can't predict what your reaction would be to the form I take in my own world."

He glanced down at his bare chest. "But it would not likely appeal to you as this body does."

Eira felt blood rush to her cheeks as she faced the truth of his words. Was her desire so plain, the ache within her so easy for him to detect?

"Fortunately"—Bosque smiled—"this is the body that would enact our union. You need never look upon the other."

Drawing a quick breath, Eira said, "But when I first opened the way for you to be in this world, you made me turn away, for fear of what I would see."

"My other form was required for the crossing between worlds," Bosque told her. "That body took your blood as a pact so that this body could be sustained here. But with the crossing complete, I may remain a man for so long as I choose."

He leaned forward, moving her onto the bed. "To provide

whatever you need." His lips touched the hollow between her ear and her jaw. "Or desire."

Eira felt her will to resist giving way, but there remained one thing she needed to know. "Wait."

Bosque stayed close, but he became still, no longer enticing her with his kisses.

"This union is a deepening of our bond," Eira said.

"Yes."

She put her hand to his chest, holding him back, though he hadn't tried to close the little distance that remained between them. "Our bond has always carried a price."

"An offering of blood," Bosque replied calmly.

"And now?" Eira asked, unsettled by his casual tone.

"The same will be required. And as before, I cannot heal your wound," he answered, his smile almost teasing. "But you need do nothing to make your offering. That task falls to me."

Eira stiffened. "What will you do to me?"

"Only what you want me to." Reaching down, Bosque gathered the hem of her kirtle. "Unless—"

Bosque began to lift her kirtle. Eira closed her eyes, barely breathing. "Unless?"

"Has another man taken your maidenhead?"

"No!" Her eyelids snapped up, and she glared at him. "Did you think otherwise?"

"I did not," he answered, still smiling. "But you were the one who pressed me about the nature of the sacrifice."

"The—" Grasping his meaning, Eira choked on the remaining words.

This time Bosque did bear her down onto the bed, his full weight pushing against her. Eira began to speak, but he stopped her words with a kiss that began gently and grew in urgency. Her lingering questions were soon forgotten.

TWENTY-NINE

**EMBER HAD WORRIED** that Agnes would take the news of her wedding badly, but the opposite proved to be true, which made Ember sick with guilt.

Secrets weighed heavy on the tip of her tongue, ready to be confessed. But she feared that revealing the coming battle would endanger Agnes more than leaving her in ignorance. Agnes wasn't the issue. Bosque Mar was.

The tall, silver-eyed man visited Agnes almost daily, despite the fact that the two sisters were busy with preparations for the wedding. Bosque would appear without notice, sometimes sitting with them, other times inviting Agnes to join him for a walk through the courtyard. Ember hated it. But she could make no excuse that would keep Agnes from accepting Bosque's offers of companionship without telling her about his origins, and that very subject was what made Ember so reluctant to share her fears with her sister. Bosque's gaze was uncanny. Ember sensed that each moment he spent in their company was one in which he delved for information, like a predator sniffing out its next meal.

If Ember alerted Agnes to the danger, Bosque would notice her changed behavior, throwing suspicion on both sisters. Try as she might, Ember found no good choices in this matter.

This particular afternoon, Bosque and Agnes were deeply

involved in a discussion of the merits of a variety of spring flowers. Why a lord of the nether realm would have any opinions on blossoms, Ember couldn't fathom, and she was relieved when a servant appeared with a message from Father Michael reminding her that she should make confession before the wedding mass.

Hurriedly excusing herself, Ember fled the chamber and made her way to the chapel. She was certain that Father Michael hadn't truly summoned her to make confession or discuss the wedding. The only benefit of so much flurry around the event was that the premise of preparation enabled Ember to avoid her betrothed. Each interaction with Alistair had become more difficult. He was constantly touching her, holding her hands, leaning in for a chaste kiss. On the one occasion when Alistair had pursued a more aggressive approach to the physical side of their betrothal, Ember insisted that she wouldn't compromise her virtue and would only surrender to her passion on their wedding night. Had that been more than four days hence, Alistair might have persisted in his efforts to seduce her. To Ember's relief, he relented.

Alistair's touch didn't revolt her, nor was his company unpleasant. But those two truths made everything worse. To see him and know what was coming twisted a knife in Ember's belly. Each interaction burdened her more than the last, so that Ember feared she might become physically sick from the tension mercilessly wringing her body.

When Ember entered the chapel, she found Father Michael at prayer. She walked along the pews quietly, waiting until he rose to speak.

The priest must have heard her approach. The moment he stood, he turned to greet her.

"Thank you for coming so quickly, Ember." Gesturing for her to follow, Father Michael crossed in front of the stained-glass window from which the archangel that shared the priest's name watched over them.

Settling into one of the front pews, Father Michael patted the wooden bench. "Please sit."

Ember took her place beside the priest. "Is there news?"

"That's why I've summoned you," Father Michael answered. "With your wedding day so close, you must be prepared for what will happen. I would not have you enter the battle like a blind lamb."

Ember clasped her hands tight in her lap.

"The ceremony will take place at the courtyard," Father Michael told her. "At the signal, your father and Mackenzie will begin their attack. Cian will assist them in leading the clan warriors."

"What is the signal?" Ember asked.

"When Alistair places the ring on your finger."

With a shudder, Ember dropped her head back against the pew. While the clansmen raised their swords, she'd be adorned in her wedding gown and flowers. Feeling a light touch on her arm, Ember turned to meet Father Michael's gaze.

"Do not belittle your role in this plan, Ember," he said gently.

Forcing a weak smile, Ember asked, "What else will happen?"

"While chaos reigns out of doors, Rebekah will open a door in the great hall," Father Michael told her. "Our hope is that the battle will hold Eira's attention long enough for Rebekah to complete her spell, closing the rift."

"And Barrow?" Ember lowered her eyes as her pulse jumped.

"He will be with Lukasz, Kael, and the Mamluks, guarding Rebekah."

Ember let her eyes close. She'd known it wouldn't be possible for Barrow to stand among the clansmen who gathered for her wedding. The chance of him being recognized was too great. But a stubborn, irrational piece of Ember's mind insisted that she needed him in the crowd, that once the battle began, she would want to shove Alistair away and rush over to fight at Barrow's side so he would know without question that the ring encircling her finger was nothing but a ruse. By her action, she would refute the ceremony she'd taken part in, purging the false promises she'd uttered as she fought at Barrow's side.

Father Michael must have surmised the nature of her thoughts, for he said, "When the fighting begins, you should see to your safety and that of your mother and sister."

Ember looked at him, nodding, though her mind clung to the hope of somehow finding Barrow.

"Mackenzie promised men to protect your family," Father Michael reminded her. "When they reach you, stay close to them. Just as you are, they will be unhappy to be excluded from the battle at large. Let these warriors fulfill the task their clan chief has given them."

Finding all her counterarguments ignoble, Ember resigned herself to playing the role of spectator in the coming fight.

Father Michael stood up. "Before that day arrives, however, I have another task for you."

Without further explanation, he walked away. Surprised, Ember hopped up and followed Father Michael out of the chapel, into his private quarters. He paused in front of a tall, narrow bookcase, looking back at her.

"Lord Hart came to make confession," Father Michael said. "From what he said, I understand you've spent little time with your betrothed."

Ember avoided the priest's gaze. "I find it difficult to be in his company, knowing I deceive him."

"I do not envy you, Lady Morrow," he said. "You've placed not only your body but your heart and spirit at great risk."

Father Michael pulled a book from the middle shelf and reached into the empty space. "For that reason, I am sorry to ask you to risk more, but fear I must."

Ember heard a click, and the bookcase whined. Father Michael took several steps back as it swung forward. "Do you remember what I asked of you at Eilean Donan?"

"You spoke of fear over the work Alistair had been doing for Bosque," Ember said.

Nodding, Father Michael continued, "And since you have found it necessary to avoid Lord Hart, I assume you have not spoken with him of this matter."

Mute with embarrassment that she'd chosen her own needs over the priest's request, Ember shook her head.

Seeing the way her cheeks colored, Father Michael said, "Don't chastise yourself, my child. I would be far more concerned if you pretended love for Alistair without a heavy heart."

Her eyes downcast, Ember murmured, "Thank you."

Father Michael beckoned Ember closer. When she reached his side, Ember saw a dark opening in the wall that had been hidden by the bookcase. "This passage leads to the catacombs where each day Alistair performs his work. He enters through a trapdoor in the cellar, but only I know of this entrance. Alistair took Lady Eira into the catacombs this morning."

"You would have me enter?" Ember gazed at the dark tunnel. "When they are still within the tombs?"

"The answers we seek lie in the corridors and chambers beneath this manor," he answered. "Your wedding takes place in four days. Alistair makes confession of his carnal desires, but not of what hides in the darkness below this manor. If there are secrets that will compromise our success within the resting place of the dead, we must know. Stay hidden in the shadows and learn what you can from listening."

Father Michael drew a dagger from the folds of his robes.

"Take this so you have means to defend yourself." He pressed the hilt into Ember's hand. "I pray that you won't need to use it."

Ember's fingers closed around the hilt. She called to mind the gathered warriors of the clans, the risk they would take by staging a decoy attack. She drew further resolve from the faces of her friends. Lukasz, Kael, Cian, and Barrow would protect Rebekah as she attempted to close the rift. If the catacombs housed some unknown weapon, it could compromise everything.

Taking a deep breath, she nodded a farewell to Father Michael and entered the tunnel. The light from the priest's quarters faded quickly, leaving Ember in darkness.

Blinking into the dark, Ember turned to follow the directional change of the tunnel and noticed a ruddy glow farther along the passage. She made her way forward cautiously. As her vision adjusted to the lack of light, she began to see the contours of the passage. When she reached the light's source, a torch in an iron sconce, the tunnel curved again, pitching sharply downward. Ember took the torch from the wall and continued on her path. The more she walked, the narrower the passage became, and abruptly Ember was facing a dead end.

Frowning, she gazed at the wall before her and wondered if Father Michael had ever used this tunnel and *knew* that it came out somewhere. She lifted the torch, searching the wall for anything she'd missed—a depression or hidden door. When she examined the corner of the wall, the shadows dancing in the torchlight grew more pronounced.

Ember pressed her hand to the wall, feeling its shape. Without warning, the stone she touched was gone and her fingers grasped at air. The gap in the wall was nearly invisible, made to trick the eye into seeing a barrier where a small space existed. The hole between the wall she faced and the one to her side barely accommodated Ember. She squeezed through and came out at the back of a statue. An effigy of the Virgin Mary at prayer loomed over Ember and disguised the place from which she'd come.

Slipping around the statue, Ember saw that she'd entered what must be the main corridor of the catacombs. The tunnel was wider, and the stone walls featured hollows at regular intervals occupied by sarcophagi. The corridor had a steep slope, and Ember began to follow the downward tilt of the path. She kept her eyes ahead.

Surrounded by so many souls laid to rest, Ember couldn't shake the sense that spirits watched as she passed by their burial sites.

A sound rising from behind the curving wall in front of her brought Ember to a halt. She listened more closely and heard voices. Every foul curse she knew jumped onto Ember's tongue, but she dared not cry out. The voices were much too close for comfort, and out of the corner of her eye, Ember caught the soft glow of lantern light spilling along the corridor. She searched the wall until she found an empty iron sconce. Quickly restoring her torch to an inconspicuous place on the wall, Ember cringed, realizing that she'd be forced to hide behind a sarcophagus. She scrambled over the cold, carved stone and rolled into the crevice between the wall and the coffin. Her shoulder dropped hard against the corner of the tomb, and she had to bite her tongue so she wouldn't shout in pain.

Ember hoped the shadows were enough to keep her hidden. There wasn't space to curl into a ball. As it was, she could barely move and worried she wouldn't be able to leverage herself from the tight space. Panic hit her like a blow to the chest. What if she couldn't get out? Fear, rolling through her limbs, almost made her yell toward the sound of the approaching group. Better to be caught than to be trapped by this sarcophagus until it became her grave as well.

Forcing herself to close her eyes and breathe, Ember beat back her anxiety. Instead of thinking about the rough stone, its cold touch reaching through her dress and making her shudder, Ember listened to the voices that grew ever closer.

"I must say, Alistair," Eira mused, "I never expected this. You're quite the innovator."

Alistair's reply was barely audible. "I only hope to please you, Lady Eira."

"You needn't worry about that," she answered him. "You've proven your worth many times over. I'll readily admit that I find you quite . . . essential."

"I'm honored," Alistair replied.

"And what do you think of our young knight?" Eira asked.

A smooth, low reply came. "I've always seen great potential in Lord Hart."

Ember went rigid. Bosque Mar's voice never failed to make her pulse spike. She was startled that he was in the catacombs. He must have left Agnes shortly after Ember went to seek Father Michael.

Keeping as still as she could, Ember prayed that the darkness was enough to hide her. She could hear their footsteps. Lantern light slid along the wall opposite her crevice. Eira and Alistair came into view first. Bosque followed, a tall guardian looming over their shoulders.

"We won't know until they're unleashed," Alistair said to Eira. "But I think they could make all the difference when it comes to a fight. The traitors will never anticipate this development."

"I agree," Bosque said. "It's an incredible feat. Something to celebrate at your wedding feast?"

Bile rose in Ember's throat as she waited for Alistair's reply, but it was Eira who spoke.

"Though we cannot share your triumph with the wedding guests, we shall toast you in secret," Eira replied.

"I am grateful, Lady Eira." Alistair added, "I hope that Rhys will soon be able to join me in the manor. He has yet to learn control, but the child is eager."

"And deeply attached to you," Eira noted. "That serves our purpose well."

There was a pause, then Alistair asked, "When will she wake?"

"After an hour or so," Bosque answered.

Eira added, "I'm more interested in when we'll know whether Rhys was able to complete the rite as you envisioned it could occur."

"As am I." Alistair's voice was tight. "We simply have to wait."

"As you wish," Bosque replied.

A blur of questions seized Ember's thoughts: Who slept while the three plotters acted? Who was Rhys, and what rite did they speak of? She realized only after the lantern light began to fade that the trio had passed her without incident. She waited until she could no longer hear their voices, then began the task of dislodging herself from the tomb. As she'd feared, in her haste to hide, Ember had wedged herself firmly between the sarcophagus and the wall. Though panic tried to keep her imprisoned by the coffin, Ember methodically squirmed and wriggled until the stones gave up their hostage. Hoisting herself onto the sarcophagus, Ember crawled back out of the tomb. She glanced in the direction that Alistair, Eira, and Bosque had gone. Their path led toward the passage by which Ember had entered the catacombs.

Given her near discovery, Ember briefly considered returning to the passage and getting away from the tombs as quickly as possible. But the snippets of conversation she'd overheard were too troubling to ignore. What had Alistair done to so greatly please Eira and Bosque? And how could they be so confident that whatever it was, it signified the demise of Ember's allies?

Turning her back on the way to safety, Ember instead faced the slight downward pitch of the ground. She reclaimed her torch from the wall and followed the path deeper into the earth.

The spiraling tunnel held nothing but the dead, and Ember's head ached with frustration until she reached the point where the passage ended, opening into a broad chamber. At first glance, this was also simply a tomb—albeit a larger one—but the sarcophagi in the room had been changed. Their surfaces were covered with objects, as though they'd been used as tables.

Ember wandered through the room, taking note of jars, vases, tools, knives, herbs, parchment, ink, and quills. She couldn't make sense of the odd assortment of items, so she left the large room to search the adjoining chambers, which were connected to the four corners of the room.

As she approached the opening to the first side chamber, Ember slowed, her nose wrinkling. Disturbing odors wafted from the arched opening—stale blood and cloying decay. Though her stomach flopped unpleasantly at the onslaught of sickening scents, Ember forced herself forward.

The rectangular chamber held four sarcophagi. Upon two of the stone coffins rested a body shrouded in cloth. Tightening her grip on the dagger, Ember crept forward. The odor in the chamber indicated that these corpses had lain here for some time, but Ember knew that they hadn't been placed here because they were meant to be buried in the catacombs.

When she reached the first sarcophagus, Ember forced herself to peel the shroud back. With a shout of fear, Ember jumped back and then clenched her jaw for allowing herself to give such a loud cry.

Reminding herself that the creature was dead, Ember ignored her screaming instincts and moved to examine the corpse. She'd seen nothing like it. From head to tail, she would have called it a wolf. But its arms and legs were those of a man, their only wolfish characteristic being the thick fur that covered the limbs and the clawlike nails extending from the fingertips.

After covering the body again, Ember went to the second sarcophagus. Prepared for another shock, Ember lifted the shroud. This corpse was similar to the first, though its anatomy revealed the creature to be female. The face of the beast was less wolflike and more human. Ember peered at its features, a nagging familiarity buzzing within her mind. Bending close to give the face a more careful examination, Ember suddenly froze as horror crawled over her skin. It couldn't be.

Dizzy and sick, Ember hid the face that so disturbed her, hurrying out of the chamber. As she stumbled toward the next side room, dreading what she'd find but compelled by necessity to continue her investigation, Ember tried to shut out the whisper that chased after her.

*Lora. Lora. Lora.*

Ember was desperate to purge the cleric's name from her mind, wanting to deny what she knew to be true. The dead woman's face, though mutilated by being somehow terribly wedded to the features of a beast, had been Lora's face. Cian and Father Michael said Lora had vanished, but any death Ember might have imagined for the cleric seemed preferable to this. How such an abomination of man and wolf came to be created, Ember couldn't fathom—though she had no doubt as to where the blame should fall. Everything she'd learned of Bosque Mar revealed the way he corrupted the earth, twisting it to his purpose. That Lord Mar had the power to effect such a horrible transformation of men and women into monsters didn't surprise Ember, but she didn't understand its purpose. Had these catacombs been the site of some horribly twisted punishment and execution? Was Alistair a part of it? This couldn't be the creation that had pleased Bosque and Eira, could it?

Ember shivered, pushing back the wave of panic that threatened to overwhelm her. Approaching the next chamber with trepidation, Ember clung to the sliver of relief she felt when the noxious odors of the last room weren't present. She crept inside, her dagger lifted and ready to strike.

Rather than housing multiple graves, this room featured a single sarcophagus upon a raised stone pedestal. It wasn't the stone tomb that drew Ember's gaze, but the cage beside it.

The large iron cage offered enough space that Ember would have been able to stand and walk a small circle within its confines. Behind the bars, Ember saw a nest of blankets and pillows. Curled up asleep within the pile of soft fabrics was a child.

The boy could be no more than three years old. His dark brown hair curled softly, and in the torchlight, it had rich pewter tones. Ember knelt beside the cage, staring at the sleeping boy.

Who would cage a child in this horrible place?

Setting the dagger on the floor, Ember gripped the iron bars with her right hand. The cage was sturdy and free of rust. She would only be able to open it with a key.

The boy's face scrunched up; his nose twitched. His eyelids fluttered and then opened. Ember stifled a gasp, not wanting to frighten the child. The color of his eyes was startling, a gold shade that absorbed the light from her torch and grew brighter.

"Dear one," Ember murmured, stretching her hand into the cage, "I'm here to help. Don't be afraid."

The boy shrank from her hand.

"Shhh," Ember whispered. She could almost grasp his hand. "Tell me who brought you here."

Blinking at her with those golden eyes, the boy snarled and then he was a boy no more. The wolf cub in the cage snapped at her outstretched fingers.

Ember reeled back onto the heels of her hands and scrambled away from the cage. She rolled over, struggling to her feet. The wolf continued to growl its warning as Ember fled the room. She ran until she reached the hidden passage. Not once did she look back.

THIRTY

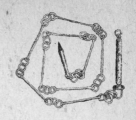

**EMBER BENT OVER,** wheezing as she tried to fight off the shock and panic that joined forces to strangle her. Though she desperately wanted to get out of the tunnel, Ember leaned against the bookcase that led to Father Michael's quarters to make sure the room was silent and likely unoccupied by anyone other than the priest.

Her pulse was still rattling when Ember pushed the bookcase forward. "Father Michael?"

No answer came, but Ember was filled with relief simply because of the gentle daylight filling the room.

Ember slipped from the tunnel and moved the bookcase against the wall until the hole was once again hidden. The chamber was empty. After taking a few minutes to collect herself, aware of how disheveled she must look after fleeing the catacombs, Ember went in search of the priest.

Making every effort to steady her breath, Ember couldn't stave off the horrific images that flashed through her mind with every blink: Lora's mutilated features, a child becoming an animal. They were nightmares brought to life, and Ember's mind wanted to reject the possibility of their existence. She wanted to purge every moment she'd spent in the tomb.

As she entered the chapel, her throat closed up. She didn't know if she could describe what she'd witnessed in the catacombs—how could she convey the twisted violence of beast and man forced into a single entity?

Voices that echoed off the chapel's vaulted ceiling disrupted Ember's troubled thoughts.

"Are you certain you wish to keep this from the others?" Father Michael asked.

The reply came from Cian. "We can't risk dissent. The alliances we cling to now are tenuous at best. As Rebekah explained, this is the only way to close the rift, to rid ourselves of Lord Mar."

"I agree with Cian." Having met Rebekah only once, Ember didn't recognize her voice but could only assume it was she who spoke. "Cian makes a noble sacrifice, but there are those who out of love would seek to stop her."

Father Michael's reply was sad. "I confess I am one of those. Lady Cian, you are needed in this fight."

"If all goes well, my final battle will end this conflict," Cian answered. "And you will need my sword no longer."

"How will you reach the great hall?" Father Michael asked. "Your absence at the wedding would be noticed."

"I'll wait until the battle begins," Cian said. "When fighting takes over the courtyard, I'll slip away."

"Try to get close to the rift itself," Rebekah told Cian. "If the spell is disrupted, the pieces of the cross will scatter, returning to the four corners whence they were called."

"I'll do as you say," Cian answered. "Let us begin."

"If it must be so," Father Michael murmured sadly.

Ember ducked behind a stone column, peeking out as far as she dared.

Cian knelt before Father Michael, wearing only her kirtle. Rebekah stood at Cian's back. The priest spoke in low, rhythmic tones, but Ember couldn't make out the words of his chanting. He held a carved wooden bowl in his hands.

Ember bit her lip to keep from gasping when Cian bowed her head and pushed her kirtle from her shoulders. The garment pooled at her hips, leaving her torso bare.

Father Michael dipped his hand into the bowl. Still chanting, he began to mark her body. With red-stained fingers, he drew first on her left collarbone and her right lower abdomen. He handed the bowl to Rebekah, who marked Cian's right shoulder and her left lower back.

Cian remained still and silent as Father Michael returned to face her.

"You make this sacrifice willingly?" he asked.

"I give my body and spirit to stem the rising tide, to turn back the dark. Blood against blood," Cian answered. "I call on the four corners of the earth we seek to protect. Give us the aid we need."

Father Michael and Rebekah joined hands, their arms forming a ring around Cian.

"*Crux ancora vitae,*" the pair intoned in unison.

Cian bowed her head. "*Crux ancora vitae.*"

Within the circle of Father Michael's and Rebekah's arms, Cian's skin began to glow. The air around her shimmered, coming alive with colors: ochre and bronze shifted to silver and pale blue that darkened until they were the deepest shades of violet and sapphire; those in turn burned from within until they gleamed crimson and gold. The cloud of ever-changing colors rose above Cian, veiling her body with its light. The nebulous hues twisted around each other, forming a distinct shape that floated above Cian's head. It appeared to be a cross, but was unlike any crucifix Ember had seen. The two ends of the lengths ended in points sharp as the tip of a sword, while the opposite ends of the beams were blunt.

The cross hung over Cian for a moment, then it descended. One of the sharp tips touched the back of Cian's neck, and she shuddered. The strange cross vanished, but Ember squinted, convinced that she had seen the identical shape branded onto the bare skin of Cian's neck.

Cian collapsed to her hands and knees, and Father Michael crouched beside her.

"It is finished," he said. "Let us get you to your chambers. You need rest."

Father Michael glanced at Rebekah. "Weave your portal in my quarters. We cannot risk your presence here any longer."

"I know," Rebekah replied, then she bowed to Cian. "Your courage humbles me, my lady."

Ember pressed herself against the column, holding her breath and flattening her body as much as she could to escape notice. Rebekah strode past her without hesitation, entering Father Michael's chamber and closing the door.

When she peeked around the column again, Father Michael and Cian had left. Ember hardly believed it could be possible, but she was more shaken now than she'd been when she emerged from the catacombs. The ritual she'd witnessed frightened her. She didn't know what it could mean, nor was she pleased that it had been performed in secret.

She'd thought to tell Father Michael everything about her strange encounters in the catacombs, but now her confidence in the priest was undermined. Too many secrets and hidden agendas made Ember question the trust she'd placed in others.

As Ember left the chapel, her head ached with indecision. Her body felt heavy, encumbered by fear and sorrow, but she couldn't think of anyone with whom she might share this burden. To confess everything to Agnes, Ember still worried, would place her sister in greater danger. She had no other friends at Tearmunn.

Ember paused outside Agnes's door, her heart squeezing tight in pain as she wished Barrow were near, ready to hold her and help her bear the weight of these ordeals. Ember let the sorrow and uncertainty wash over her, weakening her knees and making her eyes brim. Then, having given in for a few moments, she straightened, sucked in a cool, long breath, and carefully reconstructed the placid demeanor she was forced to adopt as long as these deceptions were needed.

Rapping quickly on the door, Ember waited until she heard Agnes's call.

"Who is it?"

Ember frowned, not liking the thick slur of her voice. "It's Ember."

"Come in."

Letting herself into the chamber, Ember found her sister draped across her bed. Agnes didn't sit up, but she rolled onto her side, blearily gazing at Ember through heavy-lidded eyes.

Ember hurried to her side. "Have you taken ill?"

"I don't think so." Agnes frowned, her voice still wobbling. "I'm not sure."

"How do you feel?" Ember asked. She pressed her hand to Agnes's cheek and was relieved when she felt no fever.

Agnes rubbed her eyes. "It was so strange. I remember speaking with Lord Mar, but then I must have fallen asleep." She put her hand on her belly. "This child has me napping far too often."

"You should rest as you need to," Ember told her.

"Yes," Agnes murmured drowsily. "It's strange. I dreamed of wolves."

"What?" Ember asked in alarm. Her heartbeat plunged into a breakneck pace as the boy in the cage danced before her eyes.

"Wolves," Agnes repeated. "And yet it wasn't a frightening dream. It was beautiful. I was running beside them. I felt so free."

She laughed, touching her stomach again. "I think my body fears it will be weighed down with the babe forever, enough that it prefers the lot of a wild beast."

"Perhaps." Ember forced a smile.

Agnes yawned. "You'll think me an invalid, but my eyes are too heavy to keep open."

Ember shook her head. "You push yourself too hard. Think of all the tasks you've taken on to prepare for my wedding."

"That is all my pleasure." Agnes laughed. "At least one of us should find some joy in love."

Ember's eyes burned at Agnes's words. She quickly looked away, but there was no need to hide her sudden tears. The soft sound of deep breathing told Ember that her sister had already drifted back to sleep.

Feeling utterly alone, Ember couldn't bear the solitude of her chamber, so full of evidence of her imminent marriage and the falseness of her heart. She crawled onto the bed and curled up against her sister. Agnes made a quiet sound of comfort. Closing her eyes, Ember pushed away Tearmunn and Conatus, recalling years long before, when she and Agnes were children and she didn't fear her dreams. With the present held at bay, Ember let herself drift off, hoping that, unlike Agnes, no wolves would visit while she slept.

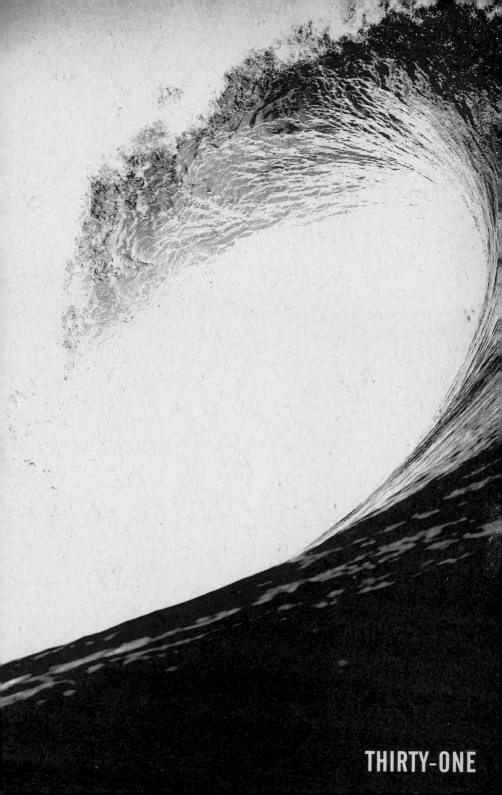

THIRTY-ONE

# EIRA LAY AWAKE, WAITING for Bosque. She didn't

care for it—the waiting. Abandoning her bed in frustration, Eira crouched before the fireplace in her chamber. She stirred the glowing embers with an iron poker and tried to think of something other than the man she hoped would soon join her.

Love wasn't something Eira had ever longed for. Nor was passion something she admired. Both struck Eira as wastes of strength and loyalty better spent on the battlefield.

So this new fluttering beneath her ribs, the sudden shortening of her breath whenever Lord Mar was near, troubled her deeply. Everything she'd dreamed of becoming since joining Conatus lay within her grasp.

But Eira had never dreamed of love. Now her body was subject to spikes of heat if Bosque so much as brushed against her. If she let his voice or visage enter her thoughts, her head was soon swimming as if she were drunk. Sometimes Eira feared she was losing control. When Bosque held her in his arms, she didn't think she would have the will to deny anything he asked of her. But there were also moments when the headiness of his kiss and caress sated Eira like no food or drink ever could, and for the first time, she knew true joy.

But Bosque was often called away, drawn into his own affairs in the nether or the work with Alistair about which, before tonight, he'd remained so secretive, leaving Eira alone or, worse, in the company of her ever-sullen sister. In his absence, doubt crept into Eira's heart, cold and slippery, making her unsure of her choices. With doubt came resentment, stirring deep within her like a restless beast.

When at last her door creaked open and Bosque's tall shadow slipped into her room, Eira stood up, brandishing the poker like a weapon.

Bosque closed the door, smiling. "Did you think me an intruder?"

"It's late." Eira kept the poker aloft.

"I had to watch over Agnes while Alistair completed his experiment," Bosque replied. He came forward, eyeing her makeshift weapon with amusement.

Eira shifted, her grip tightening until her knuckles were white. "You are often with Agnes."

Bosque nodded, continuing his cautious approach.

"Tell me, Lord Mar," Eira whispered in a dangerous tone. "How is it that our disgraced guest has come to trust you so much?"

One corner of Bosque's mouth tilted up. "You've heard that she trusts me?"

Eira looked away, fixing her gaze on the charred, smoldering wood in the fireplace. "I've seen you walking together. A day rarely passes when you're not with her."

"That's true." He paused, Eira noted, just out of reach should she take a swing at him.

"And she looks up at you with a childlike trust that borders on adoration." Eira chewed on the unpleasant words.

Bosque folded his arms across his broad chest. "You've been very observant. I thought you had little interest in Lady Morrow's fate."

"I care not of the girl and her bastard," Eira replied. "I only ask why you show so much care."

"I must say, Eira"—Bosque laughed—"jealousy becomes you. It puts fire in your blood and gives your skin a delicious scent. Honey and spice."

Eira balked for a moment before she recovered, thrusting the poker at his chest. "I am not jealous."

"You are." Bosque grabbed the end of the poker, paying no heed to the fact that it was still hot from the fire and seared his skin. With a swift tug, he pulled Eira forward. When she was within his reach, Bosque gripped her left arm, holding her still. He wrested the iron poker from her right hand and returned it to its place by the fire.

Eira tried to wrestle from his grasp to no avail.

"Why are you wriggling like a snared rabbit?" Bosque grinned at her. "Are you so eager to get away from me?"

"I was trying to have a conversation," Eira said. She stopped fighting him.

"You wanted to run me through with that iron rod," Bosque countered. "I had no choice but to disarm you."

Eira glared at him. "I did not want to run you through."

"You did." Bosque's infuriating smile widened. "And all because of a pale-haired girl who looks upon me with doe eyes."

"You admit it!" Eira snapped. "Now let me go and get out of my room."

He didn't let her go. Instead he lifted her up and carried her to the fireplace. Laying her on the sheepskin rug that was warmed by its proximity to the flames, Bosque held her still while he looked down at her.

"My lovely Eira," he murmured. "You mistake gratitude for affection. Agnes is a sorrowful girl who has been ill treated by this world. My kindness is a refuge for her, that is all."

"But why must you be so kind?" Eira asked. "Why not let Alistair care for the girl?"

"Alistair is too busy to attend to Agnes," Bosque replied. "I took it upon myself to earn her trust."

"To what end?" Eira frowned at him.

"You've seen it yourself," Bosque said. "Agnes has a priceless role to play in Lord Hart's cause with Ember. Agnes will be forever tied to us; thus, Ember will be bound as well."

Eira turned her face toward the fire and away from his gaze. She shuddered when his fingers stroked her jaw.

Not wanting to admit how his light touch affected her, Eira said, "I'm cold."

Bosque stretched his hand toward the fireplace and the smoldering embers roared into flames. "Better?" Bosque leaned down, his lips brushing her ear.

She nodded.

"Why so many questions about Agnes?" Bosque took her chin in his hand, forcing her to look into his eyes. "The truth, Eira."

Eira swallowed hard, but answered honestly. "Agnes is young . . . and obviously fertile. She could give you the heir you desire. I—"

Bosque stopped her words with a kiss.

"Stop." Eira pushed him away.

Stroking her hair, Bosque asked quietly, "Has your desire for me waned?"

"No. Never." Eira shivered. She reached up to touch his mouth, tracing its shape. "You place so much faith in me. I worry I cannot give you what you need. I am older than most brides."

"This wedding of Alistair's has muddled your thoughts, I think. Do you long to be a bride like Ember? Shall I prove my love by marrying you?" Bosque laughed, catching her wrist when she tried to slap him for making fun of her.

"Your age means nothing to me." Bosque rolled up to a sitting position, lifting Eira onto his lap. "And no other woman is suited to bear my child. Only you."

"I do not wish to be any man's bride." Eira kept her eyes downcast. "But I would be certain of your feelings."

"Have I given you cause to doubt?" Bosque asked. His arms were around her, warm and strong.

Eira shifted in his lap. "Does love hold sway in your world as it does here?"

Bosque was quiet until Eira looked up at him.

"In my world love is earned, proven," Bosque said. "It is not proclaimed or professed."

He smiled, pushing a stray lock of hair from Eira's forehead. "And if you're pestered by these questions, I have not done enough to prove my affection for you."

Eira opened her mouth to protest, but he drank in her words with a kiss.

"How shall I prove myself?" he murmured against her lips. "Like this?"

Bosque kissed her again.

As he settled her before the fire, Eira asked, "And what of my love? Have I proven it to you?"

"With every breath, Eira," Bosque said. "With every breath."

THIRTY-TWO

**ALISTAIR DIDN'T BOTHER** to seek his bed the night before his wedding. He knew sleep would elude him during the last night he had to suffer through before Ember would be in his arms. His wife. Belonging to him at last.

Forsaking his chambers, which were too full of anticipation to bear, Alistair sought distraction in the catacombs. He strode quickly down the tunnel, eager to be rid of his embarrassingly boyish fixation on his wedding night.

Despite the late hour, Alistair found Rhys awake. The young wolf was chewing contentedly on a large ox bone. When Alistair crouched beside the cage, Rhys looked up, his golden eyes intent.

"I would speak with you," Alistair said. He unlocked the cage and opened the door.

Rhys left the bone and trotted to the door. He only shifted into human form when he was free of the cage. The boy smiled as Alistair sat on the floor. Rhys dropped into a cross-legged sitting position beside him.

"Soon you'll leave your den," Alistair told him. "Do you feel ready?"

Rhys's brow knit together. "Where will I go?"

"Outside," Alistair said. "With me, of course."

"If you are there, Father," Rhys replied, "I am happy to go. May I still sleep in my den?"

Alistair's mouth twitched into a smile. The boy was so wolfish it was uncanny, but Alistair supposed it was only logical that he should be, given his origin.

"If you prefer your den, you may spend nights here," Alistair told him. "But I'll let you choose what you wish after you've seen the other places you might sleep."

"A new den?" Rhys's golden eyes gleamed with curiosity.

Alistair laughed. "Yes. A new den."

Rhys shrugged, looking at his iron cage with a fondness Alistair couldn't understand. "Maybe."

"This den isn't large enough to share with your brothers and sisters," Alistair pointed out. "And they'll be joining you soon. Are you ready to help me teach them?"

Rhys nodded eagerly.

"Good." Alistair smiled. "Would you like to run through the catacombs?"

Instantly the boy was a wolf once more, wagging his tail.

Alistair jumped up and was about to lead Rhys from the room when he heard the boy's voice.

"Is the lady coming back?"

Alistair turned, surprised that Rhys had shifted back to his human form.

"Lady Eira?" Alistair asked. "I'm sure she'll visit again, but she's very busy."

"No." Rhys frowned, his thick pewter-brown curls framing the rosy pout on his lips. "Not the serious lady. The other one who was afraid."

"Afraid?" Alistair's stomach clenched. "Of whom do you speak? Did she come alone?"

"I was sleeping." Rhys nodded, wrinkling his nose. "But the

scent of her fear was so strong, it woke me up. She was trying to get into my den."

Alistair could barely hear over the roaring of blood in his veins. "Tell me, Rhys. What did she look like?"

"She was younger than the serious lady," Rhys answered. "But she had the same fire hair, only darker."

Alistair had to brace himself in the arched chamber opening.

Rhys whimpered. "What's wrong, Father?"

"I'm sorry, Rhys," Alistair said, forcing his panic down. The child was terribly sensitive to the moods of those around him, and Alistair didn't want to distress him. "But you won't be able to run now. I have to leave you."

A wolf once more, Rhys whined. He lowered his head in submission.

"You haven't done anything wrong," Alistair reassured the wolf. "Go to your den. I promise that I'll come to take you to run soon. And you shall run under the moon."

Rhys stood up. He licked Alistair's hand enthusiastically before returning to the cage and settling back in to chew the ox bone.

Alistair managed to lock the door and clear the main chamber before he began to run. His jaw was clenched so hard, the muscles shrieked in pain, but Alistair needed the throbbing ache to stay in control of his mind and heart. Every fiber of his body screamed that he should go to Ember's chamber. He wanted to pin her where she slept and demand answers. But that was the impulse of a boy, and Alistair had to make the choices a man would. The knowledge that she'd been in the catacombs sliced Alistair's hopes to ribbons. She'd seen Rhys, but what else had she discovered? Why had she been in the tombs to begin with?

When Alistair reached Lady Eira's chamber, he banged on the door hard, expecting he would have to wake her.

Though he'd been ready to burst into the room, he was startled enough to take several steps back when Bosque answered the door. Lord Mar's torso was bare, and a sheet had been hastily wrapped around his hips.

"Lord Hart?" Bosque smiled lazily. "You look distressed. Are you having second thoughts about your bride?"

There was an unintended but cruel truth in Bosque's words that sent Alistair pushing past him into Eira's bedchamber, regardless of what had been transpiring within.

Eira gasped, gathering blankets to cover herself where she lay on the bed. "Lord Hart, you do not enter without permission!"

"Forgive me, Lady Eira." Alistair glanced back and forth between Bosque, who closed the door and went to sit on the edge of Eira's bed, and Lady Eira, whose cheeks were coloring with the rosy blush of a maid. Despite the new questions raised by this strange scene, Alistair shoved them aside. "I had to speak with you at once."

The amused expression on Bosque's face vanished. "What is it, Alistair?"

Alistair clenched his fists, reminding himself that he wasn't a lover betrayed but a commander of men. The right hand of Lady Eira and Lord Mar.

"We have a problem."

THIRTY-THREE

**EMBER WENT THROUGH THE** motions of a bride readying for her wedding day, but she felt as though she watched from above, a spirit freed from her body. Agnes stood close, smiling and dabbing at her eyes, while maidservants helped Ember into a gown of gold silk. Her hair had been carefully arranged into a mix of braids and curls that tumbled down her back.

"You rival the sun, sister." Agnes beamed at Ember. "Your hair is flames, and the gown daylight. You have never looked so beautiful."

Ember forced a smile. "Thank you."

Agnes took her hand while the servants drew the laces of the gown tight. "You look frightened."

Ember squeezed Agnes's fingers, unable to answer. Agnes looked into Ember's eyes and then said to the maidservants, "I'll finish this. Please give us some time alone."

When the servants had gone, Agnes stood directly in front of Ember. "I know many maids fear the first night with their husbands because it is known that the wedding night can be painful."

Ember's eyes widened. She was afraid, yes, but her anxiety had nothing to do with anticipation of a wedding night. If Ember ever shared a bed with Alistair, everything in her life would have gone unimaginably wrong.

Taking Ember's startled expression for confirmation of her words, Agnes continued, "You need not worry, Ember. Alistair loves you. He will not treat you like some brutes might. He will be tender and ensure that you have pleasure." Agnes was suddenly blushing. "Despite all the sorrows I've borne, I still remember the wonders that Henry wrought from my body. At the time, I thought it to be love, when it was only lust." The blush gave way to grief's shadow, and she shook her head. "But Alistair does love you, so you can take joy in the secrets of love about which maidens whisper."

Bewildered by her sister's assumptions, Ember just nodded. Her mind was filled with blades and betrayal, while Agnes spoke of love.

Agnes turned Ember to face away from her and finished securing the laces of her wedding gown. Ember's gut twisted with guilt; she could bear her secrets no longer.

"Agnes, there's something I must tell you—"

A light knock sounded, and Agnes called, "Come in!"

The door swung in, and one of the maidservants curtsied before stepping aside to allow Ossia Morrow entry.

"Mother!" Agnes cried, rushing into Lady Morrow's open arms.

Ember stood still, the soon-to-unfold plot against Eira and Bosque waiting on her lips. Her father held fast to the notion that women had no business in matters politic or military, but in this rare case, could he have shared the truth with his wife? If Ember disclosed her allies' plans to her mother and sister, would Ossia Morrow react with solemn knowing or horrified shock? More importantly, if it were the latter, would she betray Ember's confidence?

Ossia stroked Agnes's hair. "My heart is full of joy to see you so well, Agnes."

Agnes drew herself up, leaving her childish outburst behind to play the proper matron. "I am greatly indebted to Lady Eira, Lord Bosque, and especially to Ember's betrothed. I have been afforded every comfort since my arrival at Tearmunn."

"Then we are indebted to them as well," Lady Morrow answered.

Ember's mother left her elder daughter to stand before Ember. Ember felt rigid, unable to respond with warmth to her mother's arrival, as she could think only of the peril her mother would face once the clansmen began their attack.

Ossia touched Ember's cheek. "Oh, you are pale, my dear. Don't be frightened. This is a wonderful, wonderful day."

Ember hugged her mother, but the embrace felt stiff. She'd seen the shining delight in Ossia's gaze; her father had given his wife no bit of truth regarding this sham of a wedding. Neither Agnes nor their mother had any inkling of the imminent danger. Though Mackenzie had promised men to protect them, the only small comfort Ember took was in the stiletto she'd slipped into her garter when the maids and Agnes were distracted. If all else failed, Ember would protect her mother and sister herself.

"It's time to join the others," Ossia told Ember. "I'm here to escort you to the ceremony."

Ember took her mother's arm, and Agnes followed them from the room. When they reached the bottom of the staircase, Ember's knees went weak. Her mother grabbed her around the waist tightly and propped her up as they walked.

"There, there, my dear," Ossia whispered. "Don't let it overwhelm you."

Agnes came to Ember's opposite side, taking her arm to give their mother aid.

Though rain had fallen overnight, leaving the courtyard muddy, the day was the best May could offer. A cloudless sky heralded Ember's arrival. The light breeze that touched her skin was warm, its breath sweetened by blossoms that festooned the manor entryway.

Even on the most bustling days at Tearmunn, Ember had never seen the courtyard so full. Dancers whose heads were wreathed with flowers spun and jumped while pipes and bodhran filled the air with a soaring, frenzied melody.

Servants wove among the guests, bearing platters of roasted

meats and brimming cups of wine. Men and women jostled each other, lifting onto the balls of their feet to glimpse the approaching bride. Ember searched the crowd, her chest tightening. The clansmen had gathered en masse. Cian, Ember's father, and Lord Mackenzie stood at the front of their ranks.

The warriors held wine cups, but not once did Ember see a man among them drink. She found little comfort in their numbers as she realized that genuine guests were in attendance. These celebrants raised their cups when Ember passed, shouting blessings and bawdy suggestions for the wedding night. Ember bowed her head, wondering how many hapless guests would have their blood spilled that day for reasons they'd never comprehend.

Ember's gaze roamed the faces, finding mostly strangers. She knew she searched for Barrow in vain, but still she looked. Meeting his gray eyes, if only for a second, would bolster her courage, in the face of this horrid day. No longer able to bear the hollowing beneath her ribs, Ember abandoned her search to face what she feared most.

Father Michael and Alistair awaited her on a wooden dais that had been erected between the manor and the barracks. At Alistair's left shoulder stood Bosque Mar, still and imposing as a monument. On Alistair's right, Lady Eira watched the bridal party approach, a tight smile fixed upon her lips. But the figure standing at Alistair's side made Ember stumble.

The boy in the cage. He stood dressed in the fine clothing of a nobleman's child. Alistair's hands rested on his shoulders.

Ember's glance shot to the stables. If she broke from her mother and sister now, she could get to a horse and ride. Caber had been left to Barrow's care in France, but for this purpose, any swift mount would do. If she ran, Alistair would surely chase her. Maybe that would be distraction enough, serving the same purpose as the attack but avoiding the bloodbath this crowd promised.

"You must remember to breathe, Ember," Agnes whispered in her ear. "You're terribly pale."

Shaking off her coward's dream of flight, Ember did as Agnes bid, drawing long, deep breaths to steady herself. If Ember were to run, she would have little chance of making it as far as the stables. Too many people filled the courtyard to give her a clear path, and Alistair's men, if not Alistair himself, would catch her before she came close to fleeing the keep.

Agnes kissed Ember's cheek as they stepped onto the dais and then she passed her sister into Alistair's waiting grasp. Alistair took both of Ember's hands in his, bringing her gaze to his face. He brought her fingers to his lips. "You're trembling, my sweet."

Ember could only nod. Suddenly she blurted out, "I'm not well. I worry I will faint."

"I'll only keep you here a bit longer," Alistair replied. "It will all be over soon."

Ember stared at him as he squelched her last ploy to stop the ceremony. It had to be this way, Ember desperately reminded herself. The wedding and the surprise attack were the only things that could provide Rebekah the time she needed to close the rift.

Alistair gestured to the boy at his side. "Ember, this is Rhys. You'll soon know him as you'd know your own child."

The boy looked at Ember with solemn yellow eyes. "She's still afraid, Father."

Ember gasped at the way Rhys addressed Alistair. Who was this child?

Rhys watched her, calm and curious. Ember returned his gaze, wondering if she'd imagined his transformation. How could this sweet-faced child have become a wolf?

Alistair leaned down to murmur in Ember's ear. "Once we are married, you will learn who Rhys is to us, and you will love him as I do." He spoke as if the words were a threat, and Ember blanched.

"Let us begin, Father Michael," Eira commanded with a sweep of her hand toward the throng of guests.

The priest uttered the familiar words of the wedding ceremony, but to Ember they were an unintelligible jumble of sounds. She stood still as stone, trapped in this nightmare, able only to stare at the boy whom Alistair called Rhys.

When the priest prompted her, Ember managed to respond as required, but she became aware of the progress of the ceremony only when Alistair slipped a ring onto her finger. She looked down as the cool gold band touched her skin.

The signal.

Ember met Alistair's gaze. In his bright blue irises she saw many things: lust, possession, regret—but not hope or joy, and certainly not love. She tried to pull her hand back, but Alistair stepped closer, grabbing her wrist with bruising force.

"Not yet, my love," he murmured, and Ember couldn't breathe.

He knew.

A battle cry rose from the crowd at Ember's back, followed by another. The war calls mingled with shouts of alarm and fear. The bright ring of steel rose to join the screams. Wrenching her neck to look behind her, Ember saw the madness of war flood the courtyard. Clansmen hacked at Eira's guard. Wedding guests not complicit in the attack scrambled from the flurry of swords and axes. The rain-soaked ground churned beneath trampling feet. Bodies fell in the mud, some dead, others living only long enough to be crushed in the stampede.

Agnes shrieked and clung to her mother.

Bosque looked at the huddled women and laughed. "Don't be afraid, dear ladies. You're quite safe, I assure you."

Bosque lifted his palm and the muddy ground in front of the dais began to boil. Wraiths bubbled up from the muck, their shadow bodies slithering forward to take posts as sentinels between the wedding party and the embattled mass.

Rhys snarled at the appearance of the wraiths—Ember glanced down and saw the boy's lips curl back. His teeth flashed in the sunlight, canines sharp as a wolf's fangs.

"Be still," Alistair said to the child. "Remember. Not until I say."

Balling his fists, Rhys looked up at Alistair and nodded.

Seizing on Alistair's distraction, Ember thrust her foot up, sweeping his legs from beneath him. With a cry, Alistair collapsed to the dais, and Ember was free.

Without hesitation, she whirled around, grabbing her mother and sister and dragging them toward the manor. Mackenzie might have men coming to their aid, but no warrior would get past Bosque's wraiths. Ember hugged the outer wall of the building as she pulled Agnes and Ossia through the mud. Not daring to look behind her for fear that Bosque would send a wraith in pursuit, Ember could only hope that Alistair still wanted her alive.

"Keep running!" Ember shouted as she flung the manor door open. The three women stumbled inside, and Ember said, "This way."

Ember's mother and sister were sobbing as Ember pulled them down the corridor to the great hall. All Ember could think of was getting Agnes and Ossia to safety, and that meant away from Tearmunn. The only way out was Rebekah's portal.

When she reached the double doors of the great hall, Ember heard rapid footsteps behind her.

"Get inside," Ember hissed, cracking the door so Agnes and their mother could slip through. Only when they were in the great hall did Ember turn to see Alistair running at her. A young wolf loped at his heels.

Ember threw herself into the great hall, slamming the doors at her back. She desperately searched the room for a barricade. Her gaze fell upon the crescent table and its accompanying chairs.

"Mother, get a chair!" Ember shouted to Ossia. "We have to block the doorway."

Ember lurched forward as something or someone crashed into the doors. Bracing herself, Ember struggled to keep the doors from opening.

It wasn't enough.

An incredible force crashed against the doors, and Ember was sent sprawling across the stone floor.

The wind knocked from her lungs, Ember wheezed, rolling onto her side. The two doors had been blown to splinters. In the cloud of debris, Ember saw Eira, Bosque, Alistair, and the wolf standing over her.

"Wherever are you going, Lady Morrow?" Eira drew her sword. "Your wedding day has just begun."

Glancing at the wolf, Alistair said, "Stay hidden until I call." The wolf bowed its head. With ears pinned back, it slunk into the shadowed corner of the hall.

Ember scrambled to her feet, hoping to reach her mother and sister, but Alistair lunged into the room, grabbing her around the waist and pulling her back.

"You will not escape me," he hissed in her ear.

At the far side of the room, a door of light appeared.

Alistair's grip tightened on Ember when he saw the portal, and she coughed, struggling for breath.

"More guests," Alistair whispered. "How lovely."

He dragged Ember toward the door. She writhed in his arms, trying to free herself and catching only glimpses of the figures that emerged from Rebekah's gleaming door.

A battle cry filled the room, and Lukasz rushed from the portal wielding his claymore. Kurjii and Tamur were at his flank.

Ember kicked at Alistair as he wrenched her around to face Eira and Bosque. She twisted as far as she could and saw Rebekah appear from within the portal, hanging back while Kael stayed at her side. After Rebekah closed the door, Kael guided her to the shadowed staircase at the far end of the hall that led to the gallery, hoping to keep her out of harm's way while she performed the ritual. The portal was gone, but Barrow was nowhere to be seen. Ember didn't know if she was relieved by his absence or disheartened.

Alistair had almost reached his companions when a new cry of rage sounded from the outer hall. Eira whirled, raising her sword just in time to meet Cian's deadly strike. Eira's face whitened and then her eyes hardened with fury as she glared at Cian.

"You betray your own blood?" Eira hissed.

"The betrayal is yours," Cian answered. "And I have no choice but to make you answer for it."

Father Michael appeared at Cian's back, red-faced and huffing for breath. He took in the scene and tried to slide past the sword-locked pair and into the great hall.

Bosque's silver eyes narrowed. Taking one long stride, his arm shot out and struck Father Michael, sending the priest flying across the chamber. Father Michael's body slammed into the wall and fell limp on the floor. Pivoting to face the sisters, Bosque stretched his hand toward Cian, his fingers clawlike.

"No!" Eira shouted, catching his movement but not taking her eyes off Cian. "Deal with the others, but she is mine."

"As you wish." Bosque turned his palm over, and three wraiths rose from the stone floor, their bodies curling like smoke. He flicked his wrist at Lukasz, Kurjii, and Tamur. "Kill the intruders."

The wraiths oozed like tar toward the knights.

Twisting in Alistair's grasp, Ember shouted to her sister and mother, "Get to the gallery! Run!"

If Agnes and her mother could reach Kael, they would at least have some protection. A sliver of relief stole through Ember when she saw Agnes stiffen with resolve and pull their mother toward the gallery staircase.

Lifting his massive claymore, Lukasz shouted, "These creatures cannot be killed. Don't let them touch you."

Bosque threw back his head and laughed. "I shall enjoy watching you try to run from my wraiths. You will tire. They will not."

At a nod from Lukasz, the trio of knights split. The wraiths separated to follow them, pursuing their victims with a slow determination.

Eira and Cian's fight had progressed from the corridor into the great hall. The sisters danced around each other, their blades flashing through the air like streaks of lightning. Eira shoved hard, sending Cian staggering back. Eira leapt from the throne, flipping in the air to land with deadly grace at Cian's back. Cian whirled and the sisters' blades met again. The room sang with steel's bright cries as Eira and Cian rained blows upon each other.

"Come to me, Lord Hart!" Bosque called from the doorway.

Ember cried out when Alistair's grasp tightened. He swung her around, dragging her away from the swordplay.

Lukasz and Tamur had taken to weaving throughout the hall, keeping a distance between themselves and the wraiths that hunted them. Kurjii, however, backed too far into a corner, and before he could dart out again, the wraith snaked forward, wrapping itself around the knight. His sword clattered to the floor as his screams filled the room.

"No!" Ember shouted as the Mamluk warrior thrashed in the wraith's clutches.

Alistair cuffed Ember, making her head ring from the blow.

"Forget them! You are still mine, as you always will be," he growled at her. "And in my possession, you will learn the price of betrayal."

Even through the fog of her blurred vision, Ember was sickened by the hatred in his eyes. She'd done this to him, at least partly.

"Don't do this, Alistair," she pleaded. "You're better than this."

"You've barely begun to know who I am. Submit to me, and I'll spare your mother and sister," Alistair replied. "Fight me, and you'll watch them die."

Ember saw a figure looming at her left side a moment before Alistair did. Alistair shoved Ember away so hard that she fell; he reached for his sword, but he couldn't draw the blade before Barrow slammed into him, sending them both tumbling along the floor.

Scrambling to her feet, Ember reached under her skirt and withdrew the stiletto. Locked in a wrestling match, Barrow and Alistair pummeled each other, both struggling to get the upper hand. Ember held her dagger low and spun around quickly, surveying the room. Bosque blocked the way to the outer hall.

Lukasz and Tamur still dodged the wraiths that pursued them. Bosque kept his place in the doorway, watching in amusement and seemingly content to let the wraiths continue their cat-and-mouse game with the knights.

Ember's gaze returned to Barrow and Alistair. They were still a tangle of limbs and fists on the ground. Gripping her stiletto, for a moment Ember thought to intervene, but she thrust the impulse aside. Barrow was in less danger than the others whom she loved here. Ember ran to the stairs, swearing that with her last breath she'd fight to save her mother and sister.

THIRTY-FOUR

**EIRA DODGED ANOTHER** blow, gritting her teeth when
Cian parried her next strike.

"I'm happy to see you'll still fight your own battles," Cian spat
at Eira. "I thought I'd be reduced to slashing at Bosque's hideous
pets."

"I wouldn't miss the satisfaction of reminding you that I've
always been stronger," Eira snapped. "In all ways."

Their swords met again, steel rasping as both sisters pushed
toward each other.

"You mistake your ambition for strength." Cian surged forward,
sending Eira staggering.

Bosque was immediately at Eira's side, steadying her. His silver
eyes flashed as he leveled his gaze on Cian.

"Stop." Eira pulled away from him. "This is my fight."

"It is an unnecessary risk, my love," Bosque murmured, but Cian
heard him.

"What can a creature like you know of love?" Cian screamed at
him. "You seduced my sister with lust and power. You have corrupted her!"

With a screech of outrage, Eira launched herself at Cian. Their
blades met high in the air, descending into a flurry of blows.

Panting from the effort of her attack, Eira said, "How can you be
so naive? Would you live under the thumb of men forever?"

"Men do not rule me," Cian replied as their blades grated against each other. "My life has always been my own, as was yours."

"You're blind." Eira's retort came with another blow. "Gaining permission to wield a blade is not enough. I could have given you so much more."

Eira brought her sword down in a sweeping arc; Cian ducked, rolling across the floor to escape the fatal blow.

"You are the pawn of the enemy," Cian said, breathless. "I will never serve Bosque as you do."

"I do not serve him." Eira stalked toward her sister. "I love him."

Though Eira hadn't reached her, Cian reeled as if from a blow. "It is not love, sister. Love would not make you betray who you are."

Eira's laugh was bright as her blade. "You no longer see who I am, Cian. But I will show you."

Advancing on Cian, Eira brought her sword down with incredible force. Cian rose to meet the blow. Eira suddenly twisted and flicked Cian's sword from her grasp. Eira's foot lashed out, hitting Cian in the chest and sending her sprawling. As Eira stalked toward her, Cian rose, but only to her knees.

"Yield," Eira hissed.

"I yield only to death," Cian answered.

Leveling her blade at Cian's chest, Eira said, "When you draw your last breath, remember that you chose this fate."

Cian bowed her head, whispering rapid words.

"It's too late to pray for salvation, my sister."

Eira thrust, and as the sword slid into Cian's heart, she heard Bosque cry out, "No!"

Cian's body slumped over Eira's sword. Grimly, Eira withdrew the blade. The blood that covered her sword began to glow. With a cry, Eira dropped the weapon and stumbled back as the strange light blossomed from the pooling blood until it surrounded Cian's body like a cocoon.

Eira felt Bosque's arms around her, pulling her away from her sister's corpse.

An abundance of colors suffused the sphere that rose from the ground, carrying Cian with it. Spears of light shot out from the gleaming circle, striking the wraiths in the room and making them shriek, their dark mass bubbling like pitch until they burst and were gone.

Bosque roared, and the sound reverberated through the hall, its fury shaking the ground. The stone floor beneath Lukasz and Tamur shifted and cracked, sending the knights tumbling.

"Take cover," Bosque growled at Eira. He pushed her toward the edge of the hall and advanced on the sphere of light.

Eira saw that it moved with purpose, its beams growing wider and brighter as it approached the rift. As the sphere's light reached the massive dead tree, Eira gasped. The scene before her flickered; with one blink, the tree stood as it was—bone-white and bearing the gaping wound of the rift—but in the next moment, Eira could see the tree as it had been, mighty and draped in the emerald tones of its vitality.

The sphere began to descend; there could be no mistaking its destination. Eira saw that it would fill the void perfectly, its light blocking the darkness. Sealing the gate to the nether.

Suddenly Bosque loomed in front of the rift. He reached into the undulating shadows at his back, and from within the rift, he drew a sword. The weapon was larger than even Lukasz's claymore, and like Bosque's steed, this blade appeared to be forged of shadow.

As he lifted the sword, Bosque rasped in fury, "This will not come to pass."

With one stride, Bosque launched himself into the air, every muscle in his body working to power the stroke of his blade. His sword hit the sphere, barely piercing the surface of shimmering lights.

The sphere shuddered and burst. The explosion was deafening.

It sent Bosque hurtling through the air until he landed in a heap on the far side of the room. The stained-glass windows of the hall shattered. Thick branches of the dead tree cracked, groaning as they sheared off the trunk and slammed to the stone floor.

Eira fell to her knees, but not because of the explosion. Where the sphere had been, Cian was floating in the air. Eira knew it wasn't truly her sister. Whatever this spirit was, it had Cian's features, but the hovering figure was transparent.

Cian was speaking, her words in Latin, filling the room as loudly as Bosque's roar had, but not with a furious cry. Instead the air trembled as Cian's words became a song, a melody that blended aching sorrow and unflagging hope.

Stunned by her sister's transformation, Eira couldn't make sense of what Cian's spirit song meant. She was only able to discern the final phrases:

*Prolem cruces ferat.*
*Crux ancora vitae.*
May the Scion bear the Cross.
The Cross is the anchor of life.

Cian spread her arms to the side, and her body became light, so bright that Eira could barely look at her. As Eira watched, the light separated into four distinct pieces. They grew larger, taking on the characteristics of the portals that Conatus's clerics wove. Through each shimmering doorway, Eira glimpsed a different landscape. The first revealed a pine-covered slope and the dark opening of a cave.

*Haldis.*

Eira heard Cian's whisper. It hung in the air for a moment. Then the portal curled in on itself, becoming a flaring ball of light.

Through the next doorway Eira saw the snowcapped peaks of mountains and the silver-blue of ice.

*Tordis.*

Like the first portal, at Cian's whisper, the door shuddered, contracting until it too had been reduced to a ball of light.

The third doorway opened to the bluest seas Eira had ever set eyes on. More lustrous than the Mediterranean, the waters were surrounded by dense forests of a kind Eira didn't recognize. The trees were short, ropelike vines twisting between trunks. The leaves were thick and broad, gleaming jade green.

*Eydis.*

Eira gasped, stepping back at the vivid imagery held within the fourth portal. Glossy black rock and rivers of fire. The earth belching ash and molten flame.

*Pyralis.*

When the final door swirled into a ball of light, the four spheres brightened to the point that Eira found it hard to look at them. Like falling stars, they shot from the room, blasting through stone, wood, and glass as they escaped the great hall, each flying in a different direction.

And then they were gone. The chamber was silent, and Cian's body was nowhere to be seen.

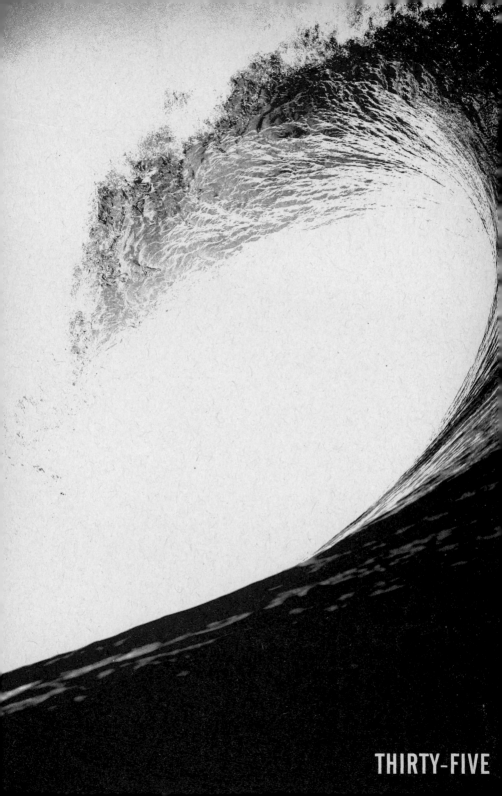

THIRTY-FIVE

**THE EXPLOSION FINALLY** ripped Alistair and Barrow apart. Their fight had been relentless and ugly. A fight with no honor, only animosity. Too close for clear blows, the knights had been reduced to biting, ripping, and tearing at each other like wild beasts. Neither gained the advantage, but both were so consumed by hatred that they willingly embraced the futility of their struggle.

Alistair didn't see Eira slay her sister. He took no note of the strange object that consumed Cian's body. All he did see was the man he despised, a man who wanted to steal what was his. He kicked and twisted in Barrow's grasp. Cursing and spitting, they wrangled each other along the stone floor.

When the room filled with light and sound, an unknown force threw Alistair and Barrow against the wall. For a few minutes, Alistair was knocked senseless. When he opened his eyes, the room was blurred, and the ground felt as if it were shifting beneath him.

"Fall back!" Lukasz's command reached Alistair's ringing ear. "Get to the portal!"

More shouts and the pounding of feet above him in the gallery compelled Alistair to rise, despite the wave of nausea and dizziness that crashed through him. He stumbled forward, drawing his sword. A single thought had taken hold of Alistair's mind.

He could not let Ember leave.

Alistair began to run, gulping air to help clear his head and clinging to his singular purpose.

"Rhys!" he shouted. The wolf leapt from the shadows to run at his heels.

Reaching the gallery steps, Alistair took them two at a time. At the top of the staircase, he threw himself forward, hurtling wildly ahead as he saw a shimmering door appear at the far end of the hall.

Barrow had reached the gallery just ahead of Alistair. Ember gave a cry of relief as she threw herself into Barrow's arms. He lifted her up, his mouth crushing into Ember's as she wrapped herself around him, welcoming his embrace in a way Alistair would never know.

Alistair opened his mouth and what emerged from his mouth was a howl of such anguish that it sounded inhuman.

Ember broke from the kiss at the sound of his cry. Grief etched across her face. Pushing Barrow toward her sister, Ember took a step toward Alistair.

"Ember!" Barrow called in warning.

Looking over her shoulder, Ember said, "Get my sister and mother to safety."

"I'm not leaving without you." Barrow glared at Alistair.

"Give me one minute." Ember took another step forward, away from Barrow. "I'll be right behind you."

Something in Ember's voice must have silenced Barrow's protests. He nodded grimly. Taking Ossia Morrow's hand, Barrow guided her to the waiting portal.

"Alistair," Ember said softly, coming toward him. Her eyes flicked nervously toward Rhys. "I don't know what's happened to you, how Bosque has twisted your heart, but I can't believe you fully belong to him. I remember the boy who taught me to fight. I remember my friend."

Alistair lowered his sword, watching Ember approach.

"Come with us." Ember stopped, just out of reach, and extended her hand. "I cannot give you what you want, but I swear you will always have my love in friendship. Is that not enough?"

"Enough?" Alistair repeated. Casting his gaze upon the wolf at his side, Alistair said, "Your time has come, Rhys. Retrieve my ring."

Ember flinched when Alistair looked at the wolf, but not quickly enough. In a flash of fur and fangs, the wolf leapt at her. She threw her hand up to guard her throat, but that was precisely what Rhys wanted.

The wolf's jaws closed on the fingers of Ember's left hand. She screamed, and Rhys jerked his head back.

Barrow had been shepherding Agnes toward Rebekah's portal, but turned at Ember's cry. He lifted his sword, but Agnes moved even faster. Her eyes had locked on the young wolf that had knocked Ember to the ground.

And suddenly it wasn't Ember's sister lunging at Rhys, but a snarling she-wolf. Her fur shone with threads of pale gold; her body was heavy with the baby she carried. Agnes snapped her teeth, and Rhys jumped back.

"To me!" Alistair shouted, and Rhys darted to his side, matching Agnes's snarls with his own.

Transfixed, Alistair stopped and then took a step back, then another. Agnes bristled, her teeth bared as she stared him down. Alistair's rage gave way to a surge of triumph.

Despite her wound, Ember uttered a tremulous cry of shock. The sound brought Agnes's head around, her ears flicking toward Ember. Then Agnes was a woman again, and her body began to shake.

"Barrow!" Lukasz shouted to the huddled trio from the edge of the portal.

Barrow scooped up Ember with one arm and stretched his other hand to Agnes. She stumbled toward Barrow, grasping his fingers. Alistair watched as Barrow dragged Agnes and carried Ember to the waiting door. Lukasz stood guard as they rushed through the portal and then he followed. The gleaming door vanished; they were gone.

"Your friendship would never be enough, my love." Like a man entranced, Alistair put out his hand, and Rhys dropped Ember's two severed fingers into Alistair's palm. One was encircled by a golden band.

THIRTY-SIX

**THE SUN DISAPPEARED** behind the mountains as Ember joined Agnes at the water's edge.

"The stew is ready," Ember said quietly. "If you're hungry."

Agnes nodded, but her expression was distant.

"It's not so different from home, is it?" Agnes gazed out over the fjords.

"I suppose not," Ember answered, not wanting to disagree with her sister, but although the Norse country was wild and rugged like the highlands, the air carried unfamiliar scents, the slope of the hills was a bit too rough, and the sky was too bright. It wasn't home, and Ember doubted she'd ever feel a true sense of home again.

Agnes sighed, her hand moving to her swollen belly.

"Are you unwell?" Ember asked.

"No," Agnes said. "Just tired."

She hesitated, the skin around her eyes tightening. "Ember, do you believe my child to be anything other than a monster?"

Ember thought of the boy in the cage. The boy who abruptly vanished and left a snarling young wolf in his place. Rhys had attacked her at Alistair's command. The wolf-child had taken two of her fingers. But Ember chose to remember the fear she'd seen in the boy's large yellow eyes when she'd first encountered him. In a moment of crisis, Agnes had transformed from woman to wolf, but she'd done so to protect her sister. There was nothing monstrous in that.

"You're not a monster, despite what Alistair and Bosque did to you," Ember said. "Why should your child be so condemned?"

"The others are afraid of me," Agnes answered. "If they fear me, they must fear what grows within me."

"No one knows whether the magics worked on you have affected your child," Ember told her. "And they aren't afraid of you, they're afraid *for* you."

"You believe that because you are my sister." Agnes sighed. "But you don't see how they look at me. You can't smell their fear."

Finding no reply, Ember took Agnes's hand. "Come to the fire."

Agnes clasped the fingers of Ember's right hand, but her gaze drifted to the sling that cradled her left arm. Her left hand was enshrouded with bandages. "Do you heal well?"

"Rebekah tells me I do," Ember replied. "Barrow thinks that I'm best off fighting with a shield strapped to my left arm and a weapon in the right."

Agnes cast a sidelong glance at her. "Are you so eager to return to battle?"

Ember nodded, offering Agnes a grim smile. She could think of little else. Before the last battle at Tearmunn, she'd been part of a resistance. Now they were truly exiles, wandering the earth until they could finish the work Cian's sacrifice had begun.

Barrow stood up to meet Ember when she and Agnes reached the encircled warriors. He kissed her, and she joined him beside the fire. Agnes wandered slightly apart, but Rebekah beckoned to her.

Ember glanced around the fire at the faces of her companions. They were so few. Lukasz and Rebekah had hoped that they would gather more allies, warriors and clerics willing to aid them as they searched for what Rebekah called the Elemental Cross—the key to sealing the rift and the magic tied to Cian's death at her sister's hand.

Each night as they gathered for the evening meal, Rebekah repeated the Latin words that Cian's spirit had intoned before her body had become like four stars. Those words were their hope, Rebekah claimed, their new purpose. While Bosque's attack had disrupted the spell before it could be completed, the power of Cian's act remained. Her body had become that which could still defeat Bosque and close the gate between the earth and the nether.

Rebekah finished this night's recitation as darkness closed around them.

"Without the Elemental Cross, the rift cannot be closed. Conatus is no more," Lukasz said. "The battle lost."

"But the war has just begun," Ember replied, and Barrow tightened his arms around her.

"The pieces have flown to the four corners of the earth, where they will rest until the Scion claims them, as Cian's prophecy foretells." Rebekah nodded at Ember. "That is when the war will end."

Solemn murmurs of affirmation answered her. It was such an impossible hope to cling to. But it was all they had. Ember closed her eyes. Though she'd been consumed by the battle, she could summon the final melody and words of Cian's spirit at will. They all could.

Only Rebekah seemed unruffled by the strange song that had been burned into the memory of each person who'd been in the great hall. It was the nature of prophecy, Rebekah had told them as easily as if she'd been reminding them that the sun rose each morning, to ensure its remembrance.

Agnes huddled on the other side of the fire beside Rebekah. Ember noticed how often her sister raised her head as if catching scents on the wind, or stared into the dark forest like it was calling to her.

The campfire spit and crackled. Ember leaned into Barrow's chest, nestling her head beneath his chin. She gazed into the leaping flames and saw only wolves.

# ACKNOWLEDGMENTS

*Rise* came into being during a difficult and tumultuous chapter of my life. Without the dauntless support of friends and colleagues, the writing of this book would have been at best a struggle. The joy of working with Penguin Young Readers Group supplies incredible encouragement for each stage of producing a novel. I'd like to give particular thanks to Don Weisberg and Jen Loja for their unwavering enthusiasm and kindness. The energy and mad talent of the sales, marketing, publicity, and school and library teams make me want to grab pom-poms and cheer them on outside their offices. Thanks especially to Shanta, Emily R., Erin, Elyse, Emilie B., Lisa, Jessica, Kristina, Molly, Courtney, Anna, Scottie, Jackie, and Felicia. A big shout-out, too, to all the sales reps who work so hard to get the Nightshade series into readers' hands.

The beautiful jackets on all of the US editions are thanks to Linda and Theresa, and the stunning interior design is thanks to Amy and Semadar. The lovely Puffin team, Eileen, Jen B., and Dana, created the gorgeous paperbacks. Thank you to everyone for the advice and encouragement about moving to New York!

My home within a home at PYRG is Philomel. Michael Green keeps me smiling and offers consolation when my sports teams are (often) in the gutter. I would wax hyperbolic for several pages about my amazing editor, Jill Santopolo, but being the talented editor she is, she would rightly have me cut all that purple prose. Thanks to Julia and Kiffin for all of their help along the way, and to Cindy, Rob, Ana and Karen, whose copyedits kept my characters honest and my writing free of double entendres.

My family continues to support my dream of a writing life and keep me steady through life's storms. Thanks to my brother, Garth, for always cheering me on. Thanks to my mom and dad for understanding their small-town-raised daughter's longing for the big city. Every day I'm grateful for my friends in the writing world: David Levithan, Eliot Schrefer, Stephanie Perkins, and Kiersten White make my heart smile. Beth Revis, Marie Lu, and Jessica Spotswood are the Breathless Godmothers of this book, and they know more about big talent than anyone else. My dear friend and colleague Casey Jarrin has made all the difference as I transition from the academic to a creative profession. She is a star.

This book is dedicated to the trio of agents at InkWell Management who've transformed my novels from spark of idea to published reality. Charlie saved Calla and the pack from a slushy death. If I find the TARDIS, Charlie will be my first phone call. Lyndsey enabled global excursions for the witches and wolves, and I hope someday we'll have an international adventure together. Richard is the bravest person I know: he dives in underwater caves— also, I adore him. I often wonder how I got so lucky to be backed by this marvelous team. Thank you for all that you do. Know that I would storm a castle for you guys.

The battle rages on in

# NIGHTSHADE

Turn the page for a sneak peek!

THE NEW YORK TIMES BESTSELLING SERIES

She can
control
her pack,
but not her
heart.

ANDREA CREMER

# NIGHTSHADE

The International Bestseller

# I'D ALWAYS WELCOMED WAR, BUT IN BATTLE

my passion rose unbidden.

The bear's roar filled my ears. Its hot breath assaulted my nostrils, fueling my bloodlust. Behind me I could hear the boy's ragged gasp. The desperate sound made my nails dig into the earth. I snarled at the larger predator again, daring it to try to get past me.

*What the hell am I doing?*

I risked a glance at the boy and my pulse raced. His right hand pressed against the gashes in his thigh. Blood surged between his fingers, darkening his jeans until they looked streaked by black paint. Slashes in his shirt barely covered the red lacerations that marred his chest. A growl rose in my throat.

I crouched low, muscles tensed, ready to strike. The grizzly rose onto its hind legs. I held my ground.

*Calla!*

Bryn's cry sounded in my mind. A lithe brown wolf darted from the forest and tore into the bear's unguarded flank. The grizzly turned, landing on all fours. Spit flew from its mouth as it searched for the unseen attacker. But Bryn, lightning fast, dodged the bear's lunge. With each swipe of the grizzly's trunk-thick arms, she avoided its reach, always moving a split second faster than the bear. She seized her advantage, inflicting another taunting bite. When the bear's back was turned, I leapt forward and ripped a chunk from its heel. The bear swung around to face me, its eyes rolling, filled with pain.

Bryn and I slunk along the ground, circling the huge animal. The bear's blood made my mouth hot. My body tensed. We continued our ever-tightening dance. The bear's eyes tracked us. I could smell its doubt, its rising fear. I let out a short, harsh bark and flashed my fangs. The grizzly snorted as it turned away and lumbered into the forest.

I raised my muzzle and howled in triumph. A moan brought me back to earth. The hiker stared at us, eyes wide. Curiosity pulled me toward him. I'd betrayed my masters, broken their laws. All for him.

*Why?*

My head dropped low and I tested the air. The hiker's blood streamed over his skin and onto the ground, the sharp, coppery odor creating an intoxicating fog in my conscience. I fought the temptation to taste it.

*Calla?* Bryn's alarm pulled my gaze from the fallen hiker.

*Get out of here.* I bared my teeth at the smaller wolf. She dropped low and bellied along the ground toward me. Then she raised her muzzle and licked the underside of my jaw.

*What are you going to do?* her blue eyes asked me.

She looked terrified. I wondered if she thought I'd kill the boy for my own pleasure. Guilt and shame trickled through my veins.

*Bryn, you can't be here. Go. Now.*

She whined but slunk away, slipping beneath the cover of pine trees.

I stalked toward the hiker. My ears flicked back and forth. He struggled for breath, pain and terror filling his face. Deep gashes remained where the grizzly's claws had torn at his thigh and chest. Blood still flowed from the wounds. I knew it wouldn't stop. I growled, frustrated by the fragility of his human body.

He was a boy who looked about my age: seventeen, maybe

eighteen. Brown hair with a slight shimmer of gold fell in a mess around his face. Sweat had caked strands of it to his forehead and cheeks. He was lean, strong—someone who could find his way around a mountain, as he clearly had. This part of the territory was only accessible through a steep, unwelcoming trail.

The scent of fear covered him, taunting my predatory instincts, but beneath it lay something else—the smell of spring, of nascent leaves and thawing earth. A scent full of hope. Possibility. Subtle and tempting.

I took another step toward him. I knew what I wanted to do, but it would mean a second, much-greater violation of the Keepers' Laws. He tried to move back but gasped in pain and collapsed onto his elbows. My eyes moved over his face. His chiseled jaw and high cheekbones twisted in agony. Even writhing he was beautiful, muscles clenching and unclenching, revealing his strength, his body's fight against its impending collapse, rendering his torture sublime. Desire to help him consumed me.

*I can't watch him die.*

I shifted forms before I realized I'd made the decision. The boy's eyes widened when the white wolf who'd been eyeing him was no longer an animal, but a girl with the wolf's golden eyes and platinum blond hair. I walked to his side and dropped to my knees. His entire body shook. I began to reach for him but hesitated, surprised to feel my own limbs trembling. I'd never been so afraid.

A rasping breath pulled me out of my thoughts.

"Who are you?" The boy stared at me. His eyes were the color of winter moss, a delicate shade that hovered between green and gray. I was caught there for a moment. Lost in the questions that pushed through his pain and into his gaze.

I raised the soft flesh of my inner forearm to my mouth. Willing my canines to sharpen, I bit down hard and waited until my own blood touched my tongue. Then I extended my arm toward him.

"Drink. It's the only thing that can save you." My voice was low but firm.

The trembling in his limbs grew more pronounced. He shook his head.

"You have to," I growled, showing him canines still razor sharp from opening the wound in my arm. I hoped the memory of my wolf form would terrorize him into submission. But the look on his face wasn't one of horror. The boy's eyes were full of wonder. I blinked at him and fought to remain still. Blood ran along my arm, falling in crimson drops onto the leaf-lined soil.

His eyes snapped shut as he grimaced from a surge of renewed pain. I pressed my bleeding forearm against his parted lips. His touch was electric, searing my skin, racing through my blood. I bit back a gasp, full of wonder and fear at the alien sensations that rolled through my limbs.

He flinched, but my other arm whipped around his back, holding him still while my blood flowed into his mouth. Grasping him, pulling him close only made my blood run hotter.

I could tell he wanted to resist, but he had no strength left. A smile pulled at the corners of my mouth. Even if my own body was reacting unpredictably, I knew I could control his. I shivered when his hands came up to grasp my arm, pressing into my skin. The hiker's breath came easily now. Slow, steady.

An ache deep within me made my fingers tremble. I wanted to run them over his skin. To skim the healing wounds and learn the contours of his muscles.

I bit my lip, fighting temptation. *Come on, Cal, you know better. This isn't like you.*

I pulled my arm from his grasp. A whimper of disappointment emerged from the boy's throat. I didn't know how to grapple with my own sense of loss now that I wasn't touching him. *Find your strength, use the wolf. That's who you are.*

With a warning growl I shook my head, ripping a length of fabric from the hiker's torn shirt to bind up my own wound. His moss-colored eyes followed my every movement.

I scrambled to my feet and was startled when he mimicked the action, faltering only slightly. I frowned and took two steps back. He watched my retreat, then looked down at his ripped clothing. His fingers gingerly picked at the shreds of his shirt. When his eyes lifted to meet mine, I was hit with an unexpected swell of dizziness. His lips parted. I couldn't stop looking at them. Full, curving with interest, lacking the terror I'd expected. Too many questions flickered in his gaze.

*I have to get out of here.* "You'll be fine. Get off the mountain. Don't come near this place again," I said, turning away.

A shock sparked through my body when the boy gripped my shoulder. He looked surprised but not at all afraid. That wasn't good. Heat flared along my skin where his fingers held me fast. I waited a moment too long, watching him, memorizing his features before I snarled and shrugged off his hand.

"Wait—" he said, and took another step toward me.

What if I could wait, putting my life on hold in this moment? What if I stole a little more time and caught a taste of what had been so long forbidden? Would it be so wrong? I would never see this stranger again. What harm could come from lingering here, from holding still and learning whether he would try to touch me the way I wanted to him to?

His scent told me my thoughts weren't far off the mark, his skin snapping with adrenaline and the musk that belied desire. I'd let this encounter last much too long, stepped well beyond the line of safe conduct. With regret nipping at me, I balled my fist. My eyes moved up and down his body, assessing, remembering the feeling of his lips on my skin. He smiled hesitantly.

*Enough.*

I caught him across the jaw with a single blow. He dropped to the ground and didn't move again. I bent down and gathered the boy in my arms, slinging his backpack over my shoulder. The scent of green meadows and dew-kissed tree limbs flowed around me, flooding me with that strange ache that coiled low in my body, a physical reminder of my brush with treachery. Twilight shadows stretched farther up the mountain, but I'd have him at the base by dusk.

A lone, battered pickup was parked near the rippling waterway that marked the boundary of the sacred site. Black signs with bright orange lettering were posted along the creek bank:

NO TRESPASSING. PRIVATE PROPERTY.

The Ford Ranger was unlocked. I flung open the door, almost pulling it from the rust-bitten vehicle. I draped the boy's limp form across the driver's seat. His head slumped forward and I caught the stark outline of a tattoo on the back of his neck. A dark, bizarrely inked cross.

*A trespasser and trend hound. Thank God I found something not to like about him.*

I hurled his pack onto the passenger seat and slammed the door. The truck's steel frame groaned. Still trembling with frustration, I shifted into wolf form and darted back into the forest. His scent clung to me, blurring my sense of purpose. I sniffed the air and cringed, a new scent bringing my treachery into stark relief.

*I know you're here.* A snarl traveled with my thought.

*Are you okay?* Bryn's plaintive question only made fear bite harder into my trembling muscles. In the next moment she ran beside me.

*I told you to leave.* I bared my teeth but couldn't deny my sudden relief at her presence.

*I could never abandon you.* Bryn kept pace easily. *And you know I'll never betray you.*

I picked up speed, darting through the deepening shadows of the forest. I abandoned my attempt to outrun fear, shifted forms, and stumbled forward until I found the solid pressure of a tree trunk. The scratch of the bark on my skin failed to repel the gnat-like nerves that swarmed in my head.

"Why did you save him?" she asked. "Humans mean nothing to us."

I kept my arms around the tree but turned my cheek to the side so I could look at Bryn. No longer in her wolf form, the short, wiry girl's hands rested on her hips. Her eyes narrowed as she waited for an answer.

I blinked, but I couldn't halt the burning sensation. A pair of tears, hot and unwanted, slid down my cheeks.

Bryn's eyes widened. I never cried. Not when anyone could witness it.

I turned my face away, but I could sense her watching me silently, without judgment. I had no answers for Bryn. Or for myself.

Keep reading to sample the first
book in Andrea Cremer's next series:

# THE
# INVENTOR'S
# SECRET

# 1.

EVERY HEARTBEAT BROUGHT the boy closer. Charlotte heard the shallow pulls of his breath, the uneven, heavy pounding of his footfalls. She stayed curled within the hollows of the massive tree's roots, body perfectly still other than the sweat that beaded on her forehead in the close air. A single drop of moisture trailed along her temple, dripped from her jaw, and disappeared into her bodice.

The boy threw another glance over his shoulder. Five more steps, and he'd hit the tripwire. Four. Three. Two. One.

He cried out in alarm as his ankle hooked on the taut line stretched between two trees. His yelp cut off when his body slammed into the forest floor, forcing the air from his lungs.

Charlotte lunged from her hiding place, muscles shrieking in relief as they snapped out of the tight crouch. Her practiced feet barely touched the ground and she ran with as much silence as the low rustle of her skirts would allow.

The boy moaned and started to push himself up on one elbow. He grunted when Charlotte kicked him over onto his back and pinned him against the ground with one foot.

His wide eyes fixed on the revolver she had aimed at his chest.

"Please," he whispered.

She adjusted her aim—right between his eyes—and shook her head. "I'm not in the habit of granting the requests of strangers."

Charlotte put more weight onto her foot, and he squirmed.

"Who are you?" she asked, and wished her voice were gritty instead of gentle.

He didn't blink; his eyes mirrored the rust-tinged gleam of the breaking dawn.

"I don't know."

"Say again?" She frowned.

Fear bloomed in his tawny irises. "I . . . I don't know."

"You don't know," she repeated.

He shook his head.

She glanced at the tangle of brush from which he'd emerged. "What are you running from?"

He frowned, and again said, "I don't know."

"If you don't know, then why were you running?" she snapped.

"The sounds." He shuddered.

"Sounds?" Charlotte felt as though frost had formed on the bare skin of her arms. She scanned the forest, dread building in her chest.

The whistle shrieked as though her fear had summoned it. The iron beast, tall as the trees around it, emerged from the thick woods on the same deer trail the boy had followed. Imperial Labor Gatherers were built like giants. The square, blunt head of the machine pushed through the higher branches of the trees, snapping them like twigs. Two multijointed brass arms sprouted on each side of its wide torso and its long fingers were spread wide, ready to clutch and capture. Charlotte's eyes immediately found the thick bars of its hollow rib cage.

Empty.

"Who sent a Gatherer after you?"

His voice shook. "Is that what it is?"

"Are you an idiot?" She spat on the ground beside him. "You must know a Rotpot when you see one! Everyone out here knows how the Empire hunts."

The screech of metal in need of oiling cooled Charlotte's boiling temper. A horn sounded. Another answered in the distance. But not nearly distant enough.

She didn't have time to mull over options. She lifted her foot from the boy's chest and offered him her hand.

The only advantage they had over the Rotpots was that the lumbering iron men maneuvered slowly in the forest.

"We need to leave this place. Now."

The boy gripped her fingers without hesitation, but he shot a terrified glance at the approaching Gatherer. They were partially concealed from view by a huge oak, but the machine was close enough that Charlotte could see its operator shifting gears from within the giant's iron skull. She watched as the man reached up, pulled down a helmet with telescoping goggles, and began to swivel the Rotpot's head around.

Charlotte hesitated a moment too long. And he saw her.

Cranking hard on a wheel, which made steam spout from the machine's shoulders, the operator turned the iron man to pursue them.

"Go!" Charlotte shoved the boy away from her. "Run east! I'll catch up."

"What are you—" he started to ask, but began to run when she pushed him so hard that he almost fell over.

When she was certain he wasn't looking back, Charlotte reached into her skirt pocket. Her hand found cool metal, and she pulled a small object from within the folds of muslin. It only took a few winds of the key before sputters and sparks leapt from her palm. She sighed and regretfully set the magnet mouse on the ground, pointing it at the encroaching machine. The little creature whirred and skittered away, its spring-anchored wheels accommodating the rough path she'd set it upon.

"Come on."

When Charlotte caught up with the boy, she ignored the puzzled look on his face and grasped his hand, forcing him to run with her into the dark western wood, away from the now bloodred haze of early sun that stretched through the forest canopy.

Between gasps of breath, his fingers tightened on hers. She glanced at him.

His tawny eyes had sharpened, and he peered at her like a hawk. "What's your name?" he asked.

Charlotte dropped his hand and gathered her skirts to accommodate her leap over a moss-covered log.

"Charlotte."

"Thank you for not leaving me back there, Charlotte."

She looked away from him, nodded, and ran a bit faster. Behind them she heard the explosion she'd been waiting for. Though they were hardly out of danger, Charlotte smiled, feeling a surge of triumph. But a moment later, a single thought chased her giddiness away.

*Ash is going to kill me.*

# 2.

**T**HE LAST BEAMS of sunlight were cutting through the forest by the time they reached the tree.

"Bloody hell!" Charlotte groped through the tangle of roots in search of subtle tactile differentiation. Her companion gasped at her outburst, and she spared him a glance. Not that he could tell. She'd tied a kerchief around his eyes when the sounds of the Gatherers seemed far off enough to risk slowing down.

The boy's face scrunched up, as if he was thinking hard. After a moment, he said, "Girls shouldn't use that kind of language. Someone told me that . . . I think . . ."

Though he appeared to be running from the Brits, she couldn't risk letting a stranger learn the way to the Catacombs. The Empire's attempts at finding their hideaway had been limited to Gatherer sweeps and a few crow-scopes, none of which had been successful. It wasn't out of the realm of possibility that they'd stoop to sending a real person out to hunt for them. And someone like this boy, who seemed so vulnerable, would be the perfect spy. If he was and this was a trap she'd sprung, Charlotte would never forgive herself.

"Well, you may not know who you are, but apparently you were brought up in polite society," Charlotte said sourly, her mood darkened by new suspicions about who he might be. "If you're planning on sticking around, you'll find girls here do a lot of things they aren't meant to do."

He simply turned his head in her direction, puzzled and waiting for an explanation. Charlotte's answer was an unkind laugh. Perhaps she should have been more compassionate, but the consequences of revealing their hideout were too dangerous. And Birch was almost too clever with his inventions. She'd never been able to locate the false branch without effort, and delays could be very costly. The Rotpots might have been stopped by her mouse, but nothing was certain. A slowed Gatherer was still a threat.

"I . . . I . . ." Beside her the boy was stammering as if unsure whether to apologize.

"Hush," she said, keeping her voice gentle, and he felt silent.

Her fingers brushed over a root with bark harder and colder than the others.

"Here it is."

"Here's what?" He waggled his head around pointlessly.

"I said hush." Charlotte stifled laughter at the boy's bobbing head, knowing it was cruel given his helpless state.

She found the latch on the underside of the thick root, and a compartment in the artificial wood popped open. Quickly turning the crank hidden within the compartment, Charlotte held her breath until the voice came crackling through.

"Verification?"

"Iphigenia," Charlotte said with a little smile. *Birch and his myths.*

The boy drew a sharp breath. "Who is that? Who's there?" He sounded genuinely afraid.

"It's all right," she whispered and leaned closer to the voicebox. "And there are two of us, so you'll need to open both channels."

There was a long pause in which Charlotte's heart began to beat heavily, once again making her question the decision to bring the strange boy with her.

"The basket will be waiting," the voice confirmed, and a little relief seeped through her veins.

The pale boy was still twisting his neck, as if somehow doing so would enlighten him as to the origin of the voice despite his blindfold.

"What's happening?" he asked, facing away from Charlotte. Rather than attempt an explanation, Charlotte grabbed his wrist and tugged him toward the roaring falls.

As the pounding of water on rocks grew louder, the boy resisted Charlotte's guidance for the first time.

"Stop! Please!" He jerked back, throwing her off balance.

"Don't do that!" Charlotte whirled around and grabbed his arms. "We're about to cross a narrow and quite slippery path. If you make me lose my footing, we'll both be in the drink, and I don't fancy a swim, no matter how hot the summer air may be."

"Is it a river?" he asked. "Where are we?"

Charlotte couldn't blame the boy for his questions, but she was close to losing her patience. Hadn't she already done enough to help him? All she wanted was to get inside the Catacombs, where they would be hidden from any Gatherers that might still be combing the forest. What did Meg always say when she was fighting with Ash?

Meg's warm voice slipped into Charlotte's mind. *Try to see it from his point of view. It's a horrible burden, Lottie. The weight of leadership.*

Charlotte looked at the pale boy, frowning. His burden wasn't that of her brother's—a responsibility for a ramshackle group aged five to seventeen—but this boy bore the weight of fear and, at the moment, blindness. Both of which must be awful to contend with. With that in mind, Charlotte said, "I'm taking you to a hiding place beneath the falls. I promise it's safe. The machines won't find us there. I can't tell you more."

The boy tilted his head toward the sound of her voice.

He groped the air until he found her hands.

"Okay."

She smiled, though he couldn't see it, and drew him over the moss-covered rocks that paved the way to the falls. As they came closer, the spray from the falls dampened their clothing and their hair. Charlotte was grateful the boy had decided to trust her and ask no further questions because at this point she would have had to shout to be heard.

When they passed beneath the torrent of water, the air shimmered as the native moss gave way to the bioluminescent variety Birch had cultivated to light the pathway into the Catacombs.

Charlotte wished she could remove the boy's blindfold. Entering the passageway that led into the Catacombs delighted her each time she returned. Not only because it meant she was almost home, but also because the glowing jade moss gave light that was welcoming. Seeing it might ease the boy's mind, reassuring him that she led him to a place of safety rather than danger.

She turned left, taking them into a narrow side passage that at first glance would have appeared to be nothing more than a shadow cast by the tumbling cascade. Within the twisting cavern, the shimmering green moss forfeited its place to mounds of fungus. Their long stems and umbrella-like tops glowed blue instead of green, throwing the cavern into a perpetual twilight.

The boy remained silent, but from the way he gripped her fingers, Charlotte knew his fear hadn't abated.

"We're almost there," she whispered and squeezed his hand, garnering a weak smile from him.

The passage abruptly opened up to a massive cavern—the place where the falls hid its priceless treasure: a refuge, one of the only sites hidden from the far-seeing eyes of the Empire. While from the outside the falls appeared to cover a solid rock base, several meters beneath the cascade, the earth opened into a maze of caves. Some were narrow tunnels like the one from which they'd just emerged. Others were enormous open spaces, large enough to house a dirigible. Far below them, the surface of an underground lake rippled with the current that tugged it into an underground river. A dark twin that snaked beneath earth and stone to meet its aboveground counterpart some two leagues past the falls.

They were standing on a platform. Smooth stone reinforced by iron bracings and a brass railing that featured a hinged gate. On the other side of the gate, as had been promised, the basket was waiting, dangling from a long iron chain that stretched up until it disappeared into a rock shelf high above them. The lift resembled a birdcage more than a basket. Charlotte opened the gate and the basket door, pushing the boy inside and following him after she'd secured the gate once more. The basket swung under their weight, and the boy gripped the brass weave that held them.

"You put me in a cage?" Panic crept into his question.

"Shhh." She took his hand again as much to stop him

from ripping the blindfold off as to reassure him. "I'm here too. It's not a cage—it's an elevator."

With her free hand, she reached up and pulled the wooden handle attached to a brass chain that hung from the ceiling of the basket. Far above them, a bell sounded, its chiming bounced off the cavern walls. A flurry of tinkling notes melded with the roar of the falls for a few moments.

Charlotte shushed the boy before he could ask what the bell meant. Now that she was out of the forest, away from the Gatherers and a short ride from home, she was tired and more than a little anxious about what awaited her on the upper platform. Not so much what as who, she had to admit.

As the clicking of gears and the steady winding of the chain filled the basket, they began to move up. The swiftness of the lift's ascent never failed to surprise Charlotte slightly, but it caught the boy completely off guard. He lurched to the side, and the basket swung out over the lake.

"Stop that!" Charlotte grabbed him, holding him still at the center of the swaying basket. "If you don't move, the lift won't swing out."

"S-sorry." The boy's teeth chattered with nerves.

Peering at him, Charlotte felt a creeping fear tickle her spine. She'd assumed his awful colorless skin had been a result of his fear, but looking at him closely, she thought it might be the natural state of his flesh. And it struck Charlotte as quite odd. Flesh so pale it had an ashen cast. She forced herself to hang on to him so he wouldn't unbalance the lift again, but she now worried his wan quality was a harbinger of illness. And that it might be catching.

Her nagging thoughts were interrupted when they passed the lip of the upper platform and the gears slowly ground to a halt.

The first sight that greeted her was three pairs of boots. The first was black, thick-soled, and scarred with burn marks. The second pair was also black, but polished and trimmer of cut and heel, showing only their shiny tips rather than stretching to the knee like the first pair. The third pair made her groan. Faded brown and featuring an array of loops and buckles that held knives in place, this pair was soon joined by a grinning face as their owner crouched to peer into the basket.

Jack, clad in his regular garb of leather breeches and two low-slung, gun-heavy belts, threaded his fingers through the brass weaving of the basket, rising with it until he was standing. "Well, well. What a fine catch we have today, mateys."

"Cap it, Jack," Charlotte said.

He pushed stray locks of his bronze hair beneath his tweed cap and continued to smile as he opened the platform gate. "A mermaid and a . . . what?"

Jack's mirthful expression vanished as he stared at the blindfolded boy.

Charlotte swallowed the hardness that had formed in her throat. Jack turned to look at the wearer of the polished boots. Charlotte was looking that way too.

The boots were mostly covered by black military pants, close fitting with brass buttons from knee to ankle and looser to the waist where they met with a band-collared white shirt and burgundy vest with matching cravat. The owner of the boots carried an ebony cane tipped with a brass globe.

Ashley wasn't wearing his usual black overcoat, but its absence did nothing to impede his air of authority.

"Pip called in that two were arriving instead of just one," he told Charlotte.

She glanced over to the wheelhouse where a slight girl wearing goggles was mostly hidden by pulls, levers, and cranks. Pip gave Charlotte a quick, apologetic wave and then ducked out of sight.

Throwing her shoulders back, Charlotte exited the basket, dragging the boy with her.

"The Rotpots were after him," she said, meeting her brother's stern gaze. "I had to help him."

"Of course *you* had to." Ash tapped a shiny boot on the stone platform.

She didn't offer further explanation but refused to look away. Charlotte didn't want to quail before her brother because rumors of her unexpected guest seemed to have spread throughout the Catacombs. From the mouth of the caverns that led to their living quarters, half a dozen little faces with wide eyes peeked out, watching Charlotte and Ashley's exchange. The children should have been at their lessons or chores, but Charlotte knew well enough that when something this unusual took place in their mostly cloistered lives, it was irresistible. When she'd been younger, Charlotte had snuck away from her responsibilities many a time for events much less exciting than the arrival of a stranger. Ash had always chided her for her impetuous behavior. Her brother had been born a leader, all sobriety and steadfastness. He was never tempted away from duty the way Charlotte so often had been.

Ash frowned and walked up to the blindfolded boy.

"And what do you have to say for yourself?" Ash asked him. "Who has my sister brought us?"

"I . . . I can't . . ." The boy strained toward the sound of Ash's voice.

Ash put the brass tip of his cane beneath the boy's chin. "I know you can't see, boy. If you'll tell me how you came to be in the forest, perhaps we can show you a bit more hospitality."

Charlotte stepped forward, hitting the length of the cane so it thwacked away from the stranger. She jerked the kerchief down so the boy blinked into the sudden light.

"Leave him be. You weren't the one being chased by an iron beast with a cage for a belly."

Ash stared at her, his dark brown eyes full of incredulity and budding fury. He didn't speak to Charlotte, though, instead turning his hard gaze on the faces peering out from the cavern opening. Ashley didn't have to say anything. The children bolted away, the pitter-patter of their speedy steps echoing in the cavern like sudden rainfall.

"Do you know if he's hurt, Charlotte?" The boy wearing the burn-scarred black boots scampered forward, peering at the new arrival.

Jack, who'd taken a few steps back as if to survey the unfolding scene from a safe distance, answered as he threaded his thumbs into his wide belt loops. "He looks fine to me. Are you sure he was really running from them?"

Charlotte ignored Jack, instead smiling at Birch, who trotted over to the boy's side.

"Let's have a look." The boots weren't the only pock-marked part of Birch's wardrobe. From his thick apron to his elbow-length gloves, the tinker's brown leather clothing boasted enough black marks to rival a leopard's spots.

The boy was shivering, but he nodded and didn't object when Birch inspected him.

"No injuries I can see. He's not feverish. If anything, I'd say he's a little clammy." Birch scratched his thatch of wheat-colored hair.

A tiny head capped by large round ears peeked around one side of Birch's neck. Its wide black eyes stared at the strange boy. The boy stared back as the bat climbed from Birch's neck onto his shoulder. Its minuscule claws fastened to one of the straps of the tinker's leather apron, never losing its grip as Birch moved.

"There's, there's something on you," the boy said, his tone wary, but also curious.

"What?" Birch glanced at the shoulder the boy pointed to. "Oh. That's just Moses. He's usually crawling somewhere on my apron. Doesn't like to roost anymore, under-standably. Fell when he was just a baby and broke both wings. I found him floating in the river one day when I was collecting guano to make gunpowder. Had to rebuild his wings myself."

Birch coaxed Moses onto his hand and then gently stretched out one of the bat's wings, which produced a soft clicking sound as the appendage unfurled. The underside of Moses's wing glinted with silver.

"The key was creating a new bone structure using hol-low tubes," Birch explained. "Light enough so he could fly."

"What proof do you have that he was trying to escape?" Ash was still watching Charlotte instead of looking at the boy.

Charlotte's charge seemed content conversing with Birch, so she gave Ash her full attention.

"Only that he was alone in the forest and running from Rotpots." Charlotte thrust her chin out. "That was good enough for me."

"How reassuring," Ash said. "And you failed to notice that he's dressed in clothes from the Hive?"

Charlotte's eyes went wide. She turned to look at her companion, feeling blood leach from her face. Her brother was right. While the trio waiting to meet them wore a mishmash of clothes cobbled together into outfits favored by each, the boy wore gray tweed pants and a matching fitted jacket with button and chain closures. His wardrobe marked him as belonging to the Hive: the artisan caste of the New York metropolis.

Ash released her from his glare, but before he said anything more, the strange boy jerked hard to the right. The sudden movement pulled his hand free of Charlotte's grasp.

Until that moment, the boy had been leaning close to Birch's shoulder, examining Moses's mechanical wing. Now he stood straight as an iron rod, gazing at Birch.

"Maker. Maker. Maker," the boy said. His limbs began to shake violently.

"What the—" Jack leapt forward, drawing a knife from his boot and holding it low, putting himself between Charlotte and the now flailing boy.

"Maker! Maker! Maker!" the boy cried. His shouts bounced off the cavern ceiling and walls, filling the air with a haunting chorus of echoes: *Maker! Maker! Maker!*

"Rustbuckets. He's having a fit." Ash raised his cane. "Easy, Jack."

"Grab him, or he'll go right over the edge," Birch warned, but Ash was already moving. While the boy's arms lashed, Ash slipped his cane through the stranger's belt and hauled him away from the precipice. With another deft movement, Ash freed his cane just before the boy flopped to the ground, lolling about with no control of his body's violent movements..

With a horrible shudder, he gave a slow, whining cry and went still.

From Andrea Cremer

# INVISIBILITY

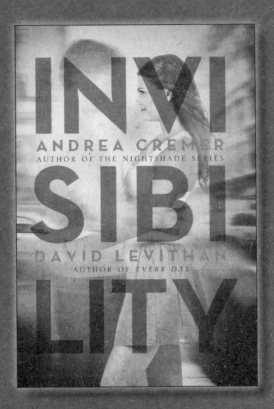

A collaboration with *New York Times* bestselling author David Levithan

# Join the hunt with the
# NIGHTSHADE series!

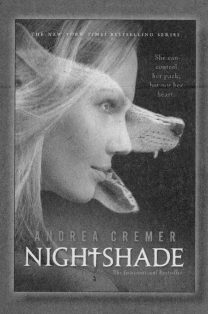

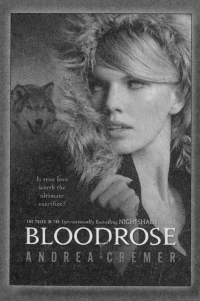
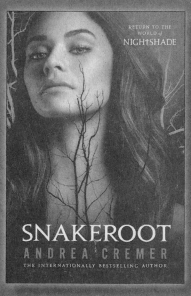